Lookin' for Love

"Recovering addicts and members of faith-based recovery programs will find a familiar—yet wholly original—protagonist to cry with and ultimately cheer for."

—Ashley E. Sweeney, author of *Hardland*

"*Lookin' for Love* by Susen Edwards is an inspiring story of harrowing trials and tribulations followed by incredible redemption. The story is riveting, leaving you wondering how Ava is ever going to dig herself out of the devastating drug-riddled, messy relationship hole she dug herself . . ."

—Ginelle Testa, author of *Making a Home Out of You*

"This roller coaster of a story has sharp turns, steep slopes, and jaw-dropping tension, careening from crisis to crisis . . . Strap on your seatbelt for this scream machine ride and witness all the drama in Ava's topsy-turvy world."

—Vivian Fransen, author of *The Straight Spouse: A Memoir*

"*Lookin' for Love* was so full of twists and turns, I forgot it was based on a true story multiple times while reading it . . . This book will remain on my list of favorites.

—Dr. Dawn Filos, author of *Tales of a Pet Vet: Stories from the Clinic and House Calls*

Lookin' *for* Love

LOOKIN' FOR LOVE

A Novel

SUSEN EDWARDS

SHE WRITES PRESS

Published 2024
Printed in the United States of America
Print ISBN: 978-1-64742-790-0
E-ISBN: 978-1-64742-791-7
Library of Congress Control Number: 2024911723

For information, address:
She Writes Press
1569 Solano Ave #546
Berkeley, CA 94707

Interior design by Stacey Aaronson

She Writes Press is a division of SparkPoint Studio, LLC.

For B & B

prologue

Kukaa, kukaa!

Eighty-two women drop their work and sink to the ground. The Swahili word means "sit" but in our world it means "squat." Those who remain standing are guards. We often squat for up to ten minutes. When we stand, the blood rushes from our heads and some of us topple over. The guards laugh and clap at our expense.

Part One

one

Natalie

My mother's love was conditional. Her unspoken words were always with me.

If you rub my feet, I'll love you.

If you get good grades, I'll love you.

If you clean the house, I'll love you.

My mother's love didn't last.

If you don't rub my feet, I won't love you.

If your grades aren't good enough, I'll hate you.

If you miss a speck of dirt, I'll ignore you.

For years I believed I wasn't smart enough, talented enough, or hard-working enough.

Maybe I reminded my mother of my birth father, her first husband, Edgar Stanton.

Courtships were almost nonexistent during World War II. Edgar was handsome, thirty-years-old, an army first lieutenant and chaplain stationed stateside. What else did my mother, Natalie, need to know? They met at a United Service Organization (USO) dance in New Jersey, married, and moved to his home state, Ohio, where I was born on March 15, 1944. Two years later, Edgar died. His record shows he "died non-battle."

I have no memory of Ohio or my birth father. What I do remember is my mother telling me that my father died in the Battle of the Bulge during the war.

What she didn't tell me was that Edgar was a bigamist with another wife and two children. It all came out when my mother was denied spousal benefits upon his death. I accidentally learned of his second family later in life. That's when I learned he died of sepsis in an army hospital in Missouri, not on the battlefield.

I suppose I should mention my mother was a habitual liar.

We left Ohio and moved to Newark, New Jersey, to live with my Hungarian grandparents, who raised me until I finished kindergarten. We lived above Central Cleaners, their dry-cleaning business. My grandparents spoiled me as did the other shop owners on our street. Each day around three o'clock, we'd head for Traflets ice cream parlor for coffee ice cream, my favorite.

In the summers we rented a house in Atlantic Highlands, where my grandfather kept a Steelcraft boat. I loved our fishing trips and spending time with this generous, kindhearted man. We'd bring our catch to the dock, where he'd give it all away.

My mother had a job as a telephone operator, a respected career for women in the 1940s. Her job accounted for her absence during the day. But where was she when I cried out for her at night? My grandmother was the only one who comforted me.

War widows were in abundance in the late 1940s. Unmarried soldiers returning from the war had their pick of women, with or without children. My mother remarried when I was four years old. I wasn't included in her courtship, engagement, or wedding. I suspect I was left at home to avoid any misunderstanding. Weren't all brides virgins? At least my mother didn't wear a white gown, a partial admission to her past and my existence.

For years I wondered why I continued living with my grandparents instead of moving in with my mother and her new husband,

Hank Wilson. Didn't my mother want me? Did her husband hate me so much he didn't want me in his life? I later learned they both worked until my mother became pregnant. It was much simpler to leave me at Central Cleaners. Had I been allowed to stay with my grandparents, perhaps my life would have taken a different course. But we can't live our lives on "what ifs."

After kindergarten, I moved into an apartment in Paramus, New Jersey, with my mother and new father. I was legally adopted and began life as Ava Wilson. A few months later, I was given a baby brother. I resented the intrusion of a screaming infant and the attention he generated but soon learned to love little Henry. I pretended he was my baby. The love I had given to my grandparents was transferred to him. There was no point in showering it on my mother. From the day I returned, she made it clear I was an unnecessary appendage. If it wasn't for my new father, I would have been sent back to my grandparents.

I'd hear the arguments at night after my parents thought I was asleep.

"She's our daughter," my father said.

"But she's not *your* daughter. She'd be better off with *Nagymama*," Natalie replied, using the Hungarian word for grandmother.

"I adopted her. She is my daughter."

"We have no room for her. We can't afford two kids," Natalie said.

"We won't break up the family."

My new father's parents divorced when he was a teenager. He lived with the stigma of a broken home and was determined not to repeat the cycle.

Their bedroom door slammed shut. All was quiet.

Please send me back to Grandma.

The apartment was silent for the next few days. As our punishment, dinner for my father and me consisted of a box of saltines. My mother ate toast and tea.

To keep the peace, my father allowed Natalie to be herself, which in most cases meant the silent treatment. The one thing he stood firm on was keeping me in the family.

Two years later, my parents bought their little piece of the American Dream—a three-bedroom tract house in Edison, New Jersey. I was eight years old.

My father worked as a union carpenter. It was dangerous work but paid well, which made my mother happy, at least most of the time. We never knew when something would set her off and she'd stop speaking to one of us. Her silences became more frequent, sometimes lasting for days, even weeks.

"Hank, tell *her* to pass the butter," Natalie would say.

I'd pass the butter.

"Henry, tell your sister to get her elbows off the table."

My brother turned to me. I moved my elbows to save him the embarrassment of my mother's silence.

"Henry, rub my feet."

She'd sit in her rocker, light her first cigarette of the evening, and glare at me. I'd close the door to my bedroom, grateful for the freedom. It was only a matter of time before Henry would be the villain, and I'd be back at work.

After everyone went to bed, I crept into the living room and counted the cigarette butts in the ashtray: twenty—a full pack after dinner. None of us knew about second-hand smoke in the 1950s. Adults believed it aided digestion. Kids . . . well . . . we coughed and made the best of it, promising ourselves we'd never take up the disgusting habit.

My father treated me with kindness and love, but like my mother, his love was conditional. He only expressed it when we were alone and only on days Natalie was speaking to me. When she ignored me or pressured me to succeed, he remained silent. *Dad, say something!* I'd pray for him to read my mind. My prayers went unanswered.

Outwardly, we gave the impression of being a good Christian family. Most weeks we attended services at the Episcopal church in town. My mother resented the church almost as much as she resented me. As a first-generation Hungarian, she was raised Catholic, but because she was on her second marriage, they married in my father's church. I wanted to believe in the peace the minister claimed came with accepting God and Jesus, but something was missing. Was it my mother's resentment I felt? Was it my innate sense that I didn't belong and was the remnant of a fraudulent marriage?

It wasn't only in church where I lacked a sense of belonging. It was the underlying theme of my life. Looking back, I'm convinced my mother projected her personal feelings of inadequacy onto me. She trusted no one, not even herself. How could she love and trust me when she didn't love herself?

The 1950s was a decade of prosperity and conformity. Insights into human behavior were rare. Had counseling been available, my mother would never have taken me. She would have seen it as a sign of failure. For her, outward appearances were everything. To please her, I succumbed to the pressure to perform.

I cleaned, walked the dog, got decent grades, and rubbed her feet. I'd do anything I could to serve my mother. It wasn't until eighth grade when I made her proud.

"Guess what, Mom? I made the twirling squad!"

My mother sat watching afternoon TV. "Ava, don't slam the door."

"Did you hear me, Mom?"

My mother popped a piece of saltwater taffy into her mouth. She hadn't heard a word I said.

"I made the twirling squad! I get to march in all the parades and football games."

I had her attention. Her daughter would be in the spotlight. My mother actually smiled.

"Here's my costume." I held up a navy blue and white uniform and placed a tall, white, fuzzy hat on my head. I grabbed my baton and gave it a twirl.

"Be careful," she said. "Wait till your father gets home so you can show us both—outside."

Life improved after that. My mother's love was still conditional, but it was there. My parents sat in the stands at our home games. They cheered and waved as I marched by. The following year I became head majorette.

By my sophomore year in high school, being head majorette wasn't enough. My mother pressured me to improve my grades. She was determined I'd be the first in the family to go to college.

"I want to see you at Moravian College," she said.

Moravian College, one of the oldest in the United States, promised prestige and success for me and more importantly, for my mother. She went back to work as a telephone operator and promised to save money for my education. Instead, she bought herself a green Ford Thunderbird convertible.

At the rate my mother spent money, I knew nothing would be left for my education. I took a job during study hall in the main office of the high school. The few dollars I earned wouldn't make much difference in our finances. But between the job and my position as head majorette, I hoped to earn points for extracurricular activities.

Working in the office gave me access to my student file. During the spring semester of my sophomore year, I pulled my records, snuck the documents home, and changed my grades from Cs to Bs. I was confident better grades would help me get into Moravian and make my mother happy.

My deceit backfired. The vice-principal caught me and contacted my parents for a meeting. I was well-liked at school and had no prior discipline problems, which kept me from being expelled. Instead, I was stripped of my head majorette title and banned from school functions for a year. Classmates shunned me. I went from popular to pariah.

My shame and guilt were all-encompassing. My parents didn't

ground me. What would be the point? I had no friends left and no place to go. I sat in my room wishing my parents would slap me, scream at me, or do something to feed my remorse. Instead, the house was silent.

That night I strained to hear my parents' voices in their bedroom.

"She's worthless. I should have left her in Newark," Natalie complained.

"I think she did it to please you," Hank said.

"Please me? Are you crazy?"

"You put a lot of pressure on her. She's just a kid," he said.

"And that makes it okay? You're no better than she is. What are the neighbors going to think?"

"I wouldn't worry about the neighbors. Try worrying about your family for a change."

I couldn't believe my father had stood up to my mother.

Drawers slammed. Something was thrown against the wall. Glass shattered. More than anything, I wished I was the one shattered. But who would pick up the pieces of me once they hit the floor?

The ubiquitous box of saltines sat on the kitchen table the next morning. When my brother asked for cereal, my mother made no move to help him. I brought him cereal and milk. He shouldn't have to suffer because of me.

"*Sit down.*" Those were the last words my mother spoke to anyone in our family for days.

Dinner progressed from saltines to toast and tea, then eventually to home-cooked meals. Conversation directed at me was utilitarian.

"Pass the macaroni."

"Clean your room. It's filthy."

After two weeks, I summoned the courage to apologize. "I'm sorry. I made a stupid mistake. I only did it to please you."

My father's eyes showed a hint of compassion. He opened his mouth to say something. My mother intercepted.

"Sorry? Mistake? You want forgiveness? Did I tell you to steal your file? You're no good. You were never any good."

Once my mother's mouth opened, it stayed open. She barked more insults at me, none of which I heard. I took shelter in my room.

My junior year in high school was spent in exile. Everyone knew what I'd done. My friends avoided me. My parents barely spoke to me. My father may have forgiven me but couldn't escape my mother's wrath. With my social life in ruin, I began taking the bus into Plainfield for dances and other teen-centered events. I made new friends, ones who hadn't heard about my disgrace or didn't care.

two

Boys

Ava, you were the best drum majorette we ever had. We want to reinstate you," Coach said at the start of my senior year.

Words of praise were alien to me. I'd been beaten down at home for seventeen years and shamed at school for over a year. How could I hold my head high and accept forgiveness when I knew I was worthless?

"I don't deserve to be head majorette," I told Coach.

He looked into my eyes and said, "You paid for your mistake. The position is yours if you want it."

"Thank you, but no thank you," I said, firm in my decision.

I was defeated and preferred to stay that way.

What I didn't tell Coach was that I had discovered bad boys. They were exciting, dangerous, handsome, and most importantly, attracted to me.

Frankie Lombardo was my first bad boy. His Italian heritage and dark good looks contrasted with my Germanic blond hair and blue eyes. Walking down Front Street in Plainfield, I'd glance at our reflection in the shop windows and imagine what our children would look like. I hadn't learned bad boys aren't thinking about the future. For them, it's all about seizing pleasure in the moment. Frankie was no exception.

My parents held the outdated belief that Italians weren't quite "white," something I suspected was a carryover from their parents' generation. When Frankie invited me to a dance at Plainfield High School, I knew I had to lie about his family name.

"His name is Frankie Lambert. I met him at the library," I told my mother.

Frankie fit my teenage image of a ladies' man. Girls flocked to him. He was the best dancer at the high school. I discovered I, too, was a good dancer.

My parents were waiting up for me when Frankie dropped me off after the dance.

"Frankie *Lambert*? You're a damn liar." My mother slapped my arm.

It wasn't the first slap, and it wouldn't be the last. Natalie's anger was rarely physical, but I almost wished it were. A slap stings for the moment. Words vibrate into your core. Silence inhabits your soul for a lifetime.

"How . . . I mean . . . ?" I saw his wallet on the kitchen table. Frankie must have dropped it as we were leaving.

"He's a damn *I*-talian," my father said, stressing the "I."

And you're superior because your skin is whiter?

"Go to your room. You're never seeing him again. Understand?" She slapped my arm again.

The next morning our family set off for church. Silence engulfed the interior of our 1955 Niagara Blue Mercury Monterey. My parents laughed and joked with friends, giving the impression we were the perfect suburban family.

The laughs and jokes remained at church. Silence returned and stayed with us as we drove home. I sat on the rattan loveseat in our breezeway, hoping for forgiveness, hoping my mother kept no record of last night's wrongs.

I heard my mother dialing the phone.

After a pause, she said, "Mrs. Lombardo? This is Mrs. Wilson. Yes, Ava's my daughter."

Another pause.

"My daughter lied about your son. Told me his last name was Lambert. We don't want her dating Italians. We prefer you keep to your own."

My parents were bigots, but I always expected they'd keep their opinions within the family. It would do me no good to stand up for Frankie and his family, for myself, for equality, or for fairness.

We all experience pivotal moments in life. This moment was one of those, but it wouldn't be my last. The number one essential human need is belonging. The second is worthiness. I felt neither. I thought about something George Gobel, a popular comedian at the time, said. "Did you ever get the feeling that the world was a tuxedo, and you were a pair of brown shoes?"

After seventeen years, I realized I was that pair of brown shoes. Nothing I did would make my mother happy. It was time to make myself happy. From now on, if my mother told me not to do something, I would do it even more.

Frankie and I continued to see each other. I'd invite him to our house when my parents went out. We drank my parents' liquor in my bedroom. I detested the taste and how dizzy it made me feel, but each sip symbolized a small victory for me and brought me one step closer to freedom.

Once I met Kevin Harrison, I left Frankie. Kevin was cuter and another bad boy. Looking back, I should have stayed with Frankie, but I had already begun my downward spiral.

Kevin and I didn't last long, just long enough for me to meet his parents and his older brother, Tom. Tom was tall—six-foot-two inches tall, thin, with blond hair and blue eyes. He wasn't as good-looking as Kevin, but we felt an instant attraction.

I had never met a family like the Harrisons. They were loud, expressive, and argumentative. An open bottle of whiskey served as the centerpiece on their Formica kitchen table. The more Kevin's parents drank, the louder they became. Tom became the centerpiece of their arguments.

"You drop outta high school to join the navy. Then you fuckin' get kicked out." Mr. Harrison slammed his hand on the table and downed the rest of his drink. He poured another before Tom had a chance to speak.

"You're good for nothin'," Mrs. Harrison screeched.

Kevin and I tiptoed into the living room. Voices transformed into a low growl.

"What happened?" I whispered.

"Tom got a dishonorable discharge from the navy," Kevin said. "It's none of my business. The sooner I get away from this family, the better."

The sooner I get away from this family, the better for me, too.

three

Tom

Kevin and I drifted apart. Tom wanted to take his place. I kept an inner dialogue going.

He's too old for me.

He's not a bad boy—he's a bad man.

The guy's a loser.

The family is bad news.

Tom never gave up, even after I left for college.

None of the private colleges I applied to would take me. I ended up at Trenton State College, about an hour from home. The freedom was intoxicating. No more hassles from my mother. No silences, bigotry, or hatred. No one knew about my past or the disgrace I'd brought upon myself.

My one success in college was playing the character of Jane Ashton in *Brigadoon*. My strong alto voice would never bring me fame as a singer, but I didn't care. I loved the lights, costumes, excitement, and attention.

My parents and brother came to opening night.

"You were great, sis," my brother Henry said after the show. "Wish I could sing like you."

"You can. Join the glee club at school. That's how I learned to sing," I said.

"Mom said you take after her. She told me she sang opera before she married Dad."

How do you tell your baby brother your mother is a liar?

"Henry, I think Mom made that up," I said gently.

"Yeah, I kinda thought so." He looked away.

"How about we take you to the diner to celebrate?" my father asked.

I wanted to hang out with the cast after the show, but my family had driven an hour to see me, so I joined them for cheesecake and coffee. I was still high from the performance and determined not to allow memories of my childhood to cloud the experience.

Meanwhile, Tom pursued me. He found a job selling flooring and drove to see me several times a week. Each visit pulled me farther away from my classes, peers, and interest in success. It wasn't only Tom pulling me away. College was my mother's dream, not mine.

I lasted one semester. My parents were furious. Once again, I was a disappointment and a disgrace. My feelings of shame, guilt, and worthlessness returned with a vengeance. I took a job at the town library. It didn't pay much, but it got me out of the house.

Tom couldn't have been happier. No more trips to Trenton, no more dorm curfews. Tom got a library card and became our most frequent patron. At first, I was impressed, knowing he was working his way toward a GED. I soon realized he was there to see me.

"Tom, you'll get me fired," I whispered when he kissed me in the stacks.

"I don't give a shit. No girl of mine should be workin'."

"You expect me to sit home with my mother waiting for you?" I couldn't think of a worse fate.

"We could get a place together," he said.

Society hadn't come to terms with unmarried couples "living in sin" in 1963. That lifestyle was reserved for artists, beatniks, and the dregs of society.

"My parents would kill me. You know how they feel about you," I replied.

By this time my parents had met Tom. His charm hadn't seduced them as it had me. They couldn't understand my attraction to a high school dropout from an alcoholic family.

"The family's got a reputation. They're a bunch of drunks," my father said. "Do you know how often the cops come to their house to break up a fight?"

"He can't help who his parents are," I said. "Tom's different."

"The apple doesn't fall far from the tree." My father loved clichés.

Are you implying I'm anything like you and Natalie?

I may not have had career or educational goals, but my main goal in life was to not become my parents. If I could break the mold, so could Tom.

The following Friday Tom picked me up after work.

"Let's go to Mario's for dinner," he suggested.

Since I was underage, he brought a bottle of Dewar's scotch to share with me on the way to the restaurant.

"Come on, Ava, have a drink."

I had no taste for scotch. When I did drink alcohol, it was usually vodka with a lot of orange juice.

"No thanks."

He shrugged his shoulders as if to say, *Your loss. More for me.*

When we arrived at Mario's, Tom rolled out of the car, lit a cigarette to steady himself, and within a few minutes, sobered up enough to escort me into the restaurant.

He ordered a double scotch and soda, gulped it down, and turned to me. "Ava—"

"Yes?" I looked into his bloodshot eyes, wondering how many of me he saw.

"Since you won't get a place with me, maybe we should—y'-know—get married or somethin'."

Was he proposing?

Tom reached into his jacket pocket and pulled out a two-inch cube. "Open it."

I looked at the ring, then at Tom.

"It was my grandmother's ring. Now it's yours if you want it."

My mind was numb. I can't say I was in love with the guy or even contemplating marriage. What I did know was Tom cared more for me than I did for him. Wasn't that a good thing? Didn't his love mean a lifetime of loyalty?

I took the ring and slipped it on my finger. The flicker of candlelight on the table cast rainbows across my hand from the tiny diamond. The ring was made for me.

Tom may have been intoxicated from the scotch, but I was intoxicated from the promise of freedom from my mother, from the disgrace that had followed me for eighteen years.

"I'll marry you," I said, sealing my fate.

four

The Wedding

I hid the ring from my parents, waiting until my mother was in a good mood to share my news. What was I thinking? My mother was never in a good mood.

It didn't take long for my secret to be revealed. My mother heard me on the phone with my friend Laura. The next thing I knew, she was tearing my bedroom apart, looking for the ring.

"Where is it?" she screamed.

"Where is what?" I continued the pretense.

"The damn ring!"

"Here." I pulled it from my jeans pocket and threw it at her. "I'm marrying Tom and there's nothing you can do about it."

"There's plenty I can do about it. Break it off or leave this house."

"I'm gone." I finally stood up to my mother. It felt great.

I had an open invitation from Laura to stay in her extra bedroom if things got dicey at home. I packed my things, called Tom for a ride, and was gone in an hour.

It was mid-January. Laura's apartment lacked decent heat, but my freedom made up for it. Tom spent a few nights with me until he arrived loud and drunk. Laura's neighbors called the cops.

"I'm sorry, Ava. Either Tom goes or you go. They'll kick me out if he causes trouble again."

~~~

I made sure I returned home when my father was there. I begged them to take me back.

"Tom's a loser," my father said. "Call off the wedding."

"If you marry him, he'll beat you up every day and twice on Sunday," my mother warned.

"I'll think about it," I lied.

I'd seen Tom's temper but never directed at me. He hadn't been given love at home. If I showed him love, I was convinced he'd change. Maybe I was mirroring my own life. Maybe I was too hopeful. Maybe I was a fool.

Our wedding was scheduled for April 27, 1963. Two months before the wedding, I learned I was pregnant. My mother continued to pressure me to cancel the ceremony. I couldn't tell her I had to get married.

Abortion was out of the question. I'd heard horror stories about backroom abortions and the damage inflicted on victims. I couldn't bring myself to have a baby and give it up for adoption. Tom would never speak to me again.

I foolishly tried hiding my condition. I faked my period by rolling up clean sanitary napkins in the bathroom garbage, thinking my mother would never check. Once again, I was wrong. Did I "glow" from pregnancy, or did my mother hear my morning sickness?

"You're nothing but a piece of trash. You deserve a bum like Tom."

My mother's words stung more than ever. Another layer of shame piled itself onto my fragile soul.

Nobody was backing out of the wedding now. But not everyone was attending.

"You can forget about your father walking you down the aisle. We will *not* be coming to the wedding," my mother informed me a few days before the ceremony.

"Fine, then we'll elope," I said.
~~~

"No, you won't. The chapel's reserved, and we paid for the reception. I've lost you but I'm not losing our money."

"I want to talk to Dad."

"He has nothing more to say, and neither do I."

Looking back, I should've gone to my father. I should've backed out of the wedding. I should've done a lot of things. But I was nineteen, pregnant, naive, and frightened.

Did my father know I was pregnant? Did he know he wasn't walking me down the aisle? No more words were spoken to me until the evening before my wedding when my mother broke her silence.

"Get out of this house, *now*!" she said, before we sat down for dinner.

"Where do you expect me to go?" I tried keeping my voice steady, and my tears hidden.

"That's not our problem. Maybe your future in-laws will take you. You're no better than they are."

My wedding dress hung on my bedroom door. Each pearl button sneered at me as I shoved it in a brown paper bag. I wiped my tears with my veil, then stuck it on my head as my final act of defiance. I grabbed the rest of my ensemble and my honeymoon suitcase, purposely slamming my mother's chair as I pushed my way through the kitchen and out the door.

I called my parents' friends, Mary and Ed, from a neighbor's. They were kind enough to open their home to me. I asked them to pick me up in front of our house—anything to humiliate my mother.

Mary and Ed drove me to the chapel the next day. In the parking lot was my mother's green Thunderbird. I should've realized they'd come to save face.

"Mary, thanks for last night. Ava hasn't been sleeping well.

Wedding jitters, you know. I thought it would be better if she had a change of scenery." My mother was at her fraudulent best.

Mary's eyes darted in my direction. She knew the truth. I suspected their friendship had abruptly ended.

A wave of nausea came over me as I started down the aisle. Was it morning sickness, doubt, or fear? I held onto my father's arm for support and stared at my satin shoes. I couldn't look at my father, the guests, or Tom, who waited for me at the altar.

I knew I was walking into the biggest mistake of my life, yet my feet kept moving.

When I said, "I do," Tom's face broke into the biggest grin I'd ever seen. When the minister pronounced us "man and wife," he crushed me in his embrace.

"Love ya, Ava," he whispered.

Maybe I was wrong. Maybe things would work out for us.

My mother was all smiles as we made our exit. She joined the small crowd on the church steps throwing rice and waving.

We hadn't hired a limo to take the bridal party to the restaurant. My mother said she wanted to save the money for our reception, giving guests the option of prime rib as well as chicken cordon bleu. What she didn't tell me was that she had canceled the dinner once she learned I was pregnant. Our guests were served hors d'oeuvres and cocktails in the smallest banquet room at Smitty's Bar and Grill.

Fifty people squeezed into a space meant for twenty. Piped-in music replaced the band I had expected. With nowhere else to stand, everyone crowded onto the miniature dance floor.

After an hour of bumping and jostling, the crowd dissipated. I asked myself who was more embarrassed: me or our guests? It certainly wasn't my mother.

My parents left without saying goodbye. I saw my father's pained expression as he looked back at me. He had to go home with my mother. I was free.

Before leaving for our honeymoon in Virginia Beach, we changed our clothes in Smitty's restrooms and stayed for a few drinks at the main bar. Tom's parents promised to pick up our wedding gear and return Tom's rented tuxedo.

If only I could have rented my gown, too.

Waves of nausea hit me once we left the bar. Tom's cigarettes, champagne, too little food, and broken shocks on his 1956 Chevy Bel Air didn't mix well with pregnancy. I left a trail of vomit along the New Jersey Turnpike. Tom's temper escalated with each stop.

"What the hell's wrong with you?"

"I'm pregnant, or did you forget?"

We said nothing more until we got close to Washington, DC.

"Tom, we need to stop for the night. We should've left tomorrow morning."

"Bitch. I wanted us to wake up in Virginia Beach. You better not ruin anything else on this honeymoon."

He pulled into the parking lot of the first motel we came to. What Tom saw was a blinking VACANCY sign. What I saw was what was known as a "motor court" in the 1930s. The room smelled of mold. Long black hairs peeked out from under the sink. I pulled the tattered bedspread down and collapsed. All I wanted to do was sleep.

Tom had other ideas.

When I turned away from him, he rolled me toward him.

"Not tonight, please? Maybe in the morning," I said.

"No, now!"

His breath reeked of stale cigarettes and too much alcohol. Another round of nausea hit me. I ran to the bathroom.

"Get out here, Ava Harrison. You're my fucking wife!"

I locked the door, sat on the toilet, and wept.

Bang! Slam! Tom pounded on the bathroom door. I knew if I didn't come out, we'd be thrown out of the motel. Cautiously I opened the door.

"That's better," Tom said.

I knew I had no choice. I took a deep breath, clenched my teeth, and let my mind drift to the days before Tom entered my life.

Is rape possible between husband and wife? My entire body ached.

We arrived in Virginia Beach early the next afternoon. I wanted to see the sights. Tom wanted to find the closest liquor store.

"C'mon, honey, let's fool around." Tom pushed me back on the bed.

Sex was out of the question. I felt bruised inside and out. Nausea overpowered me.

"Not now, Tom. I feel miserable."

"Nobody says no to me!" Tom raised his arm and slapped me across the face.

I screamed.

"Shut up and do what you're told!"

I rolled into a fetal position and cried into the pillow.

Tom lit a cigarette and poured another shot of whiskey.

"How 'bout I put this cigarette out on your tits?"

"Get away from me!"

He tried a kinder approach. I fell for it. It was over in a flash. Tom rolled off me and passed out.

The next day was more of the same. Tom had no interest in anything but whiskey and sex. My wrists were bruised from where he'd held me down. I was afraid he'd cause me to lose the baby.

Tom snuggled up to me after another round of morning sickness.

"How d'ya like bein' married to me?" he asked.

I couldn't tell him the truth. "It's nice," I whispered.

"Show me how nice."

He pulled me closer. My body recoiled in discomfort.

"Wassa matter? Too rough for ya?"

"Please, Tom. Leave me alone."

Before I knew what had happened, he backhanded me and sent me flying across the room. I landed on the floor, inches away from the corner of the dresser. I couldn't move.

The room was filled with Tom's ragged breath and my muffled sobs. Neither of us moved for what seemed like an hour.

Then he said, "Oh my God, Ava. I didn't mean to hurt you. I promise it'll never happen again."

I didn't believe him for a second. I thought about my mother's silence and how I thought a slap would hurt less. I was so wrong.

Eventually, my morning sickness passed, and I was a human being again. Tom was in a good mood and wanted to see the sights. People smiled at us and a few asked if we were newlyweds. I fantasized about us settling into an idyllic life, but I knew it would remain a fantasy. I'd move back with my parents when we got home.

As an act of respect, I rang my parents' doorbell rather than let myself in with my key. My mother glared at me through the screen door.

"What are you doing here, Mrs. Harrison?"

"Can I come in and talk to you?"

"We have nothing to talk about," she said.

"Please—" I held onto the door to steady myself.

She opened the door, turned her back to me, and busied herself at the kitchen sink.

"Can we talk?" I asked.

"About what?" Her back was still toward me.

I sat at the kitchen table facing her. "I made a terrible mistake. Tom beat me on our honeymoon. You were right about everything. I'm so sorry."

"I told you he was a bum. I warned you, Miss Smarty-pants."

"I can't stay with him. He'll keep hitting me. Can I come home?" It was the first time I allowed myself to break down in front of my mother.

She faced me. "You made your bed. Now go lie in it."

I stared at her broad shoulders, wide ribcage, and dyed blond hair freshly curled and sprayed—the classic 1960s housewife. She turned away from me and stared out the window.

five

Mrs. Harrison

We lived in a rundown apartment in Plainfield until Tom's parents gave us money for a down payment on a house. Tom took the train into Manhattan for work, leaving me to clean and repair a place that should have been condemned.

Nothing I did made Tom happy. He promised to be home at six but rarely got in before nine or ten, drunk on his ass.

"Where's my dinna?" he'd scream.

I'd reheat what had been ready at six. It was never good enough. I'd put the plate of food in front of him; he'd take a bite, stand up, and slap me across the face. Sometimes he'd grab my upper arms and shake me. Despite the warm weather, I wore long sleeves to hide the bruises.

Everything changed after our son, Tommy, was born in November 1963. Fatherhood calmed Tom and brought me more joy than I ever thought possible. I'd stare at my beautiful baby boy for hours. Every new mom believes hers is the most beautiful baby ever born. I *knew* mine was.

"I promise to love you forever. I'll always be there for you." Tommy may not have understood the exact meaning of my words, but his smiles and giggles told me he felt their message.

Tom came home sober and on time and played with Tommy before I put him down. After dinner, he'd have a few drinks and relax with me in front of the TV.

Had we become the perfect American family?

Each evening I bundled up Tommy and drove to the train station to wait for my husband. For three months he stepped off the six o'clock train, gave us a huge daddy smile, and kissed us hello.

One frigid Friday in February, it all changed. No Tom. Had he missed the train? Maybe he called after I had left the house. In the days before answering machines and cell phones, I had no way of knowing.

"Should we stay here or go home?" I asked my baby.

Tommy had no answer. We waited for the seven o'clock train. No Tom.

Eight o'clock. No Tom.

I drove back home and waited. Sometime after ten o'clock, Tom stumbled in. Scotch seeped from his pores. Instinctively I stood in front of Tommy's door. He'd never seen his father drunk.

"Missed th' train. Boss an' me worked late," he mumbled.

"Next time call, okay?" I kept my voice soft and level. "Did you have dinner?"

"Had a piss-a."

Half the pizza had dripped down his white shirt.

"Come to bed, honey," I said.

He followed me complacently into the bedroom. I steeled myself for the first slap, for the rape I knew was coming. Nothing. He collapsed on the bed.

The next day it was as though nothing had happened.

Fridays became Tom's night out. I didn't mind. It gave me more time with Tommy. Within a month he added Thursdays. By April, Tom spent three or four nights away from me.

~

"Happy Anniversary!" I kissed Tom awake on Monday morning, April 27, 1964.

From his expression I knew he'd forgotten.

"I'll make prime rib for us. Can you be home at six?"

"Sure, hon," he promised.

A bouquet of spring flowers sat on the kitchen table while prime rib roasted in the oven. I strapped Tommy in his car seat and made the five-minute drive to the train station. No Tom.

We drove home. I turned off the oven, covered the meat, and waited for a phone call.

No call, no Tom, no anniversary dinner.

A little after ten o'clock, I heard a pounding on the door. Tom lurched into the living room.

I couldn't help myself. "You missed our anniversary dinner."

"Iss still time to eat."

I knew the food was ruined, but I had no choice. He took one look at the plate of cold meat and congealed gravy and shoved it off the table.

"You call this dinner?" he screamed.

"Please, Tom, you'll wake the baby," I pleaded.

"He needs to see what a first-class bitch I married."

I ducked to avoid Tom's slap. His arm slammed into the sink.

"Now look what you've done!"

Tommy's wails sounded from the bedroom and brought me to tears. Why did I bring an innocent baby into the nightmare of my life?

I picked up Tommy and held him close.

I'll always be here for you. I'll do my very best to love you. I promise someday I'll get us into a stable home.

~~~
~~~

The 1960s were a time of change, social unrest, and women's liberation. All of that was slow to reach me. Tom had friends on the police force. Even if he hadn't, I couldn't file a complaint. Women were always at fault. Our bruises were self-inflicted or justified. I didn't know how to find a women's shelter, even if one existed. I was too humiliated to tell my friends about the abuse. I doubted anyone would believe me. All they saw was charming Tom. Maybe he drank too much, but didn't all guys?

Before Tommy was born, I had written to my mother, asking her to reconsider taking me back. I received no reply. When I called, she hung up without a word. I sent a birth announcement to my parents, hoping a grandchild would soften their hearts. I received nothing in return.

One afternoon, when Tommy was about six months old, I called home. My brother answered.

"Please don't hang up, Henry."

"Where've you been? I miss you," Henry said.

I couldn't drag my brother into the horror of my life. Instead, I said, "Would you and Mom come see my baby?"

"You bet!" Henry said. "Let me get Mom."

"Wait—" Henry didn't hear me.

"Mom! Ava's on the phone. Let's go see her baby."

The next afternoon my mother and brother met Tommy. I straightened the house, hoping to make my mother proud. I watched her harsh eyes judge our secondhand furniture, the crumbling plaster walls, the cracked tile, and corroded plumbing. But her face softened when she met her grandson.

"He's beautiful, Ava," my mother said as she bent over the crib. "He looks so much like you when you were a baby."

I wouldn't know. She'd destroyed every photo from her first marriage. I suspected she destroyed the rest of my photos after I married Tom.

That afternoon, I felt as though I were outside myself looking at a tender family scene. Did my mother want to be back in my life? How could she waltz into my life after a year and claim ownership of Tommy? She had hurt me more times than I could remember. I refused to bring my baby into her world of silence and hatred.

My mother knew about the abuse I suffered and did nothing. Now I would do nothing for her. She called several times after our visit. I hung up on her.

The phone calls stopped, but I didn't stop thinking about my mother. She was a woman trapped in her past, in a culture that provided few tools for self-growth. She was born to immigrant parents whose struggle for survival and success took center stage. By the time I entered my grandparents' lives, they had the time and money to give me love and attention, providing my mother with another reason to resent me.

Would my life have been different if I'd forgiven her? Would she have taken me back and provided a home for Tommy? Would I have been able to finish college, find a decent husband, a career? I've asked myself these pointless questions countless times.

I remembered my mother's words, "You made your bed. Now go lie in it."

My bed was made, and there I lay.

six

Barbra

When Tommy was two years old, I found a part-time job at Dryer's Pharmacy, and an elderly neighbor offered to watch Tommy for free. I now had some money of my own but more importantly, the job got me out of the house and into the community.

Mr. Beasley, my favorite customer, stopped in one day to fill a prescription.

"How're you feeling, Mr. B?" I asked.

"Good. Say, do you think your boss would let me hang a poster in your window?"

"I'm sure he would. What's it for?"

"The Elks are having a talent show in a few weeks. Mostly lip-synching, some regular singing. I remember you were a darn good singer in high school. Why don't you sign up?"

I'm sure I turned a bright shade of crimson. I hadn't sung a note in years, at least not in public.

After Mr. Beasley left, I read the poster. The Elks were offering fifty dollars to the winner. I doubted my own voice would win any contest, but maybe if I lip-synched . . .

Barbra Streisand was all the rage. Her hit single "People" was on everybody's lips. Maybe it could be on my lips, too.

I paid the five-dollar registration fee and learned I was allowed a second song. I chose "Down with Love" from Streisand's second album.

I practiced until I had every movement perfectly choreographed. Telling Tom would be the scariest part for me. To my surprise, he loved the idea.

"We'll invite my parents and all our friends," he said.

You mean those losers from the bar? I kept my thoughts private, relieved I wouldn't have to keep my performance hidden from my husband.

Stepping onto the stage at the Elks Hall felt like my Broadway debut. I held my silenced mike, closed my eyes, and mouthed every one of Barbra's words. I received a generous round of applause after "People" and a standing ovation after "Down with Love."

I won. Me, Ava Harrison, won first prize. I hadn't been this happy since Tommy was born. Tom and his parents shared my joy. For a moment, I wished my parents and my brother were there. I pushed the thought aside.

"I'm starting a college fund for Tommy with my prize money," I said.

Tom didn't argue. I knew my joy was fleeting. *Live for today and enjoy the celebration*, I told myself. And that's what I did.

For a while life improved. Tom spent more time away from me, coming home later and later, often collapsing on the couch as soon as he walked in the door. If he didn't want dinner, the food went in the garbage. My salary from the drugstore compensated for the waste.

My friend Laura noticed a change in me.

"It's nice to see your arms," she said.

"I don't understand."

"Come on, Ava, I know Tom slaps you around. Long sleeves and makeup only cover so much. Nobody bumps into doors as often as you claim."

Tears of shame poured from my eyes.

"Leave him while you're still young," Laura said.

"But what about Tommy? He needs a father."

"You call Tom a father? He's a drunk. He beats the crap outta you, and he'll do the same to Tommy when he's older."

"He'd never hit my baby," I said between sobs.

"You keep telling yourself that, honey," Laura said.

I knew Laura was right. I needed to get away from Tom before another round of violence started, but how? My boss at the pharmacy couldn't give me a raise or more hours. Other than winning the Irish Sweepstakes, I had no way to support Tommy and myself.

The only consolation came from Laura and our friend Rose. They gave me the freedom to open up about my marriage. Whenever I felt overwhelmed, they comforted me. We spent late afternoons curled up on my couch drinking coffee and sharing secrets and dreams.

One spring afternoon, Laura handed me a brochure from an organization called Project Concern. "Check this out. It's run by Dr. James Turpin. The library has a book about his work, *Vietnam Doctor: The Story of Project Concern*."

"Maybe he could help me," I said, half-joking.

"Sorry, Ava. He's working mostly with kids overseas."

"Maybe Tommy and I could move."

Laura didn't appreciate my sarcasm.

"I thought the three of us could do some fundraising for Project Concern," Laura said.

"Count me in," Rose said.

"I don't see how I could help. Between Tommy, the drugstore, and you-know-who—"

"Just read the brochure. All you need to do is get on the phone and ask for donations. It'll get you out of the rut you're in, and you'll make a difference to a lot of people," Laura said.

I'd never made a bit of difference in anybody's life, except maybe my son's. A ray of hope began to build inside me.

"I'll do it!"

Reading Dr. Turpin's book and the information about Project Concern lifted me out of my misery. I'd suffered abuse with Tom, but I always had access to food, clean water, and medical care. The poverty he wrote about broke my heart.

St. Steven's Catholic Church was the local headquarters for donations. We met with the head of volunteer operations who told us Project Concern needed medical supplies. Together we drafted an outline of an introduction we would use to solicit donations from area medical offices. Laura and Rose had full-time jobs, so most of the phone work was my responsibility.

Once Tom was out the door and Tommy fed and dressed, I sat at the kitchen table and opened the phonebook. My hand trembled as I dialed the first number, which was for Dr. Aaron. I spoke to his receptionist, who was also his wife.

"Hello, my name is Ava Harrison. I'm calling on behalf of Dr. James Turpin and Project Concern." I provided her with general information about the organization and the types of donations we were requesting.

"Of course, dear. We'd be happy to donate several first aid kits." Was it the quiver in my voice that convinced Mrs. Aaron, or the true needs of the organization?

With each call, my confidence built. By the time I called Dr. Azariti, I didn't need the script. Not every office was as amenable as Dr. Aaron's, but most offered something.

My boss at the pharmacy was eager to help. He donated a case of Band-Aids and said he'd speak to other pharmacists in the area.

By the end of the week, I'd gotten to "H" in the yellow pages, and through St. Steven's, arranged a truck to collect the donations on Saturday. Laura, Rose, and I stared in disbelief at the cases of medicine, first aid supplies, and vitamins that came off the truck.

After several months, St. Steven's ran out of room, so we rented warehouse space to store the supplies. I had called every doctor within a ten-mile radius, then set my sights on dentists. Dr. Mitchum, an oral surgeon, nearly knocked me off my chair.

"Your timing couldn't be better," he said. "I'm closing my office and retiring. I have an X-ray machine that needs a home. If you can pick it up in the next week, it's yours."

Our local newspaper heard about the X-ray machine and wrote an article about Project Concern and our successful campaign. Tom skimmed through the paper in his usual drunken stupor until he saw my photo on page three.

"What the hell is this?"

"Collecting donations. Trying to help those less fortunate," I said with pride.

"Huh, well, long as it don't interfere with your housework and your job, guess I'll let you do it. Next time ask my permission before you start somethin'." He turned the page and buried his head in the paper.

Tom's words hurt but did nothing to kill my joy. I truly believed I had found my calling.

We raised over $250,000 in donations, which were flown from McGuire Air Force Base to Puerto Vallarta, Mexico. Dr. Turpin handwrote a letter thanking us for our efforts. I cried tears of love and pride as I read his words.

And then we were done.

The next morning, I sat with Tommy at the kitchen table with nothing to do.

Perhaps I could find another cause, another way to help.

In my heart I knew it wouldn't happen. Once again, I was pregnant.

~~~

Another baby was the last thing I needed or wanted. With no morning sickness, I was able to keep my condition a secret from Tom for almost four months. I knew I'd be forced to quit my job. No self-respecting woman worked once she started to show. My boss at the pharmacy wouldn't hold my job, and even if he could, he'd want someone reliable, not a woman with an infant and a toddler. I sank into a deep depression, knowing I'd be returning to my nightmare of abuse for years to come.

Tom, on the other hand, was thrilled when he learned I was pregnant.

"Hope it's another boy," he said.

My pregnancy did nothing to change Tom's behavior. When I questioned him about working late, he claimed he and his boss were entertaining clients. Being part of the "good old boys" network was vital to getting ahead in sales. He pointed to his ever-increasing commission checks to prove his point.

He never let me know until he came home whether he wanted dinner or not. If what I had made was less than perfect, he'd slap me across the face. He was careful not to throw me across the room, careful not to damage the baby.

Ultrasound to determine the sex of a baby wasn't an option until the 1970s, so we had to rely on intuition and old wives' tales. Laura and Rose were convinced it was a boy.

"Maybe another son is what Tom needs," Laura said. "Maybe then he'll stop drinking."

"It'll take a lot more for him to stop. And what if it's a girl?" I imagined myself barefoot and pregnant until I finally gave Tom another son.

~~~

Fortunately for everyone, I delivered a baby boy, Lee, on May 1, 1967. Tom's parents were overjoyed. I made no attempt to contact my parents and received no word from them.

I prayed for freedom, my babies, and for something to change.

A year later, my prayers were answered. Tom's company promoted him to a management position and sent him to work in Stamford, Connecticut. He hopped a train on Sunday evening and came home on Friday. For the first time in five years, my weekdays were my own.

Tom's raise gave me more household income. I bought a few nice pieces of furniture, toys for the kids, and books for me. I even thought about enrolling in a class at our community college. With less than forty-eight hours a week with my husband, I began to feel like a human being.

My respite was short-lived.

"Big news!" Tom told me after three months. "I found us a house in Stamford."

"But what about our home? We've done so much to fix it up." That was an outright lie. I was the only one who'd done any work on the house.

"We'll sell it and make a profit. You'll love Stamford," he said.

Stamford was the last place I wanted to live, but what choice did I have? I had two young kids, no job, no skills, and no money of my own.

Our house sold in a matter of weeks for a $3,000 profit, which was huge in 1968. Our attorney, Michael, was Laura's cousin. Laura encouraged me to share my story with him.

"This is your chance to get away from Tom," Michael said. "The law says real estate profits must be equally divided."

So this is what hope feels like.

"God bless you, Michael."

I managed to get Tom's signature on the real estate documents, knowing he'd be in Stamford for the closing. In the meantime,

Michael agreed to loan me the security deposit on an apartment. I'd pay him back once I received my $1,500 from the sale.

I moved without saying a word to Tom. I left him with a table and chair, a knife, fork, spoon, and dish.

Have a nice life, I whispered, closing the door for the final time.

What did Tom think when he walked into that empty house? I imagined him throwing the dish against the wall and tearing through the cabinets for his bottle of scotch, which I'd poured down the sink.

Tom then drove to his parents' house. From his brother, Kevin, I later learned what had happened once Tom arrived.

"Where is she?" he screamed. "Where the hell are my kids?"

His parents sat at their kitchen table in their own drunken stupor.

"We don't know nothin'," his mother said.

"You're a liar. I know she's here."

"Have a seat, boy," his father said, "and calm yourself."

"Calm? You want calm? My wife took my kids and left me with an empty house, and you want calm? I'll show you calm!"

With one grand sweep of his arm, he cleared the table. Dishes, glasses, whiskey—it all went flying, crashing to the floor.

His mother tried making her way into the living room. Her feet crunched broken glass.

"Where you goin'?" Tom grabbed her arm and backhanded her across the face.

"Doris, call the cops." His father stood to confront his son, knocking his chair onto the floor.

His mother ran into the living room and dialed the operator. "Police! Quick!"

Tom threw a glass ashtray at his mother, missing her by inches. His father restrained him while she spoke to a police officer.

Tom spent the night in jail. His parents refused to press charges.

seven

Changes

I heard a friendly knock on my apartment door. Thinking it was a neighbor, I opened the door. Tom barged in. His face was red and distorted. Alcohol seeped from his pores.

"I'll teach you to leave me, bitch. I'm takin' the kids."

He slapped me across the mouth. I was certain he dislodged a few of my teeth.

"No, Tom, please. Leave us alone," I pleaded.

He nearly pulled my arm from its socket and sent me flying into the bedroom door. I curled into a fetal position to avoid more injury and noticed Tommy cowering behind the door, tears streaming down his cheeks. I motioned for him to hide. Tom saw me, then saw my son.

"Tommy, get out here. You're comin' with me," Tom said in a quieter voice.

"Tommy, stay with Mommy!"

Tom grabbed my bruised arm and dragged me into the kitchen. He tried kicking me in the stomach. My only defense was to return to a fetal position. I opened my mouth to protest. No words emerged. My body froze.

I lay helpless as he bundled my children, along with their toys and belongings, and left me on the floor. I don't know how long I lay there. Time and memory ceased to exist.

~~~

Sometime later, a neighbor saw my front door open and called to me. She must have heard me whimper and came into the kitchen.

"Ava! What happened?"

I couldn't speak.

I heard her call the police. Everything went dark.

The next thing I knew I was in an ambulance. A man in a white coat was speaking to me.

"We're taking you to Sweetwater Clinic," he said, referring to the nearest psychiatric facility.

I'm not crazy. Help me, I wanted to say but my jaw refused to move.

The doctors and staff at Sweetwater treated me with kindness and allowed me to rest and heal. I met with a psychiatrist, who implied my husband was the one who needed help, not me.

While at Sweetwater, I called Rose.

"Ava, you need to go to Stamford and get your kids."

"How can I? He'll kill me."

"Think of your kids," she said.

Rose was right. Once I was well enough, I went back to my apartment. Tom had emptied the place and shoved my clothing into a corner. I didn't have much to pack.

Tom was clean and sober when I arrived in Stamford.

"Let's make this work, hon," he said.

"Sure, Tom. I'm sorry." I didn't mean it for a second.

Tommy and baby Lee were overjoyed to see me.

"I'll get you out of here," I whispered, as I tucked them into bed.

Our life was stable for five days. Tom came home after work, ate
~~~

dinner, and watched TV with the family. On day six, Tom stumbled in after ten o'clock, holding a half-empty bottle of scotch.

"Whaas for dinna?"

I gave him a dried-out plate of meatloaf and instant potatoes. It did no good to reheat the food. He'd hate whatever I put in front of him.

"This ain't dinna." He threw the plate at me, missing by a foot. "You're never gonna change, are ya?"

Tom stood, holding onto the table for support. He saw a carving knife on the counter, picked it up, and came after me.

"This'll teach ya!" he screamed.

I slipped on the mashed potatoes as I ran into the living room. Tom wasn't so lucky. I heard him land in the debris that had been his dinner.

Tom lay on the floor, still clutching the knife. I hoped he'd passed out. Instead, he stood and shook the knife at me. "You'll pay for this."

I watched him hobble to the front door, grab his jacket and keys, and leave. I bolted the door and called the police. They promised to post a patrol car outside the house until I could get to safety.

The next day, I packed my kids and as much as I could carry and drove back to New Jersey. Rose took us in until I arranged to move back into my old apartment. After five hellish years, I finally found enough strength to file a restraining order and began divorce proceedings, citing mental and physical cruelty. Tom never violated the restraining order and didn't contest the divorce. My attorney arranged for child support but no alimony.

I found a job as a medical assistant, left my babies with a neighbor while I worked, and entered the next phase of my adult life.

eight

The Beginning of the End

Dr. Wendell, a family physician, trained me in every aspect of his practice. I was a quick learner and appreciated the job. We developed a business-friendly relationship, and I looked forward to coming to work. I knew I had no chance for advancement, but I didn't care. I was earning my own money.

Dr. Wendell was well-connected with medical specialists in the area and often sent me to drop off X-rays and patient files, which is how I met Dr. Bendar, a pediatrician.

Dr. Bendar was handsome; we enjoyed flirting with each other. Flirting was as far as I wanted our relationship to go. My priority was my kids. He had other ideas.

I was relaxing in my apartment one Saturday afternoon when I saw Dr. Bendar walking through my complex. I didn't exactly live on poverty row, but my home was on the low end of the economic scale. He had no reason to be there except to see me. I waited for a knock. None came.

Two weeks later the knock came. It was a Saturday evening, about seven o'clock. My kids were in bed.

"Dr. Bendar, what are you doing here?"

"Hi, Ava, can I come in?"

"Sure. Have a seat." I motioned to my one chair.

He ignored the chair and plopped next to me on the couch.

Flashbacks of Tom flooded my mind when I realized he'd been drinking. He draped his arm behind me. I slid away from him. He moved closer. I stood.

"I think you should leave," I said. "I need to get ready for bed."

"I'm ready for bed." Dr. Bendar dragged me into a stifling embrace.

"I didn't mean with you." I kept my voice soft.

I may as well have said nothing. He pushed me onto the floor and tore at my clothing. I knew if I struggled or screamed, I'd wake my kids. They'd seen enough horrors in their short lives. The last thing they needed to see was their mother being raped.

I lay there like a dead fish.

"That's better," he said, as he pulled down his pants.

As so many women of the time, my mind drifted elsewhere while he did his business. He wasn't violent. All he left was another emotional scar on my soul.

After Dr. Bendar left, I threw my clothes in the trash and lit a scented candle to remove his stench from my apartment. I soaked in the hottest bathwater I could stand, then watched the water drain from the tub, carrying my tears and his filth into the city sewer.

I thought about buying a gun for protection but knew I could never summon the courage to use it. Instead, when I returned to work on Monday, I told Dr. Wendell what had happened.

"I want to press charges and sue him." It was time I fought back.

"I'll do what I can to help you," Dr. Wendell said.

Dr. Wendell kept his word. I filed suit and won. Dr. Bendar lost his position at the hospital, and I was awarded $5,000, a huge sum in the late 1960s. I paid off my debts and bought a "new" used Mustang.

Even with my settlement and child support from Tom, I couldn't make ends meet. My salvation came from Rose.

"Hey, Ava, did you ever think about dancing?" she asked.

"You know I love to dance. I just don't get much chance to these days. Why?"

"Tina, my upstairs neighbor, told me they're looking for go-go dancers at Gentleman's Delight," Rose said.

"I don't know—"

"Tina says you can make thirty to forty dollars a night. The work's easy, and the bouncers make sure the customers keep their hands off," Rose said.

"But what about my kids? They're with a sitter all day. I can't leave them at night, too."

"Ava, think about it. One or two nights a week is all. Your kids'll be in bed before you leave, and you'll be there for them in the morning."

I had nothing to lose. I'd have to pay a sitter and buy costumes, but it was a chance to get ahead and give my babies things they lacked.

Tina helped me get started. She lent me a few costumes—complete with fringe and sequins.

Stepping out in front of the customers the first time was beyond frightening. I watched the other girls and mimicked their movements. Before the first song finished, I'd found my rhythm, but I was still a wreck inside.

"You're a natural, Ava," Tina said.

"I don't think I can do this. Some of the customers look like they want to grab me," I said.

"That's the whole idea. You'll learn the business. Give it a couple of weeks. It helps if you have a few drinks before you go on."

I took Tina's advice and sipped a weak vodka and orange juice in the dressing room. I made one drink last through my five-hour shift. I figured I'd sweat out the alcohol.

By the time I got home, I was wiped out. Mornings came way too soon.

Dr. Wendell noticed a change in me.

"Are you feeling okay, Ava? You seem tired."

"I'm okay, Dr. Wendell. I had to take a second job. I'm barely making ends meet."

"I don't see how I can pay you more," he said.

Women made less than men, especially women with only a high school education and no experience. Dr. Wendell was paying me close to minimum wage despite everything I did for him. Dancing could be my chance to make a living wage.

Dr. Wendell thought for a minute. "You've been here a year now. I suppose I could give you a twenty-five-cent-an-hour raise. Would that help?"

Ten dollars more a week before taxes? I can earn that in a couple of hours dancing.

"To be honest, I've started dancing two nights a week at Gentleman's Delight," I confessed.

Dr. Wendell's face said it all: surprise, confusion, disgust.

"Ava, how could you? You know the type of men who frequent those places. What if one of my patients saw you? I'm sorry, but medicine and dancing don't go together."

"I'm sorry, Dr. Wendell, but being a medical assistant and being broke don't go together."

My heart pounded in my chest. My breathing stopped as I waited for his response.

"Your choice, Ava. Medicine or dancing."

"Dancing, then. I'm giving you my two-week notice."

With that, I ended one career and began another.

nine

Spiraling Downward

I began dancing four or five nights a week and earning some real money—more than double what I earned with Dr. Wendell. Some nights I tended bar. I thought working nights would give me extra time with my kids. I was wrong.

My nights got later and later. At first, I'd have a drink only on weekends, but before I knew it, I had a drink every night.

After a busy shift, I needed to relax, and who better to do it with than other dancers? I looked forward to a drink, often just a Coke, with the girls at the end of my shift. We understood each other. Sometimes the sun would be coming up when we left the bar.

It would be too late or too early, depending on my point of view, to pick up my kids after work. They'd need breakfast in a few hours. By that time, I'd be dead asleep. I'd see the kids for a few hours in the afternoon, give them dinner, and send them back to the sitter. I knew I was neglecting them, but wasn't everything I did for their benefit?

Dancers chose their own costumes. Some girls preferred themes: schoolgirl, nurse, teacher, cop. Others like me went for glitz and glitter. Tina introduced me to her seamstress who custom-made my outfits. She hand-sewed crystals, beads, lace, and fringe into my outfits. They all came with little lacy stockings. It wasn't long before I had enough costumes to change six times a night. I carried a full suitcase to each gig.

Some nights were perfect. I'd find my groove and sparkle as much as my costumes. The audience would go nuts for me, and the tips would roll in. Other nights the music was all wrong; I'd trip over my feet; my costume would tear. The inconsistency messed with my head.

Competition was fierce between dancers. I had my friends, mostly Tina's friends, who took me in. When we worked together, we'd have a blast. Other nights, I'd work with total bitches. They'd try to one-up me with costumes, stage presence, and egos. I always compared myself to them, and always came up "less-than" in my mind. They crushed me during my first year until I learned to ignore them.

When I'd tell women outside the business what I did, I'd get mixed reactions. Some judged me; others envied me. The question they always asked was how it felt to be on stage with a room full of men gawking at me.

"I think of them as a bunch of perverts," I'd reply.

"All of them?" they'd ask.

"Once in a while, I meet a decent guy, but then I start wondering what he's doing at the club."

"What about the big tippers?"

"I feel obligated to hang with them on my break," I'd say. "Most guys are lonely, looking for attention. I always keep it short, saying I have to change costumes."

"I think about dancing sometimes," they'd say, "but I wouldn't let it get to me. I'd do it for a couple of years, save my money, and get out. What about you, Ava?"

"Yeah, sure, that's how I think."

I never admitted that's how I expected my life would be when I began dancing. I'd stay in the business long enough to get on my feet and keep my personal and work lives separate. I even changed my professional name from Ava Harrison to Ava Martin.

The money drew me in. The late nights drained me. The only people I spent time with were in the clubs. I saw no way out, so I stuffed my feelings deep inside and kept on dancing.

Biff Cardoba was a regular at Gentleman's Delight. He watched me dance but kept his distance. One night when I was bartending, we struck up a conversation.

"You're one a' the best dancers," he said. "What're you doin' behind the bar?"

I didn't believe him. He was either drunk or trying to pick me up.

"They rotate the dancers, in case you didn't notice," I said.

"I could getcha lots more work," Biff said. "Here's my card."

He handed me a plain white business card. All it said was: "Biff Cardoba, Agent" and his phone number.

"What's the deal?" I asked.

"Straight up ten percent. I'll getcha lotsa gigs. And no funny business. I got a wife."

More jobs, less hassle.

"I'm in," I said.

Gentleman's Delight was still my home base, but Biff got me work at clubs across Central Jersey. He didn't discriminate. A club was a club—whether big or small. Some stages were an afterthought, so small I'd have to hold on to the ceiling to keep my balance.

Other clubs had platforms behind the bar. Those were the safest. The best were runways from the bar to the tables. They got me closer to the customers, and I always made good tips.

The one thing the clubs had in common was grime. A haze of stale cigarette smoke hit me whether I entered day or night. Sometimes my shoes would stick to the floor as I made my way to the bar, where an undercurrent of cheap booze assaulted my nose. I'd douse myself in perfume to mask the stink, but no amount of perfume could hide the stench of urine wafting from the men's rooms.

Movies today portray clubs as one-off glamour. Dancers are

gorgeous gymnasts in various state of contortions swaying on perfectly placed poles. I haven't set foot in a club in more than thirty years, but I'm certain that's not how it is today.

It sure as hell wasn't like that back then.

ten

Bridgeport

My divorce settlement with Tom amounted to $200 a month in child support. It wasn't enough, but I told myself I was lucky he kept up with the payments. I knew in his heart Tom wanted to be a good father. He loved our kids. Sadly, he loved alcohol more.

After we'd been divorced about two years, Tom called.

"Hey, Ava. How ya doin'?"

I recognized his voice, but something was different. "Good, Tom. How're you?"

"I got some big news."

Oh shit. "Yes?"

"I'm leavin' Stamford. The company promoted me."

My heart rose into my throat. *Please don't come back to New Jersey.*

"I'm the new regional sales manager. I'll be movin' to Bridgeport, Connecticut next week."

Thank goodness. Now maybe I'll get more child support.

"Congratulations," I said.

"And I'm gettin' married again!"

I almost dropped the phone. My first thought was, *I'm not the only fool.*

"Her name's Elaine, and she has two kids from her first marriage. She's tryin' to help me stop drinkin.'"

"You wouldn't stop drinking for me. Why now?"

"Ava, we were too young to get married. And then you got pregnant."

"I didn't get pregnant by myself."

Static filled the moment.

"I have to go, Tom. Best of luck."

"Wait, Ava. I'm sorry how things went down between us."

"Are you apologizing?" I asked.

"I guess so. Elaine and I were wonderin' if we could have the kids for the summer. I wanna be a dad to them. Whadda ya say?"

I remained silent.

"I know it's outta the blue, but think about it," Tom said. "How 'bout Elaine and I stop by on Saturday? Once you meet her, I know you'll change your mind."

"Okay. But I'm not making any promises."

I don't know how long I sat with my hand resting on the phone. Memories of Tom floated through my mind like a bad melody. Did he think he could waltz back into my life with a new identity, new wife, new job, and new home for my kids?

For the first time in years, I wished I had a mother I could call for advice. An imaginary conversation took place in my head.

Mom, what should I do? Do I want him back in my life?

He never beat your kids.

But they saw him beat me. They have the scars.

You heard the change in his voice. The kids won't be alone with him. Maybe it's time to let go and give your babies a father.

The voices in my head faded. I tried conjuring up an image of my mother, but all I saw was the blurred outline of my grandmother who'd been dead for years. Was she my guardian angel? I'd made enough bad decisions in my life. Maybe it was time to connect with her spirit and wisdom. I decided to keep an open mind.

~~~~

I took off two nights from dancing so I'd have a clear head when I met Tom and Elaine. Tommy was six years old, so I knew he'd remember his father. Lee was a baby when we divorced. I doubted he'd recognize Tom.

My apartment was spotless. I made sandwiches and iced tea.

"Daddy!" Tommy ran to his father.

"Hey, sport," Tom said, picking up his son.

I held three-year-old Lee. "Remember Daddy?"

My baby boy studied the strange man in our living room.

Tom looked better than I'd ever seen him. He seemed taller, stronger, healthier. His eyes were clear, and his smile genuine.

"Where's Elaine?" I asked.

"Parking the car. She'll be here in a sec."

"Daddy, come see our room!" Tommy took his father's hand and led him upstairs to their bedroom.

Elaine tentatively knocked on my open door. It was an awkward moment for both of us, but I decided to do what I could to make her feel at home.

Elaine and I were polar opposites: I was petite, blond, and blue-eyed; she was tall and statuesque with dark-brown hair and eyes. We stared at each other.

"Come in." I invited her to sit on the couch.

Elaine's soft southern accent calmed me. She showed me photos of her eight-year-old twin boys, who were staying with their father until Tom and Elaine got settled.

After lunch, my kids left us to play in their room. Elaine opened the discussion I'd been dreading.

"Tom and I would love it if Tommy and Lee could stay with us for the summer. I'll be teaching kindergarten starting in the fall, so I'll be home all day."

"I know you're worried 'bout me," Tom said, "but I stopped drinkin'."
~~~~

"Why now, Tom?"

"Bad timing, I guess. I know things weren't good between us. I told Elaine all about it. It won't happen again, I promise."

I noticed he didn't apologize.

"We're renting a three-bedroom ranch. They'll have their own room, just like here," Elaine said.

Not like here. I sleep on the couch.

"I need to think about it," I said.

We said our goodbyes.

I went back to work the next evening. After my shift, I told Tina about Tom and Elaine.

"Might be good for your kids to spend some time with their dad," Tina said.

"He is sober, and I like Elaine."

"It would give you a break, too," Tina said.

I nodded. I wasn't one hundred percent sold on the idea, but it wasn't fair to keep the kids away from their father.

The next day, I called my attorney and initiated proceedings for shared custody. Two months later, I strapped the kids into the back of my Mustang and drove to Bridgeport. I held in my tears as Tommy and Lee hugged their father. I waved goodbye and sobbed the entire drive home.

eleven

Changes

My life was empty without my boys. I called them every day to reassure myself they were okay.

"Ava, you need to let go," Elaine said, after the first week.

"But they're my babies. I miss them."

"I'm here with them all day. They need to learn to trust me as their stepmother."

I hadn't thought of Elaine as a stepmother. It took some time for the concept to sink in.

"How about we arrange a time once a week for you to call?" Elaine suggested.

I hesitated for a moment before agreeing. Letting go wouldn't be easy, but it would be in everyone's best interest.

It didn't take long to adjust to the single life. I picked up day and night shifts, sometimes working ten days straight. More than ever, I needed to unwind after work. What was the harm in one more drink a night? Without my kids, I had all day to sleep and no need to go directly home.

One night I invited the girls to my apartment for drinks after work. Tina had a surprise for us.

"Check it out, ladies," she said, pulling a joint from her purse.

"Tina, marijuana is illegal!"

Don't get me wrong. I knew the hippie drug culture was in full swing. Everybody and their brother got high. Drug deals went down nightly in the bars, but I was a mom. What if the neighbors smelled pot and called the cops? I'd lose custody of my boys for sure.

"C'mon, Ava, take a hit. You won't believe how calm it'll make you." Tina passed the joint to me.

"What the hell." I took a hit.

We passed the joint from mouth to mouth. By the third pass, I'd melted into the sofa.

"So this is what all the hype's about," I giggled.

"Told ya. Maybe tomorrow night you'll join me out back for a joint before your shift," Tina said.

"Not if it turns me to mush."

"It'll turn you into a better dancer, which means bigger tips," Tina said.

I'll always mark that night as the beginning of the end.

I watched my mother go through a pack of cigarettes each night after dinner, which was enough to keep me away from tobacco. Smoking pot was different, especially through a bong. It softened the harshness of the smoke and relaxed me with fewer hits.

I loved the "not-give-a-shit" feeling I got when I was high. Sometimes my regulars tipped me with a joint and a bill. The more I smoked, the looser I got, the better I danced, and the more money I made. The more I made, the nicer my costumes. It was a win-win until my kids came home from Tom.

"No thanks, Tina," I said when she invited me out back.

"What's the matter, hon? Got a cold?"

"My kids are back. I need to stay straight."

"Suit yourself." Tina lit up.

I practically stumbled over my feet when I began my set.

Drooling wolf faces stared up at me from the barstools. Raucous cheers and yelps added to my fantasy. I wanted to run away from the bar scene forever.

I made it through my first set, caught up with Tina in the back, and asked for the joint.

"I thought pot wasn't addictive," I said.

"It's not," Tina said, "but it's the best way to get through the night. Betcha anything the day you stop dancing is the day you stop smoking."

"Until then—" I took the joint out back and lit up.

Now that my kids were home, I made sure I got high only before my shift and nursed one drink through the night. By the time I left work, I was sober and ready to be a mom again.

Tommy entered first grade and Lee began nursery school. Being a single parent wasn't an easy life, but it was better than life with Tom. I promised myself by the time Lee was ready for kindergarten, I'd find a new career and be home at night.

The monotony of my life went on throughout the school year. The summer of 1971 was fast approaching, and the kids would soon be leaving for ten weeks with their dad and stepmom. I loved my kids more than anything, loved watching them become little people, but I also looked forward to the freedom I'd experienced the previous summer.

My thoughts filled me with guilt. Was I a good mother? Was the time with Tom and Elaine in the kids' best interest? I searched my heart for answers. None appeared.

twelve

Jack

Was that Jesus sitting at the bar? I did a double take. Obviously, he wasn't Jesus, but he sure looked the part. Our eyes connected. He smiled—not a sleazy barfly smile but an honest-to-goodness smile. He never took his eyes off me.

After my set, I joined him. His turquoise eyes sparkled between his shoulder-length brown hair and full beard.

"What's your name?" he asked.

"Ava Harrison." I'd never given my real name to a customer. "And you?"

"Jackson P. Novak. Everyone calls me Jack."

"Nice to meet you, Jack." I felt a flutter in my gut. Was I falling for this guy?

We talked through my entire break. I knew I should be mingling with the customers, but I couldn't leave Jack's side.

"Can I call you?" he asked.

"I'd like that." I gave him my number—my real number.

Before I left for my next set, I added, "Gotta be up front with you, Jack. I have two kids."

"Cool. I love kids."

Had I found Mr. Perfect at Gentleman's Delight?

~~~

The following Sunday, Jack invited me for a picnic at Washington Crossing State Park on the Delaware River. We sat on an old comforter and stared at the water. A warm breeze softened the July heat. I smiled from deep inside.

"Tell me about yourself," he said.

"My boys are seven and four. They spend the summers with their father and stepmother."

"You look too young to have kids that old," he said.

"I'm twenty-seven. I started young."

Jack's eyebrows raised a notch. "I'm only twenty-three, but what the hell? Age is only a number. And besides, you look younger."

But I feel like fifty.

Jack worked at a lumber yard. He'd been staying with friends not far from my apartment.

"Someday, I wanna live down here by the river," he said. "D'ya like it here?"

"It's beautiful. Really peaceful."

"Great place to chill. Speaking of chill—" He reached in his jeans pocket and pulled out a joint.

"Aren't you afraid of getting busted?"

"Hell, no. Who's gonna call the cops?" He lit up and offered me a toke.

I'd never smoked pot in bright daylight and never in a public place.

I took a hit, then another, and grooved on the sunshine.

Jack was the consummate laid-back hippie. To him work was a necessary evil—nothing like Tom's eat-or-be-eaten mentality. Over the next few months, he introduced me to his gentle hippie friends. I had little in common with them, but they accepted me into their social circle. They stayed stoned day and night, lived in a communal house,
~~~

and did only what was necessary to get by. None of them had a clue what it was like to raise two young children as a single parent.

Jack had access to the best pot. My highs were higher, and most mornings I woke with a clear head. My dancing was spot-on, and I earned more tips than ever before. Tom and his abuse drifted into the past. I suspected it all would change once my kids came back in the fall, but for now life was good.

"I have to drive to Bridgeport to pick up Tommy and Lee," I told Jack the Friday of Labor Day weekend.

On the drive north, I wondered how Tommy and Lee would react to my boyfriend, especially after a summer with their high-pressure dad and his straight wife. Would they reject me and demand to return to Tom's suburban tract house?

Elaine opened the door but didn't invite me in.

"Say goodbye to Mama Lanie." She gave each a pat on their behind and nearly pushed them out the door.

Mama Lanie?

"Where's Tom? I need to talk to him." I'd planned to ask Tom for more child support, knowing it would be harder for him to refuse in person.

"At work. Sorry to rush you, but I have an appointment," Elaine said, locking the door behind her.

As I packed the kids into my car, I glanced back at the house and saw Tom watching from a bedroom window.

Coward.

Elaine's abrupt goodbye and Tom's absence had me worried. So did Tommy and Lee's silence in the car.

"Did you miss me?" I asked.

"I missed you, Mommy," Lee said.

I glanced in the rearview mirror. Tommy sat silently and stared out the window.

"We had fun! Mama Lanie took us to the beach, to Rye Playland, to the movies, and to . . ." Lee's voice trailed off as he listed their summer activities.

"Tommy, what about you?"

"We always ate dinner together. Mama Lanie tucked us into bed every night and made pancakes for breakfast."

My son just broke my heart.

Jack opened the door to my apartment, holding two sock puppets.

"Howdy do!" the puppets barked in unison. "Welcome home. Got some chili on the stove and Twinkies up my nose."

Each puppet grabbed a Twinkie and pretended to stuff them up Jack's nose. The kids burst out laughing.

"Tommy and Lee, this is my friend, Jack."

"The loves of your mom's life. I know all about you two. C'mon, let's eat."

Lee couldn't get enough of Jack. Tommy slowly slipped out of his shell but remained guarded.

A few days later, Tommy began second grade and Lee returned to nursery school.

thirteen

The Holidays

Jack hinted at moving in with me, but I wasn't ready for that level of commitment. It was one thing to have "Uncle Jack" stay over a few nights a week; it was another to make him a permanent fixture in my children's lives.

I was also concerned with Jack's ability to pay his own way. In the four months we'd been together, he'd had three low-paying, low-skill jobs. He had enough for rent at the communal farm and was always well-stocked with pot but rarely had enough money for nice restaurants or decent clothing. I told myself material wealth wasn't as important as kind, loving gestures. Jack had plenty of those.

Tommy and Lee loved spending time with Jack. He indulged them and hugged them more in one night than Tom did in all the years we were together.

Jack was perpetually stoned and encouraged me to join him. More and more I found myself unwinding with him after a strenuous night of dancing and in the afternoons before the kids came home from school. I'd built up a tolerance for pot and found I could still function well as a mom and a dancer. Pot also lessened my need for alcohol. Some nights I even skipped my vodka and orange juice.

With less stress and anxiety in my life, I felt I could be a better mother. I hoped my kids noticed the change in me.

~~~

Jack was like a kid when it came to Halloween. For the first time, we decorated the apartment with witches, goblins, and pumpkins. I had my costume designer create a black satin outfit with orange sequins. Black fishnets and a witch's hat completed my ensemble. I modeled the outfit for the kids before I left for work. I heard Tommy's voice on the phone as I exited the bathroom.

"I miss you, Dad."

A lump rose in my throat.

"Yeah, Mrs. Ritchie stays here sometimes. Sometimes Uncle Jack. Ooh, yeah, I'll ask Mom." Tommy called to me. "Mom, Dad's on the phone."

This couldn't be good.

"How ya doin', Ava?" Tom asked.

"Fine, Tom. How are you?"

"Me and Elaine wondered if the kids could come up for Thanksgiving and Christmas."

"That's not part of our arrangement," I said.

I heard shuffling on the other end of the phone. Elaine had replaced Tom.

"Hi, Ava. I know it's not part of our agreement, but Tommy and Lee said they'd like to come up for the holidays."

"They never said anything to me."

"Every time we call, they say how much they want to come back here," Elaine said.

It took me a few seconds to catch my breath.

"Every time you call?"

"You're usually sleeping or at work," Elaine said.

I mutely held the receiver.

"Ava?"

"Yes," I whispered.

"It would mean a lot to us. Think about it, okay?"

"Yeah, sure." I had to steady my hand as I hung up.
~~~

I wanted to rip the orange and black crepe paper from the windows and strangle myself. It was all a lie, a delusion.

"Tommy! Lee!" I called.

Who knew four little feet could make so much noise?

Lee sat on my lap. Tommy stayed on the other side of the room, a faint scowl on his face.

"Why didn't you tell me Daddy's been calling?"

"You don't like him. Why would you care?" Tommy said.

"I want to know everything about you two," I said.

Lee smiled and hugged me. Tommy folded his arms across his chest.

"You're never home. You don't love us," Tommy said.

"That's not true. You know Mommy has to work."

"You hardly ever called last summer," Tommy said.

"I called every week. Daddy and Mama Lanie said not to call more than that."

"You're a liar."

Tom's the liar, not me.

I knew better than to badmouth Tom. We sat in silence for a moment.

"Is it true you want to spend Thanksgiving and Christmas with them?" I asked.

"Yes!"

"You don't have to yell, Tommy. Lee, what about you?"

Lee shrugged his shoulders and hugged me tighter. Tommy glared at him.

"Will Santa find us at Daddy's?" he asked.

"Of course," I said.

"Okay, maybe yes," he whispered.

It would break my heart to lose my babies for Christmas. Reluctantly, I agreed.

The Halloween magic was gone. My dancing costume lost its sparkle. I grabbed a joint from Jack's stash and left for work. That was the first time I smoked while driving. I felt no pain by the time

I arrived at Gentleman's Delight. It would only be two holidays without my kids. I'd survive.

Jack invited me to spend Thanksgiving and Christmas with his mother and sister, Betty. I didn't tell them it had been nine years since I'd spent the holidays with a real family. I enjoyed the easy conversation, the jokes, the loving looks that passed between siblings, and how they immediately accepted me. I was afraid once his mother learned what I did for a living, she'd change her mind. But for now, it was all good.

After Christmas dinner, I found myself alone in the kitchen with Jack's mother.

"Jack told me what a tough time you've been having trying to support your children," she said. "You seem like a nice girl—not what I expected when I learned you were a go-go dancer."

I shuffled my feet, not knowing how to respond.

"It takes a lot of courage to do what you do," she continued. "I wish some of your ambition would rub off on my son. He's a smart man, and I love him to death, but he's so darn lazy."

Compliments rarely came my way. "Thank you."

"Don't thank me. I'm the one who should thank you. You're good people."

Why couldn't I have been blessed with a mother like Mrs. Novak?

fourteen

Separation

Jack floated from job to job. I danced in one club, then another. I finally managed to save a few dollars, which I promised myself I'd save for my kids' college education.

Tommy and Lee spent Easter and spring break with Tom and Elaine. After each visit, Tommy became angrier, Lee wilder. My babysitter complained about their behavior and quit. Jack offered to take over until I found a new sitter. I knew he wasn't the best influence, but I had no choice.

Tommy's second-grade teacher called me in for a conference two weeks before summer vacation.

"Mrs. Harrison, we've spoken about Tommy's discipline problems. He's a bright boy, but he can't stay focused. I recommend he repeat second grade."

"He'll be spending the summer with his father and stepmother. I'll speak to them and see that he gets into a summer school program."

"It's better to address his problems now rather than later. Why don't you and his father meet with the counselor?"

"We'll see." I knew Tom would never agree to a meeting.

I left the school feeling lower than ever. That evening, I called Tom and Elaine. I hated to admit failure, but I had to think of Tommy's best interest.

"Why don't you let me speak to his teacher?" Elaine asked.

I'm the mother. Who are you to interfere?

"I know I'm only his stepmother," Elaine continued, "but one teacher speaking to another might give us more insight into the situation."

"Okay, thanks." I decided to trust Elaine.

The school had agreed to a "wait and see" period to determine if Tommy would repeat second grade. I hoped a summer in Bridgeport would be what he needed to move ahead in school.

I called a few days after dropping the kids off with Tom and Elaine.

"They're doing great," Elaine said. "Day camp starts in July. They'll have a chance to make new friends and keep their minds active. It'll help calm Tommy and get Lee ready for kindergarten. My boys are going, too."

Elaine seemed to have all the answers.

That night I drowned my depression with alcohol. By the end of my shift, I was too drunk to drive home. Tina gave me a lift.

"Cheer up, hon," Tina said. "You've got legal custody, and you'll get your kids back in the fall."

Tina's words did little to cheer me. I tumbled out of her car and staggered to my front door. My apartment had never felt so empty. I cried myself to sleep.

Elaine called in early August.

"Ava, the summer camp is putting on a musical version of *Peter Pan*. I thought you might like to come see it."

"I'd love to."

She'd never invited me to anything before. Why now?

Elaine told me to arrive at one o'clock for the two o'clock show. I took the night off from work so I'd be able to spend time with my boys afterward. To my surprise, Tommy and Lee weren't home when I arrived.

"We dropped the kids at camp this morning," Elaine said. "The play doesn't start until three. Tom and I wanted to talk to you without them here."

I took a seat on the chair closest to the door. Tom and Elaine sat on the couch across from me. I had the distinct feeling they were ganging up on me.

Tom began, "Tommy and Lee tell us how much they like it here."

Despite the air conditioning, I broke out in a cold sweat.

"What's your point?"

"Since Tommy had so many problems in school last year and with Lee starting kindergarten, we thought it would be a good idea to reverse our custody agreement." Tom stared at me without blinking.

"Oh no you don't." My voice trembled.

"Our grammar school agreed to let Tommy move into third grade. If he stays with you, he'll have to repeat second. We're only thinking of their best interest," Elaine said.

"Their best interest is staying with their mother." My voice escalated.

"I love them like they're my own." It was Elaine's turn to stare me down.

"*Like* your own, not your own," I replied.

"Tommy says you're never home. You always dump 'em with a babysitter," Tom said.

"If you gave me more child support, maybe I wouldn't have to work so much!"

"And we don't like what we hear about that boyfriend of yours," Tom continued.

"And what business is it of yours who I date?"

"Just sayin.'"

"Like you were any kind of good influence," I said. "Drunk all the time, beating me in front of them. Where the hell do you get off judging me?"

"Maybe I wasn't the best husband, but I've changed. Right, Elaine?"

"Tom told me how he used to be. He's different since he stopped drinking. He has a good job, comes home every night, and treats me and the kids like gold," Elaine said.

"How do you expect me to believe you?" I asked.

"I wouldn't put up with *any* kind of abuse. Trust me," Elaine said.

"We wanna give 'em a good home. Elaine's home every afternoon, and with two incomes we can give 'em what you can't," Tom said.

"You'll never give them a mother's love. I'm the only one who has that to give."

"You can have 'em every other holiday and all summer. We'll even arrange for you to come up and visit during the school year," Tom promised.

"All we're asking is that you think about it. Talk to your lawyer," Elaine said. "We have three weeks until school starts. Camp ends next week. They can spend the rest of the summer with you and come back to us in September."

"C'mon, we don't wanna be late for the play," Tom said. "We'll take separate cars. It'll give ya time to think."

Tom stood. Our discussion was over.

My boys had minor roles in the play. Tommy sang in the chorus, and Lee was part of a group of young kids with no lines. My emotions were a minefield. It was as if I had two voices screaming in my head.

They're my children. I know what's best for them.

But I'm stressed and can't give them what they need.

They need to be with their mother.

Elaine's good people, and Tom's changed.

The dialogue continued. I was unable to decide.

~~~
~~~

I met with Michael, my attorney, two days later and explained the situation.

“What’s important is the welfare of your children. You’ve told me how tough it’s been to make ends meet, and how much time you spend away from them,” Michael said.

“If Tom gave me more money, I wouldn’t have to work so much.”

“We’ve been through this. You agreed to two hundred a month in child support. Each time you ask for more, Tom fights you. Without going to court, there’s not much we can do.”

“I can’t afford to go to court,” I replied.

“I know.”

“Children belong with their mother.”

“Provided the mother can provide a stable home,” Michael said.

“You’re telling me I don’t provide that?” My voice shook.

“I didn’t say that. Why don’t you ask your children what they want?”

I decided to take Michael’s advice.

I didn’t say a word to Tommy and Lee the first week they were home. I wanted them to adjust to being with me and stress them out as little as possible. I was scared to death. What if they agreed to spend the school year with Tom?

After a play session in the park, we came home for lunch. It was now or never.

“You know I love you two more than anything,” I began.

“I love you, Mommy,” Lee said.

Tommy’s eyes filled with tears. He said nothing.

“Daddy and Mama Lanie asked if you’d like to live with them during the school year and with me in the summer.” I held my breath waiting for an answer.

“Yes!” Tommy blurted out.

My eyes misted over.

“Lee?”

Lee looked at me, then at his brother. Tommy nodded his head and mouthed *yes.*

He shrugged his shoulders. "Me too."

Lee was five years old. He spent most of his waking hours with his brother. Of course, he'd agree with him.

"I want what's best for you, and I want you to be happy," I said.

"It's best for us," Tommy echoed.

"Come here." I opened my arms to hug them both. Lee clung to me. Tommy kept his distance.

"I can visit on my days off, and we'll spend every other holiday together. And we'll be together all summer."

I needed time alone, so I sent them to their rooms to play.

Life was a constant struggle, and my nerves were shot. I self-medicated with pot and alcohol every day. If they lived with Tom, I could find a day job, stay sober, and get back on my feet.

I'll agree to one year of reverse custody. The thought comforted me.

Jack provided the emotional support I needed. He gave me space to spend the final two weeks alone with my kids and made sure he was with me when Tom and Elaine came to pick them up.

Regret piled onto regret as we said goodbye. Tom's champagne-gold Chevy Monte Carlo pulled away from the curb with my soul in the back seat with my boys. A part of me prayed the kids would change their minds and turn back, but I knew in my heart that would never happen.

I melted into a puddle on the floor. Jack held me close.

"It's only temporary," he said. "You're not alone. You have me."

We fell asleep on the floor wrapped in each other's arms. When I woke, the sun was setting. It was time for work.

I stayed straight for my first set. I thought about my mother and her rejection of me. Had I rejected my children? Was there such a thing as generational sin? My grandmother treated me with love, but she'd never shown her own daughter love. She and her husband struggled to survive as immigrants. My mother remained in the background, unloved and unseen. Was my grandmother rejected as a child? How far back did it go? If I could break the chain, I could break the sin. But how? I'd already reversed custody.

I tripped on the dance floor and almost landed in a customer's lap, a reminder to keep my personal and work lives separate. I downed a shot of tequila as soon as I got back to my dressing room, then met Tina out back for a joint.

"My heart's with you, hon," she said. "Nobody said life would be easy. You did the right thing for your babies. Don't forget that."

"I made sure my lawyer made Tom promise he wouldn't turn the children against me. And they'll only stay with him for this school year. After that, they're back with me."

"Right."

A shiver of a premonition unsettled me. I had a second shot of tequila before my next set.

fifteen

Moving On

My days off were usually midweek, which made visiting a challenge. I took an occasional Saturday or Sunday off, but each time my income suffered. Tom and Elaine also gave me the distinct impression my visits weren't appreciated.

"Y'know, Ava, I never butted into your life when the kids were with you," Tom said at the end of one of my visits.

Elaine presented a more sympathetic point of view. "I know you miss them, and I don't blame you. But after you leave, it takes a few days for them to calm down. It's a pattern I see in my classroom. Weekend visits confuse children and send a mixed message."

I knew how rowdy my kids were after spending time with Tom and Elaine. It had to be *their* influence, not mine, causing the problem.

"How 'bout we stick to every other holiday and summers like we agreed?" Tom said.

"You also promised not to turn them against me." I suspected Tommy was lurking somewhere nearby, so I kept my voice level and low.

"I'm not," Tom replied. "I'm tryin' to stick to our *legal* agreement."

I knew I'd lost the argument.

~~~
~~~

What I didn't know was that I had lost child support. When I reversed custody, I gave up Tom's two hundred dollars a month. I also didn't realize how dependent I'd been on that money. My expenses were lower without two additional mouths to feed, but I still had rent, utilities, and insurance to pay. Instead of saving for the future, I was close to slipping into debt.

"I can't win," I said to Jack.

"Move into the farmhouse with me. You'll save a bundle."

I couldn't give up the only home Tommy and Lee had known with me to live in a commune with a bunch of hippies. Instead, I added an extra shift or two to my schedule each week, and an extra drink or two each day.

Tom and Elaine drove the kids down for the holidays we could spend together. After each visit, I sensed a greater distance between us, which I hoped would lessen when they came for the summer.

During the first week of summer vacation, Tommy spent most of the time in his room. At nine years old, he'd morphed into someone I barely recognized. He let me know how much he missed his friends and his larger room at Tom's.

Lee, now six years old, was still my little boy, but for how long?

I thought a trip to the Jersey Shore would help us bond as a family. The second week they were with me, I packed our bathing suits, beach toys, and a picnic lunch and headed to Asbury Park.

Tommy and Lee buried each other in the sand, splashed in the ocean, and played with other children they met on the beach. I kept one eye on them and one eye on the book I'd borrowed from the library, *I'm Okay—You're Okay*, by Thomas Harris. Tina thought the book would help me overcome the poor self-image I'd developed as a child. Harris wrote about how negative thoughts contaminate our adult minds, leaving us vulnerable to inappropriate emotional reactions. He provided a convincing argument about how we can change who we are and live happier, more fulfilling lives.

Maybe I could focus on the positive parts of my life and become a new person—one who could stand up for myself and my children.

I can change. I can get my life back on track. Nothing will stand in my way.

For the month of July, I enrolled the boys in day camp, which gave them an opportunity to make friends. It was an extravagance I could barely afford. Day by day, they adjusted to life with me. By the end of the month, I felt we'd made enough progress so I could bring up the topic of returning to our original custody agreement.

I called Tom. "Would you and Elaine be able to come for a visit?"

"Funny you should call. Me 'n Elaine were gonna call you about gettin' together," Tom said.

Something was wrong. I asked Jack to be there with me for support.

Tom strode into my apartment dressed in white polyester slacks and a red, short-sleeved dress shirt. His six-foot-two frame overtook every inch of my living room. Elaine, dressed in a pink, sleeveless, shirt-waist dress, stood at his side. I invited them to sit. Jack, wearing faded jeans and a tie-dyed Grateful Dead T-shirt, joined us.

"No point beatin' around the bush. The company made me East Coast sales manager," Tom began.

"It's a huge promotion. I'm so proud of him," Elaine said, squeezing Tom's arm.

"They're sendin' me to Charlotte, North Carolina." Tom waited for my reaction.

"So you want the kids to stay with me for the school year?" I asked.

"Hell, no. We're keepin' things as they are. Me 'n Elaine are here to pack their stuff."

"You're doing no such thing!"

"The company found a gorgeous house for us," Elaine said. "With Tom's raise, I won't need to work and can be home for them every afternoon. I'm from the Charlotte area. My folks are thrilled now that they'll have two step-babies to love in addition to my boys."

Jack held my hand, which did little to comfort me.

"I have them until Labor Day. You can't do this!"

"Charlotte schools open next week. They'll need a few days to get settled. We're only thinkin' of them and what's best for the family," Tom said.

"I am thinking of them. They're my family. You have no right!"

"I have every right. You signed them over to me." Tom's voice rose, reminding me of his alcoholic years.

"We reversed custody for *one year only!*"

"It's all in your head. Show me where it says that." Tom stood, indicating our discussion was over.

"Ava, please understand." Elaine's soft Southern accent taunted me.

"I'm gonna start packin'," Tom said. "Elaine, help me with the boxes."

The two of them went outside to get the boxes. I saw a small U-Haul trailer attached to Tom's car.

I sat on the couch and watched as they carried box after box to the car. I thought of the trauma and sadness I'd lived through in the ten years since I'd married Tom. None of it compared to the desolation and heartache I felt at this moment. I'd failed as a mother, a wife, and a human being.

Most everything was packed by the time Tommy and Lee came home from camp.

"Daddy! Mama Lanie!" Tommy ran to them. "What's happening?"

Tom explained the move to Charlotte.

Tommy's eyes locked with mine. "Mom?"

"I'm sorry, baby." I knew better than to bad-mouth Tom in front of him.

Lee ran to me. "Are you coming, too?"

"I can't. But I promise I'll visit every chance I get."

Lee curled into my lap. I glared at Tom and Elaine.

You're destroying my children. You're destroying me. I hope you rot in hell.

"C'mon, guys. Time to go. Don't wanna hit traffic on the George Washington Bridge," Tom said. "Say goodbye."

By now Tommy, Lee, and I were sobbing. Even Elaine's eyes were glazed. Tom held the door as Elaine gently guided my children outside.

Tommy's little hand waved to me.

Lee cried, "Mommy! No!"

My tears blurred the hard edges of Tom's car as they drove away. A surrealistic landscape was all that remained once they turned the corner. A howl of sorrow burst from my innermost being. Jack held me close and walked me inside.

sixteen

Nothing Left to Lose

"They're moving the kids out of state. Take Tom to court. You have rights," Jack said.

I thought back to the words I read in *I'm Okay—You're Okay*. Did I really believe a book could make a difference in my life? What a joke. *You're Okay—I'm a Failure* would have been a more appropriate title.

"Ava? Where are you?"

Jack's words brought me back to the present.

"I have no rights," I said.

"C'mon. Think positive."

"Sure. I'm the go-go dancing mother who dumps her kids with babysitters every night. I'm the mother who gets high every day. I'm the mother who reversed custody. What do you think a judge would say?"

"Talk to your lawyer. He'll help you."

I knew Jack was trying to help. I also knew the score. A court battle would cost thousands of dollars I didn't have. Better to accept defeat and move on.

The next day, the shock of losing my kids had worn off. Jack was right. I needed to call Michael, my attorney. Maybe he could help get them back to me before Tom left Bridgeport.

"Ava, I'm your friend and I'm on your side, but I'm also your attorney," Michael began. "We keep rehashing the same scenario. Tom's sober and has a successful career and a wife. He's got the money to fight you in court."

"But I'm their mother!"

"Your children need a stable home environment. If you were to get married again, maybe you'd stand a chance," Michael said.

"I have a boyfriend—"

"Laura's told me about your boyfriend."

I'd forgotten my friend Laura was Michael's cousin. She and I didn't see each other often, but she was witness to my downhill slide. No wonder Michael wasn't more supportive.

I opened my mouth to defend Jack. What was the point? Jack couldn't hold a job, dealt pot, and stayed perpetually stoned. Being a nice guy would carry little weight in court.

"Thanks anyway, Michael." I stood to leave.

"Go back to school, get a smaller apartment, look for a different job. Find a good man to support you. Then we can think about re-opening your case."

"Whatever." I shook his hand and left.

I went home to an empty apartment. What had seemed small and cramped the day before now loomed large. If I moved to a studio, I could save money, but I had eight months left on my lease. Eight months would bring me to the end of the school year. When Tommy and Lee came back for the summer, they'd need a place to sleep, so I'd have to sign a new lease.

I couldn't afford to go back to school. College hadn't worked out for me. Maybe I could become a beautician, but when would I study? Dancing was exhausting.

Jack loved my kids but wasn't a father figure. In all my years of dancing, he was the only decent guy I'd met. How did Michael expect me to find a good man to support me?

I curled into a ball on the sofa. I thought about praying but knew my words would fall on deaf ears.

"I give up," I said to the silent room. I closed my eyes and surrendered to sleep.

It was dusk when I awoke. Time for work. A few tokes from my hash pipe helped shake off my depression. I needed to stay positive, focus on the future, and take life one day at a time. I chose my favorite black lace costume with the gold fringe, slipped into my five-inch gold stiletto heels, teased and sprayed my hair, and left for work.

seventeen

Charlotte

Tom and Elaine were even more restrictive about my phone contact with the children in Charlotte than they were in Bridgeport.

"The kids need to get adjusted to their new home. Write them letters but please don't call so much," Elaine said.

"You're pushing them away from me. That's not what we agreed to," I replied.

"No, Ava. You're distracting them from school and their new friends. I'll make sure they answer all your letters. Come down for Christmas. We'll find a hotel room for you so you can celebrate the holiday with them," Elaine said.

"Put Tom on."

I heard shuffling and muffled conversation before Tom picked up the phone.

"You make them upset and confused, Ava. They cry after you call. Me 'n Elaine just want them to be happy. They're not happy with you."

"You're a liar, Tom Harrison."

"Prove it. Take me to court."

"But—"

The drone of a dial tone told me I'd lost the battle.

Jack offered to accompany me to Charlotte, but I felt if I could spend time alone with Tommy and Lee, I could win back their affection. I called once I got settled at the Holiday Inn.

"I thought the boys could spend Christmas Eve with me at the hotel. Then Christmas Day we could be together as an extended family," I said.

"That won't work," Tom said.

I practically screamed into the phone. "I drove six hundred miles to be with them! I took a week off from work! What happened to our agreement?"

"We're spendin' the day with Elaine's parents. You'll see 'em the day after Christmas." Tom kept his voice level.

"Thanks a pant load." I hated the sarcasm in my voice. "And what about after that?"

"We're takin' a family trip to Savannah," Tom said.

"I'm family!" I screamed.

"Not this family."

This time I slammed down the phone.

Once my tears dried, I showered, applied fresh makeup, and went downstairs to the hotel bar. After two shots of tequila, I felt my shoulders relax. I even smiled at the bartender.

"Yer a purty li'l thing once ya smile," the bartender said.

"Thanks. I'll smile a whole lot more after one more shot," I replied.

"A gal who knows what she wants. I like that. Name's Glen. What's yers?"

"Ava."

"Visitin' family for the holiday?" Glen asked.

"You might say that. Now, how about that shot of tequila?"

"On me." Glen kept the bottle close by.

Glen continued to flirt, and I continued to drink. From experience, I knew better than to go home with a customer, a lesson he had yet to learn. Before it got out of hand, I paid my check, left a substantial tip, and took the elevator back to my room.

I woke Christmas Eve morning with a nasty hangover. I swallowed two Tylenol, ordered French toast and a Bloody Mary from room service, and steeled myself for what I expected to be the saddest holiday of my life.

For the next thirty hours I drank, slept, watched TV, and cried. I sobered up Christmas evening, knowing I'd need a clear head when I saw Tommy and Lee the next day.

I couldn't believe how much the two of them had grown in just a few months. Tommy was becoming a young man, and Lee was no longer my little baby. They opened their presents in my room, then we went downstairs for lunch. I'd planned to take them to a nice restaurant for dinner, but Tommy informed me they were expected home by five o'clock.

Tom and Elaine's Charlotte home was set on a wooded lot in an upper-middle-class suburb. Holiday decorations sparkled outside the houses. Kids rode new bikes along the quiet streets. The boys jumped out as soon as I pulled to the curb.

"Bye," Tommy said. "Thanks for the gifts."

"Bye, Mommy," Lee said.

"Wait. Where's my kiss?"

Tommy forced himself to kiss me. Lee's kiss was more sincere, but even he pulled away from me.

Tom and Elaine stood on the front step. My children ran up the sidewalk into their embrace. Elaine waved. Tom's glare warned me not to come closer. As I drove away, I wondered if the neighbors knew the lies spun behind Tom's brick walls.

My tears bent the late-afternoon sunshine, creating trails of gold that nearly blinded me. At the end of Tom's street, I pulled to the curb and sat in my car for what seemed like hours. Curious vehicles slowed to stare; a few concerned faces connected with me before moving on.

It was at that moment I admitted total defeat. I'd never see the sprouting of their first whiskers, never watch them play baseball, never meet their girlfriends. I'd fade from their memories, from their plush suburban world.

I stopped at the bar at the Holiday Inn, hoping to see Glen's friendly face. Instead, an older woman behind the bar slapped a drink in front of me and went back to her conversation with another customer.

eighteen

A Future with Jack

Jack was waiting at my apartment when I returned home. Judging from the stack of empty pizza boxes and garbage can full of beer bottles, I knew he'd been staying at my place.

"C'mere, Ava. Tell me all about it." He took my hand and led me to the couch.

I'd been ready to chew him out, but for the first time in a week, somebody was there to comfort me.

"I'm a failure," I began. "I've failed as a mother, a human being, and even as a wife."

"You've been shot down your entire life. Tom's a bully. How d'you expect to fight a guy like that?"

I shrugged my shoulders and leaned into him.

"And speaking of wife," Jack said. "I've been thinking we should take things to the next level. So would you marry me?"

I'd never seriously considered a future with Jack, a twentieth century Daniel Boone. He was the guy who loved to lay back in the sunshine and dangle a fishing pole. He was my friend and my lover, not my husband.

"Ava, I don't expect an answer tonight or even tomorrow. Think about it. We'd be good together."

"I'm sorry. My head's still in Charlotte," I said, hoping not to disappoint him.

Jack left early the next morning for yet another new job. I lay in bed thinking of the pros and cons of a second marriage. I knew he'd never abuse me, but could he, a good-natured hippie, provide a stable home? Would Jack continue to drift from job to job, selling pot on the side? How would I feel about him conducting his small-time drug enterprise in our shared home?

Jack's mother was a high-powered real estate agent. More than once she'd offered me a sales position in her office. Might she become my boss and the mother I never had? Would Jack's sister become my sister?

If I stayed single, nothing would change. I'd continue to dance until my body gave out. Life would be an endless struggle until I died.

That evening I accepted Jack's proposal. I'd never seen him so happy.

"We'll have a super life together!" he said.

We set a date for the following June and booked the banquet room at the Clinton House, a historic inn in Hunterdon County, New Jersey. Jack's mother, Helen, helped organize and plan the day.

"Never thought my son would get married. You're a special gal, Ava," Helen said.

I blushed. "Thank you, Mrs. Novak."

Helen never asked questions about my parents or my children, and I never offered answers. I assumed Jack fabricated a complicated lie that included death or dismemberment.

Jack moved into my apartment for the few months leading up to our wedding. Most nights I'd come home to find him passed out on the couch in front of a full ashtray, empty pizza box, and empty beer bottles. I told myself it was a small price to pay for his emotional support and kind disposition. My only rule: he had to keep his drug deals at the communal farmhouse. As far as I knew, he honored my wishes.

I was thirty years old, not as invincible as I was in my early twenties. Dancing was great exercise and kept me fit, but it was taking a toll on my mind and body. More and more, I'd soak my feet in ice water when I came home. My legs hurt from my knees to my toes.

Tina noticed a change in me.

"Never expected you to last this long in the business. You're draggin', hon," she said.

"I'm beat," I told her.

"I've got just the thing for you."

Tina pulled a small plastic bag of white powder from her purse, followed by a single-edged razor blade, mirror, and twenty-dollar bill.

"Is that cocaine?" I asked.

"You bet your ass it's coke."

Tina laid out a small pile of powder on the mirror, then used the razor blade to chop and divide it into four lines. She rolled the bill and before I knew it, two lines went up her nose.

"Your turn," she said.

What the hell. I need all the help I can get.

Two lines went up my nose in rapid succession.

"Whoa!" The powder slid down the back of my throat.

A few grains of cocaine dotted the mirror. Tina showed me how to moisten my finger, pick up the grains, and rub them on my gums.

"Now, go out and dance your butt off." Tina gave my behind a tap and shooed me out of the dressing room.

I hadn't had this much energy in ages. I ignored the other dancers and shined on stage. When one drunk yelled, "Show your tits," I kept on dancing and playing to the crowd.

I was exploiting myself, but for the moment I didn't care. Alcohol and pot mellowed me, but cocaine gave me power and focus. For years I'd allowed other dancers to intimidate me.

That ends tonight.

~

Most of the guests at our June wedding were Jack's family, friends, and drug customers. Tina was my maid of honor, and Jack's sister, Betty, was my bridesmaid. More than anything, I wanted my children there but knew better than to ask Tom.

I was pregnant and miserable at my first wedding, so I was determined to make my second wedding the best. Mrs. Novak took me to an upscale bridal shop and helped me choose a blush-pink silk dress, gathered at the waist, with sheer sleeves that fell off the shoulders. Rather than a veil, I selected a lightweight crown of pink flowers to match the embroidered flowers on my dress. Did she suggest pink to tell the world her son wasn't marrying a virgin, or was she, like me, attracted to the nontraditional style?

My thoughts drifted to my mother and my first wedding . . . how she "punished" me with an appetizers-only reception and how she destroyed any future for us as a family. Mrs. Novak gave me hope this time would be different.

Jack wore a gray tuxedo with a pink cummerbund to complement my dress. He trimmed his hair and beard. I stood proudly at his side as we recited our vows. The congregation cheered as we made our way down the aisle.

We hired Moonglow, a cover band led by Jack's close friend, Jimmy, and rocked the night away. To this day when I hear the Eagles, Fleetwood Mac, and Doobie Brothers, I'm brought back to that day.

I often hear women say they wished they could have enjoyed their wedding but were too nervous. Not me. I couldn't have been happier.

We spent our wedding night at the Ramada Inn in Clinton. Our room would have been lackluster were it not for the flowers we brought from the reception. Jack and I joked we had created our own personalized bridal suite.

Jack had offered me two choices for a honeymoon. "We can either spend two weeks in Miami or take a six-week cross-country camping trip."

Miami sounded super but I preferred the idea of a six-week trip.

We'd have more time to spend together, and it would give my body a rest from dancing.

I hadn't renewed the lease on my apartment. Mrs. Novak offered to store what remained of my stuff in her garage.

"No rush in finding a new place to live," Mrs. Novak said. "Why don't you two stay with me after your honeymoon? You can have the studio above the garage until you get settled."

"That would be wonderful!" I said. "Right, Jack?"

From the corner of my eye, I saw Jack squirm. Living with his mother would cramp his style and likely hurt his pot-dealing enterprise.

"Yeah, sure. Thanks, Mom."

"Ava, think again about working in my real estate office. The money's good. It'll get you away from dancing and into a respectable career," Mrs. Novak said.

Finally, I thought. *Life's going to work out.*

nineteen

Camping

We chose Washington Crossing State Park as our point of embarkation. We waved goodbye to New Jersey as we crossed the Delaware River in Jack's 1968 Royal Red Volkswagen Beetle. My wedding gift to him was a tune-up on his six-year-old vehicle. His gift to me was a thorough cleaning of the interior and trunk.

We headed north through New England, crossed into Canada, and visited Prince Edward Island and Nova Scotia. Jack lavished attention on me. He never brought up Tommy and Lee or the troubles waiting for us back in New Jersey.

I hadn't been fishing since my grandfather took me out on his Steelcraft boat off the coast of Atlantic Highlands. Fishing in Nova Scotia brought back memories of those trips from my childhood. The cool Canadian winds whipped back my hair and sprayed my face with cold, fresh salt water. Ava Harrison ceased to exist. Ava Novak came alive.

On our drive south, we wove our way through New England and down to Pennsylvania, where we picked up the Pennsylvania Turnpike. We often found ourselves camping in state parks, showering in dank, dark, spider-infested stalls. But by the time we arrived in Wisconsin, the scenery, campgrounds, and fishing made it all worthwhile.

Jack was happier than I'd ever seen him.

"I've wanted to trout fish in Wisconsin since I was a kid," he said.

We fished at various spots along the Kinnickinnic River, a tributary of the Milwaukee River. Some nights we pitched our tent along the riverbank and bathed in the cool river water. I felt the power of the water—the great purifier—washing away my transgressions. I was reborn.

From Wisconsin we drove to Grand Teton National Park in Wyoming. Snowcapped mountains framed Jackson Lake. Sunsets shone grander than any I'd ever seen. Elk, deer, and mountain goats roamed without fear.

"It's heaven on earth," I said.

"With you, any place is heaven," Jack said.

"That's the nicest thing anyone has ever said to me."

Our last stop was the Yellowstone River in southern Montana. Jack couldn't get enough trout, fresh air, and time in nature. We found a campground with clean showers and friendly campers. He scored an ounce of pot from the assistant manager, enough to get us back to New Jersey.

Part of me couldn't wait for the trip to end; the other part wanted to melt into the beauty of the western landscapes forever.

Finally, reality won. We ran out of money and headed for home.

twenty

My New Life

The studio apartment above Helen's garage was sparsely furnished, but I was grateful for a free roof over my head. I was anxious to begin working in real estate and to solidify my relationship with Jack's mother.

Jack had other ideas. "We need to find a place of our own where I can get back into business. Otherwise, I'm gonna lose my customers."

"Maybe we should think about getting sober and saving some money," I said.

"That's not the gal I married talking," Jack said.

"I can't dance forever. Maybe real estate is a chance to get my kids back."

He squirmed. "Let's talk later. I'm ready to go for a ride and light up a doobie."

So much for the straight life.

The next day Helen invited me to spend some time in her office.

"Think about real estate long term. In the beginning, you can go weeks or months without an income. When you do get paid, it's good money. Plan for the lean times, but before you know it, you'll have a nice client base and steady income. I tell my sales agents to get a part-time job while they get established," Helen explained.

"I could go back to dancing a few nights a week."

"I can't tell you what to do, Ava, but you need to be available during the day and early evening. Weekends are our busiest. I imagine that's when you make most of your money dancing. I could start you in the office for three dollars an hour. I'll also take you with me on sales calls."

Three dollars an hour?

But this could be my chance to get ahead. "Okay, why not?"

At least when I worked in Dr. Wendell's medical office, I'd kept busy. At Helen's office, I sat for hours doing nothing. She'd given me a textbook to study for the state real estate exam, but the more I stared at the letters on the page, the more my eyes blurred.

I'd come home exhausted and depressed, only to find Jack zoned out. What saved my sanity was the joint we'd smoke before dinner.

"I can't take much more of this," he said after three weeks. "We can't live on three bucks an hour, and I need to get back in the game."

"Guess I'll go back to dancing. I can still be available for her on the weekends."

I reached out to Biff Cardoba, my former agent.

"Ain't a whole lotta clubs where you are. But if ya don't mind drivin', I can get ya work in Trenton and Pennsy," Biff said.

Helen would have to understand. She knew we needed the money, and her son couldn't hold a job.

I made fifty dollars in tips my first night dancing at the Pillow Talk Club in Trenton. Biff introduced me to the high rollers and drug dealers, the bouncers and club owners. By the second week I had more work than I could handle. Every dressing table held a mirror littered with lines of coke. Joints and pipes passed from mouth to mouth. The cops had to be on the take. Nobody worried about getting busted.

For once I outperformed just about every other dancer. The girls were down-and-out druggies who did little more than shake their behinds. I was a real dancer with real routines and dance steps.

"Who needs real estate? You're a shinin' star." Jack couldn't have been happier.

"I don't belong in real estate," I agreed. "What should I tell your mother?"

"Tell her it's a sucker's game," he said.

Helen's face fell when I told her I was leaving. She pursed her lips and stared out her office window. She wished us luck and said her father had a house for rent in Yardley, Pennsylvania. He was asking only one hundred dollars a month.

Looking back, I should have stuck it out in real estate. I should have insisted Jack get a real job. But when you're high every day, long-term thinking isn't an option.

Helen was cordial during the rest of our time in her apartment. She wished us well as we headed away from Flemington toward a new life.

twenty-one

New Life?

The only thing "new" about our house was us. Built in the early 1800s, the stone cottage sat across from the Delaware River on the road leading from Yardley to Washington's Crossing State Park. I'm sure passersby thought the house was "charming." To me, it was anything but charming.

Mouse droppings, cobwebs, and dead horseflies told me who'd been inhabiting the place for the last twenty years. Was sending us here Helen's perverted punishment for me not living up to her expectations?

It didn't take a genius to detect the disappointment on my face. Jack brushed a stray cobweb from my hair and hugged me.

"Hey, it's not that bad. A little soap and water, and it'll be home sweet home."

"You're okay living like this?"

"Have a little faith, Ava."

"I left my faith back in New Jersey. Come on, let's get this place cleaned up before we bring our stuff in."

"Okay, but first—" Jack pulled a joint out of his pocket and lit up. "Welcome to your new home, Mrs. Novak."

Mentally, I added one more check mark to my never-ending list of bad decisions.

We spent two nights at a local motel while we, or rather I, scrubbed, dusted, and washed windows. Jack drove to the nearest phone booth to tell his buddies where he'd be conducting business.

I was grateful for the time alone and the mind-numbing work. It took me away from the mess I'd made of my life. To my surprise, once all traces of the insect world were gone, I fell in love with the wide plank floors, the wavy glass windowpanes, and the rustic setting. I chose to ignore the dingy wallpaper, the metal tub, farm sink, and the lack of water pressure. Instead, I reflected on stories the walls could tell—stories of love, tragedy, birth, and death. Our story would now be added to the anthology.

As the days turned cool, we snuggled in front of the living room fireplace. I hated to leave the comfort of home for the club scene in Trenton, but we needed money. Jack made a few dollars selling pot and had done nothing to find a real job.

"Deer season opens in a week. If I snag a deer, we'll eat for a year. I'll look for a job after that," he promised.

The last thing I wanted to be was a nagging wife, so I kept quiet. Instead, I took him to the nearest sporting goods store and bought him a new rifle, waterproof camo jacket, and plenty of thermal underwear to keep him warm while he stalked his prey. I worried about him handling a gun when he was high, but he assured me he knew what he was doing.

The season hadn't yet ended when Jack burst into the house. "I got me a deer. Told you I'd do it!"

He grabbed me and danced me around the kitchen. "Hope you like deer meat."

I'd eaten deer once as a child and remembered it as tough and sinewy.

"Sure," I lied. "Where is it?"

"I'm getting it butchered. And you know what the best is? I'm getting the head mounted! We can hang it over the fireplace."

You expect me to sit here staring at a dead deer?

"Doesn't that cost a lot?" I asked.

"I was thinking maybe you could give it to me for Christmas."

What have I gotten myself into?

On Christmas morning I called North Carolina to wish Tommy and Lee a Merry Christmas. They thanked me for the gifts I sent, but their words were cool and detached. Day by day, year by year, I sensed the distance between us growing.

I had nothing left to do but help Jack hang the deer head above the fireplace.

Normal people would hang a family portrait. We've got a dead deer.

I turned my attention to the pot of chili I'd made for a late-day holiday party. Jack provided the grass. Our friends brought the cocaine. It was after three in the morning before everyone left. I whispered a good night to our deer head and fell into bed.

twenty-two

Changes

I became a fixture in the Trenton club scene. I missed Tina and my friends back home, but I made new friends, new drug contacts, and a following among the customers.

Because I was often billed as a "star," most of the other dancers treated me with respect. Some even asked me to help with their moves. I learned to ignore the girls who'd do what they could to one-up me.

The life of a dancer is nasty, demonic, and materialistic. More than anything it's addictive: the money, the drugs, the attention—it all feeds the ego.

I thought I could rise above it and keep my soul safe. But after so many years in the business, it had become my world . . . my identity. The deeper I fell into darkness, the more detached I became from my husband.

Jack was as sweet and loving as he'd always been, but it wasn't enough. The more money I made, the less he thought about working and the more he focused on getting high. In my sober moments, I'd see us as nothing more than a couple of dopeheads.

"Fishing season opens in two weeks," he announced one spring morning in 1975. "I've got my eye on some new equipment at Ralph's Sporting Goods. Thought maybe you could advance me the cash to get set up."

You mean give you.

"Rent's due soon and there's no food in the house," I countered.

"Rent's a hundred bucks a month. You make that on a good night. C'mon, Ava, we're a team, remember?"

Some team. I made the money, paid the bills, cleaned, and cooked when we had food in the house. I'd lost count of how many flannel shirts I'd given him. But without him, I'd have nobody.

"You win," I said. "Let's go before Ralph sells out."

In the year we'd been married, Jack had had four jobs, each of which ended after a few weeks. I'd had enough of coming home to him and his pals passed out like dead soldiers scattered amid empty pizza boxes, beer cans, and overflowing ashtrays. My feet throbbed after six hours of dancing. My head ached from too much coke, and still I tiptoed into the living room, careful not to disturb them. None of them heard me dump their trash out back or heard me stumble up the stairs and fall into bed.

Was I angrier at Jack for letting me down or at me for allowing it?

Jack talked me into a week's vacation in the Pocono Mountains to celebrate our first wedding anniversary. I deluded myself into believing a short getaway would dispel the resentment building inside of me.

A week off my feet was my greatest joy. While Jack fished, I spent my days on the front porch of our cabin, legs elevated, reading *How to Win Friends and Influence People* by Dale Carnegie. The cover promised ways to change people without offending them. Maybe I could mold Jack into a responsible adult. And maybe, just maybe, I'd find a way to get my life on track.

I was wrong again. When we got home, I decided to focus first on my dancing "career" and second on my marriage.

My efforts paid off. The Pillow Talk Club sponsored a contest. Customers cast their vote for their favorite dancer, and I won. I was officially Miss Pillow Talk! It was the first real recognition I'd had since I lip-synched Barbra Streisand years before.

"Next up, Miss Pillow Talk 1975!" Nick, the bartender, got a kick out of announcing me. He raised the spotlights as I began my set.

I played to the crowd as I danced to "Come and Get Your Love" by Redbone, but soon I was playing solely to a dark-haired man at the end of the bar. I mouthed the words to the song as I headed in his direction. He stared at me with intense black eyes, raised his shot glass, and downed the brown liquid.

Our eyes stayed locked even after the song ended. I broke the spell and moved to the other end of the stage for my next number. Was it cocaine and tequila coursing through my body, or his intense energy that brought me back to him?

I joined him at the bar after my set.

"Miss Pillow Talk, huh? What are you, some kind of celebrity?" he asked.

"It's my fifteen minutes of fame." I smiled.

"Can I buy you a drink before your fifteen minutes run out?"

Nick poured me a shot of Jose Cuervo and a shot of Jack Daniel's for my new friend.

"To you, Miss Pillow Talk." He held his glass high.

"And to you—"

"Mike. Mike Ambrose. You are—"

"Ava Mar—Novak." For the second time in my dancing career, I gave a customer my real name.

"A pleasure, Ava Mar—Novak."

It felt good to laugh. We made small talk for the rest of my break. I left to change costumes, fully expecting he'd be gone for my next set.

Mike stayed through my last set, slipped a twenty-dollar bill into my garter, and winked at me. I gave him my sexiest smile and mouthed, *Thank you.*

Mack, our resident bouncer, walked me to my car as he did most nights. Mike leaned against a fire-red Trans Am smoking a cigarette. Mack held my arm as Mike approached.

"It's okay," I whispered.

"You sure?"

"Positive." *I don't think I've ever been as positive about anything in my life.*

"Would Miss Pillow Talk be kind enough to accompany me to the diner?" Mike asked.

"I'd love to."

I hadn't gone out after work since I married Jack. Although I'd come home to my husband passed out on the sofa, I felt an obligation to be there for him.

That ends tonight.

Under the diner's bright lights, I took a good look at Mike. He wasn't just handsome, he was *handsome*—a young Burt Reynolds look-alike: lean, and muscular, with a sweep of dark-brown hair falling over his left eye. And those eyes—dark, intense, and powerful. He was impossible to resist.

Charisma—more than I ever thought possible in one man.

I was in love—actually, in lust.

"What do you do when you're not at the Pillow Talk?" I asked.

"What don't I do? I'm a mechanic by trade. Give me a motor and I'll fix it. I've been workin' at my buddy's shop the past coupla years, pickin' up work on the side. Guess you could say I'm a hustler. What about you, Ava Mar—Novak?"

I laughed. "It's Novak. Martin's my stage name. I don't do much—sleep, housework. Dancing's hard work."

"You married?"

"Yeah, but things aren't good. What about you?"

"Marriage ain't for me. Hell, I'm only twenty-four."

And I'm thirty-one.

"D'you and hubby have an open marriage?"

Other than Jack, I'd never dated a customer. I'd never cheated on Jack or Tom.

"Um, we've never talked about it," I replied.

"It's not something you talk about. You either do it or you don't—so do you?"

My heart pounded in my chest. My cheeks burned. I'd made

my share of impulsive decisions. I wasn't about to make another.

Before I had a chance to answer, the waitress brought our eggs and refilled our coffee.

I changed the subject. "Tell me more about you."

Mike took the hint. "I love to fly. Got my pilot's license at sixteen. I dig music—especially some of the tunes you danced to."

"We get to pick our own music. I like funk, rhythm and blues, anything with a good beat. I add in some Top 40 so the customers can sing along."

"Doll, nobody's thinkin' about lyrics when you dance. Come sit next to me."

I moved to his side of the booth. Mike put his arm around me and pulled me closer. His body was so *hot*.

"That's better," he said. "You and hubby have any kids?"

I couldn't lie, especially about my children. "Two. But I was married before. They're with their father in Charlotte, North Carolina, right now. It's a long story."

Was Mike smiling because he liked kids or because mine were far away? I suspected the latter.

"We'll leave that story for another time. How about we hang out in my car before I send you back to your man?"

Mike reached into his pocket for his wallet and left a ten on the table. Our check couldn't have been more than six dollars.

Bucket seats and a gear shift in his Trans Am kept us from melting into each other. Nobody had ever kissed me like Mike. I wanted us to move into his back seat, but he put the brakes on.

"You're one hot chick, Miss Pillow Talk." His dark eyes were hypnotic, even in the predawn light. "To be continued. Can I have your number?"

I didn't think about what I'd say to Jack if Mike called the house. I simply rattled off my number.

"Aren't you going to write it down?" I asked.

"What for?" He repeated the number from memory.

twenty-three

Motor Mike

The clock in my Mustang read 5:00 a.m. Would Jack realize I hadn't come home? Yesterday I would have worried about what he thought. Not today.

The thirty-minute ride home gave me time to think about the men in my life. Tom was a hard worker but also a hard drinker. He made my life miserable and was doing his best to destroy my relationship with Tommy and Lee. Jack was the sweetest guy I'd ever met. I could nag him for the rest of the century and he'd still be a lazy, pot-smoking nature boy.

Mike was ambitious, handsome, smart, and funny. I felt an explosive chemistry between us—something I'd never felt with Tom or Jack. Could Mike be my white knight—the man who would rescue me? Or would he be my black knight? I sensed he was a bad boy, maybe the baddest boy I'd ever met.

I was determined to find out exactly who Mike Ambrose was and how he would fit into my life.

Jack and three of his cronies lay passed out on the living room floor. I left them surrounded by their debris and made my way upstairs and into bed.

The next morning, I found Jack's note on the kitchen table: *Left early to fish. Probably spend the night at Stevie's pad. Didn't want to disturb you. Love, Jack.*

Other than four bodies, nothing had been removed from the disaster formerly known as our living room.

"Screw you, Jackson P. Novak!" I screamed to the empty room. I spent my morning vacuuming, wiping spills, and picking up trash. Sometime after one o'clock, the phone rang.

"Hello?"

"So you did give me your real number, Miss Pillow Talk!"

"Mike?"

"In the flesh. Whatcha doin'?"

"Cleaning—the story of my life."

"Want some company?"

I needed to think fast. I'd only met Mike the night before, and I knew what a visit meant. Jack had been taking me for granted for months and wouldn't be home until Sunday. I stared at the bags of garbage by the back door, a symbol of what my life had become.

"I'd love some company," I replied, then gave him my address.

"Be there in an hour."

An hour gave me enough time to get me and the house in order.

Fifty-nine minutes later, Mike knocked on our ancient oak door. The summer sun shone at a perfect angle, highlighting the platinum streaks in my dark-blond hair.

"Hey, gorgeous," Mike said, sweeping me into his embrace. His kiss promised much, much more.

The Delaware River was our only witness. To be safe, I led him into the living room.

"You live *here*? Not what I expected," Mike said.

For the first time in months, I surveyed my home. I didn't like what I saw.

"It's a long story. How much time have you got?"

"All afternoon."

I invited Mike to sit next to me on the sofa. Not for the first time, I felt the springs poke the back of my thighs.

"He-e-y, what's this?" Mike pulled a plastic bag of pot from between the cushions.

"My husband's stash."

Mike lifted his cushion to find a dozen similar baggies. "I take it somebody's in business."

"Jack does some deals. Small-time stuff."

"Where's he now—at work?" Mike asked.

"Fishing. Jack's allergic to work." I couldn't believe I put my husband down in front of this stranger.

Mike took another look around. "Guess that's why you live like this."

The frustration that had been building for a year broke through. I wanted to cry or break something.

"It's home for now," I said.

Mike shrugged and pulled an Altoids tin from his jeans pocket. Inside was more cocaine than I'd ever seen in one place.

"Got a mirror?"

"Upstairs." I felt his eyes follow me as I climbed the stairs.

Would he follow me? Did I want him to?

Hundred-dollar bills were rare in 1975, so I was surprised when I saw Mike had rolled one for each of us. He poured a pile of white powder onto the mirror and cut it into four wide lines.

"For you, my queen."

Mike was laying on the charm as thick as the lines on the mirror, and I was falling for it.

We sank into the cushions, and I told him the condensed version of my life story. I left out my mother, Tom's abuse, and the tragedy surrounding my kids.

"What d'you want outta life?" he asked.

I want my children. I want a kind, hard-working guy to take care of me. I want to erase the last twelve years. I want a normal life.

Instead, I said, "What does anybody want? Love, sunshine, happiness."

"Let's start with love. Take me upstairs."

I commanded my guilt to stay downstairs, but each creak of the stairs reminded me I was about to cheat on Jack.

"At least we'll hear your husband comin' up the stairs." Mike laughed.

Once Mike kissed me, I forgot all about Jack. I forgot it was our home, our bed, our sheets. We lay wrapped in each other's arms for what seemed like hours.

I wished the afternoon could go on forever, but I needed to get ready for work.

"Don't go," Mike begged. "I got a whole lot more lovin' to give you."

"Well, maybe a little while longer—"

Mike and I attempted to shower together but the lack of water pressure made it impossible.

He never took his eyes off me as I dried my hair and applied my makeup.

"You deserve a whole lot better," he said.

I laughed off his comment. I'd been beaten down my entire life. The concept of deserving didn't exist for me.

"Stick with me, doll. I'm goin' places," Mike promised.

"And where might that be?"

"I got my sights set on Florida. Lotsa boats, lotsa motors. They don't call me Motor Mike for nothin'."

"Come on, Motor Mike. Miss Pillow Talk can't be late."

twenty-four

The Art of the Deal

Mike stopped by the club that night but only for one set. He tucked a twenty-dollar bill into my garter, winked at me, and left. Inside the bill was enough coke to get me through the rest of the night and a note that simply read: *More?*

I wanted more, and he knew it.

But I also wondered where Mike was going on a Saturday night. Did he have a girlfriend? Several girlfriends? Why did I feel such intense jealousy? I'd only met him the night before, and I *was* married.

Saturday was considered "date night." If a guy had a girlfriend or wife, he was expected to spend the evening with her, which meant our customers were on the prowl. I had no intention of going home with any of them, but that didn't stop me from playing the game. I focused on making money. Thoughts of Mike would have to wait.

I woke Sunday around noon to the smell of bacon and eggs. I stumbled downstairs and found Jack cooking breakfast—a first.

"Morning, Ava, or is it afternoon? Did you miss me?" He gave me a peck on the cheek and went back to cooking.

"I did," I lied.

"I got to thinking last night. I should've been home with my wife, not in some shitty cabin with a bunch of dudes."

I needed to change the subject. "Catch any fish?"

"Threw most of them back. Like I was saying, from now on I'm spending my nights home with you."

Of all times to be falling back in love with me—just as I'm falling in love with someone else.

"I'm even gonna get serious about finding a job."

I knew he'd find another low-paying job, then leave as soon as something pissed him off . . . unless they fired him first. Today I shared his excitement. With Jack out of the house, I'd be free to see more of Mike.

Jack kept his word and found a warehouse job the next day. He proudly told me it paid $2.50 per hour, forty cents higher than minimum wage.

"That's a hundred bucks a week before taxes. Add that to the bread I make dealing, and you won't have to work as much," he said.

I knew he meant well, but I also knew my husband. Best to enjoy my freedom for now and not get my hopes up.

I didn't see Mike again until Wednesday. He planted the usual twenty-dollar bill in my garter and invited me to sit with him on my break.

"When can I see you again?" he asked.

"My husband got a job, so for now I have my daytime free."

"I work, too, y'know. We'll figure somethin' out," Mike said.

We went out for breakfast after the bar closed, but it wasn't enough. A week later, I came up with a plan.

"As long as my husband's working, I can cut back to four nights a week. Jack doesn't have to know," I said.

"I like how you think, doll," Mike said.

While Jack held his job, I spent one evening a week at Mike's apartment. The guy had money and taste. His living room was furnished in chrome, glass, and black leather. In his bedroom, he'd installed smoky mirrors on the wall behind his waterbed. A black lacquer dresser and nightstand with a lava lamp completed the decor. What impressed me most of all was Mike's stereo system. Everything from his Sony TA-1150 integrated amplifier, JBL speakers, and Thorens TD-165 turntable screamed quality.

"No wonder you cringed when you saw my place," I said.

"This is only the beginning. I've got big dreams."

Mike was more than a dreamer. He was a doer.

"I'd love to live like you," I said.

"Stick with me, doll. You'll have this and more," Mike promised.

"Jack got fired. He only lasted six weeks," I told Mike. "I have to go back to dancing five nights."

"Tell him business is off so you gotta work a coupla double shifts. Work two afternoon shifts and spend the nights with me."

Mike had an invisible hold on me from the beginning. I'd do anything he said, including cutting my income and lying to my husband.

The lunch crowd picked up in the fall. I continued to make good tips, but I was exhausted.

"We're going to have to figure out something else," I said. "I can't keep working these so-called double shifts."

"I got just the thing." Mike ruffled through his dresser drawer and handed me an Altoids tin.

"More coke? I'll have nosebleeds from here to Sunday."

"White crosses."

"Speed?"

"Yup. But it's prescription. Nothin' like meth."

"But not my prescription," I countered.

"So what? They're made in a real medical lab."

I knew it was either white crosses or bail on Mike.

"Hand me that glass of water," I said.

"This ain't a permanent solution," Mike said.

"What is?"

"Leavin' that loser husband of yours. I'll give you a beautiful life. You'll never have to work again."

How could I tell Mike that Jack had rescued me from the nightmare of my first marriage? That he'd stuck by me through the worst days of my life?

Mike laid back on the waterbed. "I know hubby's a small-time dealer. I'm a bigger dealer, did you know?"

"I thought you might be. You can't live like this on a mechanic's salary."

"How about you introduce me to Jack? Invite me to your house and tell him I've got connections for coke and grass. Everybody wins. Me 'n him'll make more bread, you won't have to support him, and we won't have to sneak around."

"Are you crazy?"

"Maybe, but it'll sure as shit be fun."

An image of Satan flashed in front of my eyes.

twenty-five

Secrets

"Try this." I laid out two lines of coke for Jack. "One of my customers turned me on to it."

So far, I hadn't lied.

"You know what I think about cocaine. I hate feeling wired," he said.

"This guy, Mike, has a business near Trenton. He wants to expand up our way. I told him you might be interested in a partnership. How will you know if the stuff is any good if you don't try it?"

"Well, okay. Just a taste."

One line went up his nose, the other up mine.

Jack lay back on the sofa. "Whoa! That's some powerful shit."

"I told you—and it's clean, too. You'll have a nice buzz going and come down real slow." I'd done enough lines with Mike to know the quality of his blow.

One taste was all it took. Two days later Jack and Mike were in business.

Mike came to our house about once a week. It hurt me to know Mike was taking advantage of my husband, but Jack's business got a major bump, which made everybody happy.

Mike had no conscience. He was more interested in getting over on Jack than making money with him. He'd sit across the table from us and shoot me seductive glances whenever Jack turned away. I knew Mike got off on our secret. To be honest, I did, too.

Mike was aggressive and assertive. He was a con man and a wheeler-dealer, everything Jack wasn't. He lavished love and attention on me, and I couldn't get enough. He was my Prince Charming, the man I'd been searching for my entire life. With Mike, I had a future. With Jack I had a roommate who offered sex when he wasn't too stoned to perform.

Mike bought me jewelry and clothes. I even spent occasional nights at his apartment. Jack never questioned where I was or who I was with.

"When're you gonna leave that dirtbag?" Mike asked me after a year.

"Soon, Mike."

"What're you waitin' for? The clock's tickin'."

"I'm worried about him. I pay most of the bills. Without me, he'd be on the street," I said.

"And whose fault is that? The longer you support him, the worse it's gonna be."

"If there was some way I could set him up. Make sure he'd be okay for a year or two," I said.

"I wasn't gonna tell you till me 'n Adam got our loose ends together, but—"

I'd met Adam, Mike's boss at the garage. Like Mike, he was a wheeler-dealer and a consummate bad boy—just not as bad.

"Some dude came into the shop a while back. We got talkin' and doin' blow. He tells us he's got a cocaine connection in Colombia. The real deal—uncut shit that'll knock us from here to Africa. All we gotta do is get down there and bring it back. Once we cut it, we'll make a bundle. I could pass some on to Jack. He'll be set for a long, long time."

It could work.

Part Two

twenty-six

Lies

"Jack, I hope you don't mind me taking a vacation with Tina."

My husband knew how much I missed my friend, so I knew he wouldn't object.

"Where?" he asked.

"Florida. Her family has a condo in Boca."

"It'll be good for you to get away." I couldn't believe how Jack put up no resistance. It was almost as though he wanted me out of the picture.

"I'll miss you," I lied.

"Yeah, I'll miss you, too."

Did my words sound as unconvincing as his?

I couldn't tell him I was flying to Colombia with Mike and Adam, nor could I tell him about the cocaine we planned to bring home.

I met Mike and Adam at Mike's apartment. From there, we took a stretch limo to the Philadelphia airport. The guys dressed in loud Hawaiian shirts, cut their hair, and did their best to disguise themselves as obnoxious American tourists. I was a mixture of nerves and excitement as we boarded the plane to Santiago de Cali, or simply Cali, the largest city in southwestern Colombia.

If the guys expected to blend in with the rest of the passengers, they were mistaken. Most travelers were families and businessmen. Colombia wasn't exactly a destination for American tourists. They agreed to dress less conspicuously for the trip home.

Pablo Escobar and his powerful Medellín drug cartel were well-known for their ruthlessness, kidnapping, and violence. I'd read about the organization and how they'd turned to trafficking cocaine in 1976. I prayed Mike and Adam had connections outside the cartel. Cocaine was a huge industry in Colombia. Other groups had to be involved in smuggling.

The airport in Cali was heavily guarded with armed police. I expected shots to ring out at any moment. We looked for friendly faces, a tourist information center, anything familiar—and found nothing.

"Let's get the hell outta here," Mike said.

Once we picked up our luggage, we made our way to the taxi stand. In broken Spanish, we asked the driver to take us to the Inter-Continental Hotel.

The InterContinental was an oasis in a sea of crime and corruption. Mike and I reserved one room, Adam another. After seeing the airport and the streets of Cali, I decided I'd relax by the pool while the guys made their connection. The less I knew about their deal, the better.

Despite the anxiety and danger, I enjoyed my first few days in Cali. I spent hours by the pool shaded by an umbrella, sipping piña coladas while Mike and Adam conducted business. They made their big score on day three.

"You won't believe the quality of this shit," Mike said.

I'd never tasted cocaine so pure. They also scored some pot, just enough to get us through the rest of the week. I thought back to the camping and fishing trips I'd taken with Jack.

Never again. This is where I belong.

Mike and Adam left the hotel the next morning and promised they'd be back by late afternoon. After a lunch of *ajiaco*, a potato and corn soup, and *arepa*, a kind of corn cake, I went back to our room to shower and take a siesta.

The phone rang. Thinking it was Mike or Adam, I answered.

"Hey, what's up?"

I was greeted with a static pause. "Mike? Adam?"

"Uh-h, Ava, is that you?"

Jack!

It was my turn to pause.

"Ava? What're you doing?"

"Jack? What're *you* doing?"

"I'm supposed to meet Mike. We got some business to take care of," Jack said. "I thought you were in Florida with Tina."

"Um, Tina bailed at the last minute. I ran into Mike at the Pillow Talk. He told me he was flying down here with his buddy from work and asked if I wanted to join them. I-I think he felt sorry for me. I didn't see any point in worrying you. I switched my ticket, and here I am."

"Huh," Jack said. "Where's Mike?"

"He'll be back later. Can I take your number and have him call you?"

"Yeah, sure."

He rattled off a number and the name of another hotel.

"Guess I'll see you later," I said.

My hand shook as I hung up the phone. I didn't know who to hate more, Mike or Jack.

"You got a phone call," I calmly told Mike later that afternoon.

"Oh, yeah, who?"

I wanted to smack the smirk off his face.

"I think you know who."

"About that—"

"You could've told me Jack was coming."

"And spoil the surprise?"

"I suppose you're proud of yourself."

"I'm tired of waitin' for you to leave that loser. Sometimes you gotta help nature along."

I was angry, but part of me was flattered that Mike went to such lengths to have me. I handed him Jack's contact information and locked myself in the bathroom while he made the call.

A few minutes later, Mike knocked.

"Jack'll be over in about an hour. Gives us a chance to get it on before he gets here."

If we were back home, I'd have walked out. But I was in Colombia with a man I was beginning to believe was a sociopath. I needed to keep cool.

"Do me one favor, Mike. Make it look like you and Adam are sharing a room, not you and me," I said.

"Okay, doll. Now c'mere. We don't have a lotta time."

Mike, Adam, and I had just lit up a joint when Jack knocked.

"What's happenin'?" Mike gave Jack a buddy slap and invited him into our room. "This here's Adam."

"Hey," Jack said, then turned to me. "Ava, so weird to see you here."

"Isn't it?" I stayed seated on the edge of the freshly made bed.

"Is that any way to greet your husband?" Mike asked.

I walked over to Jack and gave him a hug. My body felt like wood. I knew Mike was getting off on the scene.

"Enough standing around. C'mon, Jack, let's catch a buzz before we do business." Adam handed the joint to Jack. The tension in the room eased—all except mine.

"You tried this shit yet?" Mike handed Jack a bottle of aguardiente, a popular alcoholic drink made from sugarcane and anise seed. "It's the national drink of Colombia."

Jack took a drink and scrunched up his face. "Ugh, they can keep it."

"My sentiments exactly," I said.

Mike began. "Now, let's talk business. The best way to smuggle coke outta the country is to pack it in condoms and stick it up your ass. You okay with that?"

"Are you serious?" Jack asked.

"Did ya think you'd pack it in your luggage?"

"Guess I didn't think that far ahead," Jack admitted.

You never think ahead, Jack.

"What time's your flight back home?" Mike asked.

"Two hours from now," Jack said.

"You could swallow 'em and shit 'em out when ya get home. Problem is, they might break in your intestines and kill ya. You could also tape 'em inside your butt cheeks, but ya know what the airport's like. One look at you and your hippie hair, and you're toast."

"Guess I'll stick it up my butt."

The three of them went into the bathroom. I hated to think what Mike and Adam were doing to my husband.

Adam was the first to emerge about fifteen minutes later. "Piece o' cake," he said.

"Yeah, piece o' cake," Jack muttered.

"Now, here's what you do when you get home—"

"I can't listen to this," I said, and went into the bathroom.

Mike had straightened up our room, hiding all traces of his presence from Jack. Not so in the bathroom. His razor, shaving cream, and toothbrush sat on the sink, just enough to show our true living arrangement.

Jack opened the bathroom door and took my hand. "Don't worry about me. I'll be fine. I'll see you when you get back."

"Be careful," I said.

"You know me. Make sure these guys take good care of you." Jack gave me a peck on the cheek.

"What an ass," Adam said after Jack left.

"Literally," Mike laughed.

I pretended to laugh, but to me it was no joke. My husband was so indifferent that he brushed off finding his wife in Colombia with another man—someone who was his so-called business partner and friend.

That's it. I can't stay married anymore.

twenty-seven

Busted

Mike, Adam, and I spent the rest of the week getting high and touring the better parts of the city. On our last morning, Mike helped Adam tie condoms full of cocaine and stick them up his behind. I didn't ask if Mike planned to do the same, but I suspected Mike entrusted their entire stash to Adam. What was a friend for, if not to serve as a drug mule?

Adam boarded a morning flight home. Mike and I were scheduled for a later flight. I prayed Adam would make it through customs without the condoms bursting. Mike wasn't worried.

"He'll be fine," Mike said, laying out the last of our private stash.

"That's more blow than I've ever done at one time!"

"Would ya rather we leave it for the maid? We'll do a doobie before we leave. It'll balance us out," Mike said.

The two of us were wired and mellow at the same time when we arrived at the airport. I was under the illusion that the combination of drugs made me appear normal. One agent from the security service agency of Colombia, *Departamento Administrativo de Seguridad*, or DAS , disagreed. She spotted me in the restroom.

"*Ven conmigo, señorita*," the woman said in a gruff voice.

The only word I recognized was "*señorita*."

"*No hablo español.*" I must have appeared straight if I remembered how to say I didn't speak Spanish.

"Come with me, miss."

She couldn't arrest me for drugs in my system, and because I wasn't carrying anything, I knew I was safe. The best thing for me to do was comply.

"*Sí, Señora Alvarez.*" If I could read her badge and treat her with respect, I was sure she'd treat me well.

I was wrong on all counts. Señora Alvarez held me by the elbow and shoved me into a windowless cubicle lit by flickering fluorescent tubes. Rifles were stacked behind a metal table. She sat with her back to the rifles and instructed me to sit across from her.

"You are carrying drugs to America," she said.

"No, I'm not," I replied honestly.

"Strip!"

"I'm not carrying drugs!" By now I was in tears.

"Strip!"

In a space barely large enough for me to stand, I removed my slacks, blouse, and shoes. I stood wearing nothing but my bra and panties.

"Strip!"

If I thought standing naked in front of Señora Alvarez was the ultimate humiliation, I was wrong.

"Bend over."

She probed every orifice of my body. I thought of Jack and Adam and hoped they had left the country safely.

"Get dressed. Give me your shoes."

She tore the insoles from my shoes and felt for any traces of cocaine. Finding none, she returned them to me.

"Your bag."

Señora Alvarez dumped the contents of my purse on the table and ripped open the lining. Finding nothing, she handed the bag back to me. She opened my wallet and pulled out half a joint.

Holding the joint in front of her face, she screamed, "For this you will get three years in jail!"

"My God, no!" My life was over.

"How much money you have?" She handed me my wallet.

I held up my last fifty dollars.

She slipped the American currency into her pocket. "Get out and never come back."

"T-thank y-you," I whispered, and backed out of the room.

I checked the departure schedule once I was free. I still had time to make our flight. But where was Mike? Had he met a similar fate?

I saw him not too far from our assigned gate. I waved but was met with a blank expression. Maybe he didn't see me. I waved again. Mike stared at me for a moment, then his head tilted back as he began turning in a clockwise circle. He kept spinning and spinning. I ran to him.

His eyes rolled back in his head. Foam escaped from his mouth as he collapsed. He lay on the ground, his legs kicking at nothing.

"Mike! Can you hear me?"

His body continued to convulse.

"Somebody, help!"

People stopped to stare, shook their heads, and left us.

I had no idea what to do. Was Mike an epileptic? Had he shoved condoms of cocaine up his behind? Had one exploded? Was he going to die?

After what seemed like an hour, two police officers arrived. They stood over him, speaking in Spanish. One officer left, I assumed to find medical assistance.

Seconds later, Mike shook his head, opened his eyes, and stood.

"Okay, I'm ready to go now," he said.

"*What?*" I held his arm, afraid he'd have another seizure.

"I'm ready to go."

He shifted his eyes away from me and stared at the police officer, then at the crowd surrounding him.

"What the—"

"Honey, are you okay? You collapsed." I was afraid to use the word seizure. More than that, I was afraid they'd search Mike, find cocaine, and arrest us both.

Apparently, Mike had no recollection of what had happened.

"*Señor*, you cannot fly," the officer said.

"I'm fine."

"Our doctor must see you,"

This is the end of freedom, the end of Mike and me.

The medics arrived, listened to Mike's heart and lungs, then took his blood pressure. They spoke to each other and the officer in rapid Spanish. I awaited our fate.

"You have epilepsy?" one medic asked.

"I-I do," Mike replied.

Or was it too much cocaine?

"You have medicine?" the medic asked.

"I do," he lied.

"You cannot fly today, *señor*. You must return to your hotel."

Mike was smart enough not to argue.

"My wife can help me," Mike said.

Wife?

"Come with me," the officer said.

The three of us approached the ticket agent and explained our situation. It was too late to retrieve our luggage, but the airline assured us it would be waiting for us in Philadelphia. We took a taxi back to the InterContinental Hotel.

"Ava, you shoulda gone home. I'm fine," Mike said.

"And leave you? An epileptic?"

"Hell, I'm no epileptic. Too much blow is all. Guess now I know my limit."

Mike had enough money to pay for one night at the hotel. He wired his parents to send money to get us home. We flew back to Philadelphia the next afternoon.

twenty-eight

A Wasted Trip

I dreaded confronting Jack. What would he say about Colombia? How could I tell him our marriage was over?

Jack was passed out on the couch with his entourage of stoners scattered around him. He had expected me home the night before. Was he worried about me or so detached from reality that he didn't realize what day it was? I suspected the latter.

I tiptoed up the stairs and fell into bed. I wanted to sleep for a month.

The next morning Jack gently shook me awake.

"You finally made it home," he said. "What happened?"

"Mike had a seizure at the airport. They wouldn't let him fly."

"You could've come home. You could've called."

"It would've been wrong to leave him," I said.

"Ava, this whole thing is wrong. I'm not stupid."

"Jack, you're a sweet guy, but I think we both know our marriage is over."

He stared out the window and ran his hand through his hair. "Yeah, I know."

Once we exposed our truth, we both relaxed. He told me he'd left Colombia safely, but when he got home half the cocaine was ruined. I told him about my brush with the DAS agent.

"Do you have someplace else to live?" Jack asked.

"No."

"This is my grandfather's house, so I'll be staying. I don't want bad feelings between us. You're welcome to stay till you find a place."

"Thank you." Despite his faults, Jack had a heart of gold.

That evening I went to Mike's apartment, anxious to learn about Adam and to tell Mike I'd be filing for divorce.

Adam laid on Mike's bed with his legs curled into his chest. Sweat glistened on his flushed face.

"He can't shit out the condoms," Mike said.

"Jack's came out but half of it was ruined," I said.

"Yeah, we heard."

"I gave Adam a double dose of ex-lax. We hope that does the trick before the condoms break open," Mike said.

"I shoulda swallowed instead of stuffed," Adam said.

"Kinda late now," Mike grumbled.

Mike wasn't particularly compassionate toward his friend. He seemed more concerned about retrieving the stash.

I sat up with Adam most of the night while Mike slept on the couch. Around five in the morning, Adam sprang up.

"Gotta go. Get Mike!"

I turned off my imagination while they did whatever they had to do in the bathroom.

Adam hobbled out, leaning on Mike for support.

"It's ruined. All of it," Mike said.

"Never again." Adam, pale and exhausted, climbed back into bed.

"At least you're alive," I said.

"Barely," Adam mumbled.

Mike and I went into the kitchen. I made coffee.

"All that time and money wasted." Mike stared into his coffee. "The hotel, airfare, food. And for what—the scraps Jack shit out?"

"Adam almost died!"

"That, too," Mike said. "Maybe one day we'll look back and laugh."

What was there to laugh at? I almost spent three years in a Colombian prison, Mike had a seizure, Adam nearly died, and my marriage was over.

I spent the next day and night nursing Adam back to health. Once I knew he'd be okay, I left for Jack's. I needed to file for divorce and get back to work.

twenty-nine

Moving On

Jack and I filed for divorce. I continued to call the stone cottage home, though it was nothing more than a place to store my things. Jack and I were cordial to one another, but it was obvious we were both moving on with our lives.

I paid our bills two months ahead to give Jack a chance to get on his feet. Was I acting out of compassion or guilt? I wasn't sure.

The day our divorce was finalized, we sat on the sofa staring at the deer head over the fireplace.

"I'm sorry it didn't work out," I said.

"Water under the bridge," Jack replied.

"What's that supposed to mean?"

"It's nicer than saying shit happens," he said.

"That's what you thought of our marriage?" I asked.

"It wasn't meant to be. That's all."

"What're you going to do now?"

"Once you're gone, my girlfriend's gonna move in." Jack shot me a glance from the corner of his eye.

"Your *what*?"

"You weren't the only one cheating in this relationship. You think I didn't know about you and Mike?"

Truthfully, I didn't care.

"I'll be gone by the weekend," I said.

~~~

I left everything except my personal belongings with Jack and moved into Mike's Trenton apartment. I picked up three night and two afternoon shifts so I'd be able to spend more evenings with Mike. The more time we spent together, the closer we became. I'd finally found my soulmate.

"I'm ready for a change," Mike said, after we'd been living together for a month.

"Are you tired of me already?" I was half-joking, half-serious.

"Of you, doll? Never. How'd ya like to move to Florida?"

When I was twelve years old, my family took a trip to Miami. I fell in love with Florida's climate, the striking blue skies, and the ocean. I promised myself I'd move south when I grew up. My wish became buried under lies, hate, drugs, and alcohol. I'd been afraid to dream about a better life until today.

"I'm game."

"Thought so. Buddy o' mine said I could find work in the boatyards around Fort Lauderdale," Mike said.

The lease on Mike's apartment expired in November 1976. Mike sold everything except his stereo equipment. I sold my beloved Mustang to another dancer. We agreed to be on the road right after Thanksgiving.

On Friday, November 26, we said goodbye to Trenton, then climbed into the front seat of Mike's Trans Am. Mike packed a supply of amphetamines, hoping we could drive the twelve-hundred miles nonstop. By the time we arrived in Maryland, we were wired. It was all we could do to keep a soft foot on the gas pedal.

I'd taken speed when I dragged at work but never more than one pill at a time.

"How long can we go like this?" I asked Mike.

"Two days max," he said. "I got some quaaludes for when we wanna come down."

"I hate downers," I said.
~~~

"Sometimes you gotta give nature a helping hand."

Mike knew a helluva lot more about pharmaceuticals than I did. I decided to listen to his advice.

When we reached Richmond, Virginia, I saw signs for Virginia Beach. Thirteen years had passed since my honeymoon, the trip that forever changed my life. I grew silent and stared out the window.

"Why so quiet, doll?" Mike asked.

Mike knew I'd been in an abusive marriage but, other than telling him about my children, I'd never shared the details.

"Tom and I spent our honeymoon in Virginia Beach." I kept my face turned to the window, not wanting my tears to dampen our spirits.

"Wanna talk about it?" Mike asked.

"Bad memories. I promised myself I'd leave them back in New Jersey."

Most guys would have pulled off at the next exit and would have let me share my story. Not Mike. He lit a cigarette and blasted the local Top 40 radio station.

I should have taken his actions as a warning sign. But I was on the rebound, in love, and confident I'd found my Mr. Wonderful.

We'd been on the road about twelve hours when we neared Charlotte.

"Whadda ya think, Ava? Wanna take a break?" Mike asked.

The two of us were buzzed with nothing in our stomachs except coffee. My head hurt and my hands trembled. North Carolina held too many bad memories, but we needed a break. Quaaludes called to me.

We checked into the first motel we found, watched TV until the downers took effect, and slept until the next morning.

My kids were closer than they'd been in ages. The mother in me wanted to call, to beg Tom to let me visit. But I remembered how Tom had convinced me I was worthless as a parent and my children wanted nothing to do with me. Family had shown me nothing but betrayal. I told myself I'd be better off staying away.

We took turns driving the remaining seven hundred miles to Fort Lauderdale without the aid of amphetamines. We found a decent motel, then bought a newspaper, and a chilled bottle of champagne.

"To us." Mike toasted our arrival.

"To our new life. Wish we had some blow," I said.

"Your wish is my command." Mike surprised me with an Altoids tin full of cocaine.

"We could've been busted, Mike."

"But we weren't, so let's celebrate."

And we did celebrate—all night long.

The next morning, Mike set out to find a job. I scanned the want ads for rental apartments with an ocean view. Prices were outrageous, but I did find several places south of the city near the water that fit our budget.

"Got me a coupla interviews lined up," Mike said later that day. "Betcha I get a gig by tomorrow. Let's check out some apartments."

I loved Mike's confidence. He thought nothing of signing a lease without having secured a job.

We chose a one-bedroom furnished apartment on the fourth floor of a high-rise overlooking the Intracoastal Waterway. It wasn't the nicest or the cheapest, but it was a month-to-month rental, and we could move in right away.

"This place is only temporary," Mike said. "Once I start makin' the big bucks, we'll live like kings and queens."

The next day he found a job at one of Fort Lauderdale's upscale boatyards. Mike didn't wait for things to happen. He made things happen.

"I'll be workin' on yachts and some fishin' boats," he said. "I'll be top mechanic before ya know it."

I believed him. Not only was Mike a fine mechanic, but he also had excellent people skills. He could strike up a conversation with anybody, tell a few jokes, and win them over to his way of thinking—

nothing like Jack, the introvert. I chased away an image of my ex-husband staring at the deer head over the fireplace.

"I'll check out some of the dance clubs in the area. I'm sure I can get work. I packed my best costumes," I said.

"The only dude who's gonna see you in them costumes is me. Time you took a break and enjoyed life."

thirty

A Big Tip

For the first time in years, life was simple. I cleaned and straightened the apartment every morning after Mike left for work. He'd arrive home around four o'clock, lay out a few lines of coke for us, and pour a shot of tequila for me and a scotch for him. We'd sit on the balcony and watch the sunset.

Despite all the positives in my life, I knew I was an addict. I'd been smoking pot, drinking alcohol, and snorting coke every day for years. I thought about quitting, but that would put a damper on my latest addiction, Mike Ambrose.

On sunny days I sat by the pool and read *Your Erroneous Zones* by Wayne Dyer. The book promised to point the way to self-reliance and to give readers tools to free themselves from negative thinking. I wasn't ready to lose my addictions, but I wanted to avoid falling into more self-destructive patterns.

I kept a journal, using my own shorthand to keep my thoughts and feelings private. Instead of lifting the barriers to my happiness, my writing reminded me of the past I'd hoped to leave behind.

When am I going to get it—the only people helped by self-help books are the authors.

After just a few weeks, *Your Erroneous Zones* and my journal found a permanent home in the trash.

~~~

Scoring pot was easy in South Florida. We got stuck with cheap Mexican a few times but soon found street dealers with decent Colombian smoke. Mike wanted to get back into dealing but had yet to make contacts. We were also running low on cocaine.

"Dude at work told me we could score at one o' the dance clubs. Whadda ya say, Ava? Wanna put on your dancin' shoes?"

I wanted to be done with the bar scene, but we needed drugs and money. I hadn't realized how much of Mike's lifestyle was dependent upon his dealing.

"Sure, Mike, just not every night, okay?"

"And miss sunsets with my baby? 'Course not."

We found the Breakwater, a club with a Philly connection. Mike used his contacts to score the first night. He was back in business, and we were back in blow. Life was good.

After a month at the boatyard, Mike burst into the apartment. "Hey, Ava, c'mere!"

I panicked. "Are you okay?"

"Check out my tip for the day!"

Mike fanned out ten one-hundred-dollar bills on the kitchen table.

"Your tip? For what?"

"These guys had a yacht stuck in the Caribbean near the Bahamas and wanted somebody to fly out and fix it. The boss asked if I'd be interested. Said I'm his top mechanic." Mike's smile covered half his face.

"You know you're the best," I said, stroking his ego.

"They had a twin-engine plane and flew me to Bimini. Took less than an hour to get there. Got me onto this yacht called *Smooth Sailin'* and I fixed it. Piece o' cake, but I didn't let on how easy it was. We flew back, they paid my boss in cash, and tipped me."
~~~

"Congratulations," I said, "I bet your boss gives you a raise."

"Screw that. Gary, the guy in charge of boats, asked if I'd come work for him. Said the *Smooth Sailin*'s only one o' their boats."

Mike was ambitious and always looking out for himself, but something didn't feel right. He had a good job and his boss appreciated him. He knew nothing about Gary or his fleet of boats.

"Did you talk salary?" I asked.

"Hell, no. If they tipped me a grand for one afternoon, I ain't gonna worry about salary."

"What kind of business are they in?" I was afraid to hear the answer.

"The guys are from Detroit—Ben's the head of the operation. Then there's Gary, Vinnie, and Chuck. Not the mob, just a bunch o' young dudes who struck it rich. They got what they call an enterprise."

"Sounds like drug smuggling to me," I said.

"Just grass. They're bringin' it up from Colombia."

"I thought we learned our lesson with Colombia," I said.

"This is big-time. No more sticking condoms up our butts. They got a freighter loaded with thirty tons of grass, which they unload onto the *Smooth Sailin'* and other yachts, all in international water. The yachts come into Fort Lauderdale and offload onto trucks. From there it goes to safe houses, then all over the country. And once they learned I had a pilot's license, they were sold on me."

"You could get busted," I warned.

"No way. I'm just the mechanic and the pilot. I got nothin' to do with the smuggling."

I thought about the self-destructive patterns Dyer wrote about in *Your Erroneous Zones*. I had a bad feeling I was about to fall back into one of mine.

thirty-one

Seasick

Mike left the boatyard without giving notice and went to work for what he now called The Crew. Each day he came home with a pocket full of cash.

"Coupla weeks more, and we'll be able to move to a better place," he said.

"I like it here."

"Doll, we hit the big time. One of these days I'm takin' you to Ben's mansion in Palm Beach. We should be livin' large like him—yachts, planes, Maseratis."

"Just be careful."

"Nothin' to worry about. All the business is done in international waters. How'd you like to go on a deep-sea voyage?"

I'd gotten bored with my "lady of leisure" lifestyle. I needed some excitement and a change of scenery.

"They'd let me come along?" I asked.

"Not just come along. They want you to be part of The Crew. Gary says they could use a cook. I've been braggin' 'bout what a great cook you are."

"I've never cooked for more than a handful of people at a time."

"They only got six or eight onboard. They buy the best gourmet shit. All you gotta do is heat it up and put it on plates," Mike said.

"If you're sure it's safe."

"'Course it is. Gary gives us the coordinates and we sail out to meet the freighter. We offload bales of pot onto a few yachts. We get new coordinates and offload our cargo onto cigarettes and fishing boats. We scrub it all down, get rid of every seed and stem, and come into port clean."

"I won't do it unless we're clean."

"These dudes are pros. Rumor has it they're bringin' in fifteen percent of all the grass comin' into the US. Been doin' it for years and never got caught."

Pot, coke, and alcohol clouded my judgment, and made Mike's offer seem like a good idea. I rationalized I had nothing to lose and everything to gain.

Smooth Sailin', the largest and most elegant yacht in the harbor, shone in the afternoon sun. The captain escorted us onto the immaculate deck and invited us into a sunken teak living room with a full bar. Our suite was done in white leather and looked like something out of a James Bond movie.

The Crew stocked the boat with enough high-end food and wine to make me look like a gourmet chef. They even supplied us with designer outfits to wear when we returned to port. The "bosses," as Ben and Gary called themselves, wanted us to exude wealth and leisure. The guys were clean-shaven and well-groomed, the girls perky and well-dressed.

We took the *Smooth Sailin'* out for a week. We partied nonstop on the way to meet the freighter. From that point, the work began. We were one of four seventy-five-foot yachts circling the freighter, which was manned by Colombians. We'd sail close, and they'd toss bales of marijuana onto our boat. One by one, we took them below. Every closet, every empty cabin, every inch of floor-to-ceiling space was packed with our cargo. An occasional bale fell into the ocean, but nobody seemed to care. They shrugged it off as the cost of doing business. Once we filled up, we moved aside, and the next yacht picked up their share.

"Got my exercise in for the day," Mike said, as we sailed away from the freighter. "Let's party!"

"I'm exhausted," I said.

"C'mon, Ava. We're done. Won't be meetin' the smaller boats till tomorrow."

"Suit yourself."

Our cabin reeked of marijuana. I had barely enough floor space to walk from our bunk to the head. Exhausted, I fell into a deep sleep. It was dark when I awoke and time to make dinner.

The mood was festive in the dining room, especially between Mike and Melinda, one of the other women on board. I saw her whisper something to Mike before they turned around and saw me. Melinda looked away and busied herself with setting the table.

Mike was unfazed. "Hey, doll. Have a good nap?"

I glared at him and walked back to the galley.

I suspected Mike cheated on me back in Jersey, but to do it right under my nose—

"What's the matter?" he asked.

"You slept with Melinda," I said without looking at him.

I saw him flinch for a second before he regained control.

"Are you nuts? I'd never cheat on you." He held me close and ran his tongue down my neck.

Despite his obvious lie, I chose to take him at his word.

The next day, we caught up with several cigarettes and fishing boats. This time we were the ones tossing bales, and as before, a few were lost at sea. Carl, our boat captain, made note of the losses and how many bales went to each boat.

I was exhausted but determined to stay on deck.

"Tired, Ava?" Melinda asked me. "I know I was beat on my first trip. Why don't you lay down? Tomorrow's gonna be the hardest day."

I doubted she had my best interest in mind. I took a quick shower and glued myself to Mike's side for the rest of the day.

Melinda was right about one thing. The following day, every piece of bedding, every towel, every article of clothing was taken to the laundry room. We worked in bathing suits, which would be laundered once we finished. Each of us took an area of the boat and literally scrubbed it clean. We started by brushing the ceilings, followed by wiping with a damp cloth. The walls were next, followed by the floors.

Carl, the most experienced crew member, inspected every inch of space.

"Ava, remember to check behind the toilet," he said, pulling out a few seeds.

I panicked for a second. "Sorry!"

"No problem. For a beginner, you did great. Glad to have you along."

"Anything else I can do?" I asked.

"Help me open all the portholes and turn on the AC units," Carl said.

I gave him a quizzical look.

"Gotta get any traces outta the air."

That evening we sat on deck, passing joints from our personal stash.

"Tomorrow afternoon, we dock in Fort Lauderdale," Carl said. "We do a last-minute cleanup, dump our stash, and change into our white bell-bottoms and navy-blue shirts."

"Won't we attract attention, all of us dressed alike?" I asked.

"Hell, no. We're going for the preppy look. They expect it from rich brats like us," Carl laughed.

I shrugged. "Okay by me."

The next morning, we did a final cleanup and sailed into port that afternoon. We sat on deck with a bottle of champagne, toasting our journey. Nobody paid us a bit of attention.

I watched a young, nondescript guy get on board.

"That's Gary, the boat coordinator. Lemme introduce you," Mike said.

"How's it goin'?" Gary asked.

"Nice to meet you," I replied.

"Heard from Carl you did a super job," Gary said.

"Thanks."

"Here you go." Gary handed a bait bucket to me and one to Mike. "Next time, it'll be more."

The bucket was full of hundred-dollar bills. I stared at Gary, not knowing what to say.

"You worked hard. Now enjoy," Gary said.

Mike and I went below to count our cash.

"There's ten-thousand dollars in here!" I screamed.

"Twenty-five thousand in mine!"

Mike picked me up and twirled me around the cabin.

"This is only the beginning," he said.

Thirty-five thousand for a week's work was a fortune in 1977. Two more trips, and we'd have enough to buy a house and furnish it. A few more and I'd have enough to fight Tom for custody of my kids. I couldn't wait for our next trip.

Our next excursion mirrored our first: a smooth sail to the freighter, followed by three days of intense work. We changed into our blue-and-white outfits, pulled into a different marina, and played our roles perfectly.

"I could get used to this," I said to Mike.

"I already am," he replied.

Gary handed us two bait buckets. "Great job, guys."

This time my bucket held fifteen-thousand dollars, Mike's thirty thousand.

"How can they afford this?" I asked Mike. "The yachts, the waste, the salaries?"

"Like I told ya, these guys are the biggest. They're makin' millions, and they don't even own guns."

I'd never thought about guns or violence.

That night we celebrated with some of the cleanest cocaine I'd ever tasted along with a four-hundred-dollar bottle of champagne. And why not? We worked our butts off and were confident another trip was right around the corner.

Two weeks later, Gary sent us on a third trip aboard the *Smooth Sailin'*. The second day out, Carl, our captain, was in a foul mood.

"Radar's showing a storm in the Caribbean near where we're meeting the freighter," Carl said.

"Can we turn around?" I asked.

The entire crew stared at me like I was crazy.

"We're picking up seventy-thousand pounds of grass, wholesale value at fifteen million bucks. You really expect The Crew to be okay about us turning around?" Carl asked.

I tried unsuccessfully to hide my shock. "Guess not."

The storm hit the night after we connected with the freighter. Fifteen-foot waves broke over our seventy-five-foot boat. If we had stayed on deck, we would have been washed overboard. Below deck was nearly as bad. Between trips to the head, we watched the waves slam against us. The motion would cease for a moment, then return with a vengeance. My muscles burned from so much vomiting. I prayed for sleep, then I prayed for death.

When I thought life could get no worse, it did. We lost power. I had thought we could throw the bales overboard and radio for help. But with no power, we were lost at sea.

After the longest night of my life, the storm subsided. We crawled on deck to survey the damage. It was bad but nothing that couldn't be fixed. I inspected the galley. With no refrigeration, most of our food had to be thrown overboard. That day the fish ate better than most of us humans.

Damage in the engine room was significant. Was Mike talented enough to get the *Smooth Sailin'* up and running? I had my doubts. The rest of us did what we could to return the boat to some degree of normalcy. Then we had nothing to do but wait on deck for a miracle.

Our miracle came in the form of a cigarette boat. Out of the corner of my eye, I spotted the boat and someone puking over the side. Once he finished, he waved to us. I knew he wasn't part of the Coast Guard, but could we trust this man with our cargo?

"It's Ben!" Carl screamed and waved furiously. Just then we heard a rumble from below. The engine was up and running.

The Crew securely tied the cigarette boat to the *Smooth Sailin'* and helped Ben on board. He was unsteady and a little green but soon regained his composure. I went below for fresh water from our dwindling supply.

"You must be Mike's girl," he said. "Benjamin Kraus. Everybody calls me Ben. Pleased to meet you."

"Ava Novak." I held out my hand to my boss, my benefactor. I struggled for what to say or do next until we heard a scream from the bridge.

"We're saved!"

Mike had not only fixed the engine but also had our radio and command center up and running. Everyone cheered as Mike joined us on deck.

Ben slapped him on the back, "You saved the day, Motor Mike."

As if Mike needed more ego stroking.

The Crew rerouted the yacht and eventually connected with the fleet of smaller boats. We offloaded our cargo, scrubbed, cleaned, and sailed into port a day late. We made do with canned and dry food, but our fresh water supply was nearly depleted.

"Thank you, God," I whispered as I set foot on land. Everyone else thanked Mike.

Gary met us with two buckets. Mine contained twenty-five-thousand dollars; Mike's had fifty thousand. The next day Mike bought a brand-new Horizon Blue Oldsmobile Cutlass 442.

thirty-two

Bahamas

The heat's on," Mike said a week later. "Looks like we won't be doin' any more boat trips for a while."

"Fine by me." I was in no hurry to return to the high seas.

Mike kept busy with The Crew's boats, which were now all in port. He also spent time working on the engine of a Beechcraft turbo prop plane used to move money to the Bahamas and Cayman Islands. Each day he came home with a pocket full of cash, much of which went to support his lavish lifestyle.

I continued to spend most of my time at our apartment. I thought about finding work, but Mike encouraged me to stay home.

"No girlfriend of mine is gonna dance," Mike said. "People'll think I don't make enough to support us."

"I'm not talking about dancing," I said. "I thought I'd look for something in a doctor's office."

"Ava, you're high from morning to night. Any doctor's gonna spot that. Why not wait till The Crew's back in business? From what Ben says, it shouldn't be more 'n a coupla weeks."

Mike had a point. I needed coke or speed to get going in the morning. Pot in the afternoon softened the edges. Alcohol in the evening helped me sleep.

~~~

"I'm goin' to the Bahamas," Mike announced a few days later.

"Me too?" I asked.

"Sorry, doll. Me 'n Maurice are flyin'. It's a two-seater."

Maurice was Mike's new best buddy. Like most of The Crew I'd met, he was fun-loving and easygoing. I hoped Maurice would be a positive influence on Mike, but something told me Mike would be the one to influence Maurice.

"Be careful, Mike."

"Don't worry. I'm no fool."

The shrill ring of our phone woke me out of a sound sleep at four in the morning.

"Ava, it's Ben."

This couldn't be good.

"Mike called. He's in jail."

"*What?*" Suddenly, I was wide awake.

"Booked him for drunk and disorderly. My lawyer's flying down to the Bahamas to bail him out. We'll probably just have to pay a fine," Ben said.

"What happened?"

"Mike's first mistake was reserving a room at the Graycliff Hotel," Ben said.

Mike had shown me Graycliff's brochure—an eighteenth-century mansion turned into a luxury hotel. I told him he belonged in a large, corporate hotel where he could party unnoticed. As usual, he ignored my advice.

"His second mistake was turning into a loud, sloppy drunk after too many Pusser's Rum Painkillers," Ben continued.

Probably a buffet of drugs, too.

"We need to talk when he gets home," Ben said.

I imagined a drunken Mike curled into a ball in the corner of a
~~~

Bahamian jail cell. More and more I saw him for what he was: a wise guy who thought only of himself.

One thing I knew for certain: If it had been up to me, I would have left him in jail until he learned his lesson.

Sleep was a memory. I got out of bed, made coffee, sat on the balcony, and watched the sunrise. I'd come so close to having a fairy-tale life in Florida with Mike. I saw no happy ending in our future.

That afternoon, I went to the library and checked out a copy of *The Power of Positive Thinking* by Norman Vincent Peale. I needed something besides cocaine to lift my spirits. I flipped through the anecdotal stories, which were supposed to teach me how to banish negativity and live an optimistic life. It didn't work.

When will I realize a book isn't going to change my life?

Obviously, today wasn't the day. I stayed on the balcony and read until the light faded.

Back inside, I made myself a vodka and grapefruit juice and opened a can of tomato soup. As I sat down to eat, I heard Mike's key in the door.

"Well, that sucked," he said, throwing his suitcase halfway across the room. "Goddamn Maurice. It's his fault we ended up in jail."

An "I told you so" would do no good. I took Mike's hand, led him to the sofa, and brought out a pipe and a block of hashish.

"You always know what I need," Mike said.

"You're safe now. Tell me all about it."

"After we checked in at the Graycliff, me 'n Maurice took care of business for The Crew. Met our contact at some dive bar in downtown Nassau. Had a few Painkillers—"

"Drinks or drugs?" I knew but wanted to hear it from Mike.

"Drinks. You gotta try 'em. Rum, coconut milk, juice."

"Too much rum gives me a headache," I said.

"Me too. But I didn't know that till later. Anyway, seemed like we were only there for an hour or so before they flagged us. Maurice got pissed, leaned over the bar, and took a swing at the bartender. That's when the bouncer threw us onto the street."

Maurice was an upbeat, happy guy who became more upbeat and happy when he was drunk. Mike on the other hand—

I knew better than to dispute Mike's story. Instead, I passed the pipe to him. He inhaled deeply and held his breath, as though he didn't want to continue.

"We went back to the hotel, had a couple more Painkillers by the pool, then went in for dinner. Maurice said they had the best steaks in town. Y'know how much I love my steaks."

Mike could eat steak morning, noon, and night.

"Anyway, they wouldn't serve us. Said we weren't dressed properly."

"Didn't you bring a jacket and tie?" I asked.

"Hell, no. It's the Caribbean. Nobody dresses up."

I wanted to shove the hotel brochure in his face. The dress code was right there in black and white.

"Maurice started in, sayin' we had every right to be there. I kept quiet at first, but Maurice kept at it. He said we're guests at the hotel and can dress any way we like."

"Why didn't you just leave?" I asked.

"I wanted to, but Maurice stood his ground. The maître d' yelled to somebody to call the cops. 'C'mon, Maurice, let's split,' I said, but they wouldn't let us leave. The cops hauled us into the station and stuck us in a cell."

"If you didn't cause any trouble, why did they arrest you and not just Maurice?"

"Well, maybe I got into it, too."

Mike's whole story was a fabrication.

"They allow you one local phone call. Maurice called one of his pals on the island who called Ben."

"You're lucky Ben bailed you out. Is he pissed?"

"Nah, cost of doin' business."

Even a night in a Bahamian jail did nothing to tame Mike.

"Gotta call Ben and let him know I'm back."

Mike was no longer my white or my black knight, but I was still in love and lust with him. Without him, I'd have to go back to New Jersey, back to dancing and a life of cheap drugs and booze.

Mike joined me back in the living room.

"Ben wants to meet with us," he said.

"Is he firing you?"

"Hell, no. I'm too valuable. He invited us to his mansion for dinner tomorrow night to discuss business."

I'd heard stories about Ben's palatial home, his cars, and lavish lifestyle. Much as I was nervous about Mike's fate—and in turn, mine—I was flattered to be invited, and curious to see how his boss lived.

thirty-three

Peacocks

Gary Nielsen, the boat coordinator and one of "the bosses," was our main contact at The Crew. Mike envied Gary's penthouse condo with views of the ocean and Intracoastal Waterway. Every piece of furniture and work of art reflected quality and good taste. And why not? The Crew grossed millions every month.

"We'll be livin' like Gary before you know it," Mike said on the way to Ben's the next day, "but I'm more interested in livin' like his boss."

"One step at a time, Mike," I said. "We've only been in Florida a few months. You don't know what Ben's got in mind."

We drove north on A1A, eventually crossing the Lake Worth Lagoon and Bingham Island. From there, Mike made a left onto Flagler Drive. A few twists and turns brought us onto a quiet, tree-lined street. Sprawling homes were set back from the road, some barely visible through manicured landscapes.

"Here we are," Mike said as he drove his Cutlass down a shaded driveway, eventually parking behind a white Rolls Royce convertible.

A fire-red Ferrari and a sleek black Maserati were parked in front of a three-car garage. Tennis courts and a hot tub were off to the left. Tall palms graced the sides of the house. A two-story, carved, teak door with beveled glass sidelights welcomed us.

"Where's Robert Redford?" I joked.

The teak door opened and Ben, not Robert Redford, stepped outside. I found it hard to believe this young, scraggly guy was the head of a multimillion-dollar drug ring.

"Nice wheels," Ben said to Mike.

"You, too, man," Mike replied.

The entrance foyer was decorated with potted palms, bringing the natural landscape of the property indoors. A geometric crystal chandelier hung from the sixteen-foot ceiling and shone onto the cream, ceramic-tiled floor. An antique Venetian mirror reflected it all, adding even more elegance to the room.

"Your home is gorgeous," I said.

"Thanks. C'mon back to the lanai."

We walked through a formal living room, done in white with a few accents of coral and black. To the right was a library, complete with leather sofas, a massive partner desk, and built-in mahogany shelves. I imagined Ben sitting at the desk arranging shipments of tons of marijuana from Colombia to Florida.

A black lacquer table served as the centerpiece for the dining room. Twelve white satin upholstered chairs waited for the next round of guests. A glass cabinet held shelves of cut crystal, which reflected the light from another chandelier. Everything was immaculate.

When we first arrived, I wondered what Ben's place cost. Now I wondered what it cost to maintain.

Ben opened a set of French doors, and we stepped into the lanai. Gary and another guy were sitting at a glass-top table, sipping red wine.

"Help yourselves to wine and food." Ben escorted us to a sideboard with several bottles of French wine, a cheese board, a basket of bread, caviar, and an assortment of fruit.

I poured wine for Mike and me, then arranged a plate of food for us. We joined the men already at the table.

"How's it goin', Ava?" Gary said. "By the way, this here's Vinnie Lasseter."

"Pleasure." Vinnie stood and offered his hand to me.

"Ready to get down to business?" Ben asked.

Three male heads nodded. I sat quietly observing the dynamics. Ben controlled the room, exuding power and wealth. The acoustics created a slight echo when he spoke, adding to his dominance. He never raised his voice, never criticized, and never bad-mouthed anyone.

Gary and Vinnie mirrored Ben with thin builds and dirty blond hair. All three were in their mid-twenties, confident, relaxed, and focused. Mike was the odd man out. His good looks were no match for the others.

"We've got a situation here in Florida," Ben said. "Word on the street is the DEA is onto us."

"What else is new?" Gary said.

"Yeah, but now they have extra agents watching the marinas. They know the *Smooth Sailin'* and the *Olympia*," Ben said, referring to two of his yachts.

"We move operations north or south," Gary suggested. "We trade the boats in and buy some new ones."

"Forty tons of product in one week on the *Olympia* might've been pushin' it," Vinnie said.

"Forty tons, fifty tons, what's the difference? Everybody's on the payroll. Problem now is we got some new agents on our trail. Mike's hot after he got busted in Nassau. There's gonna be trouble anywhere he goes," Ben said.

"Sorry, man," Mike said.

"Apology accepted," Ben said. "It was bound to happen. I think the incident brought things to a head."

"You're an excellent mechanic, Mike," Gary said. "The Crew doesn't wanna lose you."

"We take care of our own," Ben continued. "Now, before we get to new business, I wanted to talk about that last shipment. Chuck Fedder says sales are up, and demand is higher than ever."

From their conversation, I assumed Chuck Fedder was another boss in The Crew, and along with Ben, responsible for keeping the books. I wondered why he wasn't at today's meeting.

Ben started talking numbers. Other than hearing "millions" repeatedly, I tuned him out and stared through the row of sliding glass doors leading from the lanai to the back of the property. A guesthouse matching the design of the main estate sat off to the side of an expansive kidney-shaped pool. Two peacocks strutted across the lawn, adding a touch of magical elegance to the scene.

I wanted to join the peacocks, stroll the grounds, and dangle my feet in the pool. I wasn't part of the conversation, so why did they want me at the table?

"Ava, whadda ya think?" Mike asked.

I snapped out of my daydream. "About what?"

The guys laughed. I turned a bright shade of scarlet.

"Kenya," Mike said.

"Sorry, I've been watching the peacocks." I imagined the guys thinking, *Typical female.*

"Vinnie's our man in Asia—Hong Kong, Singapore, Bangkok—made us a fortune with Thai sticks," Ben said. "He's getting us set up to grow our own in Northern Thailand."

I'd begun to master the art of acting nonchalant, but my brain was doing backflips. Here I was, Ava Novak, in the company of worldwide drug smugglers.

"We're looking for another country with the right climate, poor farmers, and a cooperative government," Ben said. "We think Kenya's the place."

"Kenya's not for me," Vinnie said. "Got my hands full in Asia. Ben thought you and Mike might be interested."

"I'm game," Mike said.

"Why us?" I asked.

"You proved yourself on the *Smooth Sailin'*," Ben said. "I think a nice young couple would do well over there."

"And since Mike's hot, it'll get him out of the country and allow us to get back to business as usual," Gary said.

Ben must have noticed my worried expression. "Gary's got a point but, more than that, I think you two are perfect for the job.

You've only been in Florida a few months, you've got no family, no ties, nothing to hold you here."

No family except two kids who've forgotten I'm alive.

"How 'bout we do a few lines, fire up the grill, and give these two a chance to talk about it?" Vinnie said.

A Baccarat crystal box appeared on the table along with a gold-plated coke sniffer for each of us. Ben laid out lines on a gold-handled mirror, which we passed around the table. Ben signaled to someone in the kitchen, who wheeled a cart laden with steaks and shrimp out by the pool.

I'll always remember the beauty of that day, Friday, May 1, 1977. For a short while, I felt as though I'd entered paradise.

thirty-four

Decisions

A slender, young blond woman in a mint-green sundress appeared from around the corner. Ben stood as she joined us at the table.

"Mike, Ava, my girlfriend, Donna," he said.

Donna smiled shyly and giggled. "Nice to meet you."

I asked myself how a guy like Ben caught a long-haired beauty who looked like she stepped off the cover of *Seventeen* magazine.

"I parked the Mercedes behind the Maserati," Donna said.

Donna answered my question. *Money, what else?*

"I hear Ben's sending you and Mike to Mombasa," Donna said.

"Where's Mombasa?" I felt like a fool.

"Kenya."

"We haven't made up our minds yet."

"Are you serious? I'd give anything to go to Mombasa, but my place is here with Ben."

Talk about subservient. Then again, I wouldn't expect Ben to have a liberated woman as a girlfriend. Powerful guys almost always preferred submissive women.

What did that say about me? I knew I'd missed the women's lib boat, but I'd made my own way since I was nineteen, despite two failed marriages and a drug and alcohol addiction. This wasn't the time for self-reflection. The stakes and I were much too high.

"I'll show you the brochures," Donna said. "It's a city in Kenya's harbor on the Indian Ocean. The beaches and seafood are to die for, and the hotels are incredible. Weather's kind of like here, but it's all so exotic."

"Once you and Mike get settled, Ben and I'll come visit," Donna said.

Ben was deep in conversation with Gary and Mike. I had a feeling he had no interest in leaving the United States.

Mike was on his second steak while I feasted on Gulf shrimp grilled to perfection. I couldn't remember ever enjoying myself so much. If we decided to go to Kenya, I was confident our lives would mirror this night.

The setting sun cast a pink glow on everyone and everything. A soft breeze rustled the palm fronds, the quiet broken only by the occasional screech of a peacock. I watched the chef wheel away the remnants of our dinner and counted at least six empty wine bottles. Had I drunk an entire bottle of wine?

Wine usually put me to sleep, but the combination of quality wine and cocaine kept me relaxed yet alert. The angel on my right shoulder whispered, *Go home and sleep on Ben's offer.* The devil on my left shoulder shouted, *Say yes tonight before Ben changes his mind.*

Conversation paused as the chef wheeled out a cart stocked with Courvoisier, Grand Marnier, crystal aperitif glasses, and miniature pastries. I was stuffed but accepted a Grand Marnier and a cannoli to be polite.

"We'll book flights for you in a couple of weeks," Ben said. "Mike'll head out first, then you'll join him. That'll give you time to get your lives in order, and time for me and Vinnie to iron out the details."

"But—"

"But what, Ava?" Ben asked. "Are you telling me you want to send Mike into darkest Africa alone?"

"Um, no. I guess I missed part of the conversation."

I glared at Mike, who was too full of himself, wine, and steak to notice. Even though the angel on my left shoulder would have eventually won the argument, I'd have appreciated time to discuss my future with Mike.

"Stop over tomorrow afternoon, and we'll iron out the details." From Ben's tone I understood the evening was over.

I had too much to think about on the ride home to get into it with Mike. What would be the point? He thought only of himself and had no clue he should have consulted me before agreeing to Ben's plan.

"Can you imagine—the bosses sendin' us to Africa? Shows how much they value me."

"You really think it's a good idea?" I asked. "Africa's not America. We won't know anybody. We don't speak the language."

"Ya think lions 'n giraffes are runnin' down the street? They speak English. We'll be livin' in a goddamn hotel on the beach."

Mike went on and on about the outrageous life we'd have in Africa. I was still angry he hadn't consulted me, but the more he said, the more intrigued I became.

We slept until almost noon the next day. Over coffee, I read the brochure from the Mombasa Beach Hotel. Ocean views, turquoise water, sparkling blue skies, rooms decorated in sophisticated African decor. If I didn't know better, I'd think the hotel was in the Caribbean. Until last night, I had no idea where Kenya was located. I studied the map Ben had given us. The country lay on the Indian Ocean, midway down the continent. From there, we could visit Egypt, Madagascar, even book a safari—and it would all be on The Crew's dime.

If we supervised the farming, we'd oversee the shipments out of the country and never get our hands dirty. I'd never have to go through another airport check like in Colombia. The more I read, the more enthusiastic I became. How could I say no to a once-in-a-lifetime adventure?

"Whadda ya think, Ava?" Mike asked.

"I think *yes*!"

"I knew you'd come around," Mike said. "This is our chance to make it big. Let's get over to Ben's."

I greeted Ben with an enthusiastic smile.

"Guess you're on board, Ava," Ben said. "Let's talk business. Gary's waiting for us in the library."

I sat quietly while Ben and Gary discussed logistics with Mike. The Crew would reserve a suite with an ocean view for us. We'd arrive with enough cash to cover our expenses and to bribe local officials, cabdrivers, and drug dealers. Once we were settled, they'd ship seeds to us.

"Mike, you'll fly to London first to meet with Vinnie," Ben said. "Thought you'd enjoy the Dorchester. Supposed to be the ritziest hotel in town."

"Thanks so much, Ben. We won't let you down." I felt like a twentieth-century Cinderella.

"I know," Ben said. "Gary, take Mike out back and have him look at Donna's Mercedes. She says it's making some weird noises."

Gary stood, gave Ben a strange look, and left with Mike.

"I'm gonna level with you, Ava," Ben began. "Mike's trouble. If he wasn't such a good mechanic, we'd have dropped him after the *Smooth Sailin'* fiasco. He saved our shipment, our boat, maybe our lives. But he's got a big mouth and a bigger ego. If we don't get him out of the country soon, we're all toast."

My instincts were right about Mike. The bosses wanted him out of the way before he destroyed their worldwide enterprise.

"Will we be okay in Kenya?" I asked.

"We need somebody with a big mouth," Ben replied, "somebody who'll make the right contacts and fast. Everybody's on the payroll in Kenya, from the top government officials to the cabdrivers. The farmers are poor and will do anything to make ends meet."

"What about me?"

"You kept your cool on the *Smooth Sailin'* when most chicks would've lost it. You're friendly, outgoing, and not afraid to get your hands dirty. People'll see a rich American couple living large. Mike by himself is trouble."

"Wow, thank you!" For once, someone believed in me.

"Don't thank me. You've got a bigger job ahead than you realize. Kenya's like the Old West. You need to stay cool and keep Mike in line. And remember, we never resort to violence."

"You think there's gonna be violence?"

"As long as we play our cards right, we'll be okay," Ben said. "Money always wins over guns. Remember that, and make sure Mike remembers. We've been at this for years in the States and Asia. Never owned a gun, never needed one. If somebody gets kidnapped, we pay the ransom. If an official threatens us, we pay him off. If somebody rips us off, we walk away and don't do business with him again."

It dawned on me that Ben was nothing more than a peace-loving hippie with a head for business. Like Jack, he started dealing to pay for his own habit. But unlike Jack, his enterprise grew nationally, then worldwide. And unlike Jack, he knew how to treat people.

"I won't let you down," I said.

"I know. You're good people, Ava," Ben said. "Now, how about some blow?"

"You read my mind." I smiled.

The Baccarat crystal box appeared along with the gold coke sniffers and mirror. Ben laid out four lines and handed the mirror to me.

"Just so you know, we only deal in pot. Never anything stronger. This is my personal stash. You catch Mike dealing anything else, you let us know."

"I promise." I was sure they'd warned Mike, too, but it was good to know.

"Stick with me, play by the rules, and you'll be a rich woman."

"Thank you."

A few minutes later, Gary and Mike joined us.

"Ready to go, my African Queen?" Mike joked.

I saw Gary and Ben exchange looks.

"A last piece of business," Ben said. "Mike, you'll fly to London on Monday, the eleventh. Ava, you'll fly out the following Monday. By that time, Vinnie will be gone, and Gary'll be joining you. You'll fly to Nairobi the following Sunday. We'll get together once more before you go to iron out the details. And Ava, one last word—"

"Meet you out front," Gary said.

"But—" Mike began.

"Out front," Ben said with authority.

Once they left the library, Ben said, "Keep your eye on the money. Make sure Mike doesn't do anything stupid. If he does, you wire me immediately."

I was in over my head, but the pull of excitement and adventure kept me moving forward.

thirty-five

London

I packed a few things for London's cooler spring temperatures and some tropical basics. The Crew fronted us $25,000, more than enough to buy everything we needed once we arrived in Kenya.

I popped a quaalude while I waited at Miami International Airport. A downer and a couple of drinks put me to sleep for most of the flight. I arrived at Heathrow Airport early the next morning and took a cab to the Dorchester Hotel.

My driver spotted me as an American tourist and drove past one historic site after another. I tried playing it cool, but once I spotted Buckingham Palace, it all evaporated.

"Do you think we'll see the queen?" I asked my driver.

"She'll be having her morning tea," he replied. "Give her a ring once you settle in."

He was having fun with me, and I played along. I was in Mayfair, the heart of London. Hyde Park, Trafalgar Square, the Thames—I wanted to see it all. Five days wouldn't be enough.

Within seconds of my arrival at the Dorchester, a concierge grabbed my luggage and escorted me into the lobby. Marble, fine antiques, fabulous artwork, floral arrangements—everything spoke of understated luxury and class. I pinched my arm to make sure I wasn't dreaming.

"Welcome, Mrs. Ambrose. Your husband's suite is on the eighth floor adjacent to Mr. Nielsen's," the desk clerk said. "Your personal butler is James. He's been trained to Royal Household standards and is available for your every need."

"Thank you," I said.

The desk clerk snapped his fingers and a white-gloved bellhop appeared.

"I'll take you to your suite, madam," he said.

James was waiting for me when we got off the elevator.

"Mr. Ambrose is in a meeting," James said, unlocking the door to our suite. "He will be joining you shortly."

A meeting at this time of morning? Was Mike lying already?

"May I give you the grand tour?" James asked.

"Thank you."

James's voice was a blur. I stared at the highly polished parquet floors, the perfectly appointed living room, the luxurious queen-sized bed, and marble bathroom. I couldn't imagine Buckingham Palace being any finer.

Once I was alone, I plopped onto the bed and stared at the ceiling. Here I was in London, in the lap of luxury with all expenses paid. All that was missing was Mike.

I knew I should unpack, shower, and call Gary's suite, but I was exhausted. I wrapped myself in the feather-stuffed duvet and let my head sink into the down pillows. The sheets were cotton but so soft, they felt like silk. I was either in heaven or sleeping on a cloud.

After what seemed like minutes, I opened my eyes and glanced at the time. Was it eleven o'clock in the morning or at night? I tried calculating what time it was back home, then let it go. I was in London and starving.

I turned and saw Mike lying beside me. I wanted to kiss him awake but decided to let him sleep. I crept out of bed and showered in our marble and glass walk-in shower. Our towels and two terrycloth robes hung on a heated rack.

Mike was awake when I came back into the bedroom.

"Hey, doll. I missed you," he whispered.

"Missed you, too." I joined him back in bed.

"How about we order some breakfast?" Mike suggested.

"I'm starving. I haven't eaten since yesterday."

We looked at the room-service menu and decided on a full English breakfast. I assumed we'd ordered bacon and eggs. Instead, our server wheeled in a cart laden with stewed fruit, eggs, sausages, baked beans, grilled tomato, mushrooms, toast with marmalade, tea, and coffee.

"I'll never eat all this," I said, "Who eats baked beans and tomatoes for breakfast?"

"Lemme help." Mike finished every speck of food. "Before we do anything else, we should call Gary."

Gary had left us a message saying he'd be out until teatime.

So very British.

Mike was content to stay in our suite until we met Gary. I headed for Hyde Park.

Gardens, fountains, and magnificent greenery—all set in the center of London. I felt a sense of contentment as I strolled down shaded pathways. At three o'clock, I made my way back to the Dorchester.

Mike and I joined Gary in his suite, which was as large and luxurious as ours. Was he married? Did he have a girlfriend? At that moment I realized how little I knew about Gary or the rest of the bosses.

"Welcome to my humble abode," Gary laughed.

"I could get used to this," I said.

"Don't get too comfortable. We have a lot of work ahead of us," Gary reminded me. "Vinnie scouted out the area around Mombasa, so we have a good idea of where we want to start operations. I've got all the info right here."

Gary handed us a packet of information. Mike shoved it aside and poured himself a generous amount of Glenfiddich single-malt scotch.

"We're good," Mike said.

"*Read it!*" It was the first time I'd heard Gary raise his voice.

"Yeah, yeah, don't worry," Mike said.

I leafed through the information while Gary and Mike talked business.

"Ben said he gave you twenty-five grand. You're gonna need more than that to get things up and running, so I'll give you extra cash before you leave. They love the American dollar in Kenya."

I was getting used to outrageous sums of money tossed around like confetti.

A gentle knock sounded on the suite door. Gary's butler wheeled in a tea trolley stocked with tiny sandwiches with crusts removed, warm scones with clotted cream and preserves, a selection of cheeses, and a variety of teas.

"May I, madam?"

I nodded.

The butler poured me a cup of Earl Grey tea, then said, "Our sandwiches include smoked salmon with cream cheese, cucumber and butter, and chicken salad. Today's scones are blueberry, and we have petit fours for the end of your meal."

He bowed and left us to our feast. Gary and Mike played it cool, but I felt like a kid in a tea shop. *Live for the present*, I told myself. I had enough life experience to know moments like this were rare.

After tea, Mike and I returned to our suite. All I wanted to do was relax in bed and watch some British TV until I fell asleep. Mike had other plans.

"Gary wants to go pub hoppin'," he said. "He's gonna introduce me to some of The Crew's drug contacts."

"They have contacts in London?"

"Shit yeah. How d'ya think they afford all this?"

"Have fun. I'll probably be asleep when you get back."

~~~
~~~

I fell asleep not long after Mike left and woke around midnight. He hadn't returned. I hoped he hadn't gotten in trouble.

Mike tiptoed into our room sometime after two o'clock. By the way he slammed into the furniture, I could tell he was drunk. He crawled into bed beside me reeking of whiskey and cheap perfume.

Will he ever change?

We established a pattern. I'd wake early, have a small breakfast, and set out to see the sights. I'd return by midafternoon and join Mike for tea, then we'd head to one of the hotel bars for cocktails. Gary joined us each day before flying back to Florida.

With Gary gone, Mike had no excuse to leave me the next evening.

"How about you and I catching some night life?" I asked him.

"Sorry, doll. Gary connected me with some dudes. Gonna do a coupla deals. Can't have ya along."

"Do these 'dudes' wear cheap perfume? I know you're cheating on me."

Mike had mastered the art of the innocent look. "I'd never cheat on you."

"Sure, Mike. Whatever you say." *No point in arguing with a sociopath.*

I couldn't sleep that night. Around two in the morning, I had a craving for hot chocolate and rang for room service. Twenty minutes later, our butler wheeled in a silver service cart with a pot of cocoa and a dish of miniature marshmallows.

"Anything else, madam?" he asked.

"I have a few things that need washing. Should I wait till morning?"

"Certainly not," he said, "I'll have them returned first thing."

If it hadn't been for Mike, I'd have believed I died and gone to heaven.

I finished my cocoa and fell into a deep sleep. The next morning, I found Mike crashed on the living room sofa next to my freshly laundered and pressed clothing. I ignored him and took my things into the bedroom.

Not only were my clothes pressed to perfection, but the hotel had also repaired a tiny rip on the pocket of my jeans. The small gesture almost brought me to tears.

Mike was so out of it that he didn't hear our butler wheel in the breakfast cart. I tried picturing the scene from the butler's point-of-view: a lonely woman sipping hot chocolate while her no-good boyfriend roamed the seedier side of London. The lonely woman enjoying a full breakfast cart while the no-good boyfriend slept it off. Truthfully, I didn't care. It was my last day in London, and I intended to take advantage of everything British.

thirty-six

Welcome to Kenya

A taxi brought us to Heathrow International Airport, where we caught a late evening flight to Jomo Kenyatta International Airport in Nairobi, Kenya. I wasn't looking forward to another overnight flight, but I popped a quaalude and managed to get a good amount of sleep on the plane. Even though Mike slept most of the day at our hotel, he slept through most of the night as well.

Our flight arrived on time, and we made our connection to Mombasa International Airport, which was clean, modern, and efficient. We found our luggage, sailed through customs, and were nearly blinded by the tropical sunlight as we exited the building.

Gary had suggested we chat up some taxi drivers to find local drug connections. We knew better than to approach the driver who took us from the airport to the Mombasa Beach Hotel. To him, we were American tourists on holiday. We needed to gain the trust of a few locals before asking any direct questions.

Mombasa was a mix of new and old, wealth and poverty, beauty and squalor. Traffic crawled. Our cab had no air conditioning. We sat in traffic for nearly an hour with open windows, breathing fumes and listening to the alien sounds of the city. Magnificent high-rises sat adjacent to crumbling buildings. Businessmen strolled alongside ragged street vendors. I'd get a glimpse of the Indian Ocean, and in the next instant I'd be drawn down a dark alley.

"Is this paradise or hell?" I whispered to Mike.

"We'll make it our personal paradise," Mike replied.

I had my doubts until our taxi left the main highway and headed toward the ocean. The city released us into greenery, fine buildings, and ocean views. Once I saw the sign for Mombasa Beach Hotel, I knew we had entered paradise.

The hotel was as luxurious as any in Southern Florida. Whether facing the ocean or the pool, each room had a large balcony. The lobby was decorated in vibrant greens, reds, and gold. While it wasn't as elegant or sophisticated as London, the hotel oozed luxury.

"Welcome to Mombasa Beach Hotel. My name is Oliver. How may I serve you?" The front desk clerk's English had a pleasant, lilting accent.

"Mr. and Mrs. Michael Ambrose checking in," Mike said.

I knew better than to give his introduction any special meaning. I'd read most Kenyans were devout Christians. Registering as an unmarried couple would raise eyebrows and was probably forbidden.

"You are in Suite 400, one of our finest," Oliver said. "I understand you have an open-ended stay."

"Yeah. We got business here in Mombasa," Mike said.

"Yes, sir. We have instructions to bill your company, Sunstar Industries, for all expenses."

Sunstar Industries?

"Obuya, please take Mr. and Mrs. Ambrose to their suite." Oliver motioned to a bellhop.

"*Siku njema bwana, madam.* Good day, sir and madam. I am Obuya, here to serve you."

Everyone we had met had been genuinely friendly and kind. London was becoming a distant memory.

"Anything you need, please call on me," Obuya said as we rode the elevator to the fourth floor.

"Thank you." I had a feeling Obuya would be the one to open doors for us in Kenya.

"Your room." Obuya opened the carved double door to our room.

Ben had booked a suite for us overlooking the ocean. Our bed was draped in sheer mosquito netting, though I doubted a mosquito could find its way into our new home.

"Mike, it's perfect," I said, after we generously tipped Obuya.

He picked me up and spun me around. "If we play our cards right, we just might be here forever. Before we unpack, let's celebrate."

Mike stood with his back to me, unbuttoned his shirt, and slipped out of his pants.

"I need a shower before we do anything," I said.

"Later, doll." When he turned to face me, I saw he'd taped bags of cocaine to his chest and stomach. "I was sweatin' so much in that cab, I thought the tape would melt offa me."

"You could've gotten busted," I said. "Why take a chance?"

"Nobody gives a shit when you're leavin' London. And nobody gives a shit when you get here. With all the cash we got, I ain't worried."

He had a point, but I was glad I didn't know what he was up to.

"I don't know about you, Mike, but all I want to do for the rest of the day is catch a buzz and relax on the balcony. We can start work tomorrow."

"Tomorrow? Are ya nuts? We're on Sunstar's dime. Work can wait."

"Speaking of Sunstar Industries—what is it?" I asked.

"One of Ben's covers. He's got all kinda corporations."

"Smart guy," I said.

"I'm learnin' all I can from him," Mike said.

"What does Sunstar do?"

"Ben said Sunstar's into agriculture. Makes sense, right? I'm thinkin' 'bout sayin' we're into diamond mining," Mike said.

"Do they have diamond mines here?"

"I dunno. If not, we can say we're lookin' to start one."

"Better stick to what Ben said. We don't want to attract too much attention."

Mike didn't like me telling him what to do, but I wasn't taking any chances. Ben and Vinnie had done the research, and they were a lot smarter than Mike.

"Yeah, yeah. Let's do some lines, call room service, and relax."

Mike's answer to everything was to get high. In my heart, I knew it was my answer to everything, too.

We decided to order *samaki choma*, a roasted fish dish recommended on the room service menu. It came with collard greens and coconut rice. Mike ordered a bottle of Johnnie Walker Black scotch for him and a bottle of Smirnoff vodka for me.

Without pot to put me to sleep, I drank more vodka than I had in a long time. I knew I'd have a nasty hangover, but honestly, I didn't care.

In the past week I'd traveled nearly halfway around the world. I'd eaten strange food, drunk too much alcohol, and snorted substandard cocaine. I needed time to relax and get my life back on track. Mike and I spent much of the next day at the pool. Even though we had an ocean view, Nyali Beach was about a mile from the hotel. Between the heat and humidity, a hangover, and the great unknown, I decided a visit to the beach could wait a day or two.

Obuya took care of all our needs. We rewarded him with generous tips. By the end of our third day, we felt confident he could be trusted.

"We're lookin' for somebody who can show us the city," Mike told Obuya.

"My friend, Waititu, is your man. He knows every street, shop, and ruin. He speaks English, Swahili, and many dialects and languages of our country. May I call him?"

"Yes, please," I said before Mike had a chance to say something stupid like, "My good man."

A short while later, Obuya informed us that Waititu would meet us in the hotel lobby at ten o'clock the next morning.

"And away we go," I said, quoting an old line from Jackie Gleason.

thirty-seven

Waititu

A short, angular, mid-thirties man sat in the hotel lobby the next morning. When he spied us coming out of the elevator, he jumped from his seat.

"*Siku njema bwana, madam.* Good day, sir and madam. I am Waititu. At your service." He smiled and bowed deeply.

Despite his formality, he was warm and welcoming. I liked him instantly.

"*Siku njema bwana.* I'm Ava. Pleased to meet you." I bowed and smiled, hoping to get a laugh from Waititu.

"I'm Mike. Glad to meet ya. I'm not much on bowin'." Mike extended his hand.

"Obuya says you need a guide. What can I show you?" Waititu spoke with the Kenyan accent I was beginning to love.

Mike and I had discussed our strategy the night before. We would warm up to Waititu, have him show us the city, ask questions about the countryside and farming, then mention drugs.

"My wife wants to visit the markets. Then maybe you could drive us past some ruins," Mike said.

"Of course. *Twende zetu.* Let's go."

Waititu wore faded blue jeans, a striped polo shirt, and scuffed leather sandals—all of which were clean but had seen better days. I noticed he was missing a few teeth in his lower jaw. I was confident he would welcome our dollars and do whatever he could to help us.

"My car is not new, but it is clean. Madam, it would be best to sit in the back. Your husband has long legs and needs the front." Waititu opened the rear door to a dark-green Toyota with a dented rear bumper and several scratches on the doors.

"Thank you," I said.

Mike climbed in the front.

"I will drive you around the city and show you our history and markets. When you want to stop, you tell me."

"*Asante.*" Obuya had taught me to say thank you.

"*Karibu.* You are welcome," Waititu replied.

Mike wasn't looking too happy, but I was having the time of my life.

Waititu wove his Toyota through narrow streets, pointing out shops, ruins, and street vendors. I felt I'd entered a time warp: no McDonald's, no billboards, no upscale shopping malls. Most men dressed like Waititu, though I did see a few in military outfits.

Some women we saw wore traditional brightly printed robes and headdresses. Others wore sundresses, still others wore skirts and tops that often didn't match. What surprised me was the number of women in saris. Everywhere was color, vibrancy, and smiles.

"You may like Today's Market. It is under a tent and will be safe for you," Waititu said. "I will let you out here and return in an hour."

Safe? Were we in danger? I looked at Mike for reassurance. He winked at me.

"Cool, man," Mike said. "One hour."

Stepping out of the car was like entering another dimension. The streets were hot and dirty. We were hit with one smell after another—gasoline fumes, urine, spices. People stared. Apparently, this part of town saw few American tourists.

I was grateful to enter Today's Market. The tented roof shielded us from the midday sun. Fruits, vegetables, spices, and grains lay in baskets, on blankets, and in wooden boxes. Women cooked soups, stews, and snacks, and called to us to sample their foods. We'd been warned about eating street food, so I smiled and shook my head.

At the far end of the market were the local crafts. I bought several strings of colorful beads, two wooden bowls, and a small, handwoven basket. The vendors spoke little English. I sensed they wanted to bargain with me, but I was content to pay the highest price. We had an endless supply of cash, so why not share the wealth?

"Whadda want this crap for?" Mike asked.

"Souvenirs. Maybe I can help some of these people."

"You're payin' top dollar for junk."

I held in my temper. Mike thought he was better than these people. He was so wrong.

An hour passed in a flash. As promised, Waititu was waiting for us.

"I'm gonna start chattin' him up," Mike said.

"Are you sure you don't want to wait? I thought you wanted to chill out for a while."

"If this is Africa, you can keep it. Sooner we get rollin', sooner we get outta here."

"Be careful, Mike."

"Yeah, doll, y'know me."

I sure do.

I was tired, hungry, and needed a drink but didn't want to be the one to pull the plug on the day. I decided to trust Mike's decision to get down to business with Waititu.

"What is next for you?" Waititu asked.

"D'ya know anywhere by the ocean where we can get somethin' to drink? We'll buy ya a beer and we can talk," Mike suggested.

"I will take you to my favorite place. It is popular for locals and tourists," Waititu replied.

He drove onto the main highway and from there onto Link Road. We passed our hotel and made a left turn, taking us to the ocean. Several thatch-roofed huts stood on wooden platforms on the beach. We had returned to the twentieth century and paradise.

Waititu waved to the bartender. "He is my brother-in-law. I will order Tusker beer for us."

"I don't drink beer," I apologized. "Maybe white wine?"

"I will ask for the best wine."

A short while later a waitress brought our drinks and a plate of samosas.

"*Asante*," I said.

"*Karibu*," she replied.

Everything tastes better at the beach; this meal was no exception. Once we'd eaten our fill, Mike got down to business.

"Thanks for today," Mike began.

"You are most welcome," Waititu said. "I can show you more of the city, beaches, and countryside."

"Actually, we're here for work," Mike said.

Waititu put down his beer. "Yes, that is what Obuya told me. May I ask what is your business?"

"Sunstar Industries. We're into farming."

My heart pounded. *Don't blow it, Mike.*

"Kenya has much farmland. What is your crop?"

Seconds of silence surrounded us.

"Marijuana," Mike whispered.

"*Bangi*. You know it is illegal here in Kenya." Waititu didn't appear surprised.

"Yeah, same as the States, but that don't keep us from growin' and smokin'," Mike said.

Waititu smiled. "Many things are illegal, but many people are for sale."

"Are you for sale?" I asked.

"I can help you, but it will take time and money," Waititu said.

"We got both. I'll start by buyin' you another beer." Mike signaled the waitress, who brought another round of drinks.

"To new business ventures," Mike said.

"Cheers!" Waititu said.

We gave Waititu a generous tip. He promised to meet us with an update in a few days.

"I hope you had a pleasant day," Obuya greeted us back at the hotel.

"We did." I showed him my treasures from Today's Market.

"Something to remember your visit," Obuya said.

"Thank you for introducing us to Waititu. He was very helpful," I said.

"Yes, he knows many people." Something about Obuya's smile told me he knew what we were up to.

"C'mon, doll. Time for a shower." Mike nudged me toward the elevator.

Once in the elevator, Mike said, "Be careful what you say to him. We don't wanna blow our cover at the hotel."

"I have a feeling word travels fast around here. Anyway, like Waititu said, everybody's for sale."

"He said many people, not everybody," Mike argued.

thirty-eight

Farmland

Obuya left us a message to meet him in the lobby the next morning.

"*Habari za asubuhi.* Good morning, Mr. and Mrs. Ambrose."

"Good morning, Obuya," I replied.

"My friend Waititu has a message for you. He will be traveling the next few days to find what you need for your business," he said.

"Great, thanks." Mike slipped Obuya a ten-dollar bill.

"My pleasure. Please let me know if I may help you further," Obuya said.

Once Obuya was out of earshot, I turned to Mike. "We could be in big trouble if Waititu told him why we're here."

"Don't sweat it. 'Course he knows. What could go wrong?"

"Famous last words," I said.

"Obuya's not gonna blow it. He's gettin' rich offa us."

"I've got a bad feeling," I said.

"Trust me. It's all good."

Maybe Mike was right. He'd spent more time with the bosses and knew more about the operation than I did.

We spent the next few days playing tourist. We'd scored some pot on the beach and used up our supply of cocaine.

"Maybe Waititu can turn us on to some local blow," Mike said.

"You're putting a lot of trust in the guy," I warned him.

"What's your problem?"

"Nothing, I guess." I shrugged off my concern.

"Mr. Ambrose," the desk clerk called to Mike. "I have a letter for you."

The handwritten note was from Waititu.

I have located some farmers. I will meet you tomorrow morning at eight o'clock. Please to wear comfortable shoes and clothes.

"Looks like we're in business!" Mike said.

"*Habari za asubuhi.* Good morning, Mr. and Mrs. Ambrose," Waititu greeted us the next morning.

"Please call us Mike and Ava. And *habari za asubuhi* to you, Waititu," I said.

"Shall we go?"

"Wait, man. We ordered food from the hotel for the trip," Mike said.

"We can buy food at a shop along the roadside," Waititu said.

Mike and I looked at each other.

"I understand. You have American stomachs. May I suggest we buy food so we do not offend the villagers. One day soon you will have Kenyan stomachs."

I visualized myself puking or worse behind an acacia tree while a lion waited to devour me. I laughed.

"What's so funny?" Mike asked.

"Nothing. C'mon, let's go."

We took the Mombasa-Malindi Highway north through tourist and residential neighborhoods before leaving Mombasa. It may have been the fastest route out of the city, but it took us nearly an hour to travel fifteen miles. At a nondescript point in the road, Waititu made a left turn. Within seconds we were in the countryside.

The paved road turned to dirt. Sparsely treed plains slowly gave rise to soft hills and farms. We saw men and women bent close to the ground working the soil. Everyone stood to wave as we drove by.

"They're so friendly," I said.

"Very friendly," Waititu said. "They do not often see a car—or Americans."

Eventually, we came to a paved road, a few shacks made from corrugated metal, a market, and gas station.

"We need gas," Waititu said. "I will also buy Pepsi and food."

Mike handed Waititu some Kenyan money and an American twenty-dollar bill.

"Did you think Kenya would look like this?" I asked Mike.

"Don't know what I thought, but this ain't it."

"We are so blessed—" I began, then looked around. The few people I saw wore second- or third-hand clothing, lived in shacks or worse, yet they all smiled and looked at peace.

"Yeah, we're blessed," Mike said. "I'll be more blessed when we get back to the hotel and into the pool."

Waititu returned and handed us each a can of Pepsi. "Here is your change, Mike."

"Keep it."

Freshly fueled, we drove farther into Kenya's farmland. Then, in the middle of nowhere, we came to a village. Nothing prepared me for the reality or the uniqueness of this tranquil community. Villagers lived in round mud huts with grass roofs. Each had a single open door. Apparently, they felt no need to lock their homes.

A few elderly men and women sat in the village center with young children; I assumed everyone else was working in the fields. None of them wore traditional garments. Instead, they dressed in T-shirts, skirts, and shorts.

Waititu waved to an elderly man, who motioned for us to sit next to him under a tree. Mike and I greeted him in English.

"This is Amara," Waititu said. "He speaks no English."

"*Habari za asubuhi.*" I had no idea if it was still morning but wanted to attempt to speak his language.

Amara smiled a toothless grin. Maybe our dollars would bring him out of poverty, but would it make him happier?

Waititu and Amara spoke in what I assumed was a dialect of Swahili. Occasionally, Waititu would translate for us.

"He is asking about seeds for your crop," Waititu said.

"Tell him we'll send for seeds and pay the farmers once the seeds arrive," Mike said.

More Swahili was spoken.

"Amara knows the crop is illegal," Waititu said. "He wants to know what protection they have against the police."

"Tell him we'll pay the police to keep quiet," Mike said.

Amara nodded. Two small boys ran to him. He hugged them and motioned us to stop talking. Waititu and Amara spoke playfully to the children before Amara shooed them away.

Should we be involving these innocent farmers in our illegal activities? What if they get arrested and we can't help them? I lived with enough guilt about my own family. I didn't want to be responsible for destroying their harmonious lifestyle.

Waititu turned to Mike. "Amara wants payment before the seeds arrive. He says it is a promise to keep the farming with his village. When the seeds arrive, he wants another payment."

"What the—" Mike began.

Maybe they're not so innocent. I motioned to Mike to talk to me in private.

"Mike, honey, I think we should do what Amara wants."

"They're takin' advantage of me," Mike said. "I don't like it."

"These people have nothing. You'll be getting rich off their labor. It's Ben's money, not ours."

"You know I don't like it when somebody gets over on me." He paused. "Well, okay, seein' as we're the ones makin' the big score."

Mike, it's about you—always.

We rejoined Waititu and Amara.

"It's a deal," Mike said.

I left the men to work out the details and joined the two boys playing a game in the dirt. "Game?" I asked.

One boy understood. He made motions with his hands to show how to play.

"Marbles!" I smiled. The boys used nuts and stones and were perfectly content.

Waititu and Mike discussed the farming operation on the ride home. The village could devote five-hundred acres to growing marijuana. Mike didn't think it was enough land.

"Let us see how it goes with Amara before we speak to another village," Waititu suggested.

Mike had enough sense to take Waititu's advice.

They sat in silence for a while before Mike asked the question that had been on both our minds.

"Me 'n Ava wanna buy some smoke for us. Bought some *bangi* at the beach but it ain't quality."

"I can get you the best *bangi* tomorrow," Waititu said.

"What about cocaine?" Mike asked.

"It is not so easy to buy, and not so good. Do you like quaaludes?" Waititu asked.

"Sure, man. Downers, uppers. It's all good."

Mike gave Waititu a handful of cash when we returned to our hotel.

"I will see you tomorrow my friends." Waititu waved goodbye.

Back at the hotel, Mike wired Ben for seeds and money. I was curious how the seeds would arrive but asked no questions. The less I knew, the better.

thirty-nine

Weeds and Seeds

When the seeds arrived, Mike left me at the hotel while he went off with Waititu. I spent most days at the pool reading magazines. Hotel guests came and went, providing little distraction.

After several weeks, I approached Mike. "I can't take much more of this. Can I come with you and Waititu on your next trip?"

Mike hesitated. I knew him well enough to know he was hiding something. Had he met another woman?

"You really wanna go back out there? I'm lookin' out for ya, doll, keepin' ya safe."

Now I *knew* he was cheating on me.

"I do. I'm part of this operation." *And I promised Ben I'd keep an eye on you.*

"Well, okay. To be honest, things ain't goin' good with the crops. The seeds won't grow."

"Why haven't you told me? Does Ben know?"

"Waititu said to give it another week," Mike mumbled.

"I'm calling Ben today."

I'd never seen Mike panic before. "Don't—"

"He deserves to know," I said. "It's not your fault. It's gotta be something wrong with the seeds or the soil."

We called Ben with the news. He said he'd fly Maurice, Mike's buddy and one of The Crew's horticulturalists, to check on the fields.

Several days later Maurice joined us at the hotel. I was overjoyed to see someone from home. Waititu said he would drive us to inspect the crops.

Maurice joined me in the back seat of Waititu's Toyota on the way to the farmland.

"Is your family into farming?" I asked him.

"I grew up on a dairy farm in Mississippi, but my relatives back in Jamaica grew pineapples, avocados, and other fruit crops," Maurice replied.

"Do you know anything about growing pot?" I asked.

Maurice smiled. "I thought you meant legal farming. My brothers and I have been growing pot for Ben for a few years. First, we grew only outdoors, now we have greenhouses."

"Maurice's the best," Mike said from the front seat.

As we left the city, Maurice peered out the car's rear window. He shot me a worried look. I turned and saw a late-model gray Toyota driven by two large white men.

"Shhh," Maurice whispered.

Were we being followed?

The car followed us when we left the Mombasa-Malindi Highway, then slowed to leave more distance between our two vehicles. The two men were either inept at tailing or wanted us to know they were there. If Waititu was aware of them, he didn't let on. Mike was oblivious.

"I will stop for gasoline before we go to the village." Waititu pulled into the row of businesses serving Amara's village.

The gray Toyota stopped on the roadside.

"I'm gonna get me some smokes," Mike said.

"What's going on?" I asked Maurice, once Mike was out of hearing range.

"Those dudes are Ben's mercenaries," Maurice said. "Ben said he needed somebody besides me and you to keep an eye on Mike."

"Are they paid assassins?" I tried keeping my voice from rattling.

"I doubt it," Maurice said. "You know Ben doesn't support violence, but he does need to protect his investment."

"What are we supposed to do?" I hoped Maurice didn't hear the panic in my voice.

"Nothing," Maurice said. "Pretend they don't exist. They want us to see them—kinda like a conscience."

"One thing Mike doesn't have is a conscience."

"Looks like he's got one now," Maurice said. "Don't say a word. Let Mike figure it out for himself."

The Toyota continued to follow us until we pulled off the paved road toward the village.

"*Habari yako?* How are you?" I greeted Amara when we arrived at the village.

"*Sijambo, asante,*" he replied, telling me he was fine. He then spoke to Waititu.

"He is worried. Most seeds are not growing. Those that grow are tiny, sick plants," Waititu translated. "He wants to take us to the farm. He hopes Maurice can help."

Amara crowded into the back seat with Maurice and me. We bounced along dirt trails until we reached the fields. I knew nothing about farming, but even I could tell something was wrong. How did Mike let things go so far without intervening—unless he'd been lying and hadn't been here with Waititu.

Waititu, Amara, and Maurice approached two farmers while Mike and I remained by the vehicle. We watched Maurice examine the soil and a few straggly plants.

The farmers nodded and smiled. Amara grabbed Maurice's hand and gave it a squeeze. I felt the stress leave my body.

"Bad seeds," Maurice said. "Soil this rich should grow anything.

I'm no chemist but I bet if you get some different seeds, your plants'll grow like weeds."

We drove Amara back to the village and headed back to Mombasa.

"Does the village have more farmland?" Maurice asked.

"None to grow *bangi*," Waititu said.

"We'll have to find more villages," Maurice said. "We need at least twice as much farmland, maybe more. Can you help us, Waititu?"

"It will take money," Waititu replied. "The larger the business, the more people we must pay, and the more chances we must take."

"Money ain't a problem," Mike said. "The bosses send whatever we need."

Mike loved to be the big man and often spoke without thinking.

Keep your mouth shut about money. The more the locals think we have, the more they'll demand.

Back at the hotel, Mike and Maurice called Ben. After the call, they invited me to join them for drinks and smoke.

"I hear the coke sucks here," Maurice said.

"Pot, uppers, downers, that's about it," Mike said. "Speakin' of which, are ya interested in some 'ludes?"

Mike had developed a taste for quaaludes, or 'ludes, as he called them. Downers made him stupid and obnoxious and made me want a one-way ticket home.

"Business first," Maurice said. "Ava needs to know what's happening."

"Okay," Mike said reluctantly. "Ben's gonna get in touch with Vinnie Lasseter in Hong Kong. Vinnie's got contacts all over the world. He'll send us as many seeds as we need."

"How do you know they'll grow?" I asked.

"Ben talked to some expert who says Hawaiian seeds are what we need," Mike replied.

"How will the seeds get here?" I asked.

"Don't worry about details, doll."

"But I do worry. I don't want to get busted."

"We don't know details," Maurice said, "but Ben's no fool. He's gonna protect our operation."

I decided to trust Ben. He hadn't let us down yet, which was more than I could say for Mike.

While we waited for the seeds, Waititu scouted out more farmland. Mike and Maurice spent most afternoons and evenings away from me. Were they with Waititu or getting into trouble on their own? I didn't know and didn't ask. All I knew was we had higher quality pot and pills.

Speed made me edgy and magnified my loneliness, so I stayed away from it unless I needed a bump from the numbing effects of too much pot and alcohol. I was living in paradise with an unlimited supply of cash, yet unhappiness overwhelmed me. I thought about getting clean but couldn't do it alone. Most people have family or friends for support. I'd never had the support of my family, and my friends were all back home.

Once we get home, I'll get sober. My words felt hollow. I poured myself another glass of South African chardonnay and returned to our balcony. Who was I kidding?

Several days later, Mike and Maurice met me at the hotel pool.

"They're here!" Each guy held a large cardboard box.

"Shhh. Not so loud," I warned.

"Get off it, doll. Nobody's gonna say nothin'," Mike said.

"We head to the villages tomorrow. We'll be rich before you know it," Maurice said.

Obuya and several other hotel staffers worked nearby. I caught Obuya's eye and waved. His smile told me he'd been well-paid to keep quiet.

~

Our first trip took us to Amara's village. The two mercenaries followed us, this time in a blue Honda. It was the first time I'd seen them since my last trip to the farms, but I suspected they'd been keeping a close watch on Mike. He had to be aware of them but never said a word to me.

In the village, several women in traditional dress cooked in the shade of acacia trees. Young children played nearby. One woman called to Amara, who exited one of the round huts.

Waititu handed Amara a box of seeds and an envelope of cash. The two men spoke like old friends.

"The best seeds on the planet," Maurice said to me. "Just wait a month. The plants'll be gigantic."

"Hang here, doll. We're takin' the seeds to the fields," Mike said. "Be back in a flash."

I walked over to the women, who invited me to sit with them. They continued to prepare food, which included several types of greens and ground corn. We sat in comfortable silence while the children ran in circles around us.

The kids were curious about a white woman in their village, so I motioned them over. I made a soft fist with my left hand. With eyeliner, I drew black dots for eyes on my index finger and a red mouth on my thumb with lipstick. I moved my thumb up and down, which opened and closed the mouth.

We all broke into fits of laughter. I drew faces on each of the kids' hands, which led to more joy. It was one of my happiest moments in Africa. Before we left the village, I gave the women my makeup case.

Mike was surprised to see me with the villagers when he returned. "What are you doin' with those women?"

"They're good people," I said.

"Watch yourself," he hissed.

They're better human beings than you'll ever be.

"We must go now," Waititu called to us.

We piled into Waititu's car, made our way back to the paved road, and headed north.

"Our next village is not far," he said. "It is larger and more prosperous. They are excellent farmers."

We came to a shopping area, somewhat larger than the one near Amara's village. These buildings were wooden—some even had two stories. Billboards advertising cigarettes, Coca Cola, beer, and diapers hung everywhere. Food and household merchandise lay piled in front of each store. I wanted to take photos but sensed I'd embarrass the locals.

Waititu pulled into the gas station. He turned to Mike, who handed him a pile of Kenyan bills. After Waititu paid the attendant, he pocketed the rest of the money, something I'd seen him do several times.

We made a left at a faded wooden sign. This dirt road had fewer ruts and potholes. A village appeared in the distance. I saw little to distinguish this village from the last one until we drew closer.

Like Amara's village, the walls of the round huts were made of mud, but many had been whitewashed. A few even had windows. The earth in the common area had been packed and cleanly swept. Trees gave the village a cool, peaceful energy.

Waititu parked in the shade and waved to a thin, elderly man, who stood to greet us.

"This is my good friend, Tumaini," he said.

"*Habari yako?*" I had been studying Kenyan phrases but was not ready to practice more than, "How are you?" on a stranger.

"*Nzuri asante na wewe?*" Tumaini smiled.

Waititu translated, "Good, thank you, and you?"

We all smiled. As in Amara's village, the men left me alone while they discussed business. I waved to a group of elderly women, who waved back but did not invite me to join them.

While I waited, I thought about the choices I'd made in my life that led me to this remote village in eastern Kenya. I thought about my mother and my little brother, who had to be in his twenties by now. Did they wonder where I was? And what about Tom and my kids? Was I lost to them?

"Hey, Ava? How many times do I gotta call ya? We're leavin' unless you wanna stay here." Mike snapped me out of my daydream.

"Okay, Mike."

We celebrated with joints and a bottle of Smirnoff vodka on the ride back to Mombasa, confident our new seeds would bring us success.

forty

Company

What would ya say to some company?" Mike asked me two weeks later.

Mike thought nothing of leaving me at the hotel day after day. Of course, I wanted company.

"I'd love some."

"Carl's comin', and so's Edie," Mike said.

I hadn't thought much about Carl, the captain of *Smooth Sailin'* since we left Florida. I'd never met Edie, his wife.

"For how long—a week?"

"They're comin' to live in the hotel," Mike said. "Me and Maurice can't manage this by our lonesomes. Told Ben we need help, so he's sendin' Carl. It'll be a free ride for him and Edie."

I craved female company. Maybe Ben would be open to sending another friend for me.

"Do you think I could invite somebody?" I was thinking of Tina, who had moved to Sacramento, California. From her letters, I knew she was ready for a change.

"Why not? The plants are growin', and we'll be makin' millions for The Crew. Are ya thinkin' about Tina?"

My gigantic grin told Mike he was right.

"It's a deal," Mike said.

"Thanks, sweetie."

Carl arrived first, followed by Edie and Tina a week later.

I squealed with delight when I met Tina in the hotel lobby. A friend from home was the greatest gift I could imagine.

"Welcome to your new adventure!"

"This is not how I pictured Africa." Tina surveyed the upscale hotel I'd called home for the past few months.

"You're gonna love it here." Kenya had much to offer, but it wasn't home. I hoped Tina's presence would change how I felt.

Edie arrived later that afternoon. She and Carl embraced. The love between them was palpable. I turned away, wishing someone loved me as much.

Once everyone unpacked, they joined Mike and me in our suite. We'd ordered a full bar setup and every appetizer on the menu. Mike lit a joint and passed it to Maurice.

"Aren't you afraid of gettin' busted?" Carl asked.

"We got everybody on the payroll," Mike bragged. "Couldn't be safer."

Carl shrugged and took a hit.

We celebrated for hours. The longer we partied, the louder we became. Sometime after midnight, we heard banging on the wall of the adjoining suite and a muffled, "Keep it down!"

Mike banged back and yelled, "Screw you, man."

"Don't push it, Mike," Carl said.

"We're cool." Mike turned up the volume on the stereo he'd recently purchased.

A few minutes later, Theodore, the night manager, knocked on our door. "Please, I know you are enjoying yourselves, but I have received many calls from guests complaining of the noise."

"We're payin' customers. Just havin' a little fun." Mike reached into his pocket to tip Theodore.

Carl held him back and said, "I'm sorry. We'll keep it down."

The rest of us nodded and mumbled our apologies. Mike was obviously annoyed, but it was the five of us against him.

"Thank you, sir," Theodore said.

"Don't let these people push you around. We're the kings around here," Mike said.

Carl took Mike aside. The two spoke in whispers, after which Mike turned down the music and gave a pretend yawn.

"I'm fadin'. Let's call it a night," Mike said.

"It's been a long day. See you guys in the morning," Carl said.

Anybody who could tame Mike deserved my respect.

The next day, Waititu rented a van to take the six of us to the fields.

"We have had good rain. I am sure your seeds will be grown to young plants," Waititu said.

Mike sat next to Waititu in the front seat. Maurice and Carl sat behind them. I sat squashed between Edie and Tina in the rear seat. Like most vehicles in Kenya, the van had no air conditioning.

I could see everything was new and exotic to my friends. They held on to me as we exited the main road and drove onto the dirt trails.

"Where're we going?" Tina whispered in an anxious tone.

"To the farms. Nothing to worry about." I realized how numb I'd become to the primitive conditions and landscape.

We bounced along until we arrived at the small group of shacks serving the business needs of the local villages.

"We always stop here for gas," I told my friends. "Waititu likes to do business with the locals."

"We're not eating here, are we?" Edie asked.

Carl turned to his wife. "The hotel packed a lunch for us."

I felt Edie's body relax.

Waititu introduced our friends to Amara when we arrived in the village. Several young children ran to greet us. I handed packages of cookies to each of them.

"*Asante.* Thank you!" they yelled in unison.

The warm welcome relaxed our friends. I introduced Edie and Tina to a small group of women preparing food.

"This is nothing like I expected," Tina said.

"We're goin' to see the fields. Wanna come?" Mike called to us.

Several weeks had passed since the farmers had planted the seeds. From the cheerful welcome we'd received, I assumed the crops were doing well.

The fields were an explosion of green. Some plants stood knee high with buds and flowers already forming. Farmers greeted us with huge smiles. Waititu spoke in Swahili to a few men and translated for us.

"They are very happy with the new seeds. It is still the rainy season, so the plants will continue to grow. They have cut some back, so they will grow larger. Soon you will not believe what you see."

"They'll be big as Christmas trees before ya know it." Mike clapped Carl on the back. "We're gonna be rich!"

I wondered how much Carl would share in the profits. Mike and I had done all the work. Was he cutting me out?

Back in the village, Mike, Waititu, and Amara spoke in hushed tones. Money was exchanged, everyone smiled, and we returned to the van.

On the ride to Tumaini's village, we passed a joint and celebrated our success. Tumaini greeted us with the same exuberance as Amara. We visited the fields, exchanged more smiles and money, and headed back to Mombasa.

forty-one

Party Night

Every night was party night now that our friends had joined us. Theodore, the night manager, was a frequent visitor at our door, asking if we could please keep the noise down. Although he always left with a handful of American dollars, I suspected he wanted us gone.

"Mr. Mike, if it is up to me, you and your friends can make noise and have fun every night. But many of our guests are not happy. My boss asks every day why so many people complain," Theodore said.

"We're your best customers," Mike replied. "We spend more money than anybody else. You're gettin' rich off us, too. Watch your step or we'll be checkin' out."

"Mike, chill out," Maurice said. "He's just doing his job."

"If they don't like the noise, they shouldn't rent the suites on either side of us," Mike said.

"Maybe we should think about moving out," I said.

"And what—find a Holiday Inn?"

"Maybe find a house," I suggested.

Five pairs of bloodshot eyes stared at me.

"A house! Great idea, doll. We'll show these hotel assholes. See how they like it when our money's gone," Mike said.

Mike must have been wasted that night if he actually listened to something I had to say.

Mike, Maurice, and I met with Waititu the next day.

"You are tired of hotel living?" Waititu asked.

"Yeah, man, we wanna make Kenya our home," Mike said.

From Waititu's expression, I knew he wasn't taken in by Mike's lie. He had to know about the trouble we'd been causing at the hotel.

"What sort of house do you want?" Waititu asked.

"Big enough for all of us," Mike said. "Money don't matter. We got plenty and more whenever we need it."

I shot a warning glance at Mike.

"Let me see what I can do," Waititu said. "I will call you soon."

After Waititu left, Maurice turned to Mike. "Where are we gonna get money for a house?"

"Ben, where else? Lemme call him. What time is it in Florida?"

"Middle o' the night. Better wait. You don't wanna piss him off," Maurice said.

"Ben'd never get pissed at me," Mike bragged.

Then why are mercenaries following you?

"Mike, honey, let's go upstairs and figure out our strategy." I snuggled up to him, giving everybody the impression I wanted more than a consultation.

"Can't say no to you, babe." Mike winked at Maurice. "Catch ya later at the pool."

I managed to distract Mike until after lunch. I sat next to him when he called Ben. To my surprise, Ben loved the idea and called it an investment in The Crew's future.

"He said make sure it's a place he'd wanna live. Y'know what that means, doll!"

"A real home!" I smiled.

"Not just a home, a palace!"

I'd settle for a bungalow with a white picket fence. Anything to bring some peace and sanity into my life.

Waititu connected us with a realtor who drove us north from our hotel through winding streets in gorgeous residential neighborhoods. For the first time since we arrived in Africa, I sat in an air-conditioned car. It was heaven.

"I think you will like this property. It has everything you need: six bedrooms, gardens, a pool, and privacy." The realtor pulled into a circular driveway in front of a grand two-story, stucco villa with a red-tiled roof.

"Mike, this is perfect!"

"I was hopin' for somethin' more," Mike said.

You greedy SOB.

"Let's take a look," I said.

"We are in luck. The owner is here. He is a prominent attorney in Mombasa," the realtor said.

The minute I stepped onto the property, I felt at home. Massive trees sheltered the house from the midday sun. I imagined myself sitting on the wraparound veranda sipping an afternoon cocktail.

A fifty-something Indian man greeted us at the front entrance. "Rajiv Devi. Pleased to meet you."

He shook hands with Mike and the realtor, then nodded in my direction.

"Come, let me show you my magnificent home," Rajiv said.

Ceiling fans and cross ventilation brought the outdoors inside without the intensity of the tropics. My high-heeled sandals made a pleasant clicking sound on the parquet floors in the rooms on the first floor.

"It comes furnished, though if you prefer your own furniture, I can arrange to move things out," Rajiv said.

"Furnished is perfect," I said, before Mike had a chance to speak.

Each of the six bedrooms on the second floor came with its own tiled bathroom.

I nudged Mike. "I love it!"

Mike shrugged. "Nothin' like Ben's house."

"But a lot nicer than Gary Nielsen's condo." I could see my comment got Mike thinking. Gary was Ben's second in command. If Mike lived here, he'd have one up on Gary.

"Let's see the outside," Mike said.

The dining room opened onto an enclosed backyard with a garden, patio, and pool.

"The pool's bigger than Ben's," Mike said.

Always a competition with you, isn't it?

"What about the landscaping? We can't take care of this ourselves," I said.

"The house comes with a cook, housekeeper, and gardener. They live behind the fence." Rajiv opened the back gate and showed us two small shacks.

My heart went out to the poor families who cared for this magnificent home.

We went back inside and sat with Rajiv and the realtor.

"The price is $250,000." Rajiv and the realtor exchanged glances. I suspected Rajiv had just raised the price.

"No problem," Mike said. "We can give you a $50,000 deposit. I need to wire my partner for the money."

Rajiv's eyebrows lifted ever so slightly. "You are very easy with the money, sir. May I ask your business?"

Mike hesitated long enough to raise suspicion. "We're into ah—commodities."

"That is a very broad term. What sort of commodities?" Rajiv asked.

"Gemstones and ah—diamonds. We're lookin' to start a diamond mine here in Kenya," Mike said.

The corners of Rajiv's mouth tilted upward. "Excuse me, Mr. Ambrose, but Kenya is not known for diamonds. May I suggest you consider rubies or other colored stones?"

"Been there, done that," Mike backpedaled. "My sources told me diamonds are next."

Rajiv held his hands in prayer in front of his heart. "I'm sure you will succeed, sir. Now, let us discuss the sale of my home."

forty-two

Safari

It wasn't long before we left Mombasa Beach Hotel and became homeowners. I knew Ben and one of his shell companies were the real homeowners, but I didn't care. I had been living in chaos for so long, any chance of stability was a blessing.

"Ben's sendin' me to Hong Kong and Thailand," Mike announced one morning. "I'm meetin' with Vinnie Lasseter. Gonna bring him a sample of our crop."

"Who'll oversee the farms?" I asked. *And what about carrying drugs on the plane?*

"Maurice and Carl'll take care of stuff. The plants are already up to my waist. I'll be back in a coupla weeks," Mike said.

I'd had a love/hate relationship with Mike from the beginning. Since we'd been in Kenya, the scale had tipped toward hate. Time apart was exactly what I needed.

"You got your girlfriends," Mike said. "Don't go cheatin' on me while I'm gone."

"With the girls? You know I'm not like that."

Tina, Edie, and I relaxed by our pool after a breakfast of spiced chai, fruit, and *maandazis*, spiced fried dough, all prepared by Mary, our cook.

"I don't know how you put up with Mike," Tina said. "He's the biggest bullshit artist I've ever met."

"Thank goodness Carl's not like him," Edie replied.

"Have you been on a sight-seeing safari yet?" Tina asked.

"I want to. Just never got around to it," I said.

"Let's do it," Tina said. "I bet Waititu could set us up."

"Shouldn't we wait for Mike to get back?" I asked.

"He wouldn't wait for you," Tina said.

A week later, Waititu arranged a three-day trip for us to Tsavo East National Park, several hours inland from our home.

"You will see a different side of Africa," Waititu told us. "The Tsavo River flows through the park, but you will also see desert. It is the most beautiful place I know—except for the ocean."

"Will you join us on safari?" I asked.

"No. It is for tourists. I will stay with my cousins in Wundanyi, a town close by," Waititu said. "Today we drive to the park, tomorrow is your safari, and the following day we drive home."

"Will we be safe without him?" Tina whispered.

I shrugged. "I sure hope so."

Our accommodations were simple but not as primitive as I had anticipated. Tents rested on raised wooden platforms behind stockade fencing. Each came furnished with two single beds with mosquito netting, a small table, two wooden chairs, and a dresser. A ceiling fan with a dim bulb provided minimal air circulation and lighting. Restrooms were communal.

"How cool is this!" Tina exclaimed. "Never thought I'd go on an African safari."

"I'm glad Mike's not here," I said. Mike would've demanded a suite with the amenities of the Dorchester in London.

Several other guests joined us for dinner in the large public tent.

The food was simple: grilled meat, roasted sweet potatoes, collard greens cooked in oil, bottled beer, and soda. Our hosts encouraged us to make it an early night as we'd be leaving first thing the next morning.

Sunrise was magnificent. Fuchsia, baby pink, and ruby rays lit the sky. The morning dew caressed my skin. What more could I ask from life?

Breakfast was another simple meal: a variety of fruit, coffee, chai, samosas, sweet potatoes, and *uji*, a fermented porridge made from millet.

"You will have many opportunities for photography," our guide explained. "We will drive along dirt roads, but our vehicle has special shock absorbers to make the ride more comfortable."

The five of us, along with an older British couple, piled into one safari vehicle. I thought briefly of Mike but forgot him when I saw my first herd of red elephants.

"This is what I expected Africa to be like," Edie said. "Reminds me of *National Geographic* magazines when I was a kid."

Periodically, we'd stop for pictures of cape buffalo, cheetah, giraffe, and antelopes.

"You will see a pride of lions to your right," our driver said. "They are nicknamed 'man-eaters of Tsavo.' But don't be afraid. They have already eaten breakfast."

Nervous laughter erupted from the back of the vehicle.

"I can't believe all the birds," I said.

"We have more than six hundred species of birds in the park," our driver explained.

We stopped for lunch at a lodge with spectacular views of the distant mountains. An occasional acacia tree in the foreground added to the beauty of the vistas.

"I never want to leave," I said.

"Another day and you'll be screaming for a hot shower." Tina laughed.

"Maybe. But for today, this is my heaven."

Back at camp I showered under a sputtering outdoor faucet and joined my friends for an early dinner. With no alcohol or drugs in my system for two days, I slept deeply and dreamt of a reunion with my kids.

forty-three

Home Again

A Mercedes was parked in our driveway when we returned home from safari. From my seat in the back of the van, I noticed glances pass between Carl and Maurice. I assumed the car belonged to one of their local drug contacts.

"Looks like we've got company," I said.

"It might be the pool service," Carl said. "You ladies stay in the van. Maurice and I'll check around back."

"The pool company wouldn't drive a Mercedes," I said.

"Carl's lying. I can always tell," Edie said.

"Something's going down, and I'm gonna find out what," I said.

"Madam, why don't you stay with me?" Waititu urged.

"I'll be fine."

I tiptoed through the first floor. Nothing had been disturbed. Maybe Carl had told the truth about the pool service. I peeked out the dining room doors and saw Carl and Maurice deep in conversation. They knew something I didn't.

I went upstairs. Each bedroom door was open, except for Mike's and my room. *I could swear I left the door open.* Maybe Fatima, our housekeeper, had closed it.

The bamboo shade was drawn, giving an air of twilight to the room. The musty odor of sex filled my nostrils. In the dim light I noticed our bed was unmade. I flipped on the light switch, confident I could outrun anyone waking from a nap.

Mike! I clapped my hands over my mouth to keep from screaming.

He was naked and he wasn't alone. He straightened his leg, which had been draped across the other body and sat up.

"Where ya been, doll?" he asked innocently.

"On safari. What—what're you doing home? *And who's with you?*"

The other figure stirred. "What's going on, baby?"

A young woman squinted and sat up. I stared at her naked breasts before meeting her gaze. She was petite, blond, and looked a lot like me.

"It's not whatcha think," Mike said.

My composure surprised me. "What am I thinking?"

The woman covered herself with my robe and walked into the bathroom.

"I know it looks bad, but nothin' happened."

"I catch you naked in bed wrapped around some bitch, and you tell me nothing happened. I'm not stupid."

"Lemme explain."

I planted my feet in front of Mike, crossed my arms, and stared into his face. "You have two minutes. Ready? Go!"

"Vinnie took me shopping in Bangkok. I bought all new furniture for the house. Wait'll ya see it."

"Ninety seconds."

"Vinnie said I better get back here before the shit arrived, so I flew home a coupla days early. I couldn't wait to see you and tell you about the trip. When I called, Fatima said you were away. I thought about takin' a cab, but then I thought about callin' Liz."

"I assume that's Liz in the bathroom *in my robe*. One minute left."

"Rajiv introduced me to Liz after we moved here. Thought she'd be able to help us with the business. She's a big shot in the government."

"Oh, really?"

"Yeah. She gave me a ride home. Told her she could use the pool, get somethin' to eat, relax a bit before she left. I was beat. Came up here and fell right to sleep. Guess she musta been tired, too. I had no idea she was here till you came in. That's the God's honest truth."

"You're a liar. You've been cheating on me since the day we met. But to do it in our own bed—screw you!" I slammed the door and ran downstairs.

My breath came in gasps. My heart pounded in my chest. I wondered if Edie and Tina knew the truth. Carl and Maurice had to know. I felt like a fool.

I met my housemates by the pool where they had already lit joints and made a pitcher of vodka and tonic.

I was well on my way to oblivion when Mike joined us—alone. He pulled up a lounge chair next to me, rested his hand on my knee, looked into my eyes, and said, "I missed you, doll. Couldn't wait to get home."

I didn't want to start anything in front of our friends. "Missed you, too."

How many lies had I told Mike? How many had he told me? I had no one to depend on except Tina and Edie. Here I was, living in luxury with more money than I'd ever had, yet I was miserable. I thought about the Kenyans in the farming villages. They had nothing, yet their smiles and gratitude were genuine.

All I ever wanted from life was to be loved and live in peace. But the longer I lived, the more love eluded me. All I could do right now was forget what happened and make peace with Mike.

forty-four

Cutting the Grass

Because we paid our mortgage in cash wired to us from Ben, Rajiv stopped by to collect his payment promptly at ten o'clock the morning after Mike arrived home from Thailand.

"Good morning, Mr. and Mrs. Ambrose," Rajiv greeted us. "Do you have your payment?"

"Yeah, man, right here." Mike pulled out a wad of American bills in excess of what was due.

"I see you have a great deal of money. You do not need to pay more than one installment but if you are so inclined, I will happily accept it all." Rajiv smiled.

"This is nothin'," Mike said. "We got a bottomless pit for cash, but I need the rest for other stuff."

"Perhaps to pay those large white gentlemen who followed me here." Rajiv no longer smiled.

Now that Mike was back, the mercenaries were, too.

"Whadda ya mean?" Mike asked.

"Your bodyguards? Your babysitters? Who are those men?" Rajiv asked.

"They work for me."

Rajiv's expression told me he didn't buy Mike's lie for a second.

"Somethin' else," Mike said. "I bought new furniture for the house. It'll be here any day. What should we do with what's here?"

"I can arrange to have it moved, but it will cost you. Best to notify your contact in the States for more cash," Rajiv said.

Two days later the furniture and another new stereo system arrived, as did more cash for Rajiv. I sat on the veranda and watched as heavy pieces of carved, dark wood entered the house. I would miss Rajiv's tropical pieces, but I was in no position to argue.

"Excuse me, madam, but I must trim the lawn," Peter, our gardener, said to me after the delivery truck left. "Is this a bad time?"

"It's fine," I replied.

Peter used a sickle to hack away at the grass.

"Don't you have a lawnmower?" I asked.

"No, madam."

"We'll buy you a lawnmower tomorrow, and while we're in town, we'll buy new beds for all of you."

A grin spread across Peter's face. "You are most generous."

"I'll do what I can to help," I said.

Now that our grass at home was getting cut properly, we took a drive to the farms to check on our other grass. It was late October and the first time I'd seen the crops in nearly a month. I stared at marijuana plants as tall as me. Some buds were as large as my fists.

"I had no idea pot could grow like this!"

"Kenya has rich soil, lots of rain and sunshine, and farmers who know what they're doing," Maurice explained. "They've been cutting the plants back, which makes them grow larger. By Thanksgiving, we'll have our first harvest!"

"Americans'll go wild for this shit," Mike said.

"Can we try some?" I asked.

"The farmers harvested a few plants for us to try," Maurice said. "Some are already dried. The rest we'll take home and dry ourselves."

We said our goodbyes, packed the pot in the trunk, and set off for our second village. Our personal mercenaries were never far behind.

forty-five

Everything Changes

Waititu drove the guys to the fields twice a week. Tina, Edie, and I spent most of our time at home. By now, I'd had enough of Kenya, Mike, and our artificial life. I missed my kids. I missed Florida. I even missed dancing, or at least earning my own living.

Mike made up one excuse after another to go into Mombasa. I knew he was seeing his "side piece," Liz, and I knew confronting him would do no good. I also knew Ben needed me in Kenya until the fields were harvested.

By now Rajiv realized we weren't into gems. His visits became more frequent, his payoffs larger.

"Mike's gonna get us into a lot of trouble if he doesn't keep his mouth shut," Maurice said.

"I think we're already in hot water," I replied.

"Don't say anything to anybody else, but I'm flying home tomorrow," Maurice said.

"Who'll keep Mike in line?" I asked.

"I don't think anybody can. Ben needs me back home."

"Wish I could join you."

"You keep Mike out of trouble until the plants are harvested, then ask Ben to bring you home. You should be outta here by Christmas."

"I'll miss you." I hugged Maurice.

Once Maurice was gone, the mercenaries also disappeared. Were they on vacation or did Ben need them back home?

"Glad to see them mercenaries are gone," Mike said. "Betcha they were after Maurice for some shit."

You're delusional, Mike.

"Not to change the subject, but I'm gonna ask Rajiv for help gettin' the crop outta the country," Mike said.

"You'll do no such thing!" It was rare for me to stand up to Mike.

"He's a lawyer and knows everybody," Mike argued.

"Exactly. He'll have us busted."

"Y'know this whole country's corrupt. We've been payin' off Rajiv since we got here. He's on our side."

"Talk to Waititu," I suggested. "Or call Ben. He may already have something arranged."

Mike stood over me, raised his hand to slap my face, then pulled it away. "I'm in charge here, get it? This is my operation and don't you forget it."

"I get it all right."

Two more months and I'm gone. Those words would keep me going.

"What're you gonna be for Halloween?" Tina asked me.

"I don't think they celebrate Halloween in Kenya," I replied.

"Remember how we used to dress up when we were dancing?"

"I do." I couldn't believe I was looking back fondly on my dancing days.

"I don't care if we dress up. I'm just thinking about breaking up the monotony," Tina said.

"Me and Carl are thinking about going home. This is getting old," Edie said.

"You can't leave me here alone," I pleaded. "And Mike needs Carl."

"Carl said they'll harvest after Thanksgiving," Edie said.

"They don't celebrate Thanksgiving here either," I said.

Halloween was on a Monday in 1977. We'd given our housekeeping staff the night off and decided to have a party without costumes. The guys opened a bottle of single malt scotch. I made a pitcher of vodka and tonic for the girls. Mary, our cook, had made us trays of appetizers earlier in the day. And the pièce de résistance, our freshly dried pot.

A party was exactly what we needed to lift our spirits. We spent happy hour by the pool, then moved indoors after sunset. Around nine o'clock, we heard several vehicles pull into our driveway.

"Did you invite anybody?" I asked Mike.

"I didn't tell nobody about tonight, not even Waititu," Mike replied.

Bam! Bam! Bam! Fists, or something heavier, pounded on the door.

We sat, frozen.

"*Open up! Police!*"

"Flush the pot!" Edie whispered.

We could flush the soup bowl of pot in front of us, but what about the five-plus pounds drying in the closet upstairs?

"*Open up or we break down the door!*"

Carl grabbed the bowl and ran for the bathroom. Mike opened the door.

"Police. We're searching for guns, ivory, drugs."

At least twenty police officers crowded into our living room.

"*Stand!*" they commanded.

We all stood. They slashed the cushions on our new furniture and pulled open every drawer, dumping the contents on the floor.

I thought about asking for a search warrant, but I had no idea if warrants were needed in Kenya.

Three officers held Mike, Edie, Tina, and me at gunpoint. Carl was still upstairs. The other officers split into groups of two or three and tore apart the rest of the house.

"*Up here!*"

So much for Carl flushing our evening's stash. They'd found the mother lode.

Two officers carried the bulk of our marijuana into the living room. "You are under arrest for international smuggling and possession with intent to distribute."

"That's our personal supply. We're not smugglers!" Mike screamed.

"Hold out your hands!" the officer commanded.

Each of us was handcuffed. With guns pointing at our backs, we marched outside and into police cars.

We were allowed one phone call before they locked us up. Mike called Rajiv, who promised to bail us out in the morning.

"Why not tonight?" I whispered.

"Just be glad he's comin'," Mike said.

Tina, Edie, and I were pushed into a dank, dark holding cell that reeked of urine and unwashed bodies. A mattress, ripped at the seams, lay on the floor next to a concrete bench. Flies slept on a toilet in the corner. A large plastic bin of stagnant water was home to more flies.

Edie burst into tears. Tina and I clung to her.

"It's only one night," I said.

"But what if it's not? What if Rajiv doesn't come? What if we stay here forever?"

"Shh, Edie." I stroked her back and prayed she was wrong.

"At least we're alone," Tina said.

Except for the flies.

Rajiv didn't come for us until late morning, but he kept his promise and bailed us out.

"You made the front page of the paper." Rajiv showed us a copy of the *Standard* newspaper. The headline read, "Five Americans

Arrested for Drug Trafficking." Fortunately, our photos weren't included, but a photo of two police officers and our private stash were.

Rajiv drove us home and waited while we showered. We joined him in the kitchen where Mary had prepared a welcome-home brunch.

"I am not worried," Rajiv said. "The government has no proof of intent to distribute or international smuggling. You had five pounds of marijuana. I will make sure you only pay a fine."

"I can't spend another night in jail," Mike said.

"Don't worry, you won't," Rajiv promised. "The government doesn't want a scandal, especially with Americans."

"Cool, man." Mike was back to his cocky self.

"You have a court date in three weeks," Rajiv said. "It will take money for the judge and my fee. Will that be a problem?"

"Not a problem," Mike replied.

Mike gave Rajiv the bulk of our cash, which covered our bail and his so-called legal fees.

After Rajiv left, Mike called a meeting.

"Well, that sucked," he began.

"It don't sound like we've got anything to worry about," Carl said.

"What're you gonna tell Ben?" I asked.

"The truth," Mike said. "He won't care."

Just don't tell him how you shot off your big mouth to Rajiv.

"What do we do between now and then?" Edie asked.

"Go back to our lives. You heard Rajiv. We'll get a slap on the wrist, pay a fine, and harvest our crop," Mike said.

And then I'm outta here.

forty-six

Crop? What Crop?

Mike called Ben, who wired us $25,000 to cover our living expenses and pay off everybody until our court date. I was sure Mike lied about why we needed money, but I was in no position to confront him or Ben. That money was necessary for our survival.

A few days after our arrest, Waititu stopped by for a visit.

"I am certain you will have no further trouble with the police," he began. "Rajiv will get your conviction reduced to possession. You will only pay a fine."

"We have enough money behind us to pay off everybody right up to the president," Mike said.

Waititu's eyebrows lifted in surprise. "I think payment to the judge and police will be enough."

"Back to business as usual," Mike said.

"I am not so sure. I visited the villages after your arrest. They are scared. Unlike you, they have no protection against the government."

My heart went out to the farmers who had become my friends. They depended upon us for their livelihood and didn't deserve to be punished because of our mistakes.

"We should visit them today or tomorrow," I said.

"They got nothin' to worry about. We'll take care of them. Once the plants are harvested, they'll be rich," Mike said.

"Your wife is right. You need to reassure them. I can take you now."

Mike shot me a glance that seemed to say, *Mind your own business.*

"This ain't no time for games. We need to get out there," Carl said.

"Tina and I are staying home," Edie said. "What about you, Ava?"

"I need to see this through," I replied.

Conversation was minimal on the ride to the villages. Amara did not look happy when we arrived. He and Waititu spoke at length without smiling.

Waititu approached us looking at the ground, shaking his head. "I have bad news. The crop—it's gone. All of it."

"Oh my God. Have the police been here?" I asked.

"No. But once the farmers heard about your arrest, they burned the fields. Everything is destroyed."

"Who the fuck do they think they are?" Mike screamed. "Those were our plants. We gave them seeds and money. We had a deal!"

"They cannot go to prison. They worry for their women and children," Waititu said.

I turned away from Amara and Waititu so they wouldn't see me cry. Not only had we made a mess of our own lives, but we had also ruined the lives of these innocent people.

"Waititu, please tell them I am sorry," I said.

"I think Amara would appreciate it coming from you. Tell him, '*Samahani.*'"

"*Samahani.*" I took Amara's hand.

"*Samahani*," Amara repeated.

"Let's get outta here. Maybe the rest of the farmers won't be so stupid," Mike said.

"*Kwaheri.* Goodbye," I said.

"*Nenda na mungu*," Amara said.

I turned to Waititu for a translation.

"Go with God."

"*Nenda na mungu*," I repeated.

~~~

I had never seen Mike so angry. I sensed he blamed Waititu for showing the newspaper to the farmers. I prayed our other fields would still be intact.

Tumaini greeted us with a desperate look when we arrived at his village. His fields had been burned to the ground as well. Tumaini was furious and lashed out at us in Swahili.

"Let's get the hell outta here." Mike shot an angry look at Tumaini and walked away.

"*Samahani*," I mumbled through my tears.

Mike slammed his fist onto Waititu's car. "Six months we wasted. All that money down the toilet. Time to find some new farmers."

"Why don't we wait till after our hearing?" Carl suggested. "We don't wanna bring more attention on us."

"It'll take that long to get more seeds anyway," Mike said.

"Now to figure out what to tell Ben," Carl said.

Back at the house, I told Tina and Edie what had happened.

"We need to get out of the country," Edie said. "It's been one bummer after another. I'm going to talk to Carl about one-way tickets home."

"What about you, Tina?" Tina had been my best friend for years. Would she desert me?

"Me, too," Tina replied. "If I were you, Ava, I'd do the same."

"I can't tell Mike I'm not coming back."

"Then get a round-trip ticket and don't use the return," Edie said. "I promise not to say anything to Carl."

"How about we get out of the country before our hearing?" Tina asked.

"With an arrest hanging over our heads? And more bribe money due?" I hated to be the bearer of bad news, but we needed to face reality.
~~~

"Shh—I hear Mike and Carl coming," Edie said.

"Guess ya heard the bad news," Mike said as he walked into the room. "I'm gonna tell Ben what fuckups the locals are. Tell him we need cash and more seeds. Then we'll find some farmers who won't screw us."

Four pairs of eyes stared at Mike. Four pairs of eyes knew who the true fuckup was.

forty-seven

Surprise of a Lifetime

Our hearing was set for Monday, November 21. Ben sent $50,000 to pay our fines, additional bribes, and five round-trip tickets back to the States.

In less than three weeks, I'd be celebrating Thanksgiving at home. *Not that I have any family to celebrate with*, I thought, but that was the least of my worries.

I expected we'd meet Rajiv to discuss our hearing. But when he came by the next week to collect our mortgage payment, he shrugged off our questions.

"No need to worry. It is a misdemeanor. A small fine will be paid to the government, and a payment will be made to the judge. I will take care of you," he promised.

The crops were destroyed. The police had found no guns or ivory and no proof of international trafficking. We decided to enjoy our last days in Kenya.

Waititu kept Mike supplied with quaaludes and the rest of us with pot. The weekend before our hearing, we stayed straight so we'd be fresh and alert when we went to court.

"When we get back home, we'll have a party to end all parties," Mike said. "We'll have Mary and Fatima prepare a feast."

Despite my outward confidence, I was apprehensive. Kenya truly was the Old West where anything could happen.

Federal agents arrived at our home in two separate vehicles the morning of our hearing. The drive to the courthouse took an hour. To me it felt like days.

Mike and Carl had purchased suits for the hearing. Tina, Edie, and I dressed in simple dresses that landed slightly below our knees. We left most of our jewelry and money at home.

The courthouse reminded me of official Florida buildings with a white stucco exterior, gently arched porticos, and clock tower entrance. Graceful palms shaded the exterior. My legs trembled as we were escorted into a utilitarian courtroom.

Rajiv waited for us and motioned to join him. "Have a seat on the bench behind me. The judge and I will be hearing several cases this morning. You are third on the agenda."

Rajiv seemed relaxed and confident. I wished we were first so we could pay our fine and get on with our lives.

The first two cases were minor offenses. Each defendant stood while Rajiv and the judge discussed the case. A small fine was issued to each.

"See, all they want is money," Mike whispered to me.

"Michael Ambrose, Ava Novak, Carl O'Reilly, Edith O'Reilly, and Christina DaSilva, stand," the judge ordered. "Mr. Devi, how do your clients plead?"

"Not guilty, your honor," Rajiv said.

"Approach the bench."

Rajiv followed the judge's orders.

While they spoke, I turned to observe the courtroom. A handful of people peppered the benches. Most were black, a few were Indian and white. I spotted a blond female in the rear corner. Liz! Mike's side piece. A feeling of dread crept from my heart to my head. I turned my attention forward when I heard the judge say my name.

"Ava Novak, Carl O'Reilly, Edith O'Reilly, and Christina DaSilva. You are charged with possession of an illegal substance with intent to distribute abroad. I find you guilty and sentence you to nine months in prison. At the end of your sentence, you will be deported."

I reached for Mike's hand to keep from collapsing. He kept his hands folded at his waist. Tina took my other hand. The look on her face mirrored my inner terror.

"Michael Ambrose, you are free to go. Next case."

The judge banged his gavel. An officer of the court motioned us to follow him.

"Don't worry. I'll get you out." The casual tone of Mike's words belied the horror of the moment.

The four of us paraded across the front of the room like the condemned criminals we had become. I turned for a last look at Mike, the sociopath, in whom I'd put my trust. His attention was turned to the back of the courtroom, where Liz smiled and waved at him.

How much did you pay Rajiv to let you go and leave us to die?

I'd never truly hated anyone until now—not even my mother or my ex-husband, Tom. I only hoped Mike would keep his word and find a way to get us out.

Two vans waited for us outside the courthouse. Before we boarded, Rajiv approached us.

"Your judge has little mercy for drug trafficking," Rajiv said. "Mike has promised to speak to your boss when he returns to the States. He says your boss has great influence in Kenya. Don't worry."

A guard planted himself between Rajiv and us.

"Do not give up hope. We will do what we can to get you out before nine months," Rajiv said.

"Over here!"

Another guard dressed in olive drab holding a machine gun motioned to Carl. At gunpoint, he was pushed into one van. He took a last look at his wife and mouthed, *I love you*, before he disappeared.

Edie screamed, "*No!*"

"Shut up!" Another guard hit Edie with his machine gun.

"We're gonna die," Tina whispered.

"You three, get in the van. *Now!*"

We climbed into the back of a white windowless van. Splintered wooden benches lined both sides of the rear. Metal bars separated us from the front of the vehicle. Two guards climbed in front. The motor turned over. We were on our way.

forty-eight

Kukaa! Kukaa!

To this day, I can't explain my state of mind. Fear, denial, confusion, sadness, shame, and guilt blended with anger at Mike and even more anger at myself. I flashed back on my life and the missteps that led me to this point in time. I silently thanked God for not giving me insight into my future. I asked for forgiveness for what I'd done and strength to face what would soon be done to me.

Without windows, I had no idea where we were going. From the courthouse, we traveled on a main roadway before making a sharp turn onto what felt like a pockmarked dirt road. The van slowed and turned onto a gravel driveway. The engine died.

I wished I had died.

"Get out!"

The guards opened the rear door of the van. Two rectangular concrete block buildings stood in the middle of an arid plain. A few weeds struggled for survival around the compound. From what I could see, security was minimal. An escape meant death from exposure or dehydration unless a wild beast came along first.

At gunpoint, we were escorted into a concrete room lit with a naked hundred-watt bulb.

"Strip. Everything off," one guard barked. "Clothing on table. Stand under light. The matron will inspect you."

I'd watched enough movies to know we needed to act tough and in control. But right now, that was impossible. Tears rolled down our cheeks. Our one consolation was the male guards left us to undress in private.

A few minutes later an unsmiling matron and her assistant entered the cubicle. Both women had seen better days. Their lumpy bodies clad in gray cotton shifts spoke of poor diets and poverty. I suspected both were in their late twenties but appeared twenty years older.

We stood naked and vulnerable, our dignity a memory.

"You—" the matron pointed to Edie. "Bend over. Spread your cheeks."

Edie's tears dripped onto the dirt floor. I thought of the cavity search I endured at the airport in Colombia. All it took to secure my freedom was fifty dollars. Mike needed to secure a lot more this time. Could he convince Ben our lives were worth saving?

"You're clean." The matron confirmed what we already knew. She turned to her assistant. "Give them dresses. Their white bodies make me sick."

While we waited, the matron recited the prison rules. I was too traumatized to focus on most of what she said until . . .

"We hate Americans. You think you are better than Kenyans." She spat where Edie's tears had landed. "Your government says we cannot touch you. But that does not mean you cannot be punished. We have ways to teach you lessons."

Like feed us to the lions. A lion's lunch almost seemed preferable.

The assistant returned with three faded orange dresses, three pink scarves, underpants, used flip-flops, and three bars of soap.

"Your uniforms."

The matrons threw them on the dirt floor, forcing us to pick them up and brush them off before putting them on.

"Put soap on head and tie scarf around it," the assistant said.

What?

"You get one soap. If you drop, another prisoner will steal," the matron explained.

Our belongings were boxed and taken away. The matron then handed me a little blue Bible. "Read and repent. Now, come with me. Mealtime."

She shoved us into a fenced-in outdoor area where a large group of women dressed like us sat on the ground eating with their fingers from metal plates. We took our place in line and were handed plates filled with rancid vegetable scraps and gray, dried-out mystery meat.

Edie, Tina, and I stared at each other in horror. Our food scraps at home were more appetizing than what we were expected to eat. I picked at what appeared to be rotting carrot tops and boiled potato skins.

Three guards in gray dresses stood on a bench in front of the prisoners and yelled, "*Kukaa! Kukaa!*"

Every orange-clad woman dropped her plate to the ground, stood for a second, then squatted. A fourth guard walked over to us, kicked Tina, and repeated, "*Kukaa! Kukaa!*"

We joined the rest of the squatting prisoners. What remained of our lunches fell into the dirt.

Five minutes later the guards yelled, "*Simama!*" Everyone stood, then went back to eating.

I felt the blood leave my head when I stood. I toppled to the ground. The entire prison yard broke into laughter.

After lunch we were taken to see the matron.

"We give you choice of work. Work in sewing room or work in fields," she said.

Almost in unison the three of us said, "Sewing room."

"Come with me."

The matron led us to one of the concrete buildings. Inside were dozens of women, heads bent, sewing by hand. She pushed us toward the front of the room where female guards stood watching the prisoners. She spoke in Swahili, then turned to us.

"We make table linens and sell to pay for food." She handed each of us a tablecloth with faint blue outlines of flowers and leaves, and a large basket of colored thread. "Follow lines. Your work must be perfect."

Try as I might, I couldn't get the knack of embroidering. By the end of the day, I'd completed one flower. The front was acceptable, the back a disaster.

Twice during the afternoon, the guards yelled, "*Kukaa! Kukaa!*" Everyone stood, then came to a squat. I managed to keep my balance but saw several women fall to the ground, causing a round of laughter and applause from the guards and some of the prisoners.

Dinner was a repeat performance of lunch with the addition of lumpy, gelatinous porridge. I couldn't decide what was worse—the rotting odor from our food or the foul odors coming from the other prisoners. We picked at the vegetables, ate the porridge, and avoided the meat.

After dinner, we had time to walk around the prison yard and talk.

"Today's Monday. Mike's flight leaves Wednesday," I said. "He'll be back in Florida on Thanksgiving. I doubt Ben'll be around. That means we won't be out of here till Friday."

"I'm sure he won't leave us here that long," Edie said. "I can't stop worrying about Carl. At least we have each other. He's all alone." She broke down. We hugged her close.

"*No touch!*" a guard called to us.

"They're everywhere," Tina said. "Edie's right. The money's probably on its way. We'll be out tomorrow."

I expected Mike would spend the rest of Monday with his side piece. Then, if we were lucky, he'd remember to wire Ben on Tuesday. We'd have to trust him to get the money to Rajiv before he left for the States. Any number of things could go wrong.

"Let's check out what the Bible has to say before it gets too dark," I said.

I flipped through the pages until I came to Psalm 34:4. "'I sought the Lord, and he answered me; he delivered me from all my fears.'"

"It's not the Lord we need. It's Mike," Edie said.

"*Kukaa! Kukaa!*"

We stood, we squatted, we toppled over, and were herded to bed.

forty-nine

Bedtime

Did I say bed? Dirt floor was more like it. As the new kids and the only white women in the prison, we were the target of the most violent and insane prisoners. We cowered in one corner, breathing into our tiny circle to lessen the stench of unwashed bodies and excrement. Rough hands roamed along our bodies until a guard clapped two boards together as a warning to stop.

I recited the words from Psalm 34:4, hoping they would ease me into sleep. I'd begun to doze when I felt something crawl up my arm. A scream escaped my mouth as I swatted the creature toward another prisoner. What freak of nature was sharing the space with me?

"*Nyamaza!*" a guard commanded.

Exhaustion finally overcame me, and I slept. By morning, my body ached and was as filthy as the other prisoners'. A series of red bites littered my one arm.

"*Kuoga!*" A guard pushed us outdoors and led us to the showers. Toilets consisted of holes in the ground and were located throughout the prison. I almost cried when I saw modern showers. We were instructed to strip and wait our turn. The water was lukewarm with a brownish tint and a faint metallic odor. I didn't care. I removed the bar of soap from my head and scrubbed the best I could in the few minutes before the water shut off. We'd been given a comb and toothbrush but no shampoo or toothpaste. I dressed in yesterday's underwear and dress and waited for the next horror.

Breakfast consisted of porridge with the consistency of mucous. An occasional lump kept the meal interesting. I expected each lump to be a worm, insect, or worse. To the prison's credit, the lumps were nothing more than poorly cooked grain. The three of us retched as we ate but kept it down, knowing we needed our strength for the day ahead. The day we hoped would be our last in this hellhole.

After breakfast, we joined the rest of the women in the sewing room. Small windows set high in the walls let in the morning light. The doors were kept open to keep the air circulating and lessen the stench. We sat on wooden benches and made sure our tablecloths didn't touch the dirt floor. Soft Swahili conversation surrounded us, then some of the women broke into song. If I closed my eyes and held my breath, I could almost believe I'd joined a sewing circle in Amara's village.

Lunch was a repeat of yesterday's meal. We choked on the vegetable scraps and gave our meat to other prisoners.

Back in the sewing room, one of the prisoners smiled and asked in English if she could sit next to me. I squeezed closer to Tina to make room for her.

"My name is Elizabeth," she said.

"I'm Ava. These are my friends Tina and Edie."

"Americans?"

I nodded.

"I think you are the first white women to enter our prison. You must have committed a terrible crime."

"We don't belong here," Edie said.

"Everyone says they are innocent." Elizabeth laughed.

"But we really are," I said. "We were charged with international smuggling of *bangi*, but it was a mistake. Our lawyer's coming soon to get us out."

Elizabeth cackled until tears rolled down her cheeks. "My lawyer said the same thing. Once you are here, they forget about you."

Edie and Tina looked up from their sewing. Panic spread across their faces.

I took slow deep breaths to stay calm. It didn't work.

"Why are you here?" I asked.

"Embezzlement. Fraud. Not like most prisoners."

"What do you mean?" I asked.

"Some are prostitutes, thieves, or murderers."

The more Elizabeth spoke, the more frightened I became. "All of them?"

"No. Most are here for brewing and selling alcohol. You know, *busaa* and *chang'aa*," she laughed. "They are poor and trying to feed their families."

"They're victims like us," Tina said.

"Yes, we are all victims," Elizabeth replied. "My boyfriend and I stole the money. He paid the judge to stay out of prison. But no money was left to pay for me."

Just like Mike.

"*Kukaa! Kukaa!*" We stopped our conversation, stood, then dropped to a squat.

"To be continued," Elizabeth whispered.

At the end of the workday, Tina, Edie, and I comforted each other with words of support and uplifting psalms.

"Something must have gone wrong," Edie said. "Ben must be away for Thanksgiving, or maybe the money got held up because of the holiday."

"There's always somebody at Ben's house who'd know where to reach him," I said. "Mike screwed up."

Tina began to cry. "We're gonna die in here!"

Exactly what I'd been thinking.

"Mike wouldn't desert us," Edie said.

"Let's take it one day at a time," I said.

~~~

Over the next week I came to the realization that we'd been abandoned. I spent my days in a malnourished, sleep-deprived fog. Each night, we'd fend off other prisoners and oversized insects. Each day, we gagged on porridge and vegetable scraps. We did our best to conduct ourselves like model prisoners, hoping we'd be released early for good behavior.

By the second week we learned who of the eighty-two prisoners and fifty-two guards we could trust. Elizabeth was the only prisoner we'd met who spoke English, but we learned to communicate with others through smiles and gestures.

"I don't like to criticize," Elizabeth said, "but the back of your tablecloth is a mess. You will get two more days in jail for each mistake."

The look on my face said it all.

"Let me help you," she said. "Carefully tear out your work, and I will show you how to make it perfect."

"Thank you." I hugged my friend.

"*No touching!*" a guard yelled.

"*Kukaa! Kukaa!*"

The entire room was punished for my transgression.

That evening after dinner, we sat outdoors reading the Bible until the light faded.

"This little blue Bible is the only thing keeping me sane," I told Edie and Tina. "I promised God if we ever get out of here, I'm going straight. No more drugs. No more booze. I'm gonna make it up to my kids."

"Do you really think there is a God?" Tina asked.

"This has gotta be God's punishment for the mess I've made of my life," I said.

"Ava, you'd have to be a mass murderer for punishment like this. And what about me and Edie?" Tina asked.
~~~

Our conversation ended abruptly as we heard the guards shouting in Swahili. The only word I understood was "Elizabeth."

One guard grabbed Elizabeth by the arm and dragged her into the center of the courtyard. The guard kicked the back of Elizabeth's legs, forcing her onto the ground. We watched in stunned silence as four guards beat the crap out of my friend. One of Elizabeth's Kenyan friends moved to help. A guard slapped her face and kicked her into submission.

Elizabeth lay curled in a fetal position. Her friend and another woman we'd become friendly with were taken into the center and beaten. The three received final kicks to the head. The guards retreated, laughing, and congratulating each other for a job well done.

Elizabeth and the other women weren't at breakfast or in the sewing room the next day. Did the prison have an infirmary? Had they survived?

A woman I'd never seen before sat next to me. "You did Elizabeth."

"*Sielewi*. I don't understand."

"You. Friend. Bad," she said.

"*Sielewi*."

"No touch American. Touch friend." A guard hit two sticks in warning. She moved away from me.

Now I understood. The guards couldn't touch us because we were Americans, so they punished us by hurting our friends.

fifty

Hope

I'd lost so much weight I never expected to have a period, but Mother Nature surprised me after nearly three weeks in prison. Fortunately, I was taking a shower at the time. I asked a guard for a pad.

"It goes on ground. Use scarf from head." Her laugh was evil.

I grabbed a wad of toilet paper, knowing it wouldn't last long.

When the guard turned away, another prisoner motioned to me. I followed her outside where she showed me a pile of rags—discards from the sewing room.

"*Asante*. Thank you." She disappeared before my words reached her.

The next day the matron approached us at lunch.

"Come with me," she said with her usual scowl.

We exchanged looks of concern as we followed her to the concrete cubicle that served as her office. What new punishment was she about to inflict on us?

I almost fainted when I saw Rajiv. He stood as we entered the room. I stared at him without speaking.

"Please, sit," Rajiv said. His expression spoke volumes about our appearance and odor.

The three of us squeezed onto a splintered wooden bench across from him.

"I am here to give you an update on your situation." He cleared his throat before continuing. "I have heard nothing from Mike. When no money arrived, I expected him to return to Mombasa. Something has happened to him."

"We'll die if we stay here much longer," I cried.

"I see that," Rajiv said. "Mike promised he would wire your boss for money the day of your hearing. When none came, I thought he would fly back to the States and send money in a day or two. My intention was never to have you stay in prison."

Your intention? I had suspected Mike and Rajiv had conspired against us. Now I knew it to be true.

"Is there anything you can do for us?" Edie asked.

"I can find a new judge and schedule a new trial," he continued. "I will ask to drop the exportation charges and charge you with possession, a misdemeanor. It will be expensive."

"We exported nothing," I said. "Our crops are gone. You know that."

"I know," Rajiv said. "Until this incident, you were fair and generous with me. I believe I can trust you."

"Once we're free, we'll wire our boss for money," I said.

"I'm sure you will. Be advised if anything goes wrong, you may end up back here."

"Will you help Carl, too?" Edie asked.

"Of course."

"How long will it take?" I asked.

"I will make phone calls when I return to Mombasa," Rajiv said.

Tina, Edie, and I extended our filthy hands to him. He winced, hesitantly clasped each one, and promised to stay in touch.

As we walked back to the sewing room, I said, "I don't know how much he'll do for us if we can't come up with some cash."

"But he promised—" Edie replied.

"Maybe I'm being too negative." *Or maybe I'm being realistic.*

That evening, it was Tina's turn to find a Bible passage to lift our spirits. She read to us from Proverbs 3:5-6: "Trust in the Lord with all your heart and lean not on your own understanding; in all your ways submit to him, and he will make your paths straight."

"See," Tina said, "we gotta trust."

A week later the matron summoned us to her office.

"Your lawyer left message." She handed us a scrap of paper.

I read her chicken scratch to my friends. "Court appearance Tuesday, December 20, 10:00 a.m. Come for you at 8:00 a.m. Wear street clothes and bring possessions. Rajiv Desi."

It was the first bright moment in almost a month. We kept our cool in front of the matron but screamed for joy once we were out in the yard. Immediately, a guard yelled, "*Kukaa! Kukaa!*"

We squatted and nearly passed out, but our smiles stayed plastered to our faces.

We skipped breakfast on December 20 and changed into our own clothes while the matron watched. Our ribs and hip bones protruded through our loosely fitting dresses.

Carl was in the car with Rajiv when they arrived at the prison gate. Edie ran to greet her husband, who looked as emaciated and downtrodden as we did.

Rajiv explained he had found a new judge and requested our charges be dropped to possession. With no crops and no history of exportation, he was confident we'd be fined and freed from prison.

I remembered our last court appearance and how Rajiv made the same promise. Could we trust him this time with no money behind us?

"Will we still be deported?" Tina asked.

"I've asked to have the deportation charge dropped. I am not sure how the judge will rule," he said.

I didn't care. I'd seen enough of Kenya to last a lifetime.

We sat in silence for the rest of the drive.

As we entered the courthouse, I prayed this time would be different. Tina, Edie, and I stopped at the restroom. For the first time in nearly a month, we used real toilets and soft toilet paper, washed our hands with hot water, and saw ourselves in actual mirrors.

No makeup could disguise who we'd become. Our hair was knotted and filthy. Our rough, scabbed cheekbones protruded beneath sunken eyes. Red swollen insect bites covered our arms and legs.

I opened my handbag for a comb and lipstick, hoping to improve my appearance. My cash, jewelry, watch, and makeup—everything was gone.

"The matron stole all my stuff," I said.

Tina and Edie's belongings were gone, too. "One more indignity to add to our collection," Tina said.

Everyone stared as we made our way to the front of the courtroom. We took our seats behind Rajiv.

The judge summoned us. "Carl O'Reilly, Edith O'Reilly, Ava Novak, Christina DaSilva, approach the bench. Mr. Desi, I understand you have requested a reduced sentence for the defendants."

"Yes, Your Honor."

"After careful consideration, the court accepts your request. The defendants are now charged with possession of five pounds of marijuana. All charges of exportation are dropped."

"Thank you, Your Honor," Rajiv said.

"Your clients have served nearly a month in prison," the judge continued. "No fine will be imposed. Deportation charges are dropped. You are free to go."

"Congratulations," Rajiv said.

We stood, stunned and unable to move.

"Next case," the judge bellowed.

"Time to go." Rajiv escorted us through the courtroom to freedom.

I shuffled down the aisle, devoid of thought and feeling.

Once outside, I told Rajiv we had no money.

"Not a problem. I will pay for your taxi ride home and call you in a few days."

"Thank you," we mumbled in unison.

fifty-one

Charity

None of us spoke on the ride home. Edie and Carl snuggled close. I sat in front next to the driver and never once looked behind me.

Peter, Mary, and Fatima greeted us with forced smiles when we arrived at the house. They turned away from us so we wouldn't see their pained expressions.

"We prepare special dinner tonight," Mary said after a moment. "Shower, relax, and tell us how we can help."

We nodded and headed for our bedrooms.

My bedroom was exactly as I left it, minus any trace of Mike. I shed my clothing, stuffed it in the waste basket, and went into my spotless, tiled bathroom. While the water heated for my shower, I stepped on the scale.

Eighty-five pounds! I've lost twenty-five pounds!

The shock of the weight loss sent me over the edge. I stood in the shower and sobbed silent tears. How could I put the events of the last month into perspective and then behind me?

Could I trust Rajiv, the judge, the Kenyan government? What if Ben refused to send money to pay Rajiv and whomever else? What if he abandoned us? How would we get home?

I stayed in the shower for an hour before I felt the filth of prison leave my body. I dried off with a thick, white towel and dressed in a thin, silk robe. My emaciated body was still covered with bites and sores, but I was beginning to feel human again.

Despite my fatigue, confusion, and nausea, I knew my next priority was to contact Ben. The clock read 2:00 p.m.—6:00 a.m. in Florida. I'd wait three hours before calling.

As exhausted as I was, I couldn't sleep. I thought about a glass of wine, then realized I hadn't eaten anything since the day before. Instead, I made lists in my head of what I needed to say to Ben, what I needed to do before leaving Kenya, what I'd do when I arrived in the States.

At five o'clock, I dressed in a cotton sheath and went out by the pool. I saw only Mary, who asked if I needed anything.

"Maybe some water."

She brought me a pitcher of water with ice and lemon, and a plate of biscuits. The simple gesture brought me to tears.

"You are safe now," she said.

My smile was a lie. *I'll never feel safe again.*

It was time to call Ben. His girlfriend, Donna, answered the phone. "Ava! Are you okay?"

I ignored her question. "Can I speak to Ben?"

"Ava, we had no idea you guys were in prison," Ben said.

"But—didn't Mike tell you?"

"Now isn't the time to talk. Are you home?"

"We got home this morning," I said. "We need you to wire money to pay our lawyer and God knows who else."

"Not necessary. Now, how about coming home for the holidays?"

I'd completely forgotten about Christmas.

"I'll wire you money for tickets this afternoon. Play your cards right, and you'll be home by Christmas Eve."

"Thank you."

"It's over, Ava. Lemme know your flight info, and we'll see ya soon."

~~~

Mary and Fatima prepared a seafood dinner unlike any I'd seen since arriving in Kenya. We expressed our gratitude but left most of the meal uneaten. After a month of rotting vegetables and porridge, the first bit of protein caused my stomach to cramp.

"Please share the meal with your families," I said. "Maybe some soup would be better."

An hour later, they presented us with pumpkin soup, which we sipped slowly. After dinner, Edie and Carl excused themselves and went upstairs to their room. Tina and I stayed by the pool.

"I'm in a weird space," Tina said. "I feel like we should be celebrating, but all I want to do is sleep."

"Me, too," I agreed. "I can't imagine what it must be like for Edie. Knowing the person you love most in the world might be dead has gotta be the worst."

"What do you think happened with Mike?" she asked.

"I don't know what to think. Ben said Mike's in Philly with his parents. I'm gonna call him once we get our flight info and ask him to meet me at the airport."

"Seriously? I thought you'd be flying to Florida."

"It's Christmas," I said. "I can't impose on Ben. Tom and my kids don't want me. I've got no money for a hotel. What else can I do?"

"I've decided to go back to California. All my stuff is there."

"So this is it." I stared at Tina in the fading light.

"For now, yeah."

"I need to lie down. See you in the morning." I hugged Tina, knowing on some level our friendship would be forever altered.

Ben's money arrived the following afternoon. The four of us booked a flight from Mombasa to Nairobi, which would leave the next morning. From Nairobi, we'd catch a flight to London. Edie and Carl decided to spend a night in London before flying home to their family in Detroit. Tina would fly to Chicago, then California. I was the only one flying to Philly.
~~~

My fingers trembled as I dialed Mike's parents, who lived in a suburb outside Philadelphia. His mother answered.

"Hello, Ava. Mike told me you decided to stay on in Africa. He's still asleep. Can I give him a message?"

I gave Mrs. Ambrose my flight information and asked if Mike could meet me at the airport.

"You're welcome to join us for Christmas," she said. "You may not recognize my son at first, but I'm sure he'll recognize you."

"Um—okay." *What the hell did she mean?*

It took all my strength to pack my belongings. Much of what I'd bought in Kenya, I gave to Mary and Fatima. They thanked us and prepared *vibibi*—a rice and coconut pancake—soup, chapati, and sweet bananas. They offered to make us *uji*, or porridge, but we'd seen enough porridge to last a lifetime.

In prison, we had talked about the grand celebration we'd have once we were free, but all we wanted to do was sleep or sit in silence by the pool. Would our friendship continue once we flew back to the States, or would we go our separate ways to whitewash our prison experience?

The next morning Peter, our gardener, drove us to Mombasa Airport. At any moment, I expected the Kenyan police to arrest us and send us back to prison, but we boarded the plane to Nairobi with no hassle.

The same fears haunted me while we waited for our London flight. Once again, our boarding was seamless. Bit by bit, I felt the tension leave my body.

Tina and I said tearful goodbyes to Edie and Carl at Heathrow. We vowed to stay in touch but in my heart, I doubted we'd meet again.

Before leaving for my gate, I hugged Tina and confessed, "I couldn't have gotten through this without you."

"Same here."

"I'll write once I'm settled," I said.

"I know you will."

I watched her walk away. She turned, waved, and blew me a kiss.

If it hadn't been for me, Tina would never have come to Kenya, never would have gone to prison. Guilt overwhelmed me.

Had I been thinking clearly, I would have asked Ben for money for a hotel in London, but all I could think of was getting home.

Home—that was a joke. I had no home. All I had was Mike. What lies would he tell me? What lies had he told his parents? What do you say to someone who left you to rot in prison?

Despite these thoughts, I was filled with gratitude. My prayers had been answered. Even though the flight home was packed, it was the first time since April I felt comfortably alone. I slept, read my Bible, and contemplated a sober life.

fifty-two

Where Are You?

I wasn't prepared for the cold weather or the man who met me at Philadelphia Airport.

"Ava!"

I looked for Mike's familiar handsome face, his dark hair, and mustache. The only person I saw was a blond priest standing near the luggage carousel.

"Doll, it's me." The priest approached.

"Mike? What the—"

Mike had bleached his hair and mustache and sported a pair of wire-rimmed glasses with no lenses, barely concealing a healing black eye. He wore a pair of black jeans and a black shirt with a priest collar. Anyone giving him more than a casual glance would recognize he was no clergyman.

"I'm hot, babe. How d'ya like the disguise?"

"Great, Mike." *You're only fooling yourself.*

"I'd kiss ya but us priests ain't supposed to do shit like that."

And you're not supposed to leave your friends to die.

"Let's get out of here." I grabbed my suitcase from the carousel.

Mike walked with a limp and led me to a beat-up Buick sedan. "Sorry, the heat ain't workin'."

"I'm freezing," I said. "Don't you have a blanket or something?"

A gentleman would offer a lady his jacket. Mike gave me a moth-eaten blanket from the trunk. It brought back memories of prison, but I welcomed the warmth.

Neither of us spoke until we left the airport parking lot.

"I've been so worried," Mike said. "I'm glad you're okay."

"I'm not okay. Neither are the rest of your friends."

"Speakin' of my friends, where's Carl?" Mike asked.

"In London."

"And Tina?"

"California. What happened, Mike?"

"It's all Rajiv's fault, the greedy bastard," he began.

"Don't bullshit me."

"I'm not," Mike said. "Rajiv knew we had millions behind us. He kept askin' for more dough, sayin' if we didn't pay him, he'd turn us in. It got to the point where I couldn't pay anymore. That's when he sent the cops to bust us. He pretended to be our buddy and promised we'd get a slap and a fine."

"That's not what happened."

"No shit." Mike turned to look at me. "I couldn't believe the judge sentenced you and not me. I wanted to scream, to say, 'Take me.'"

"But you didn't."

"I was afraid if I said anything, I'd get locked up, too. One of us had to stay out to get in touch with Ben. I tried callin' him once I got back to the house. The lines were down so I figured I'd fly home for Thanksgiving and talk to him."

"We rotted for almost a month. I lost twenty-five pounds."

"I thought you lost some weight."

"I lost a lot more than that."

"Soon's I got back, I told Ben. He said he'd take care of it. When I didn't hear nothin', I figured you guys were partyin' your asses off and forgot about me."

"You could have called," I said.

"You got no idea what's been goin' down here. The Feds are after Ben and everybody in The Crew. That's why I'm in disguise."

"What about your other girlfriend? What was her name?"

"You're my only girlfriend," Mike lied.

"You remember—the blond bimbo I found in our bed. The one I saw waiting for you in the courtroom."

Mike pretended to think for a moment. "Ya mean Liz? She was there for Rajiv in case somethin' went wrong."

I saw no point in arguing. Eventually, I'd learn the truth.

"What happened to your eye, and why are you limping?" I asked.

Mike hesitated. "Um—it's part of what's goin' down with The Crew."

"I thought Ben didn't believe in violence."

"Wasn't him. It ain't just the Feds after Ben. It's some rival gang. They beat the crap outta me."

Liar.

"Dudes couldn't get to Ben, so they came after me since I'm his number two man."

You're number two, all right.

It was time to change the subject. "What do I tell your parents?"

"I told them me and you are workin' for Sunstar Industries," Mike said. "They sent us to Kenya to grow cotton."

"And what about your disguise?"

"I told them I came home 'cause some drug cartel was workin' in Kenya, and I looked like one of the dudes in charge. That's why I got beat up and needed to disguise myself."

"They believed you?"

"Yup. Are they stupid or what?"

Stupid like their son.

"You had to stay to finish up business," he said. "Next week, we're goin' back to Florida."

"That's a relief. I know your parents don't like me."

"It ain't that they don't like you. They think you're a bad influence on me."

If they only knew.

fifty-three

Back in Florida

Mike made up a story about my need to rest while we stayed with his parents. He and I flew to Florida on New Year's Day. We spent a week at the Pier 66 Hotel on Fort Lauderdale Beach before renting a furnished, two-story condo with a magnificent view of the ocean.

"Can we afford this place?" I asked Mike.

"'Course we can. I'm back workin' on Ben's boats and planes."

"He's not mad at you for Kenya?"

"Hell, no," Mike said. "When ya bring in two mill a week, ya gotta expect to give some up."

"Does Ben want to see me?"

Mike squirmed for a second, then regained his cool. "Nah, I told him you were safe. He said to take some R&R."

Now that I was back in Florida, I wrote to my kids in Charlotte, North Carolina. The letters came back undelivered. I called Tom's number and learned it was disconnected. No forwarding address or number was provided. Without hiring a detective or calling Tom's parents, I saw no option but to wait and hope they'd find me.

The sores and bug bites on my body had healed, and my weight shot up to ninety pounds. Each day I felt stronger and more like myself. I began to question my future. While in prison I promised myself I'd leave Mike, stay sober, and find meaningful employment.

Day by day, my resolve weakened. Mike had returned to his charming, charismatic self and slowly lured me into his world of sex, drugs, and rock 'n roll played on the finest stereo money could buy.

For the first two weeks, Mike and I shared a midmorning breakfast before he left for work. He'd arrive home for a late dinner. We'd share a bottle of wine, the only alcohol I'd tasted since my imprisonment.

After dinner, Mike would light up a joint. He said he needed a smoke to relax before bed, but I suspected he'd been doing speed or cocaine and needed pot to sleep. I resisted for the first few days until the lure of peaceful surrender overtook my wish for sobriety.

One night, Mike didn't come home. He stumbled in the next morning looking like he'd slept in his clothes. His kiss smelled like coffee and stale alcohol with a female bottom note.

"What happened, Mike?"

"Late night. Had to fly to the Bahamas. Crashed there and flew home this morning."

"Next time call if you're not coming home," I said.

"Sure, doll, whatever."

Mike's nights away became more frequent. Had he found a new girlfriend or was he screwing anything in a skirt? Was he making business deals, trying to compete with Ben? I realized an ocean view was spectacular only if shared with someone special.

I needed a plan for my future. Instead, I found Mike's cocaine.

I dipped the coke spoon into the box, transferred the white powder onto a small mirror, and listened with inner pleasure to the subtle crunch of tiny rocks beneath a single-edged razor. I formed two white lines and slowly inhaled. The rush was instantaneous.

An addict can rationalize anything: a drug habit, a cheating boyfriend, a life alone. What I couldn't rationalize was what came next.

One afternoon in late March, Mike stood in our front doorway holding a ball of sand-colored fluff. "Surprise!"

"A puppy, Mike?"

"Thought ya needed some company. Feel like I'm neglectin' you."

"I can't take care of a puppy."

"Sure ya can. This here's a pit bull pup. Treat him right, and he'll protect ya from all sorts of bad people."

I named the puppy Buddy, and that's what he became, at least for a while. Druggies are not good pet parents, so I knew I needed to find him a stable home.

I met other dog walkers and retirees on our walks to the beach.

"What a sweet little pup!" An elderly man stopped to pet Buddy.

"He's a lover boy," I said. "I'm looking for a good home for him."

"Why? You'll never find a better friend. Lost my Bowser last month. Just about broke my heart."

My heart had been broken too many times. I couldn't risk another fracture.

"Would you like him?"

"Seriously, miss?"

"He's yours."

Buddy's tail wagged furiously as the man bent to pet him.

"My name's Ava. Meet me back here in an hour, and I'll bring his papers and toys."

"I'm Al. I'll be waiting."

I couldn't believe my luck. Al stood waiting for me on the beach.

"C'mere, Buddy," he called.

Buddy ran to Al's waiting arms, and without so much as a look back, planted doggy kisses on his new dad's face.

"How can I ever thank you?" Al asked.

"How can I ever thank *you*? Here's my name and number in case you change your mind."

He took my information, but I knew I'd never hear from him. It was love at first lick.

Mike staggered in around midnight. From the bangs and slams in the kitchen, I knew he was wired and drunk.

I heard the shatter of broken glass. "Where's my friggin' Johnnie Walker?"

I put on my robe and joined him in the kitchen. His dime-sized pupils glared at me.

"Shh, you'll wake the neighbors."

"Maybe they got my Johnnie."

"It's right here, hon." I handed him the bottle.

He poured a hefty shot, sat the scotch on the edge of the counter, and knocked it to the floor.

"Ah, shit. Clean it up, doll."

What am I, your slave? I knew better than to get into it with Mike.

"Where's Buddy?"

"I found a new home for him—an elderly man I met on the beach."

"*You what?*" Mike struck me across the mouth.

Mike had lost his temper plenty of times, but this was the first time he'd hit me. I held on to the counter to keep from falling.

"I can't keep a puppy, and you're never home," I said.

"I'm home now, ain't I?"

"For the first time in a month."

"Don't smart-mouth me, bitch." Mike swung his fist. This time he missed.

"Finish your drink and come to bed. I'll clean up the kitchen."

He poured more scotch into a glass, downed it in two gulps, and headed for the bedroom.

I swept up broken glass and wiped the floor clean. I'd found Mike's Altoid's tin of black beauties and white crosses, so I knew he was using speed daily. I almost wished he'd go back to quaaludes. 'Ludes made him sloppy and stupid, which was a lot better than what he'd become.

I laid on the couch for most of the night and contemplated my future. Once I left Tom, I promised myself I'd never stay with another man who beat me. Even if Mike had no memory of hitting me, I was certain he'd do it again.

My Bible had kept me sane while in prison. Tina, Edie, and I had read Psalms and verses daily. I hadn't opened the book since I'd gotten home.

Flecks of Kenyan dirt drifted onto our living room rug as I opened the Bible for the first time in four months. I stopped at Psalm 121:7-8.

"The Lord will keep you from all harm—he will watch over your life; the Lord will watch over your coming and going both now and forevermore."

Could I trust in the Lord? Time would tell.

fifty-four

The Truth Comes Out

I fell asleep as the sun came up. Not long after, I heard Mike tiptoe into the kitchen for his morning coffee. I felt him in the living room staring at me but refused to acknowledge his presence. He kissed my forehead. Was he looking for forgiveness or was he oblivious to what had happened the night before?

Once I heard him leave for work, I got up. I decided to spend the day sober and map out my future. I sat with my morning coffee, pen and paper in hand, when the phone rang.

"Hello?"

"Hey, Ava, it's Ben. Did Mike leave yet?"

"Mike left a while ago."

"Good," Ben replied. "It's you I want to talk to."

"Me?" I hadn't heard Ben's voice in months. I'd made no effort to call and thank him for sending the money to release us from prison. How could I thank someone who left me to rot for almost a month?

"I've wanted to call since you got back, but Mike said you weren't strong enough to leave the house."

"I'm fine. I've been fine for months."

Ben paused. "Can you come to my house this afternoon?"

It was my turn to pause.

"Ava? We need to talk."

"Okay," I agreed.

My thoughts were rolling faster than the incoming tide. Did Ben blame me for the mess in Kenya? Did he want reimbursement for the bribe money he paid to free us from prison? Mike had lied about my health. What else had been happening behind my back?

The only way to learn the truth was to meet Ben. I took a deep breath and called for a taxi. Before leaving, I snorted a few lines of coke—so much for a day of sobriety.

Ben greeted me at his front door. "Ava, it's great to see you."

"You, too."

Ben's forehead was deeply creased. Frown lines outlined his mouth, even though he was still in his twenties.

"C'mon in. I've got lunch waiting."

"Thanks for everything," I said, despite what I really felt. "I don't think I can ever repay you."

"We'll think of something." Ben laughed. "And by the way, you look great. From what Mike said, I thought you'd contracted some tropical disease."

"Just malnutrition and bug bites."

Ben mumbled something, then escorted me to the lanai where his chef had arranged a buffet of chilled seafood, salads, cheese, and bread.

"You didn't need to go to all this trouble," I said.

"It's the least I can do. Let's have a bite to eat, then we'll get down to business."

A bottle of sauvignon blanc chilled in a silver bucket. He poured a glass for himself, then offered one to me.

"Maybe later."

"Bon appétit." Ben's wine glass and my water glass clinked. I had no idea what we were toasting.

Once we'd eaten, he led me outdoors.

Tell me your version of what happened in Kenya," Ben began. "Then I'll tell you mine."

The last thing I wanted to do was relive the worst month of my life. I told him about the bust, the trumped-up charges, the courtroom scene, the time in prison, our meeting with Rajiv, and our ultimate release. I finished by saying, "We would have died if you hadn't gotten us out."

"I wish we'd gotten to talk sooner. You're not gonna like what I have to say, but you deserve the truth."

I gave him my full attention. "Shoot."

"Mike called me the day after your arrest. He said you guys would be issued a small fine and you'd be home for Thanksgiving. I didn't give it a second thought."

"You didn't know about the sentencing?"

"Nope. Right before Thanksgiving, Mike wired that he'd be flying home on the Concorde. That's when he showed up with Liz."

The woman from my bed? The woman from the courtroom?

Keeping cool and focused was becoming more difficult. "Didn't you wonder why he was flying home with another woman?"

Ben shook his head. "Not at first. I thought she was a friend you had flown over."

My shoulders tensed.

"Mike asked if they could stay in the guesthouse over Thanksgiving. Me and Donna were spending the holiday with my folks in Detroit, so I was glad to have somebody watching the place.

"When we got home, Mike and Liz were all over each other. I asked about you. Mike said you two decided on a trial separation. Something about you meeting somebody else."

"That never happened." I took a deep breath, then lifted my empty wine glass. "I think I'll have that glass of wine now."

The first chilled sip coursed through my veins.

"Tell you the truth, I was glad to hear you split," Ben said. "Mike's bad news."

"If he's such bad news, why keep him around?" *And why do I keep him around?*

"He's the best mechanic I know."

"But you asked him to supervise the farming," I said.

"It takes a certain kind of person to travel halfway around the world to grow pot."

A fool. "But why didn't you send the money to free us?"

"I don't know if you're ready to hear this—"

"I'm ready." *At least I think I'm ready.*

"It had to be about three weeks after Mike came back," Ben said. "He and Liz were partying with me and Donna. Mike was outta control—too much blow or something. I asked about you, Carl, and the girls, wondering if you were coming home for Christmas. Mike broke down. Started crying and confessed you were in prison."

"*Excuse me?*"

"I'm sorry, Ava. You know I'm a peace-loving guy. If somebody screws us in business, I walk away. This was different. I needed to act."

"You're the one who beat him up?"

"No. I needed to keep on Mike's good side to get you out. Liz had no idea, either. She smacked him across the face and walked out. He ran after her like a little puppy. I heard lotsa screaming, then a taxi pulled up, and she was gone."

"Smart girl." *I should be so smart.*

"Once they left, I called Rajiv," Ben said. "He said Mike had been making noise about the crop and the unlimited money behind him. Your arrest was nothing more than a plan to extort more money from me.

So Rajiv and Mike did cook this up.

"Mike sacrificed his friends for money?" My hand shook with anger as I poured myself a second glass of wine.

"Afraid so. After Rajiv, I got on the phone with my contact in the Kenyan government. I'd been paying him to turn his head on our operation. Why do you think things went so smoothly?"

"I—I had no idea."

"Nobody did. Least of all, Mike."

"Can I use your bathroom? I need a breather."

I locked myself in the guest bathroom and stared into the mirror. I thought of Judas, the disciple who had betrayed Jesus for thirty pieces of silver. I'd hurt a lot of people in my life, but I'd never betrayed anyone like Mike, my Judas, had betrayed me.

I needed to get back to Ben and the rest of the story.

"You okay, Ava?" Ben asked, when I returned.

"As good as can be expected."

"I called Rajiv and told him what I'd told the government official—that if you weren't released from prison, I'd have my people blow up the country."

"And he believed you?"

"Damn straight. He knew we had the power and money to follow through. I had mercenaries in place."

"The guys following us?"

Ben nodded. "Them and more."

I poured myself another glass of wine. I longed for the numbing effect of alcohol to envelop me so I could handle the truth.

"It took a few days to work out the details. None of us wanted to raise suspicion by pardoning you without another hearing. By the time you went in front of the second judge, everything was in place. No fines were issued and neither Rajiv nor the judge got a dime."

"What about your government contact?"

Ben smiled. "Scared shitless. He'd already gotten plenty from me. End of story."

I shook my head. "Not the end of the story for me. What about Mike?"

"You have no idea how pissed I was at Mike, even before you went to prison," Ben said. "His big mouth cost me millions. I went ballistic when I heard the fields were destroyed. All he had to do was keep his trap shut and keep everybody happy. But no, Mike had to be the big man."

"He's not so big now, is he?"

"Hardly. It wasn't so much the money. It was Mike's cockiness. If it'd been him in jail, I'd have left him there."

"I never heard you talk like this."

"Can't remember the last time I was this pissed."

"I want to hear about Mike, but first . . . I think I need some grass."

"I don't blame you." Ben reached for a box of pre-rolled joints. He lit one and passed it to me.

"Once I knew you were out and safe, I took care of Mike," Ben said. "My mercenaries beat the crap outta him. I think they would've killed him if I gave the order."

"What about his hair and that stupid priest getup?"

"Here's the bad news. Mike wasn't lying about everything—we're hot. Not Mike so much, but he doesn't know that. I'm letting him think the Feds are after him. It'll keep him in line till I decide what to do."

"And what about me?

"I've got a proposal for you, Ava. Please don't say a word to Mike."

I felt my heart flutter. "Um—okay."

"Vinnie Lasseter and I think we can salvage Kenya."

"Are you kidding?"

"I know it sounds crazy, but things were going great until Mike opened his big mouth. You've got Waititu, and I can guarantee Rajiv won't pull any more stunts."

"Just thinking about Kenya gives me chills," I said.

"This time'll be different. You're the only person who has the contacts, and the only one I can trust. Gary's agreed to go with you. Two weeks there and back. Whadda you say?"

"Do I have to give you an answer right now?"

"Think about it—but not for too long."

"What'll I tell Mike?" I asked.

"Don't tell him anything. I'll send him to the Bahamas while you're away."

"And what if he finds out?"

"I'm gonna get rid of him as soon as I can find a replacement,"

Ben said. "This could be your chance to get away from him."

I promised Ben I'd give him an answer in a day or two.

On the ride home, my thoughts bounced between the truth of my imprisonment and my future. I knew Mike was a two-timer, a liar, and a sociopath, but I never thought he was evil enough to desert his friends in a Kenyan prison.

As crazy as Ben's scheme sounded, it would be my opportunity to get away from Mike.

Back at the condo, Mike lay on the couch watching TV, his bottle of Johnny Walker at his side.

"Where ya been, doll?"

"Ben wanted to see me."

A look of fear passed across his face.

He sat up. "How many lies did Ben tell you about me?"

"Why would he lie?"

"He's still pissed about burnin' the fields. He'll do anything he can to make me look bad. Tell me what he said."

"That's between me and Ben."

Mike shifted and reached for his scotch. "I been tryin' to protect you from him."

"Is that why you told him I was sick?"

"Yeah. You been through enough."

"It had nothing to do with 'forgetting' to tell Ben we were in prison?"

"He's a fuckin' liar." Mike downed his scotch and poured another shot. "I told ya Ben promised to send the money. I trusted him, and he let me down."

"What about Liz?"

"Who?"

"You know, the bitch you flew back with instead of me."

"I can explain—"

"Shoot."

"I told ya, she's tight with guys in the Kenyan government. I thought if she came with me, we'd have a better chance of gettin' you guys outta jail."

"Where is she now?"

"Beats me."

Mike's body language told me he'd popped a quaalude. Besides Kenya, I wanted to confront him about his slap the night before. But I knew I'd never get anywhere.

Once Mike passed out on the couch, I called Ben.

"I'll go," I said.

"That was quick. Thought you needed time to think."

"It didn't take long. I chose the lesser of two evils."

After a moment of silence, Ben said, "Me and Gary need about two weeks to get our act together. In the meantime, don't say a word to Mike."

fifty-five

Kenya Redux

A week later, Gary picked me up in a new, deep-red Corvette. He'd taped a hundred-dollar bill onto the passenger side of the dashboard.

"I love the car, but what's with the bill?" I asked.

"You'll see."

Instead of driving north on Route 1 to Ben's place, Gary drove south for a few miles and pulled onto the interstate. The Corvette went from zero to infinity in a matter of seconds. I held onto my seat to keep from flying into the windshield.

"You asked about the bill," Gary said, "I'm gonna punch it. If you can grab it, it's yours."

"I'm game," I laughed.

The car picked up more speed. Each time I leaned forward, I was thrown back, unable to grab the bill. Finally, I gave up.

"This car moves!" I squealed.

"Damn straight." Gary slowed to a legal speed. "Can't risk speeding for too long. The Feds are everywhere."

I shot Gary a worried look.

"Don't worry, Ava. They don't know where any of us live. We've been usin' pay phones, talkin' in code, doin' business in different hotels."

Speeding in a red Corvette didn't fit my definition of keeping a low profile. I hoped Gary knew what he was doing.

We exited the interstate and headed toward Pompano Beach, eventually pulling into a motel that had seen better days. Gary parked behind the building and escorted me to room 122. Gary knocked three times, paused, then knocked three more times. Ben cautiously opened the door. We hurried inside.

"I've been moving around a lot lately," Ben said, "trying not to do business at home."

"Have a seat, Ava," Gary said. "We wanna discuss Kenya."

Ben handed me an envelope. "Here's your ticket to New York. You'll be leaving on April 24. From there, you'll be flying on the Concorde to London."

"I'm leavin' on the nineteenth," Gary said. "I'll meet you at the Dorchester."

"I'm having déjà vu," I said.

"But this time, no Mike, no five days in London, no open-ended trip to Mombasa," Ben explained.

"Two weeks and we're back home," Gary said.

Ben sent Mike to the Bahamas, which allowed me to leave without an excuse. Coming home would be another story. I'd deal with that when the time came.

My flight to New York was unremarkable. And then I saw the Concorde. I'd heard about the remarkable plane that would bring me to London in three hours, but nothing prepared me for the delta-winged, drooped-nose, supersonic spaceship waiting at JFK International Airport. Despite its magnificence, the plane was small . . . maybe a hundred seats. I walked through the front section, passed the restrooms, entered the rear section, and sat next to a tiny window. The entire plane was first class.

The noise on takeoff was deafening, but I didn't care. The crew treated me like royalty with endless flutes of champagne, caviar, and steak tips. I felt spoiled, loved, and valued. Mike, prison, and the real reason for my trip evaporated.

The Dorchester was as I remembered: polished and luxurious. Gary and I shared a two-bedroom suite with a common living room. Gary left a note saying he'd be back later that evening. Since we'd be leaving the next day for Nairobi, I wanted to take advantage of every amenity the hotel had to offer. I treated myself to a hot bath in the oversized marble tub, then ordered from room service.

The next morning, we ate a hurried breakfast and took a cab for Heathrow, where we boarded a plane to Nairobi. Our flight was smooth, and we arrived in time for our connection to Mombasa.

I had mixed feelings on the taxi ride to my former home. The city and countryside were frozen in time, but I was someone new. The exuberance I'd felt last year had faded into the reality of our visit. I knew the dangers the country held and was determined to avoid a repeat of the prior year.

Ben had alerted Rajiv and our household staff to our visit. Mary, Fatima, and Peter greeted me with smiles and hugs. They escorted us to the dining room, where they had laid out a welcome-home feast rivaling our return-from-prison meal. This time I ate with relish.

"I had no idea you guys lived so well," Gary said. "I could get used to this."

I tried imagining the setting from Gary's perspective: the tropical gardens and pool, luxurious furnishings, and a kind, loyal staff. He was in heaven. I had returned to my personal hell.

I gave Gary first choice of bedroom. I chose Tina's old room and vowed never to set foot in my former bedroom.

~~~
~~~

Waititu joined us for breakfast the next morning.

"Where is Mr. Mike?" he asked.

Gary and I had decided it would be best to keep the truth in Florida.

"He's busy back home," I said.

Waititu squirmed. "To be honest, I never thought he was the right man for farming. I hope I do not offend."

Gary and I exchanged glances.

"No offense taken," Gary replied. "Ava has spoken highly of you. With your help, we hope to save the operation."

"I will do what I can," Waititu said. "But please know our farmers are frightened."

"Can you find us new farms?" Gary asked.

"I will try."

I appreciated Waititu's honesty. I had a sinking feeling our trip would be another waste of time and money.

Gary and I spent the day sightseeing with Waititu. We ended the day at the seaside café where his brother-in-law tended bar. He ordered Tusker beer for the guys and white wine for me. I felt as if I were in a time warp. If only I could rewind the tape that was my life and return to this scene a year ago. I would play my cards much differently.

I left the guys to discuss business and took a walk on the beach. As the sun began to set, a light breeze blew from the west, cooling my emotions. I couldn't imagine a more tranquil scene, but I promised myself it would be my last sunset on Mombasa Beach.

Gary and I spent the next day at the house. I read by the pool, while Gary spent much of his time on the phone with Ben. I thought about the cost of the calls, then looked around me. Ben was willing to spend $250,000 on a house he'd never seen. What were a few international calls?

Gary left with Waititu the next morning. He arrived home in the evening with a bag of pot that I suspected had been harvested before the fields were burned. We enjoyed Mary's superb Kenyan food, chilled South African white wine, and tokes from a hand-carved pipe.

My days became monotonous and lonely. Gary spent his time with Waititu; the household staff left me alone except at mealtimes. Gary shared little with me about the operation, but from what I overheard on his calls to Ben, it didn't sound good.

I was right. After ten days, Gary brought me up to speed.

"This Kenya thing is done for," he said. "Ben wants me home. Guess we'll do a rewind in a coupla days."

"Rewind?"

"Y'know, Kenya to London, London to New York, then back to sunny Florida."

And a rewind back to Mike.

"Are you okay?" Gary asked. "Not ready to go home?"

"I don't have a home."

"Sure you do. You're one of us."

Gary's words did little to comfort me.

fifty-six

The Price of Freedom

I asked Fatima to pack some personal things I'd left in my former bedroom. None of us would return, so I gave the furniture, linens, dishes, and Mike's stereo to our staff. I assumed they'd sell what they couldn't use. Rajiv would get the house back. In the end, he was the big winner. I didn't care. All I wanted was my freedom and a chance to begin again.

I never learned the truth of why the operation wasn't resurrected, and I never asked.

Ben put me up at the Pier 66 Hotel while I worked up the courage to return to my condo and face Mike. Not only did Ben pay my room and board, he also kept me supplied with enough drugs and alcohol to keep me high around the clock. To my credit, most days I waited until midafternoon before indulging.

I needed to put an end to my destructive behavior, but how? My Bible offered some comfort, and I returned to it daily. I thought about joining Alcoholics Anonymous, but I wasn't ready to air my problems in a room full of strangers.

I hadn't read a decent book since I went to prison, so I borrowed *Looking Out for #1* by Robert J. Ringer from the library. I read the introduction, which appeared to have been written just for me. Ringer would teach me how to make rational decisions leading to long-term happiness. The book promised to bring about dramatic changes—exactly what I needed.

I'd read countless self-help books, but this one felt different. Or maybe it was me who was different. As the days went by, I hatched a plan, but first I had to summon the courage to return to my condo and confront Mike.

Ben and the major players in The Crew were in hiding. They moved from hotel to hotel, from pay phone to pay phone. I had to wait for someone to contact me before I could make a move.

Eventually, Ben called and agreed to meet me at a diner in Deerfield Beach. I checked out the booths—no Ben. I looked in the parking lot for Ben's Maserati—no car. Had he deserted me?

"Ava, over here!"

The only person I saw was a scruffy guy wearing a baseball cap and aviator sunglasses. "Ben?"

"In disguise. C'mon, I'll buy you lunch."

Ben escorted me to a back booth and sat facing the door. I slid in next to him.

"Wouldn't you be more comfortable in the other seat?" he asked.

"Ever since I got out of prison, I can't sit with my back to the door."

He nodded in understanding. "You and me both."

We ordered.

"What's up?"

"I want out," I began. "I want to go back to New Jersey, but I'm not sure how it'll happen."

"What about Mike?" he asked.

"I was gonna ask you the same question."

"We still have him on the payroll. Like the rest of us, he's moving around trying to evade the Feds."

"Is he living at our condo?"

"Hard to say. You'll have to confront him sooner or later."

"It's time," I said.

"What can I do to help?" Ben asked. "If it's money you need, all you have to do is ask."

A gangster with a heart of gold. I smiled.

"It's good to see you smile," he said.

"You're a good person, Ben."

"You, too." He hugged me. "I'll call you by the end of the week."

The condo was a disaster. Filthy clothing, including three sets of bras and panties, were scattered across the living room floor. Rotting garbage overflowed in the kitchen and bathroom. Thank goodness Mike had left the AC on high and the sliding glass door open; otherwise, I wouldn't have been able to breathe.

I walked through the rooms in a state of detachment. Any feelings I'd had for Mike were either gone forever or buried deep inside me. I'd have to face him sooner or later—and whoever belonged to the lingerie.

Two days later, Mike blew in, looking like he hadn't slept or bathed in days. He registered no surprise at my presence or at his immaculate surroundings.

"How ya doin', doll?"

He moved to kiss me on the mouth. I moved aside.

"Fine, Mike. Where've you been?"

"Here 'n there. Heat's on, in case ya didn't know. Where ya been?"

"Here and there." I found great pleasure in mocking him.

"I'm beat. Catch ya later." He began shedding his clothes and climbed into bed.

I didn't join him.

Once I heard him snoring, I called Tina in California.

"Great to hear your voice," Tina said. "What's up?"

"I'm leaving Mike."

She snorted. "About time. What's that son of a bitch been up to?"

I recounted Mike's betrayal. "Ben said he'll help me get back to Jersey, but I need your help."

"What can I do?"

"I need a place to stay until I get settled and find work," I said. "Any idea who I could call?"

Tina thought for a moment. "Remember Tammy?"

"Our partner in crime?" I regretted my words as soon as I spoke.

"Crime was hardly the word for it," Tina replied. "We were three dancers out for a good time."

"Sorry." I apologized. "I'd give anything to go back to those days."

"You might be able to. Did you know she got married to that furniture salesman?"

"Danny? He was the biggest BS artist on the planet."

"That's him," Tina said. "They bought a place in the country. Betcha they'd let you crash there."

"But I haven't talked to her since I left Jersey."

"Tammy and I are close," Tina said. "She asks about you all the time."

I scribbled down Tammy's address and number. "What about you, Tina?"

"It's been tough getting back on my feet. Money's tight."

"Maybe I can help," I said. "Ben feels bad about what happened. He offered me money to get out. I'm sure he'll come through for you."

"And Edie, too?"

"And Edie."

"I'll give Tammy a call," Tina said. "Love you, Ava."

When was the last time someone said those words to me?

"Love you, too."

When was the last time I'd said those words to someone?

Ben had given me a secret code to use when I needed to get in touch. I called one of his safe houses and later received a coded message to meet the next afternoon at a Days Inn near Miami.

Ben had ditched the scruffy look for a neatly trimmed beard and ponytail. He wore brown leather pants and a tailored shirt.

"I like the look," I said.

"Me too. In a few days it's gonna change. Gotta keep one step ahead. C'mon in."

I stepped over the threshold and into Ben's latest home.

He offered me a seat at a cheaply veneered table. "What's going on?"

"Were you serious when you offered to help me get out?"

"Absolutely."

"I think I have a place to stay in Jersey, but I'm gonna need a little money to get on my feet."

"Name your price."

My palms began to sweat. I dropped them to my lap to hide my anxiety.

"How about $5,000?"

Ben grinned, then broke into a laugh. "That's it?"

"Maybe $5,000 for Tina and $5,000 for Edie. They're struggling, too."

His grin remained. "You're sure that's it?"

I nodded.

Ben reached into a knapsack and pulled out a manila envelope stuffed with hundred-dollar bills. He counted out three piles of fifty bills.

"I suppose you're gonna wire the bread to your friends."

I nodded again.

He added two more bills. "This'll cover the cost of wiring."

"You have no idea how much this means to me," I said. "I'll repay you as soon as I can."

"It's a gift, Ava."

"You're an angel."

He walked me outside.

"Stay safe and thank you." I hugged him.

Before going back to his room, he turned to me. "Y'know, I would've given you a hundred grand if you'd asked."

I stood in the parking lot and stared into space.

Part Three

fifty-seven

Back to the Past

Mike was waiting for me when I returned from my meeting with Ben.

"How 'bout me and you have a night out?" he asked. "Maybe I'll even buy ya a diamond necklace."

"No thanks."

"C'mon, doll. You've been avoidin' me for weeks."

I considered his offer, not because I wanted to reconnect with Mike, but because I could sell the necklace and boost my nest egg.

"I'm done," I said finally.

"Done? Nobody says done to me."

"I just did."

"You'll be sorry."

"I already am."

I expected Mike to strike me, rape me, or destroy my belongings. Instead, he grabbed his wallet and moved to the door.

Before slamming the door, he said, "You'll live to regret this."

Mike was right on two counts: I was alive, no thanks to him, and I was living with regrets.

I waited nearly an hour to call Tammy, afraid Mike would come home and hear my conversation. I contemplated how I moved from one abusive relationship to another and vowed to change my life once

I got back to Jersey. I felt strong and invincible until I remembered other promises I'd made and broken. Would this time be different?

Tammy and I spent an hour on the phone. She knew I wasn't ready to talk about Kenya, so we kept the conversation light. She invited me to stay in their finished basement until I got back on my feet.

My next call was to the airline. After booking a flight to Philadelphia the following week, I moved onto the balcony and stared at the ocean. I'd lose the gorgeous views, tropical weather, money, luxury . . . and Mike.

No amount of money or natural beauty is worth a lifetime with Mike.

Mike drifted in and out of my life for the next few days. I waited until the morning of my flight to come clean.

"I'm leaving," I began.

"For how long?"

"Forever," I said.

"*What?*"

"You heard me. I'm heading back to Jersey."

"But why? We've got a great thing goin'."

You're a narcissist and a sociopath.

"Do I really have to explain?" I asked.

He looked at me, clueless. "Please don't."

I caught myself before I clung to his crumbs of affection.

"It's over." I unlocked the front door and threw the keys at him.

"No, Ava."

Were those tears in his eyes? I turned away before I could change my mind.

"Goodbye."

I slammed the door and ran for the elevator. He didn't follow.

I glanced up at our balcony once before my taxi left. The glare from the morning sun partially blinded me, but I swore I saw Mike framed in the doorway.

~~~

I cried when I met Tammy at the luggage carousel. Her smiling face meant freedom from Mike and the opportunity to start a new life.

"I'm so happy to see you! You're gonna love our new house! You're gonna love Danny! You're gonna love your new digs . . ." Tammy had always been hyperactive but never as hyper as she was that day. She chattered on and on.

A headache appeared behind my eyes. I hoped this wasn't her daily demeanor.

"Danny's waitin' in the car. You're gonna love him. You're gonna love our car. You're gonna . . ."

She's my salvation. Stay calm.

Tammy's motormouth went into high gear when we met Danny at the car. The two of them talked over each other, discussing my future.

"I'll getcha back to dancin' soon's you're ready. Money's outrageous these days. We'll getcha a car. We'll find ya a boyfriend. Maybe an agent . . ."

"Thanks, Tammy," I said. "First, I need to find my kids, then I'll find a job. Don't think I want to dance."

"Not dance? Who are ya? Rules are looser now. Skimpy costumes. Pole dancin'. Lap dances. You'll make a fortune . . ."

"They need a bartender at Dream Girls," Danny said. "How 'bout that?"

"Yeah, yeah, Dream Girls . . ."

"I'll think about it." I'd hoped to put an end to the conversation, but the two of them rambled on.

Tammy and Danny lived in a small ranch house on a country road between Trenton and New Brunswick, a perfect location for dancing in either town or anywhere in between.

If I want to dance, that is.
~~~

Their basement had been converted into a windowless, paneled family room with a pull-out couch, a tiny TV, dresser, and a full bathroom. For a moment, I missed my luxury condo and ocean view; then I remembered Mike.

"Get unpacked. Then we'll party. Then we'll show ya our wedding pics. Then we'll—" Tammy never paused for a breath.

I wanted to sleep undisturbed for a week, but Tammy and Danny had other plans. They offered me crystal meth, which I politely refused.

She shrugged. "More for us then."

The powder vanished up their noses. Within minutes, their verbal rant accelerated.

Vodka, hashish, and cocaine were next on the menu. I resisted the urge to snort a few lines of coke, knowing how much I needed to rest. I needed food, too, but knew better than to ask. Food ranked low on the priority list of speed freaks.

The party went on and on, as did their so-called conversation. A little before midnight, I excused myself and went to bed.

I slept intermittently. Each time I awoke, I heard pacing and voices above me. How long had it been since they'd slept?

fifty-eight

A Car, a Job, and a Home

I bought a 1974 silver Ford Galaxy. The purchase took a bite out of the $5,000 from Ben, but without a car, I was helpless. I took Tammy up on the offer to tend bar at Dream Girls in North Brunswick, where she was a regular dancer.

In the two years since I'd stopped dancing, clubs had become raunchier and costumes more revealing. Boundaries between customers and dancers were looser, the tips larger.

Tammy earned twice what I made tending bar. As more and more of her money went up her nose, her behavior became more and more erratic. She and Danny would crash and burn one day soon. I didn't want to be around when that happened.

If I wanted to get my own place and reconnect with my kids, I'd need more money. I finally let Dave, the manager, talk me into two dancing nights a week.

I resurrected my dance costumes, which I'd stored at Ben's place in Florida. Compared to the newer styles, they were laughable. I practiced my old routines in Tammy's basement until I felt confident to take the stage.

I was a wreck until the music entered my soul, and I began to move. After the first song, I felt powerful and confident. Once again,

I was hooked. I promised myself I'd only take a short detour from my goal of sobriety. But the more I danced, the more alcohol, pot, and coke coursed through my body.

By spring 1979, I'd returned to full-time dancing and had enough money to get my own place. In Plainsboro, I found a gorgeous second-floor apartment with a balcony overlooking a golf course. It was time to reconnect with Tommy and Lee.

I summoned the courage to call Tom's parents.

"Hello, Mrs. Harrison," I began. "It's Ava."

"Ava?"

"Your former daughter-in-law."

"Whadda ya want?" She sounded old and drunk.

"I've been trying to reach Tom and my children. Their number in Charlotte is disconnected, and my letters came back."

"They moved."

"Can you tell me where?"

"Why should I?"

"I'm their mother."

"That ain't what Tom says."

"Please?" I couldn't keep the tremor out of my voice.

"Thas up to Tom."

"Can you tell him to call me?" I rattled off my number. Was she capable of writing it down?

"Don't bug me no more." Mrs. Harrison slammed down the receiver.

I'd saved enough to send Tommy and Lee to summer camp. If I hired a private investigator, I'd have nothing to give them. I prayed for a miracle.

My miracle came two months later. By that time, I'd gotten on the circuit and booked gigs from Trenton to New Brunswick. One afternoon, I was dancing at the Rainbow Lounge in Piscataway when a familiar face smiled at me.

Kevin Harrison—Tom's brother! I joined him on my break.

We spent a few minutes catching up before I summoned the courage to ask, "What happened to Tom and the boys?"

Kevin's face darkened. "Tom and the kids are in Bridgeport, Connecticut. They left North Carolina maybe two years ago."

"How are Tommy and Lee?"

Kevin looked away.

"What happened?"

"How much time d'you have?"

"Ten minutes before my next set."

"I'm sorry, Ava."

Panic seized my heart. *Were my kids dead? Injured?*

"Tom started drinking again and getting violent," Kevin began. "He started slapping Elaine around and making life miserable for Tommy, Lee, and Elaine's kids. Elaine filed for divorce. She tried getting custody of the boys, but because she's the stepmom, the court left them with Tom."

I stared numbly at Kevin, tuning out the sounds and sights of the club. *Why hadn't I been there for my children?*

Wait a minute! It was Tom who locked me out of their lives. He told me I wasn't wanted. Tom was the consummate father who'd taken a vow of sobriety. How could I have known?

"What about Tommy and Lee?"

"Surviving," Kevin said. "Not the happiest kids on the planet, but they're smart and ambitious, especially Lee."

His words eased some of my anxiety.

"What should I do?"

"I'll give you Tom's number and address. From there you're on your own."

It was time for my next set. I downed two shots of tequila and pushed Kevin's news to the back of my mind.

fifty-nine

Reunion

My wastebasket overflowed with drafts of apologies and explanations to Tom and my kids. The one thing missing was the courage to take the first step.

School would end in a few weeks. I wanted to send them to summer camp, so I needed to act quickly. On a Wednesday afternoon, I took a deep breath to stop my hands from shaking and dialed Tom's number.

"Hello?" A young man answered.

"Hi. I'm looking for Tommy," I said.

"This is Tommy." My fifteen-year-old son sounded so mature.

"It's your mom." My voice trembled.

"Mom?"

I sensed confusion in his voice. "I've been looking for you for two years," I said.

Silence.

"I wrote. I called. Your dad never told me you moved."

"You deserted us." Tommy finally spoke.

"No, honey. Dad told me to stay away."

"That's not what Dad said."

Your father's a liar and a drunk. "Can we start over?"

Silence.

"I want to visit you and Lee," I said.

"You'll have to ask Dad. He gets home at six."

"Is Lee home? I'd love to say hi to him."

"He's not home, either," Tommy said. "I have to go now. Bye."

I curled into a ball on my sofa and sobbed until I fell asleep. The sun was beginning to set when I came to. I'd wanted to call Tom before he entered a drunken stupor. I hoped it wasn't too late.

Tom was cordial to me, which told me he was in that liminal space between feeling no pain and inflicting pain. He agreed to a visit on Saturday.

Two trains and a taxi took me to Tom's 1960s split-level in Bridgeport. As I stood on the sidewalk summoning the courage to ring the bell, I reminded myself I'd survived a month in a Kenyan prison. Finding the courage to visit my children paled in comparison.

A teenage version of Tom opened the door. Tommy greeted me with cool suspicion.

"Come in." His invitation was guarded.

I knew better than to ask for a hug. Instead, I said, "You've become a handsome young man."

And I missed watching your transformation.

An athletic twelve-year-old boy stood in the living room. "Hello, Mother," Lee said formally.

"Lee, I hardly recognize you." As soon as I spoke, I regretted my words.

"That's what happens when you abandon your children." He stood with his arms crossed in front of his chest.

"I hope we can change all that."

The three of us sat stiffly until Tom joined us.

"Ava, you look good," Tom said.

I couldn't return the compliment. Tom looked like he'd aged twenty years.

I asked about their lives, interests, school, and friends. Tommy slowly warmed to me. But not Lee. He cocooned himself in a wing chair at the far end of the room.

"Can I treat you two to lunch?" I asked.

"Okay!" Tommy quickly agreed. "Can we go to Bernie's Place? They make the best sandwiches."

At the mention of Bernie's, Lee perked up.

"Don't keep them too long," Tom warned.

After more than two years, I deserved more than lunch, but I was on Tom's "turf."

For me, lunch was pure joy. I doubted Tommy and Lee felt the same. I told myself to take things slowly. So many questions remained unanswered. So many explanations and apologies remained unsaid.

For a while Tom allowed me to visit every other weekend. I took the boys shopping, to lunch, and to the movies. I felt our barriers lift and hoped I could invite them to spend some of their summer with me.

As summer vacation approached, I asked Tom if I could give each of them $1,000 for camp.

A gradual rage spread across his face. "I don't want you bribing them."

"I'm trying to make up for lost time," I said.

"You mean jail time."

"*What?*"

"I know what happened in Africa. Don't worry, your secret's safe with me. But it's gonna cost you."

"I was set up." I doubted he believed me. "How did you find out?"

"None of your business how I found out. Do you really think I'm gonna let the kids stay with you?"

"It's better than living with a drunk."

Tom raised his hand to slap me, then retreated. "Maybe I drink but I never abandoned them."

"It's your fault. You took them from me."

"Bullshit. Since you're back, they're actin' out. You're messin' with their heads. It's time you backed off."

"I want to hear it from them," I said.

"You won't. I raised 'em to be polite."

Tom still had power over me. I'd never learned how to fight for my children or for myself. Maybe he was right. Maybe I needed to back off.

I convinced myself teenagers don't want their mom in their faces on the weekends. I continued to call, write, and visit less frequently. Whenever I had extra cash, it went to them—or to Tom. I was never sure.

sixty

New Friends

Not only were clubs seedier, costumes skimpier, and dancing sexier, the other dancers were younger and tougher. Some of them thought I was a loser, a leftover from the generation of go-go bars. I'd always found it challenging to compete with younger, cuter girls with better routines. But now in my mid-thirties, they often got the better of me. On those nights, I'd stumble, miss a beat, or tear my costume. I needed a strategy to compete, to rise to the top of the garbage heap.

Who'd have thought my month in prison would be my ticket to triumph? On most shifts, I'd have at least one ally. But one night at Dream Girls, it was me against the next generation. I needed to assert myself, or I'd be finished as a dancer.

"Hey, grandma, think you can get a rise outta the customers?" Amber, an eighteen-year-old bleached blond taunted me.

"You think you're tough, Amber?" I clenched my fists and dug my feet into the ground to stop trembling. "When I was in prison in Africa, the natives showed me how to kill a person with two fingers right here."

I pointed to a spot on my neck below my ear. "No gun, no knife, no blood. Just pressure."

Her eyes opened wide, and she backed away. "You were in prison?"

"For international drug smuggling. You learn a lot behind bars."

Word got around. From that point on, nobody bothered me.

Diana, Ricki, and Missy—tough druggies in their late twenties—became my new friends. Like Tammy and Jack, they drank, inhaled crystal meth and cocaine, and lit a joint when they wanted to come down.

Big Eddie supplied our drugs. Eddie's merchandise was focused on quantity rather than quality, but nobody seemed to care.

When we weren't dancing, we partied. Diana and her boyfriend rented a house on a country road, a perfect setting for her July Fourth bash in 1981. She asked Ricki, Missy, and me to arrive early to help with food preparations.

"Ricki, you're gonna be the centerpiece," Diana said.

Missy, Ricki, and I exchanged confused glances.

"C'mon out to the back porch, and I'll explain."

Instead of a picnic table set with paper plates, she'd covered the table with a sheet and placed a pillow on one end. Tupperware containers of food and a roll of Saran Wrap sat nearby.

"Okay, Ricki, strip but leave your panties on. Then climb onto the table," Diana instructed.

Ricki was high enough to blindly obey Diana's orders.

"Now let's wrap her with Saran Wrap and decorate her with food."

"Won't she be too hot?" I asked.

"Nah. We're gonna keep the AC goin' and blow the cold air out here."

"You thought of everything," Missy said.

"And it's only appetizers," Diana said. "Once we fire up the grill, she can get up."

We decorated her breasts with sliced tomatoes and surrounded her body in chips, crackers, and greens. Ricki's stomach was concave enough to support a bowl of blueberries, and in her crotch, we placed a bowl of yogurt dip.

"Red, white, and blue!" Missy screamed.

Ricki was the hit of the party until Diana's biker friends arrived and decided they needed to dig deeper for the yogurt dip.

"Get the fuck out of there!" Ricki sat up, scattered garnish everywhere, and threw dip at the offenders.

A round of laughter and cheers exploded as she ran in the house. Missy and I followed.

Ricki was furious. I helped her into the shower and found her clothes in Diana's bedroom.

"Bunch of lowlifes. Let's get outta here."

Missy and I had had enough, too. We said a quick goodbye to Diana and piled into my car.

I knew cops would be on the lookout for drunk drivers like me, but what choice did we have? I spotted a police car in my rearview mirror and did my best to stay focused and drive at a reasonable speed. It didn't work. He flashed his lights and pulled me over.

I rolled down the window and thanked God we weren't smoking.

The officer opened his mouth to ask for my license and registration. When he saw the three of us, he winked and smiled.

"Celebrating the Fourth, ladies?"

We smiled our sexiest smiles and nodded.

"How far are you going?" he asked.

"Only a few miles to my place," I said.

"You look like nice girls. How about I follow you and make sure you get home okay?"

"Thank you." I felt my body relax.

"That was close," Ricki said.

"And we didn't have to show our tits!" Missy burst out laughing.

To my surprise, the officer kept his word, followed us to my apartment complex, and left us to celebrate the rest of the holiday.

If only the Kenyan police had been so kind.

sixty-one

Ava Novak?

Most days I was able to leave Florida, Mike, and Kenya in the past. I was now fully immersed in the 1980s world of dancing and strip clubs. The money was fantastic, and I was my own boss. After paying my bills, I sent money to Tommy and Lee—hoping to win back their love.

I hadn't forgotten the promise I made to myself to get sober, but the longer I stayed in the industry, the longer I delayed my vow.

One afternoon in late August 1981, a straight-laced customer sat at the bar and watched me closely through my last set. He approached me as I left the stage.

"Ava Novak?"

Everyone in the business knew me as Ava Martin. Who was this man?

"Agent Miller, DEA." He discreetly showed me his badge.

"I have nothing to say to you." My voice shook.

"If you don't talk to me, I'll have to arrest you."

"On what charges?" I sounded confident, but inside, my heart pounded.

"I know about the *Smooth Sailin'*. I know about your connections to Ben Kraus and South Florida."

"What do you want with me?"

"We need to talk." His voice was firm.

Agent Miller allowed me to change into street clothes and waited for me in the parking lot.

"The entire crew's been arrested and awaiting trial," he said.

"I've been in New Jersey for years."

"We need you to testify. If you don't cooperate, we'll hold you in contempt of court. You could spend three years in jail."

"Do I have a choice?" I asked.

"As I said, testify or go to jail."

"They'll kill me."

"No," he replied. "You'll be one of fifty-two corroborating witnesses. We'll fly you to Florida. I'll escort you."

Agent Miller continued with details about dates and times, but my thoughts had taken me to another time and place. Could I trust the DEA to keep me safe? Would I be tried and sent to prison? Had Mike been arrested? If so, would I have to testify against him?

"Ava?" Agent Miller snapped me back to the present.

"Sorry. You need to know how upsetting this is for me."

"I'm sure," he said unsympathetically. "The trial's set to begin in early September. I'll meet with you once more before we fly you to Florida."

"What for? Seems like you have all the information you need."

"Remember, if you don't cooperate, a warrant will be issued for your arrest."

"I didn't say I wouldn't cooperate." I stared him down with false courage.

We arranged to meet a few days later at a local diner.

"I wasn't sure you'd show." Agent Miller greeted me.

"Do you understand how I felt when you confronted me?"

He nodded. "I get that a lot."

The waitress took our order. He ordered a full breakfast. All I could manage was coffee.

"I don't know how much you know about Benjamin Kraus's operation," he began. "His smuggling ring was responsible for bringing in nearly fifteen percent of the marijuana into the United States between 1972 and 1979. What you witnessed was a small part of the operation."

So far Agent Miller hadn't told me anything I didn't know.

"We arrested Kraus in 1978, but he jumped bail. We tracked him to Seattle and got him to plead guilty last month. He's agreed to testify against four key members of his operation."

I had to ask. "What about Mike Ambrose?"

"Arrested him back in March. He failed to make a court appearance and wasn't abiding by the terms of his release. He surrendered last month."

Mike was finally getting his due.

"Can you tell me more about Mike?"

He smiled for the first time. "I thought you'd be interested in Mike. A magistrate set his bail at $50,000 and required him to post $5,000 in cash. His father had to post his $72,000 home as collateral on the remainder of the bond. He was a no-show in court last month to answer allegations that he wasn't living up to the conditions of his bail."

"That sounds like Mike," I said.

"Mike's probation officer said he was revoking his bond. His Florida attorney said he's never met Mike. And now his father could lose his house."

Mike would turn on his own parents to save his neck, just like he turned on me and his friends.

"I'll accompany you on a flight to Fort Lauderdale at the end of the month," he said. "We'll put you up at the Marriott. We expect this part of the trial to last four days. I can't say when you'll be called, but once you've testified, you'll fly home."

"And that's it?"

"Most likely."

~~~

I told my friends I was taking a short vacation. The only person I confided in was Tina in California. I hadn't seen her since Kenya, but we stayed in touch with letters and occasional phone calls.

I assured her I was the only one who needed to testify. She wished me luck and convinced me I was doing the right thing.

Agent Miller sent a car to bring me to the Philadelphia Airport. He was kind enough to have booked a seat several rows ahead of me, giving me one less thing to worry about.

Worry was hardly the word for what I was feeling. Anxiety, fear, apprehension, and terror were more like it. The bosses had treated me with kindness and generosity. I knew them as peace-loving guys who found a way to make millions from a product they believed harmed no one.

Ben had saved my life, and now I was testifying against him. Would his mercenaries hunt me down? Would they kill me, beat me senseless, make my life more of a living hell than it already was?

Agent Miller and I took a taxi to the Marriott, where we met Angela Falcone, Assistant US Attorney and prosecutor for the case. I learned Ben was one of eighteen named in a twenty-eight-count federal indictment. He'd been in jail since March on a $4,000,000 bond. Gary and Vinnie were fugitives. Others in the case were unknown to me.

"Most questions will require a yes or no answer," Ms. Falcone said. "As a corroborating witness, we expect you to confirm or deny allegations. Do you understand?"

"I do."

"And remember, you'll be under oath."

She and Agent Miller left me to unpack and stew in my misery.

The United States Federal Building and Courthouse was an imposing, unfriendly structure designed to intimidate. Agent Miller led
~~~

me through security and into an elevator, which opened to a bustling corridor. I walked with my head down, hoping my hair would disguise who I was and why I was there. Periodically, I peeked out through my blond curtain to reassure myself no one was gunning for me.

I expected to be ushered into a full courtroom with Ben, Mike, and others shooting daggers in my direction. Instead, we entered a cubbyhole of a room furnished with a table, a leatherette office chair, a coffee maker, and a stack of outdated magazines.

"You'll stay here until you're called to testify," Agent Miller said. "If you need anything, Officer Martinez will help you."

He waved to a police officer across the hallway.

"How long before I'm called?"

"Hard to say. An hour, maybe two."

"I don't know if I can go through with this. Couldn't I be placed in witness protection?"

"You're one of fifty-two witnesses. We can't place all of you."

"But—"

"Ava, you'll be in court by yourself," Agent Miller said. "You'll have no contact with the accused or other witnesses as long as you stay put."

He closed the door, leaving me in yet another prison cell. After pouring myself a cup of what tasted like yesterday's coffee I flipped through the stack of magazines. *Guns & Ammo* was the featured publication, along with last year's holiday edition of *Good Housekeeping* and several issues of *Parents*.

I barely made it through *Good Housekeeping* when Agent Miller came for me. As we made our way down the corridor, I imagined I was in one of those nightmares where the hallway continues into eternity. I wondered if a dream sequence was preferable to my current reality.

Agent Miller handed me to Assistant US Attorney Angela Falcone, who led me to the witness stand. After swearing to tell not only the truth, but the whole truth, my mind turned to Jello.

"Were you part of the crew on the *Smooth Sailin'*?" Ms. Falcone asked.

"Yes."

She fired off question after question about my work on the boats before switching topics.

"Were you in a relationship with Michael Ambrose?"

"Yes."

"What is your current relationship with him?"

"I haven't seen or heard from him in several years."

Ms. Falcone asked me about Ben, Gary, Vinnie, and other members of The Crew, whom I'd never met.

"Did Mr. Kraus send you and Mr. Ambrose to Kenya?"

"Yes."

Angela Falcone knew everything about the Kenyan operation. All I needed to do was corroborate her information.

"Yes."

"Yes."

"Yes."

My testimony went on and on.

"After your stint in a Kenyan prison, you mentioned you were so grateful to be back in the States that you literally kissed the ground. Is that true?"

"Yes."

"Then tell me, Ms. Novak, why would you return to Kenya only a few months later?"

"I-I don't know," I stammered. I felt like a fool.

I sunk into the witness chair. My hands trembled. Yesterday's coffee rose into my throat.

Her questions continued. Finally, I heard the magic words, "Thank you, Ms. Novak. That's all."

I held onto anything to keep from falling as I left the witness stand. My ordeal was over. I'd let down Ben, one of the kindest, most generous men I'd known. He'd lost his empire, tens of millions of dollars. Most of all he'd lost his freedom.

In silence, I rode back to the Marriott with Agent Miller. On behalf of the United States government, he thanked me for my cooperation.

I ordered a bottle of wine with my dinner and drank myself to sleep.

The next morning, I said a final farewell to Fort Lauderdale and to a life I hoped to leave behind. For good this time.

sixty-two

TIME Magazine

"Where's your tan?" Diana asked, my first night back at Dream Girls.

"I spent most of my time indoors." I winked at her.

"Who's the lucky guy?"

"I'll never tell." How could I tell Diana about Agent Miller and the true reason for my trip? Better to let her fantasies run wild.

"Big Eddie scored some fine blow. Welcome home." Diana passed a mirror with four lines of cocaine to me.

"Just what I need." The powder flew up my nose.

The world of dancing may have been dark and dirty, but it was heaven compared to what I'd been through in Florida.

I doubted if news of the trial would reach Philadelphia news networks, but I wasn't taking any chances. For the next three months, I avoided all national newspapers and TV news programs. I knew my friends would be sent to prison due in part to my testimony.

But what about Mike? Did he eventually have his day in court? Would he serve time, or would he find a way to weasel out of a conviction?

My phone rang one late November afternoon in 1981.

"Hi, hon, it's Tina!"

After catching up, Tina revealed the real reason for her call.

"Have you seen the latest issue of *Time* magazine?" she asked.

"Um, no."

"You'll never guess what's on the cover."

"Let me guess—The Crew?"

"Bingo!" Tina laughed. "Mostly it's about the drug trade in Miami, but there's an article about Ben's arrest. It's probably too late to buy a copy, but I bet the library has one."

I sat on my couch to keep my knees from buckling. "I don't think I want to read it."

"It's one for the scrapbooks," Tina said.

"Not for mine. I want to forget the whole mess."

Tina chattered on. I half-listened until she mentioned Mike.

"What about Mike?" I asked.

"Well, the *Time* article got me curious. I went to the library to read Florida newspapers. You wouldn't believe the coverage the trial got."

"What about Mike?"

"The *Miami Herald* from December 5 said Mike failed to show up for sentencing. Seems he's home in Pennsy suffering from mental and physical problems."

A shiver shot down my spine. Mike was less than an hour from me.

"I'd like to give that asshole some real mental and physical problems." Tina giggled.

"It's not funny. He could show up here any minute and beat me senseless."

"He wouldn't," Tina said.

"Like he wouldn't leave us in prison? I testified against him!"

"Why don't you call your DEA buddy?" Tina asked. "He'll give you the lowdown."

"Good idea. Thanks."

We chatted a while longer, then said our goodbyes.

~~~

I waited until February to call Agent Miller. I learned Mike was serving time at Allenwood Federal Correctional Complex near Allentown, Pennsylvania. I asked no further questions. Agent Miller supplied no further answers.
~~~

sixty-three

The Visit

The next year or two blur in my memory. Dancing, drugging, and drinking occupied most of my time. I continued stalking the self-help shelves of the library, hoping to find a way out of my self-induced misery. I'd find sobriety for a day or two, but then the bottle, pipe, and line called to me. The substance was stronger than my will.

My fortieth birthday in March 1984 came and went. No one in the clubs knew my true age. Dancers hit their peak in their mid-twenties. Most died or retired before they reached thirty. I knew I was on a path to destruction and couldn't last much longer.

In my clearheaded moments as Ava Novak, I prayed my soul would be reborn. The rest of the time as Ava Martin, I ran on automatic. Depression and insecurity governed my world.

A phone call that spring changed everything.

"Hey, doll, guess who?"

"Mike!" It took a moment to realize I was hyperventilating.

I sat on a kitchen chair to keep myself from collapsing. Was he out of prison? Out to kill me?

"That's all ya have to say?"

"W-why are you calling?"

"Just wanna say hi. Catch up on old times."

"How did you get my number?"

"I got my ways," he said.

"Where are you?"

"Allenwood. Y'know, the country club ya sent me to."

"You sent yourself."

"No hard feelings. I been thinkin' 'bout ya. Gets awful lonely here."

I stayed silent.

"How'd ya like to come for a visit?"

"In prison?"

"I thought maybe we could start over. Let bygones be bygones."

"I don't know—"

"Please, doll. It'd mean a helluva lot to me."

"I guess I could." I couldn't believe I was falling for Mike's bullshit.

Two days later, armed with a large coffee and a road map, I set out on the two-hour journey. I fantasized about our meeting and rehearsed what I'd say to Mike, until my car came to a stop on the Pennsylvania Turnpike. I watched as police cars and ambulances hurried past.

An accident. I'll be stuck for hours.

A light turned on in my brain. What was I doing? I wanted Mike out of my life. He didn't deserve a visit from me.

The traffic began to crawl. I made my way to the next exit, turned around, and headed home.

sixty-four

Another Visit

Whenever Tom granted me permission, I visited Tommy and Lee. Tommy now attended Pace University. Lee, still in high school, had become a super-athlete and a scholar. The older they became, the less time they wanted to spend with me.

How could I blame them? I'd missed most of their childhood and adolescence. Against my will, I'd turned them over to an alcoholic and abusive father, but that's not how they saw things. Tom had convinced them I'd deserted my family, that I didn't care enough to fight for them.

I invited Lee for a visit to celebrate his graduation from high school in 1985. To my surprise, he accepted. I cleaned my apartment and locked my stash in a jewelry box, which I hid in the back of my closet. In my mind, it was a step toward sobriety.

My handsome son arrived in a beat-up 1978 Ford Fiesta. I watched him scan the complex searching for my apartment.

"Over here, Lee!" I called from my balcony.

No smile or wave—he simply nodded in my direction and headed for my building.

"Congratulations, graduate!" I opened the door and reached to hug him. Subtly he backed away, and stiffly accepted my gesture.

"I thought we could have lunch, then I'll take you shopping. Can't have my son starting college without the right clothes."

"I have plenty of clothes."

"But nothing from me." As soon as the words exited my mouth, I knew I'd made a mistake.

"That's right," Lee said. "Nothing from you."

I brushed off his comment. "C'mon in. I made chicken salad, your favorite."

"I haven't eaten chicken salad since I was ten. But you wouldn't know that. What do you really know about me?"

I scrambled for words to save the day.

We sat—two strangers staring at each other, struggling for conversation. I learned Lee had received a full athletic scholarship to Fordham University. He planned to major in political science.

"I'm so proud of you," I said. "Where did you get your ambition?"

"Not from you or Dad," he said. "I've had to fight for myself since the day you left us."

"I didn't leave you." I scrambled for the right words. "Your father took you and Tommy from me. He beat me, destroyed me."

"Dad's got his problems, but he's always been there. Always gave us a home."

My plans for the day—shopping, dinner, maybe even an overnight stay—evaporated. Lee itched to be on his way.

He stood to leave. "I don't want to hit traffic on the George Washington Bridge."

"Before you go," I said, "I've been saving money to help you with college."

"I told you I got a full scholarship."

"But you'll need clothes, books, maybe even a computer. Please, Lee, let me help you."

"I don't want anything from you."

His words pierced my heart.

"If you change your mind, you know where I am." I touched his arm as he walked out the door.

"Thanks for lunch."

I didn't know it then, but that would be the last time I saw my youngest son.

sixty-five

One More Visit

ne Tuesday afternoon not long after Lee's visit, my friend Diana stopped over for coffee. I busied myself in the kitchen, while she relaxed on the balcony.

"Ava, come here, quick!"

I took a step onto the balcony.

"Stop right there," she said.

"What—"

"I think Mike's in the parking lot!"

Diana had never met Mike, but I'd shown her photos. She had to be mistaken.

"Mike's in prison," I said.

"You tell me." Diana stepped aside to give me a clear view.

"It is Mike!" I stumbled back inside but not quickly enough.

"Hey, Ava!" Mike called.

"I'll tell him you don't want to see him," Diana said.

"That'll only piss him off. I'll meet him in the parking lot. If anything happens, call the cops."

With Diana watching from above, I went outside to meet Mike.

"Ava! Great to see ya." Mike moved to hug me.

I stepped back and crossed my arms in front of me. "What are you doing here?"

"I'm a free man. Out on parole."

"I thought parole meant you couldn't cross state lines."

"I don't know nothin' about that," he said. "I missed ya."

My neighbor's four-year-old daughter rode past on her tricycle. "Hi, Miss Ava."

I waved and smiled, grateful for the distraction.

"Sorry the guards didn't let ya in to see me."

"Excuse me?"

"The day you were supposed to come visit. Sons a bitches kept you away from me."

"I didn't—" Mike thought the guards wouldn't allow me to visit him in prison. I couldn't tell him I'd never made it to Allenwood.

"Didn't what?"

"Um—I couldn't get in," I lied.

"That's all gonna change now." He took a step toward me.

"Stay away from me, Mike."

His "charming" smile turned bitter. I felt rage stream from his body.

"Nobody says no to me."

"I just did." The sun hid behind a cloud. I wished for my own cloud.

"I know where ya live," he threatened. "I got your phone number."

"If you don't leave now, my friend's gonna call the cops."

"You'll come around. We got a history."

"That's right. A history. A past, not a future." I started walking away.

"I'll be back."

That's what I'm afraid of.

My bravado was fading. I needed to get to the relative safety of my home.

I expected Mike to lunge at me, grab me, drag me to his car, and rape me. Instead, he planted himself between me and the door. I smelled the summer sweat on his skin.

"You go in that door, and we're done."

"Goodbye, Mike."

I hurried past him, unlocked the door to my building, and slipped inside. Once I knew I was safe, I crumbled to the floor and sobbed until my ribs ached.

Diana met me where I sat.

"I think he's gone," she said. "Are you gonna call the cops?"

"If he comes back."

Once I convinced Diana I was okay, she left for her four o'clock shift at Dream Girls. My shift began at six o'clock, which gave me two hours to take care of business.

That business was to contact Agent Miller from the DEA. He listened to my story and promised to intervene.

Agent Miller kept his word. He called me two days later.

"I got in touch with Mike's parole officer," he began. "I told him Mike frightened and threatened you."

I wished he hadn't used the word "frightened." It made me feel like more of a victim than I already was. But Agent Miller had come to my rescue and gone out of his way to ensure my safety.

"He won't bother you again."

"How can you be so sure? Mike doesn't believe the rules apply to him."

"His parole officer said to call him immediately if you see or hear from Mike. If he contacts you once more, he's going back to prison."

I actually have someone in my corner.

"One more thing," Agent Miller said, after he gave me Mike's parole officer's name and number. "If I were you, I'd change my phone number, make it private. You don't want him harassing you from pay phones."

"Should I get a new apartment?"

"I don't think it's necessary."

I wasn't sure I agreed but decided to trust his judgment.

"Thank you," I said. "You didn't have to go out of your way for me."

"You put yourself out on a limb for us. Just repaying the favor."

sixty-six

Warren

At forty-one, my body was breaking down. More and more I opted to work the lunch and early-evening shifts. The crowd was older, calmer, and less raunchy.

Not only was I addicted to drugs and alcohol, I was also addicted to the lifestyle dancing afforded me. A piece of me went to the devil each day, but I didn't care. My bills were paid, my drugs were free, and I had a beautifully furnished apartment to go home to every night.

I still longed for stability, sobriety, and a life in which I wasn't constantly assessing myself and my audience. I prayed for a miracle, a guardian angel, a prince charming to sweep me off my feet.

Angels come in all shapes and sizes. Would I recognize mine when he or she came along?

Dream Girls was my home base, but more and more I drifted toward other clubs catering to the lunch crowd. Grady's Bar and Grill in New Brunswick became my second base. Customers continued to whistle and shout, "Show your tits!" but I knew their requests were hollow and part of the game.

Grady's stage was located behind the bar and had wings projecting on either side. I danced the full length of the stage, connecting with the closest customers. Repeatedly, I tried to catch the eye of an older, white-haired man in jeans and a plaid shirt who was a regular fixture at Grady's. He'd plant himself on the barstool in a back corner with a beer, sandwich, and fries. Unlike most other customers, he kept to himself.

The bar was empty on Wednesday, July 3, 1985. Most people had taken an extra-long holiday and left for the Jersey Shore.

Felix, the bartender, and I sat at the corner of the bar waiting for someone to come in.

That someone turned out to be our solitary, white-haired customer. He surveyed the empty room and asked, "Are ya closed?"

Felix jumped to attention. "Waitin' on you, Warren."

Warren gave us a half-smile and sat on his favorite stool. "Ham 'n cheese on rye and a Bud."

"You got it," Felix said.

I stood and stretched. "Any song you'd like me to dance to?"

"Rest your feet, little lady. No point in dancin' just fer me."

I glanced at Felix. "You heard the man. Take it easy."

"Thanks." I turned to Warren. "Would you like some company?"

Warren stared into his beer before replying. "Guess so."

I sat next to him and asked Felix for a seltzer with lime. It was too early for alcohol, even for me.

"I'm Ava."

"Warren Anderson."

"Pleased to meet you." I held out my hand. We shook.

Something nagged at the back of my brain. His name had a familiar ring.

"Do I know you from somewhere?" I asked.

"I got no kids, so ya wouldn't know me that way."

"Where do you live?"

"Got me a couple acre farm in Piscataway."

"A farmer? Here in New Jersey?"

"Yup. 'Least now I am. I'm a retired carpenter. Local 19."

Local 19! The union my father had belonged to. Blood rushed to my face. I held on to the bar to keep from toppling over.

"You okay there?" he asked.

I nodded, unsure what to say. Fortunately, Warren changed topics.

"I been watchin' ya. You seem different from other dancers."

"And you seem different from other customers."

We laughed.

"I take it you been at this racket a while."

"Too long."

"Why not do somethin' else?"

"I need the money," I said.

"Smart gal like you could find a million ways to earn a livin'."

"Like what?"

"I dunno. Maybe be a lady barber, y'know, a beautician."

I smiled at his four-syllable pronunciation—bee-you-tish-un. "That'd mean going back to school. I'm too old."

He snorted. "Dearie, ya ain't old till ya get to my ripe age. I'm turnin' seventy next month."

I did the math. Warren was eight years older than my father. No doubt he and my father had worked together at some point.

I decided to take a chance. "Did you know Hank Wilson from Local 19?"

Warren did a double take. "Hank? Sure I 'member him. Always had a pocketful o' pistachios."

It was my turn to do a double take. My father loved pistachios. His hands were permanently stained pink from the dye on the shells.

"He—he was my father." Long-suppressed tears filled my eyes.

"Was?" Warren asked. "Did he pass?"

"Sorry, no. I should have said 'is.'"

"Ya get to be my age, ya never know. How's the ol' boy doin'?"

"Okay, I guess. I haven't seen him in a while."

Warren gave me a quizzical look.

"It's a long story."

Just then a half-dozen young guys walked in. Felix gave me the eye, meaning it was time to get back to work.

Warren understood. "To be continued."

I circulated through the small crowd on my next break and made sure to connect with Warren one last time before he left. The link to my real father scared me to death. I hadn't seen or heard from my parents in twenty-two years. I had no wish to revisit the events that had led me to the present, yet I sensed Warren was about to play an important role in my life.

sixty-seven

Lunch and Dinner

Warren had recently lost his wife of fifty years. Sadness covered him like a shroud, but he always came to life when we sat together on my breaks.

He tipped me fairly but not extravagantly, which I appreciated. I had no desire to be beholden to an older man, or any man, at that point in my life. As summer progressed, Warren brought me tomatoes and other vegetables from his garden. His sincere offerings meant more to me than all the jewelry and gifts I'd received from Mike.

One afternoon in late August, Warren asked me if I had any children.

"They're hardly children. My oldest will be twenty-two this November. My youngest is starting college next month."

"You're lucky. Me 'n the wife never had no kids."

"Not so lucky. They live with their father, my ex—" I stopped before I dumped my life story on this kind, older man.

Warren mumbled something.

"Excuse me?"

"Never mind. Say, would ya like to have lunch with me tomorrow?"

"I can't stop to eat while I'm working."

"Ya got me wrong. How 'bout I take ya someplace nice fer lunch?"

"Um-m, thanks but no thanks. I don't date the customers."

"Ava, it ain't a date. Heck, I'm old enough to be your dad, granddad even."

"I don't know—"

"I won't pester ya, but I'd sure enjoy your comp'ny. Tell ya what. I'll meet ya at Alfonso's. No strings attached. I promise."

I almost didn't recognize the well-dressed man waiting in Alfonso's vestibule. Warren had gotten a haircut, shaved his stubble, and dressed in a navy sport jacket and khaki pants.

"Warren, you look so nice!" I hoped he wouldn't take my compliment the wrong way.

"So do you, Ava. C'mon, I reserved a table on the patio."

Warren may have been rough around the edges, but he was a gentleman. He made no advances and asked nothing personal. By the end of the meal, I felt I'd made a new friend.

We both reached for the check. "Lunch's on me."

"Thank you, Warren."

"I'd sure like to see ya again. Are ya busy next Tuesday?"

Warren and I met for lunch every Tuesday for the next few months. I opened up about my two marriages, my boys, and how I got into dancing.

"I've seen a big change in you," Warren said one day in October. "Ya seem happier. Them tension lines are gone from yer face."

I laughed. "I could say the same for you. I was thinking you look lighter and happier."

"I'm startin' to think o' you as the daughter I never had."

"You are the sweetest man I know, Warren."

"Now that we got that outta the way, maybe you could tell me what you plan to do fer the rest o' yer life."

"I wish I knew. I can't dance forever."

"Don't put yerself down, young lady. You got a lot goin' fer ya."

I shook my head. "No, I don't. You don't know the half of it."

"I know a lot more 'n ya think. How 'bout we meet fer dinner next week?"

Dinner would mean a date. I had no interest in dating a man I'd come to think of as my surrogate father.

Warren sensed my hesitation. "Same rules, Ava. We'll take separate cars. Dinner'll give us more time to talk. You've made a huge dif'rence in my life, and I wanna think I can do the same fer you."

"You've done more for me than you know."

Could Warren be my guardian angel?

Dinners brought us closer. Warren shared intimate details of his life and persuaded me to do the same. I rarely shared confidences with anyone, but a voice inside me told me this time I'd be safe.

"I lived through some bad times back in the late '70s," I began.

"Ya told me 'bout yer marriages and losin' yer kids. How much worse could it be?"

"You may not want to see me anymore."

"What happens to us ain't always our fault. Ev'rybody makes mistakes, but it don't change who ya are inside."

"How did you get to be so wise?"

"Fought in WWII, seen a lotta changes in the world. I'm an old man. Like to think I learned somethin' over the years."

"I got involved with the wrong people in Florida—"

Once I began my story I couldn't stop. I told Warren about Mike, Ben, Kenya, and prison.

"I promised myself I'd get sober once I got back to the States. I failed."

"You didn't fail." Warren consoled me. "You been up against a whole lotta obstacles. Yer only human."

Nobody had ever said anything like that to me before. All the self-help books I'd read over the years—none had the impact of Warren's simple words.

"Are you saying none of this was my fault?"

"Didn't say that. What I'm sayin' is ya ain't perfect. Nobody is. Own yer responsibility and move on."

One minute Warren had absolved me, the next he'd blamed me. Which was it?

"'Member, Ava, ya can't change what happened. All ya can do is change yer way o' thinkin' and move on."

I put my fork down and stared into space.

"You don't hafta say nothin'. Another thing ya learn with age is the value of silence. You just sit there, darlin', and do yer thinkin'."

Warren's words brought back thoughts of my mother. I needed to take responsibility for my life. But until this moment, I realized I never had. I still blamed my mother for the disaster otherwise known as my life.

If my mother hadn't disowned me, I wouldn't have stayed with Tom and suffered his abuse. I wouldn't have left him for Jack, the polar opposite of Tom. I would have gone back to school and found a real career . . . and never met Mike. Florida and Kenya never would have happened.

I could have raised Tommy as a single parent with the help of loving grandparents. And Lee would never have been born.

"Lee!" I snapped back to the present.

"What's that?" Warren looked at me quizzically.

I decided to level with Warren. "I realized my mother's actions set my downhill slide in motion. I thought about the mistakes I wouldn't have made if she'd allowed me to come back home. And then I thought of Lee—"

"Your little one?"

"Not so little anymore. If she'd taken me back, Lee wouldn't exist. Even though he wants nothing to do with me, I can't imagine a world without him."

"There ya go. Look at the good that's come outta your life."

sixty-eight

Gifts

Missy, Ricki, and Diana invited me to spend Christmas Eve with them. The idea of another all-night drinking and drug fest was more than I could handle.

"Gonna spend time with your sugar daddy?" Diana asked during a break at Dream Girls.

"Warren? He's not my sugar daddy. And I'm sure he's spending the holiday with family."

"Suit yourself. You'll be missing the best party of the year."

Diana left me to hustle some customers.

Spending a lonely Christmas in my apartment would bring up memories of holidays I had spent without my kids and holidays I had spent in a drug-induced stupor.

Did I have the courage to spend this Christmas alone? To face myself?

A few days before Christmas, Warren stopped at Grady's for lunch. He plopped onto his usual stool and ordered a beer and a burger. Once my set ended, I joined him.

"Any plans fer Christmas?" he asked.

Should I be honest and admit I had nowhere to go?

"I'm not sure yet. What about you?"

"My sister and her son's family are comin' over. How'd ya like to join us?"

It had been years since I'd spent a holiday with a real family. What kind of emotions would it bring up for me?

"I can't intrude on your family."

"Ain't like that. I been tellin' my sister 'bout you. Said she'd like to meet ya."

Warren's invitation scared me to death, but it was time to move past my fears.

"Well, then, I'd love to."

"Come fer Christmas Eve and spend the night. You can have the guest room and bath. We do a big brunch Christmas mornin'."

I knew I'd be safe at his home, especially with his sister and family.

Warren's sister Sally made a shrimp scampi dinner for Christmas Eve. The family reminisced of past holidays and discussed current events. They included me and made me feel welcome.

Christmas morning, I offered to help with brunch preparations, but Sally shooed me out of the kitchen.

"Spend time with my brother," she said. "He loves your company."

I joined Warren in the living room. We listened to Christmas carols on his record player and said little.

When the record ended, Warren turned to me. "I been wonderin' if you got any money stashed away fer hard times."

"Not much." I kept a small savings account but nothing for hard times.

"Ya need somethin'. I wanna help ya. You got no idea how much yer friendship means to me."

"I can't take anything from you."

"I got a pension and investments. Think I earned the right to share some with who I want."

Warren walked to his desk, pulled out his checkbook, and began writing.

"Pass it on when ya git to my age." He handed me a check for $30,000.

"Warren, this is a fortune. I can't accept this."

"Sure, ya can. Might be just whatcha need to get yerself back on track."

"You're a wonderful man." I hugged him.

A week went by before I saw Warren again. I'd written him a heartfelt thank-you note. Had I embarrassed him with my gratitude?

I needn't have worried. Warren invited me for dinner the week after New Year's. I met him at Murphy's Steak House, one of his favorite spots.

"Did ya enjoy the rest o' yer holiday?"

"Not as much as I enjoyed Christmas with you and your family. Thank you again—for everything."

"Ain't nothin'. Listen, Ava, I gotta make a confession."

I felt my shoulders tense.

"I had an ulterior motive for invitin' ya to Christmas."

"I don't understand—"

"You've been like a daughter to me. Spendin' time with you's helped me get past my wife's dyin', but I think ya know that already."

I reached across the table for his hand. "You don't have to go there."

He nodded. "What I didn't tell ya is that my sister works at the county college in the career center."

I was even more confused.

"You got a whole lot more goin' fer ya than dancin' in dive bars. I wanted to see if my sister agreed."

"Your sister and I never discussed careers."

"Didn't hafta. She's a good judge o' character. Said you were a sharp cookie and thinks she can help ya. They got this aptitude test at the college. Even though you ain't a student, she said she could finagle things and let ya take the test."

"But why? I earn a good living and when I can't dance anymore, I can always tend bar." Did my words sound as hollow to Warren as they did to me?

"Yer on borrowed time and ya know it. Let me 'n Sally help ya."

"Life doesn't work out for people like me."

"Cut the crap, Ava!"

Diners at nearby tables stared at us.

"I've tried getting sober. I can't do it."

"Take it one day at a time. Go fer the test, then think about the rest."

I lay awake that night thinking about Warren's words. He believed in me. Apparently, his sister did, too. The next day I made an appointment to take the exam. I had nothing to lose but time. I'd already wasted enough time in my forty-two years on Planet Earth.

The exam took less than an hour to complete. Sally sent me for coffee while she ran it through her system.

"Have a seat, Ava."

"Did I pass?" I tried keeping things light.

"It's not pass or fail," she said. "But I think you know that."

I nodded.

"The test shows you're a people person. Since you're an extrovert, a job in a lab or private office wouldn't suit you. You don't like routine, so you need to find a career that's different every day."

"So far it sounds like dancing is my perfect job."

Sally ignored my comment. "You don't have a mechanical bone in your body, and you're not cut out for math or science—or agriculture."

Guess that's one reason I failed in Kenya.

"You're telling me what I'm not cut out for. Does the test show *anything* I can do?"

"You love beauty, music, and the arts. Here's your list of best careers." Sally handed me a printout with her findings.

At the top of the list was cosmetology. Other career choices were sales, advertising, and social director.

"I have no training in any of these areas. I can't go to school and work full time."

"Don't sell yourself short. We work with Athena Beauty Institute. They have a three-month nail technician program starting the end of January. I know my brother gave you some money. Use some of it to get an education. I promise you won't be disappointed."

I knew Warren was lonely, which was why he treated me with kindness. But why Sally? What was in it for her?

"I'll think about it," I promised.

"Do more than think. I have Athena's information somewhere around here." She rummaged through her desk and handed me a crumpled flyer. "Give them a call, or I'll call for you."

"I can call."

"Tell my brother what we discussed. I'm sure he'll be supportive."

"Thank you."

It wasn't the first time I'd thought about a career in the beauty industry. I knew I had an eye for color, hair, and nails. And I did have $30,000 from Warren. The nail technician program was $2,500, which would only put a small dent in my savings.

I should have taken the night off from Dream Girls but didn't. While I danced, I thought about those cartoons where an angel sits on one shoulder, the devil on the other.

The devil: *You're nothing, broken, worthless.*

The angel: *I can change. Warren believes in me.*

The devil: *You've failed at everything. Made a mess of your life.*

The angel: *I can't change what happened, but I can change my future.*

The devil: *You're too old, too stupid, and you're an addict.*

The angel: *Shut up!*

I tripped and nearly fell off the stage. A nasty laugh erupted from a customer at the end of the bar.

Don't you dare laugh at me.

Something clicked in my fog-encased brain. Was I so desperate for love and acceptance that I would allow these sleazy men to judge my self-worth?

The only people in my life were customers, other dancers, and addicts. I needed to move into a world with new people who lived straight, normal lives. But could I?

I'd become comfortable in chaos—even craved it. Catcalls from customers replaced words of love. Alcohol and drugs bound me to my friends. My body ached, my feet throbbed, and my lungs filled with second-hand smoke. When and how would it end?

I drove directly home after work, telling my friends I had an early-morning appointment. I didn't lie exactly. My appointment was with my application to Athena.

The only person I shared my decision with was Warren. I saw him the next afternoon at Grady's.

"I did it, Warren. I enrolled in nail school."

His smile nearly broke my heart.

"Good fer you, darlin'. You won't regret it." He reached into his wallet, pulled out a folded piece of paper, and handed it to me.

"Warren, no!" It was a check for $3,000.

"It's a check fer tuition and other expenses."

"But you already gave me so much."

"It's yours with one stipulation. If ya drop out, I expect a full refund."

"You are my guardian angel." I kissed him on the cheek.

"I ain't no angel. Stay in school. That's all I'm askin'."

sixty-nine

Nails and Ricki

If I danced three nights a week, I could pay my bills and attend school during the day. It wouldn't be easy, but the program lasted only three months and could be my ticket to survival.

All the students at Athena were recent high school graduates, except for two women in their late twenties and me. Homework was minimal, classes were fun and interactive. I took to nails like I'd taken to dancing. Customers in our student clinic asked for me, which boosted my self-esteem and enthusiasm for my new career.

I needed a clear head for class, which meant I needed to limit my drug and alcohol intake. I still had a drink before each set, and I still partied on the weekends. But now I had a goal, maybe a reason to live.

A clearer head meant I saw my friends from a different perspective. Missy, Ricki, and Diana were barely thirty years old. At the rate they were partying, they wouldn't see forty, especially Ricki.

Speed and cocaine kept Ricki going through her shifts; alcohol and downers helped her sleep. She rarely ate. A bottle of Jack Daniel's balanced between her legs when she drove. Her hands shook, the circles under her bloodshot eyes deepened, and her speech became less and less coherent.

Ricki had always been one step ahead of me in the drug world. When I needed to reassure myself I was okay, I'd think, *At least I'm not as far gone as Ricki.* But the night she tumbled off the stage at Dream Girls, I knew something had to be done to save her.

Ricki's mother lived in Atlanta with Ricki's daughter, Tiffany. Her mother had an inkling of her daughter's substance abuse, but I doubted she knew the severity of her condition. Would I be betraying Ricki's trust if I reached out to her mother? Probably, but it didn't matter. My friend's life was at stake.

I drove Ricki home that night and tucked her in bed with her bottle of Jack. An ashtray of pills sat on her nightstand. I thought about removing them, but they could be downers, which would help her get the sleep she needed.

I went through her things, found her address book, and her mother's number.

It was close to two o'clock in the morning when I called from Ricki's kitchen. A muffled voice answered.

"Mrs. McHenry, I'm sorry to call so late. It's about Ricki."

The woman's voice snapped to attention. "What happened? Is she alive?"

I explained Ricki's condition as kindly and rationally as I could. "She needs help."

"I'm sure I can get a flight in the morning," she said. "Can you stay with her until I get there?"

"Of course." I'd miss class the next day, but my friend's life was more important.

I found an extra blanket and pillow and lay on Ricki's couch. Every hour or two, I checked to make sure she was still breathing.

In the morning I made myself a pot of coffee and scanned the Yellow Pages for rehab centers. I was surprised to find an entire column of centers throughout central New Jersey. I tore the page from the book.

Ricki lay comatose, alongside her bottle of Jack, until late afternoon when a taxi dropped Mrs. McHenry at the apartment.

"You may have saved my daughter's life," Mrs. McHenry said. "Thank you."

"I'd do anything for Ricki. Will you be taking her to rehab?" I handed her the Yellow Pages list.

"First, I think we need to get her to a hospital. Ava, can you dial 9-1-1?"

I made the call, then helped Mrs. McHenry awaken and dress her daughter. When the EMTs arrived, I showed them into the bedroom.

Ricki's mother and I waited in the living room. "You may as well go, Ava. I'll ride with her in the ambulance and call when we have more information."

Part of me felt I was abandoning my friend, but I was confident she'd get the help she needed.

That evening, Mrs. McHenry called to say her daughter would be hospitalized for a few days, then moved to a rehab facility.

"Where will she be? Will I be allowed to visit?" I asked.

"Ricki and I have your number. We'll be in touch."

I waited a week before calling Ricki. I wasn't surprised when no one answered. A call to Mrs. McHenry went to her answering machine. I received no return call. I drove past Ricki's apartment. Her car hadn't moved since Diana and I had brought it back—a sure sign she'd been taken to rehab. I decided to wait out the month before reaching out again.

By mid-March 1986, no one had heard from Ricki. I called her number and learned it had been disconnected. Mrs. McHenry's number in Atlanta had been changed to an unlisted number. Ricki's car was gone and a FOR RENT sign hung in her apartment window.

If Ricki had died, someone would have contacted me. I suspected she'd gone to Atlanta with her mother, who was restricting contact with her druggie pals.

~~~
~~~

I graduated from Athena in April, passed my state licensing exam, and found a part-time job at Bella's Salon in Princeton. I enjoyed the work and the calm vibe of the shop. Instead of the pounding rhythm of the bars, soft new age sounds wafted from overhead speakers. I found a friend in Martie, the owner, who was about my age.

"I'd love to hire you full time, Ava," Martie said.

"Thanks, but I don't think I could pay my bills as a full-time nail tech." I wasn't ready to quit dancing, the only world I'd known for more than fifteen years.

"Then go the full cosmetology route. You'll have your choice of careers—hair, makeup, facials—I'll even help with tuition."

"I'll think about it. And thank you." I hugged her.

I did think about it—a lot. It was almost as though God was handing me a plan for redemption. All I had to do was say "yes" and my life would work out. What was holding me back?

I reflected on the past during my drive home that evening. I'd never known peace or serenity. I'd lived an anxiety-filled life since I was a teen. Fear of abandonment was my reality. The tighter I held onto false crumbs of love, the worse my life became. I'd gone from one abusive relationship to another.

My thoughts drifted to Ricki. *If she's sober, there's a chance for me. If she's dead, I'll mourn her and follow in her footsteps one day soon.*

When I got home, I wrote Ricki a letter. I kept it simple and caring. On the envelope I wrote, "Please forward." At best, it would find her. At worst, it would go to her mother and add to her heartbreak.

seventy

A Letter Changes Everything

On Monday, May 19, 1986, a thin envelope waited for me. My name and address were clearly printed, but no return address. I stood next to the bank of mailboxes and carefully ripped the seal.

Dear Ava,

Hi, it's Ricki. Thank you for saving my life. I would have died if you hadn't called my mom, who got me into a thirty-day rehab program. It wasn't easy, but I had no choice. I worked really hard in the program and was scared shitless when I left.

You asked about meeting for coffee. I'm sorry but I can't. I had to make a clean break, which is why I never called you or any of the old gang. That's why I didn't put a return address on the envelope. I think about you guys all the time, but I'm afraid to get sucked back into the life.

I have a new apartment—more like a studio—since I'm not making the big bucks anymore. I'm working in an office. Life isn't easy, but I'm alive, and maybe one day I'll even get custody of my daughter.

I go to Alcoholics Anonymous meetings every night. I have a sponsor and get support from other members. On the weekends, I sometimes go to two meetings a day.

If you want to see me, here is a list of my meetings.

I love you,
Ricki

I leaned against the cool bricks of my building and stared at Ricki's note. If Ricki could get sober, maybe I could, too. I scanned the list of AA meetings and for a minute considered attending one. But then I thought about the meetings I'd seen on TV. Bad coffee, stale cookies, and alcoholics chain smoking and sharing their dirty laundry in a church basement.

I'd been a private person my entire life. I couldn't imagine standing in front of a room full of strangers, confessing my addiction.

Back in my apartment, I stuffed Ricki's letter and list of meetings in my junk drawer and poured a hefty shot of tequila. I told myself I'd already cut back on my drinking and drug use. What more could I do?

Warren invited me to spend Memorial Day with him and his family. Much as I appreciated his kindness, I knew his sister Sally would bug me about going full time into cosmetology. Warren would look at me with sad eyes and worry about my survival.

Dancing on Memorial Day would be a waste of time. Bars would be empty until midnight, when drunks stopped in for a nightcap on their way home from family gatherings. Diana invited me for another raunchy picnic. I turned her down, too.

I envisioned a quiet holiday reading by the community pool. Instead, I partied with my drug pals, sans Ricki, until four in the morning the night before. I stumbled into my apartment, dropped the blinds, took the phone off the hook, and fell into bed. I woke at noon with one of the worst hangovers of my life.

I downed nearly a pot of coffee, which made the pounding in my head even worse. I washed down three Tylenol with a pitcher of Bloody Marys. By late afternoon, I felt ready to face the holiday crowd at the pool.

Kids splashed in the shallow water while moms chatted and dads grilled burgers and hot dogs. I'd missed a magnificent day of sunshine and the joy of family and friends—again.

I smiled falsely at familiar faces and soon returned to the solitude of my apartment.

What was the purpose of my existence? Why was I taking up space on the planet when the food I ate could be given to someone more deserving? Who would miss me if I disappeared? Disappear—I laughed at the irony. Die was more appropriate.

I pulled out the list of AA meetings and saw that Ricki's meeting had been in the morning.

AA's for suckers, at least that's what I'd told myself for years. *I can get sober on my own, and if I can't, I'll leave a good-looking corpse.*

For the next few days, I managed to avoid alcohol, pot, and pills. But on Saturday, May 31, I found myself back at Dream Girls with the usual crowd of burnouts. My resolve disappeared. Life was so much easier if I gave in to the will of my friends.

But it wasn't. Something shifted in my consciousness, and I knew I'd reached the end of myself. I had two options: slit my wrists or meet Ricki at her Sunday AA meeting.

I chose the less messy option. I stumbled into my apartment, put my things down, and fell to my knees.

"God, please help me," I said in total surrender.

seventy-one

A Meeting

Ricki's AA meeting was scheduled at four o'clock at the Presbyterian church not far from Dream Girls. Only a handful of cars sat in the parking lot. I'd been hoping for a huge crowd so I could observe unnoticed.

I was also nervous about seeing Ricki. Would she welcome me or shun me in favor of her new sober friends? And what if Ricki didn't show? How would I explain myself? Could I find the courage to stand up and admit I was an alcoholic?

As it got closer to showtime, more cars appeared. I stared at the people entering the building: teens and seniors, men and women, rich and poor. Other than a few who appeared to have been beaten up by life, I'd never suspect any of them to be alcoholics.

I opened my car door and slowly walked to the entrance. I hung back, hoping to find the courage to take the next step.

I can't do it. I turned around and bumped into Ricki.

"Ava!" Ricki's hug was the warmest, most sincere hug I'd ever received.

I knew at that moment I was exactly where I needed to be.

"C'mon in, honey. The meeting's gonna start." Ricki took my hand and led me inside. Before we got seated, she said, "You saved my life. Maybe I can do the same for you."

I saved someone's life! I'd made a difference not only in Ricki's life but the life of her mom and daughter—and who knows how many others. Until that moment, I assumed I'd destroyed everything and everyone I touched.

I turned my attention to the speaker, who was celebrating one year of sobriety. He spoke of his personal journey and invited others to share their experiences. Some had hit bottom; others were encouraged by friends or family to attend a meeting before they further damaged their lives. Each story was different, yet all had the same theme: They wanted to stop drinking and knew they couldn't do it alone.

Hello, my name is Ava, and I'm an alcoholic. I whispered the phrase to myself, hoping I'd find the courage to publicly admit my addiction.

All faces looked at me when it was my turn to introduce myself. I saw kind, supportive eyes and friendly smiles. *God, give me courage to admit my frailty.*

"Hello, my name is Ava, and I'm an alcoholic."

It's hard to explain the miracle that followed my admission. I felt God's presence in the room and in me. Looking back, it was as though God had removed my obsession to get high.

I learned the concept of staying sober today—not tomorrow, not next week, not ten years from now. The Twelve Steps were mentioned with emphasis on the first step: Admit we are powerless over alcohol . . . that our lives had become unmanageable.

One day at a time. Would I struggle with addiction every day until I died? Life seemed so much easier without a plan, without daily goals.

Some members left immediately after the formal meeting, while others, including Ricki and me, stayed for coffee. Ricki introduced me to her sponsor and a few of her new friends. Everyone was warm and welcoming. No questions were asked, no answers expected. When the lights flickered, indicating the end of our time, I didn't want to leave.

Ricki didn't pressure me to attend another meeting and didn't invite me for coffee or to her apartment. I understood our friendship, at least for the present, would be confined to meetings.

We hugged before getting into our cars.

"Take care of yourself," she said. "You know where I'll be."

"Thank you, Ricki. Great seeing you."

A sense of calm followed me home. Knowing I was powerless wasn't a new concept, but until that day—June 1, 1986—I'd tried everything I could think of to regain my power. Self-help books were Band-Aids. I'd been numb to reality and my feelings. I didn't know how to live a sober life. But if Ricki, the biggest party girl I knew, could do it, so could I.

Alcoholics Anonymous has saved hundreds of thousands of lives since its inception in 1935. They create an atmosphere of camaraderie and sharing, with respect for individual privacy. They believe in turning your will and life over to a higher power—not necessarily the Christian God, but your own personal concept of God.

With God's help, and the help of AA, I was ready to give sobriety a try.

I made myself a salad when I got home and searched through the mess in my freezer for something to microwave for dinner. Two bottles of chilled vodka waited for me to take the first drink of the evening. I poured the liquid down the sink with no regrets and no congratulations.

One step at a time.

Even though I drank mostly vodka, tequila, and wine, I had a fully stocked liquor cabinet for friends. One by one I emptied the bottles in the sink.

I poured a chilled glass of seltzer with lime to accompany my nuked burrito and enjoyed the clear-headed after-effects of my meal. I grabbed a few cookies and tuned into *60 Minutes*.

My phone rang midway through the show. I jumped to answer but decided to let it go to my answering machine. Diana's stoned voice called for me to join her and the gang for another lost evening.

I deleted the message and went back to TV.

After *60 Minutes*, I went for a walk. The air was clear and warm; the setting sun cast golden rays above the neighboring golf course. I knew better than to declare sobriety, but something had shifted in my soul. A nagging voice in the back of my mind told me I was only fooling myself, but a stronger voice told me I'd found my home.

Back in my apartment, I piled my dance costumes on the bed. Some had cost as much as $200. Each was a work of art, a hand-stitched masterpiece. I could sell them to other dancers or give them to my friends, but that would mean I'd have to enter a bar or risk being sucked into another all-night party. One by one, I dropped them into a garbage bag. Before I walked to the dumpster, I thought about emptying my kitchen garbage into the bag to ensure I wouldn't do a dumpster dive and retrieve them in the morning. But an inner voice told me that wouldn't be necessary.

A fleeting sense of nostalgia passed through my heart as I tossed the bag, but it was soon replaced with a sense of lightness and freedom.

seventy-two

A New World

I considered myself fortunate to have my job at Bella's. Once again, my boss, Martie, encouraged me to attend cosmetology school and offered to help with tuition.

"I've been seriously thinking about it," I told her several days after my first AA meeting.

"Think fast, Ava. Athena Institute's next program begins June 16."

The sixteenth was less than two weeks away. Would I be able to manage work, school, and AA meetings? I thought about the hours I'd spent partying, nursing hangovers, and recovering from painful nights of dancing. *Yes, I'll find the time.*

I still had $30,000 from Warren and a small savings account I'd started for Tommy and Lee. If necessary, I could borrow from either of those to pay my bills. Yes, I'd be able to afford school.

Martie was thrilled when I announced I'd quit dancing and would start at Athena. "You won't regret it."

Self-doubt still rose to the surface, but I now recognized it for what it was—chatter and nonsense.

I'd avoided Warren since before Memorial Day, unsure what I'd say to him. I knew he'd rejoice at my transformation, but would I disappoint him if I went back to my old ways?

I'd been sober for ten days when Warren called. Picking up the phone, I realized his was the first call I'd answered since June 1.

"Been worried about ya," Warren said. "Ev'rything okay?"

"More than okay. I have lots to tell you."

"Wanna meet fer dinner at Mickey's Tavern?"

I wasn't ready to set foot in a bar. "Um-m, how about we go someplace else? Maybe Michael's Ristorante?"

"Sure thing. I'll bring a bottle o' wine. They ain't got a liquor license."

"No wine. I'll explain when I see you."

"Ya look dif'rent somehow," Warren said, once we sat down. "Dif'rent hairstyle or somethin'?"

Was my sobriety that obvious?

"I've been going to AA. I haven't had a drink since May 31."

"No kiddin'? Good fer you." Warren reached across the table and squeezed my hand.

"I quit dancing, too."

Warren raised his eyebrows, accentuating the lines in his forehead.

"And I'm starting cosmetology school on the sixteenth."

"Holy smokes, girl! I'm proud o' you."

Warren's words nearly brought me to tears.

"I got a confession," he said. "I never told ya, but my wife was in AA."

Warren's revelation blew me away. "Why wait till now to tell me?"

"Didn't wanna make ya feel guilty 'bout drinkin' and dancin'. Anyways, it was a long time ago."

"She didn't mind you drinking?" I asked.

"Never brought it home. Only had a beer or two after work. Wasn't till she passed that I'd have a beer at lunch."

I knew if I asked, he'd offer more information. But I thought it best to let him decide how much to tell me. He brought the conversation back to me.

"How ya fixed fer funds? Need help payin' fer school?"

"Martie at the salon is helping. I'll pay for the rest," I said.

"No, I'm payin' the rest."

I knew Warren thought of me as the daughter he never had, but now I realized he saw his wife in me, too. My sobriety would mean nearly as much to Warren as it did to me.

One day at a time. I turn my will and my life over to God. My new statements gave me hope and confidence.

I wanted to share my sobriety with my children, but then remembered Lee's last words: *I want nothing from you.* I hadn't seen him in a year, but Tommy and I had opened an awkward line of communication. He was about to graduate from Pace University. To my surprise, he invited me to his commencement.

I noticed Tom a few rows ahead of me at Tommy's ceremony. Whatever had attracted me to him was long gone. All I saw now was an out-of-shape, middle-aged alcoholic. My instinct was to hide in the bushes and make a quick exit after Tommy received his diploma. But I couldn't do that to my son.

Tom turned to watch Tommy walk down the aisle and spotted me. We made eye contact; he nodded and turned away. After the ceremony, he made his way to me.

"Nice of you to attend." His voice dripped sarcasm.

"I've missed too much of my son's life. I want that to change."

"You really think you can waltz back in after all these years?"

"I'm not the same person I was. I—" I didn't need to explain myself to Tom.

"You're what? Ready to be a mother now that your boy's fully grown?"

Despite the years and distance between us, Tom still had the power to hurt me.

Tommy joined us before we could say more. I longed to hug him and never let go. Instead, I plastered a smile on my face and said, "I'm so proud of you, baby."

I was broken, Tommy, I wanted to say. *I had no survival tools. I'm working my way back, one day at a time. Please, let's start over.*

Tom stood like a petulant child. Did he take any responsibility for the mess we'd made of our lives? Would it change anything if he did?

Before I knew what had happened, Tommy took both our hands and looked at us through moist eyes.

"I can't believe both my parents are here." He tried to smile but instead clenched his lips together to hold back his tears.

None of us said a word. I squeezed his hand, hoping my love would pass to him.

The moment faded as we exited the auditorium. Neither invited me to join them for whatever festivities they had planned.

"Thanks for coming, Mom," he said, before we parted.

I wanted to make plans to get together again. Instead, I thanked God for my sobriety and for the blessings I'd received that day.

seventy-three

More Changes

I attended more than ninety AA meetings in ninety days. I received my thirty-day, sixty-day, and ninety-day chips, which I've kept all these years.

AA helped me distinguish between true friendship and party pals. I realized I had almost no true friends besides Tina in California, Martie at the salon, and Warren. Diana, Missy, and Big Eddie called during the first few weeks but then gave up. I wasn't surprised.

The longer I stayed sober, the clearer my thoughts became. It wasn't easy, but I now had a support network, a job, and the promise of a new career. Through AA, I learned to trust in God and made the decision to turn my life and my will over to him. I accepted the concept of "one day at a time" and made a commitment to work the Twelve Steps.

On June 1, 1987, I celebrated one year of sobriety and completed cosmetology school. I received my one-year chip from AA and sat for the state cosmetology licensing exam. With the help of Warren and Martie, my education was paid for.

"Congratulations!" Martie and Bella's staff shouted as I opened the door to the salon.

My station was filled with balloons and bows. A bottle of sparkling cider sat next to a sheet cake. It dawned on me that I must have passed my exam.

"Now you can work for me full time!" Martie hugged me.

I thought back to celebrations in my former life. Martie would be cutting up lines of coke, while someone else would be passing out hits of speed.

I continued to attend AA meetings daily and began sponsoring new members. Warren and I met for dinner every week or two. Our friendship grew stronger the longer I stayed sober. He was my gift from God, the first person to give me unconditional love.

seventy-four

Nicholas

The next three years flew by. Bella's provided me with a good living. Warren became the father I never had. Sobriety became my new way of life.

And then I met Nick at an AA meeting.

"My name is Nicholas, and I'm an alcoholic." The older man's voice trembled as he made his testimony.

I'd rarely dated since I'd become sober. I wasn't afraid of dating; I just wasn't interested. I loved my work, and my life was full of wonderful people. What more did I need?

Apparently, Nick was exactly who or what I needed. He was tall and lean, with thinning gray hair tied in a ponytail, and kind, green eyes. He reminded me of a poet.

Nick chatted me up after the meeting. Before we knew it, we were the last two in the building.

"Would you like to go for coffee?" he asked.

"I'd like that." Something about his invitation felt like the right thing to do.

We took separate cars to the nearest diner and grabbed a booth. I began the conversation. "Are you looking for a sponsor?"

"I have one."

"Tell me about yourself."

"Well," he began, "as I said at the meeting, I'm fresh out of rehab, and I'm determined to make it stick this time."

"This time?" I asked.

"It's my fourth rehab in the last ten years."

I struggled to hide my surprise. *Maybe coming here with him wasn't such a good idea.*

"Does this time feel different?"

"Kind of. My sister and her husband have been real supportive. I can't let them down."

I decided to give him the benefit of the doubt. After all, my past was littered with flaws.

"You've got them, your sponsor," I reached across the table and took his hand, "and me. Call me anytime."

"Thanks." His deep green eyes locked onto mine.

We exchanged phone numbers and talked for nearly two hours. I learned Nick had been a freelance reporter for years. Since his release from rehab, he had secured a permanent job at the *Princeton Packet*.

Nick consumed my thoughts on my ride home and my dreams that night. *It'll pass*, I told myself.

But it didn't.

I saw Nick at several AA meetings over the next few weeks. He'd break into the sexiest grin whenever he caught my eye. I was falling hard for the guy even though we'd never exchanged last names.

I arrived early to my regular Tuesday evening meeting and was chatting with Chad and Gloria Peterson, one of my favorite AA couples, when Nick walked in. He waved and approached us.

"Hey," he said to all of us, "I see you've met Ava."

I looked at him, confused. How did he know Chad and Gloria?

"*This* is the Ava you've been talking about?" Gloria asked.

"Ava, meet my sister and brother-in-law."

I wanted to melt into the linoleum.

Chad and Gloria appeared as surprised by his announcement as I was. I had no idea what he'd told them. At that point, we were only a couple in my mind. I was determined to take it no further.

Nick took a seat next to Gloria and patted the seat next to him. I shook my head and sat in the back of the room, hoping to make my exit once the meeting ended. He joined me.

"Gloria and Chad are cool," he whispered. "I told them I met someone special, but I didn't have the nerve to ask her out on a real date. They told me to go for it."

That was before they knew it was me.

"I really like you, but I'm an alcoholic," I said. "You should be with someone outside of AA."

"That's what makes it all so perfect. So, how about it—would you go on a real date with me?"

I nodded and turned my attention to the speaker. The meeting had come to order.

seventy-five

In Love

The more we saw of each other, the less I thought about Nick's four rehab experiences. We shared our sobriety stories; he didn't flinch when I told him about Kenya.

We'd been dating for six months when he invited me to spend Thanksgiving with Gloria and Chad.

"I'm cooking the entire meal," he said proudly.

"You're cooking?" I couldn't hide my surprise.

Nick was as much a genius in the kitchen as he was with the written word.

For the past few years, I'd spent the holidays with Warren and his family. Warren knew I'd met someone, but I hadn't gotten up the nerve to introduce him to Nick.

"I'm disappointed, but I understand. Ya wanna spend time with yer fella."

"I knew you'd understand."

"When am I gonna meet yer sweetheart?"

"Soon, I promise." With everything Warren had done for me, I owed him an introduction.

~~~

My relationship with Nick went from casual to committed over the next few months. An occasional overnight at my apartment turned into an occasional night apart. Things were easy between us, probably because we'd been friends before we became lovers.

I reflected on the abuse I had suffered with Tom, the dysfunction with Jack, and the over-the-top insanity with Mike. Being with Nick had a calming effect on me—at least most of the time. I did my best to ignore his occasional mood swings, telling myself it was part of his sobriety struggle.

The biggest blessing was that we didn't need drugs, alcohol, or chaos to keep us together.

Nick called one night about six months into our relationship. "I'll be working late tonight—some big political meeting."

He always reported on local politics and attended evening meetings. Why was this night any different?

"Can you wait up for me? We need to talk," he said.

A wave of anxiety passed through me but quickly dissipated.

"Okay. See you later, sweetie."

"Love ya, Ava."

He tiptoed in around one in the morning. I listened for drunken sounds, but his footsteps were solid. Nothing toppled over. Nothing broke. I felt my shoulders relax.

"Thanks for waiting up." He sat next to me on the bed.

"Is everything okay?" I asked.

"I hope so." He turned toward me with an expression I couldn't describe, then reached into his jacket pocket and pulled out a small box.

"I've never met anyone like you," he began. "You're my soulmate, my lover, my best friend. I'd never have stayed sober without you. Will you marry me?"

He opened the box to reveal a small solitaire diamond ring. "I hope it fits."
~~~

My prior life had been full of surprises. I thought I'd put the unexpected behind me.

Guess I was wrong.

I told myself if the ring fit, we were meant to be together. It did.

"Yes," I whispered.

He held me close. "You've made me the happiest man on the planet."

The more I thought about us as a married couple, the more perfect it seemed. I knew he'd been married three times, but I told myself this time would be different. He was sober, attended regular AA meetings, and had a secure job.

And I've had my share of failed relationships. I convinced myself we'd make it work.

Martie and the rest of the staff congratulated me at work the next day. I noticed imperceptible glances pass between them. They'd warned me about Nick's past. Was that all that worried them, or was there more?

I told myself they didn't know Nick like I did.

I called Warren with my news.

"Can't wait to meet the fella," Warren said.

"You're gonna love him as much as I do. Nick and I want to invite you for dinner at my place. Nick's agreed to cook for us."

"I wouldn't miss it."

We made plans for the following week.

seventy-six

A Wedding

Nick and I set a date for Warren to come to my apartment for dinner.

Nick went out of his way to create a dinner rivaling any five-star restaurant: salmon wrapped in phyllo with a sour cream dill sauce, haricot vert, lyonnaise potatoes, homemade sourdough bread, and crêpes suzette for dessert. I bought a pink damask tablecloth and matching napkins, which Nick folded to look like birds.

Nick was in his element. I was a nervous wreck.

Warren kissed me on the cheek when he arrived.

"Where's this man o' yers?" Warren asked.

"Still in the kitchen," I said. "Wait till you see the feast he's prepared!"

"Smells scrumptious."

Nick heard our voices and came out of the kitchen, drying his hands on an old dish towel.

"My two favorite men in the world! Warren, meet Nick Ravelli."

Warren had a face that never lied. His eyes shot over to me, then to the floor. He shuffled his feet, took a deep breath, and finally offered Nick his hand.

"Nice to meet ya," Warren said.

"Likewise." Nick smiled broadly at Warren. "Ava can't say enough about you."

"Same here," Warren mumbled.

"Gotta get back to my salmon. Dinner'll be ready in a few minutes." Nick hurried back to the kitchen.

I'd rarely seen Warren annoyed. The look he gave me shouted disappointment and confusion.

"He's an old man," Warren said in a stage whisper. "What the hell are ya doin'?"

"Age is only a number, and he's only sixty."

"What's gonna happen in ten years? Ya wanna be pushin' his wheelchair?"

"You never know what life will bring," I said. "I found somebody I love, somebody who makes me happy."

"I ain't gonna tell ya what to do with yer life," Warren said. "Sixty ain't old like it used ta be, but from what you've told me, the guy's more like eighty inside. If yer dead set on him, live together but please don't marry him."

"Dinner is served!" Nick's announcement brought an end to Warren's warnings.

The meal was spectacular. Warren put his feelings aside and changed back into the Warren I loved.

Nick was anxious to set a date for our wedding. I urged him to wait a year. Much as I was in love, Warren's words lingered in my mind. Nick reluctantly agreed, provided we could continue to live together. We picked Saturday, June 20, 1992, as our date and booked the Titusville Inn on the Delaware River as our venue.

Visiting the Delaware River brought back memories of Jack and my disastrous second marriage.

This time will be different. I was twenty years older, sober for six years, and marrying a talented, sober, kind man.

Warren agreed to walk me down the aisle and give me away. Martie and Warren's sister, Sally, were my bridesmaids. Chad and Gloria had accepted me into their family. I was confident life and marriage would work out for me as Ava Ravelli.

I thought it best not to invite Tommy and Lee. Tommy had become increasingly distant. Lee had ignored me for years. Still, a large part of me wished they could share my joy.

"I know yer upset about the kids," Warren said when I told him they weren't coming. "Think about it from their point o' view. Tommy won't know nobody there. Lee told ya years ago he wanted nothin' to do with you."

"I know, but they're the only family I've got," I said.

"Ya got me, Nick's folks, and a ton o' friends."

Warren was right. Family wasn't bound by blood.

What I remember about my third wedding day is a sparkling blue sky, two hundred well-wishers, and a spectacular feast prepared by the Inn.

We toasted with sparkling grape juice, which tasted sweeter than champagne. After the reception, a limo drove us to the Philadelphia Airport Hilton. We left the next morning for a week in Barbados.

Our gifts and cards were waiting for us when we returned. Most guests had given us money.

"We should do something special with this money," I said.

"How about we buy a condo?" Nick suggested.

Where did that *come from?* I hesitated before asking him, "Don't you like it here?"

"This is your apartment," Nick said. "I want a place that's *ours*. Between the gifts and what we have in the bank, we've got a nice down payment. We even have enough for some new furniture."

Owning our own home would give us roots and stability, two things I longed for. "Let's do it!"

"My boss knows someone in Willingboro who's got a condo for sale," Nick said.

"But we've got jobs and friends here."

"Our friends will still be our friends. And it's only a forty-five-minute drive to Princeton," Nick said. "Condos are cheaper down there. And wait'll you see pictures of the place."

seventy-seven

New Home, Old Life

I fell in love with the condo almost as quickly as I fell for Nick. Two months later, we were homeowners.

I hated the forty-five-minute drive but told myself Nick was making the same commute. As he got busier at the paper, I saw less and less of him.

Most evenings, Nick would wake me when he got home. Those midnight moments were special for both of us. Then, one night several months after we moved, he didn't come home.

I woke at five in the morning to an empty bed. I panicked. Had he been in an accident? On life support in the hospital?

I called the newspaper and spoke to one of the pressmen.

"Sorry, Mrs. Ravelli, nobody's here but us guys in the press room."

"Thank—" I heard Nick's key in the front door.

Nick's uneven footsteps sounded on the stairs. I turned off the light and pretended to be asleep.

He tiptoed into the bedroom, tripping over nothing. I was used to cigarette odor on his clothing, but that morning another odor wafted into the room—marijuana. He ignored me and headed for the bathroom.

Should I question him? Accuse him? Maybe he'd given someone a ride. Maybe he'd been out with friends from work. I decided to wait for him to say something.

Freshly showered, he came to bed and kissed me awake.

"Hi, hon, how'd you sleep?"

"Hi, Nick," I whispered, pretending to come to consciousness. "What time is it?"

"Almost morning," he replied. "I stayed at the office to finish my story."

Liar. This wasn't the first time I suspected Nick of using drugs. His behavior had become increasingly erratic since we moved, his mood swings and impulsiveness more noticeable.

"I'm exhausted," he said.

I took the hint. "I'll let you sleep, Nick. See you tonight."

Nick had left his jacket and shoes on the floor just inside the front door. When I picked up his jacket, a baggie fell out. It contained half a dozen pre-rolled joints.

I wanted to shake him awake, throw the baggie in his face, and send him packing. He told me he'd been attending AA meetings on his way to or from the office. He knew I'd struggled with sobriety for years. Why couldn't he share his struggle with me?

He probably thought he'd let me down. Like me, he was a flawed human being. I decided to say nothing until we had time for a heart-to-heart talk.

I left him a note on the kitchen table: *Can we talk when you get home tonight?*

Halfway to the salon, I regretted leaving the note. He'd know I'd found his stash and have time to concoct an excuse. He'd think I was invading his personal space and accuse me of not trusting him. But the damage was done.

When I arrived home from work, Nick was long gone. His reply read: Working late. Let's talk tomorrow. Love you.

I spent another lonely evening in front of the tube, and another solitary night in bed.

We both had the following day off. Once he was awake, I brought him coffee and began the conversation.

"I found your stash."

"I thought that's what you wanted to talk about," he said. "It's not mine."

An addict's famous excuse.

He knew I didn't believe him. "Seriously, hon, it belongs to one of the cub reporters. He's trying to go straight and asked me to hold it for him."

"But he knows your history, right?" I asked.

"That's why he asked me. He knows he can trust me."

I wanted to believe my husband. I took his hand, looked into his eyes, and said, "It's okay if you slipped. Come to my meeting this morning. Get back on the program."

"*I'm not using!*" Nick had never raised his voice to me before.

I didn't want to argue. "I believe you but come with me. We haven't been to a meeting together in weeks."

"I'm sick of those damn meetings. Nothing but a bunch of drunks crying the blues."

"Then I'll see you when I get back." I hated the anger in my voice.

He hugged me. "I'm fine, just tired."

After my meeting Nick was in an upbeat mood. "Sorry about before."

"No problem." What else could I say?

"I've got an idea," he said. "You know how we've been wanting to redecorate? How about we get started?"

He knew just how to lift my spirits. "Can we go to Kachina Village?"

Nick and I were enamored with the Southwest and had talked about traveling to the Grand Canyon and Sedona, Arizona. Life kept getting in the way, so we fed our fantasy at Kachina Village, a shop devoted to everything Arizona.

From dreamcatchers to Kokopelli, from desert scenes to turquoise accents, we transformed our condo into a southwestern paradise.

"I love our new home, and I love you," I said.

"It's perfect, and so are you," Nick said.

All it took was a trip to Kachina Village.

"All we need now is a new couch," I said.

"Maybe we could hold off on the couch and take that trip to Arizona we've been talking about."

"It's a deal." I couldn't think of a more perfect way to cement our relationship and get Nick away from drugs.

We both had two weeks of vacation coming up in July.

"It'll be hot out there," Nick said.

"It's not a problem for me," I said.

"Me neither."

seventy-eight

Arizona

Nick and I fell in love with Arizona's wide-open spaces, piercing blue skies, and majestic sunsets. We began our trip in Scottsdale, drove to Sedona, and from there traveled to the Grand Canyon.

"Can you believe it's one-hundred-and-ten degrees?" I thought back to my years in Florida when I'd break a sweat at eighty. "This is paradise."

"We have to move," Nick said.

"Were you thinking of Scottsdale?"

"Where else? There's money here, and I'm sure I can find work."

Money wasn't a priority for me, but a wealthy area meant more demand for manis and pedis.

"I picked up one of those real estate magazines in the lobby," Nick said. "Let's call a realtor and check out some properties."

"We're leaving tomorrow. Let's take the book with us and think this through."

"Are you backing out?" Nick's impulsiveness often got the better of him.

"We need to sell our condo before we can think about buying another place."

Disappointment registered on his face. "You're right. It's just so perfect here."

"It'll happen," I said. "I want this as much as you."

~~~

We met with a realtor when we arrived back in New Jersey. He explained we'd take a hit since housing prices had fallen and encouraged us to wait a year or two.

"He's full of shit," Nick swore as we left the Century 21 office. "Let's talk to somebody else."

"I think we should listen to him. Do you really want to lose $20,000?"

"It's only money. This is our life." He stormed across the parking lot. I followed at a slower pace.

Nick's moodiness meant trouble. I wasn't surprised when he skipped our evening AA meeting and met some friends from work. My sober spouse was slowly disintegrating.

We saw little of each other over the next few days. I knew it was up to me to reestablish our line of communication.

"Can we talk?" I began.

"About what?" Nick continued to brood.

"Arizona. I think we should listen to the realtor."

"I know," he said. "I'm just disappointed."

"Me, too, but if it's meant to be, it'll happen. God's timing isn't always the same as ours."

"God? What does he know?"

"More than we'll ever know," I said.

Reluctantly, Nick came around to my way of thinking. We decided to give it a year.

A year turned into almost two.

"Ava, guess what?" Nick surprised me early one evening in the spring of 1995. He picked me up and danced me around the living room.

"You sold the condo and we're moving to Arizona?"

"Better. I found a new job!"
~~~

A new job meant he'd lost interest in moving. I hid my disappointment and pretended to share his enthusiasm.

"Tell me," I said.

"I met with the editor-in-chief of the *Burlington County Times* right here in Willingboro. He was impressed with my writing and asked me to come on board. I can practically walk to work. I'll be making more money, too. Maybe we can afford that couch we wanted."

All I wanted was to leave New Jersey. A couch wouldn't make a bit of difference.

"Now that I'll be working close to home, maybe you should look for something here in town," he said.

Martie had made me the manager at Bella's. She planned on opening a second salon and hoped I'd transition to manage the new location. Martie believed in me and had been there in the early days of my sobriety. I felt a responsibility to stay with her until we moved to Arizona, but each day I tiptoed farther from my dream of life in the Southwest.

"And we'd have more time together," Nick said.

More time with my husband was enough of a reason to switch jobs.

"Maybe I'll check out Blissful, that salon down the street."

Blissful had a HELP WANTED sign in the window.

Please let it be a nail tech job.

A young, bubbly blond greeted me. "Are you here for an appointment?"

"I'm here about a job."

"We're looking for a mani-pedi person," she said.

"That's me! Oh, sorry." I held out my hand. "I'm Ava Ravelli."

"Katie Winslow. C'mon back and we can talk."

Katie and I immediately hit it off. I agreed to start in two weeks.

~

Martie, my coworkers, and clients had been my family for nearly nine years. Giving my notice wasn't easy.

"You'll always have a home here," Martie said.

They threw me a small going-away party. My tears were a mixture of grief and relief.

If I thought I'd see more of Nick, I was mistaken. Most days he left the house around eleven in the morning and didn't get home until after midnight.

When I expressed concern about the long days, he said he had a few free hours each afternoon.

"Is that when you go to your meetings?" I asked.

"Screw those meetings. I'm too busy."

Each time I brought up Alcoholics Anonymous, he had an excuse. I knew Nick well enough to keep silent, at least for now.

seventy-nine

Surprise, Surprise

Katie welcomed me to Blissful and did what she could to make me feel at home. "Ava, meet Suzi, our other nail tech. I think you two will hit it off."

"Let me show you the ropes." Suzi smiled and led me to the mani-pedi area.

Katie was right. Suzi and I clicked immediately. She even looked like me—thin and blond—but with a huge smile and a great sense of humor.

Our schedules were staggered most days, but on Wednesdays we both got off at five o'clock.

"Hey, Ava, how'd you like to go for a drink after work?"

I'd shared some of my life with Suzi, but not my sobriety story. "Sorry, I don't drink. Believe it or not, today is my ninth anniversary of sobriety."

"Then we definitely need to celebrate. No alcohol necessary."

"I like the way you think!"

We left our cars at the salon and walked to Pitch Perfect Café, a favorite spot for non-drinkers. The coffee house served light meals and light jazz and allowed patrons to linger long after their plates and cups were empty.

"Don't you want to get home to Nick?" Suzi glanced at her watch. "It's after nine."

I snorted. "I'll be lucky if I see him before midnight."

"What kind of marriage is that?"

"I've been asking myself the same question."

On my way home, I thought about the past nine years. For the most part, life was good. I was secure in my sobriety and my career. I had my AA friends, friends from work, and now Suzi. Nick wasn't perfect but had always been there for me. We were a team, even though one player was absent most of the time.

To my surprise, my husband was home waiting for me.

"Where've you been?" Nick was sprawled on the couch watching CNN.

"Suzi and I went out to celebrate my ninth anniversary."

"Huh?"

"Of sobriety."

Was that a look of guilt passing across his face?

"Right, sorry I forgot. Congratulations!" He hugged me.

I swore I smelled alcohol on his breath before he turned away.

"Be right back, then we can celebrate for real." Nick went into the bathroom. When he returned to the living room, he'd brushed his teeth, used mouthwash, and washed his face.

I pretended to ignore his deception.

Two weeks later, on a Friday evening, I waited for Nick to come home, I relaxed on our recliner and thought about a move to Arizona. I'd turned fifty-one in March. Nick's sixty-fourth birthday was around the corner. How many years did we have left? Didn't we deserve to spend them in the Southwest, not in some glorified New Jersey living room?

The real estate market was still in a slump, but what was more important—our happiness or our wallets? I promised myself I'd talk to Nick that night.

Nick arrived home long after I fell asleep.

"Wake up, hon. I've got a surprise." A faint odor of alcohol nudged me awake. "Hmm—" I struggled to wake up. "I want to talk, too."

He ignored me. "Guess what! I booked a trip to Cozumel!"

Nick's impulsiveness continued to surprise me. "Seriously? We just started new jobs. I can't take off work, and neither can you."

"I told my boss we had the trip booked before I started at the paper. Tell your boss the same thing."

"I can't lie."

"Then tell her the truth," he said. "Tell her I surprised you for our anniversary."

I shrugged. "If I lose my job over this, I'll never forgive you."

"You won't. Now, what were you going to tell me?"

"Nothing." I knew better than to bring up Arizona.

Katie couldn't have been more supportive. "Go, Ava, have a blast. We'll be closed over the Fourth of July holiday, and it'll be a morgue in here the rest of the week."

"Thanks, Katie. You're the best."

"I know," she smiled.

Nick and I had a fantastic time in Cozumel. Our room overlooked the ocean. We ate breakfast in bed each morning, then left for a day of sightseeing or the beach. I never once suspected him of drinking or drugging. The trip was exactly what our relationship needed.

Once we returned home, my husband became distant and irritable. I began smelling alcohol on his breath again and pot on his clothing. I knew he was stressed and tried to coax him back to AA.

"I'm fine," was his usual response.

Pressuring him would only make him angry, which could lead to more substance abuse, so I let it drop.

~~~
~~~

Early one evening two weeks after our trip, my phone rang.

"Hello?"

"It's me." Nick never called from work.

"Are you okay?"

"I'm fine. Just wondering if you'll be home later. We need to talk." Nick's voice sounded artificially cheery.

"What's up?"

"We'll talk when I get home."

A knot formed in my gut. "Okay. Love you."

"Right." The line went dead.

I assumed he wanted to talk about getting back to sobriety. I'd never confronted him about his recent lapses. Or maybe he, like me, was ready to move to a warmer climate. All I could do was wait.

Nick was ready to move on, but not to Arizona. He stumbled in around ten o'clock, righted himself, and headed for the bathroom. He wasn't smiling when he joined me in the living room.

He looked at me, then turned his gaze to the opposite wall. "I want a divorce."

Once the shock wore off, I turned to him. "*What?*"

Calmly, he repeated, "I want a divorce."

"Can we talk about it? Is it something I've done?"

"No, and no. I don't want to be married anymore."

"We can work things out. Maybe go for counseling?"

"Nope."

Timidly, I asked, "Is there someone else?"

He answered without hesitation. "The office manager at the *Times*."

A deluge of emotions passed through my head and into my heart: hurt, jealousy, loss, but most of all, confusion. I knew things hadn't been great between us, but how could I have missed the signs?

"But we just had a blast in Cozumel. We talked about moving to Scottsdale."

"Cozumel was Cozumel. Scottsdale was your dream."

For a moment, I doubted my sanity. It *was* Nick who planned our vacation. It was Nick who shared my Arizona dream.

"I'll get a few things and get out of your hair," he said.

"Nick, please—"

"Don't make this any harder than it needs to be. I'll be back for the rest of my stuff in a few days."

I couldn't bear to see him leave, so I went into the kitchen to make a cup of tea. I clenched my teeth to hold back my tears and waited for the slam of the front door. All I heard was a gentle click of the lock. Seconds later the tea kettle whistled, signaling the end of my third marriage.

eighty

A New World

On Sunday morning, I headed to my regular AA meeting. I'd gotten no sleep the night before, but I needed the group support. I can't say the meeting lessened my pain, but I left with new resolve, which lasted until I came home to an empty house. Most of Nick's things still coexisted with mine, reminding me of yet another failed relationship.

Although Warren and I were still close, we saw less of each other since I'd moved. Distance wasn't all that was keeping us apart. He'd found a girlfriend, who was now his fiancée.

I needed to hear his voice, so I called him.

"Hi, Warren."

"Ava! How's it goin'?"

"Terrible." I broke into a wave of tears.

He waited patiently for me to regain control. I told him about Nick. Although he gave me words of support, I sensed an "I told you so" in the background.

"Do ya want me to come down and sit with ya?"

"No, just hearing your voice makes me feel better." I didn't want to take him away from his new life, nor did I want him making the long drive by himself.

We talked until I was spent.

I'd stayed alone many nights, but this time felt different. I wanted to wall off Nick's side of the bed and pretend it didn't exist. I fell into a difficult sleep, filled with images of my past.

It was dark when I awoke. I checked the time—four in the morning. I'd slept eight hours but was still exhausted. While my coffee brewed, I pulled out a notebook and made two columns. The first I titled, "What I've Done Wrong," the second, "What I've Done Right."

Column one went on for three pages, starting with my marriage to Tom and ending with my marriage to Nick. I had two entries in column two: career and sobriety.

Through all my sadness, I never craved a drink or any kind of drug. And I never thought about changing careers.

For the moment, my depression lifted, but it returned full force when I arrived at work. Suzi immediately knew something was wrong. She comforted me as only a true friend could.

"That bastard doesn't deserve you," Suzi said. "You've always been there for him. When was he there for you?"

I knew she was right. "But why didn't I see it coming?"

"You're in love with the idea of him. That clouded your vision."

"How'd you get so wise?"

"Been there, done that," she replied. "C'mon, we've got a busy day."

I immersed myself in work and pushed Nick to the back of my mind.

When I got home that evening, Nick's personal things were gone. He'd left me with everything but our large-screen TV. I searched for a note but found none.

Sadness overwhelmed me. I imagined myself a lonely old woman living out her days in a New Jersey suburb.

Reality hit two weeks later when I sat down to pay our monthly bills. I called Nick at the paper to ask for his share of the expenses.

"I can't help you, Ava. I've got bills of my own to pay."

"I can't do this alone!"

"Your name's on everything. The bills are yours."

I nearly threw the phone across the room.

"And I've got a divorce to pay for. Don't call me again."

And with that, Nick Ravelli was out of my life.

Money was tight but I managed to keep up the mortgage payments. I bought nothing but a second-hand TV. I lived on frozen dinners and went out only to work and AA meetings. By October, I'd resigned myself to my new life.

Then I received the divorce papers.

Nick asked for nothing. The condo and everything it contained belonged to me. If I could hold on until the real estate market picked up, I could sell and move to an apartment. But day by day, my finances dwindled, and my depression flourished.

It was another lonely evening—just a TV dinner and me—when my phone rang.

"Hello?"

"It's Lee."

"Lee! It's wonderful to hear your voice." *Was my son calling to reconcile with me?*

"I'm calling to tell you Tommy's getting married."

My boy is getting married!

"His fiancée's parents have no money. I asked Dad for help, but he can't pay for the entire wedding. I'm asking you to chip in."

"I'm so sorry. This couldn't have come at a worse time. My husband left me with nothing except bills."

"Another husband? How many is that?"

I ignored his question and asked, "How are you doing?"

"This isn't about me. It's about doing what's right for my brother, your son."

"I just can't. When is the wedding?" *Why wasn't I invited? Why hadn't Tommy called?*

Lee's voice took on a bitter note. "Can't say I'm surprised."

"Lee, I—"

My son interrupted. "Don't misconstrue my call. I want nothing to do with you. This is only about Tommy."

His bitterness drove a knife into my heart. "I'm sorry you feel that way. I want to make things right with you."

A hollow dial tone was his response.

If I thought my depression couldn't go deeper, I was mistaken. Lee's words broke my heart into more jagged pieces. I knew I'd lost him ten years ago, but I thought Tommy and I had a chance. How could he leave me out of his wedding?

I left him out of my weddings. Guess he learned by example.

eighty-one

Counseling

If I called Tommy to ask about his wedding, he'd know Lee had called. I decided to wait for a call from him. None came.

Finally, in November, I called Tommy to wish him a happy birthday.

"What's new?" I asked.

"Not much. I'm getting married."

I feigned surprise. "That's wonderful, honey! Tell me all about it."

"There's not much to tell. It's gonna be a small ceremony. We don't have much money."

I wanted to be part of my son's wedding, to watch him take his vows, to share his excitement. I waited for an invitation, but none came.

We chatted a few minutes more before saying goodbye.

I thought my heart had broken when Nick left me. It was now completely shattered.

Our divorce was simple, quick, and painful. At my attorney's office, I put pen to paper and signed *Ava Ravelli.*

Who am I? Ava Ravelli had a nice ring to it, but it was not who I was or who I wanted to be.

I began life as Ava Stanton, a name taken from me when my

mother married my stepfather. Tom gave me his last name, which I kept until I married Jack. Although our marriage was short-lived, Jack's name stayed with me through Florida, Kenya, and the end of my dancing career. I'd eagerly taken Nick's name, hoping to erase my past. His name now felt like a curse.

Suzi took me out to dinner to celebrate, or mourn, my divorce.

"You can celebrate your freedom or live in the past," she said.

Neither extreme felt right.

"I need a new start. I'm thinking about changing my name."

"And go back to Ava Novak?"

"The only name that feels right to me is Stanton, my birth father's name."

"Ava Stanton. I like it!"

The name flowed from her tongue. "I like it, too. It's a name no one can take from me."

"Own it, Ava."

"I will." I promised myself for the rest of my life I would remain Ava Stanton.

Although I had much to be grateful for, I couldn't shake my depression or the dream of Arizona I'd shared with Nick. I plowed through my days and cried myself to sleep at night.

At an AA meeting in November 1995, a woman shared how counseling helped keep her sober. I approached her after the meeting and asked for more information.

"Her name is Dr. Brenner, and she specializes in counseling alcoholics."

"I'm secure in my sobriety," I said. "I have other issues I need to work on."

"Dr. Brenner will be perfect for you. She understands our dynamic." She handed me a business card. "No need to mention my name. Just say you heard about her at a meeting. She'll get it."

"Thanks." For the first time in months, I felt a glimmer of hope.

~~~

Dr. Brenner was supportive and understanding. She coaxed information from me slowly, as I learned to trust her. I shared my earliest memories, the trauma of my first marriage, and my life as an addict.

"You know God created you as a perfect human being," Dr. Brenner began, "but even the most perfect person breaks down. Think about a new car. You drive it out of the showroom and across the country. You fill it with gas but never maintain it. Eventually, that car will break down. You can wax it, but it still won't run properly. You open the hood and look inside. You know something's wrong but without the proper tools, the car will never run properly."

"I'm the car, correct? And AA is the wax?"

"You can look at it that way. Ava, you've been fighting for your life with no tools. You've experienced trauma, which has affected your body and soul. I'm sure you've heard the old saying about insanity—"

"I don't think so."

"The definition of insanity is repeating the same thing over and over, expecting different results. You're a bright, capable, beautiful woman. But without proper nurturing, you'll continue to be stuck in the past."

Dr. Brenner's words hit home.

"So, because I received no love from my parents, I continue to look for love from people who are incapable of returning that love."

"Exactly."

I thought for a moment. "You could say my people-picker is broken."

She laughed. "Your people-picker may be broken, but you are finding your tools."

Each week Dr. Brenner and I dug deeper. I learned I'd been codependent upon each of the men in my life, putting their needs in front of mine.
~~~

"Think about what the flight attendant teaches you about your oxygen mask. Put your mask on first. If you can't breathe, you can't help anyone else."

I nodded in agreement, then leaned back into my chair without another word.

"What's going on for you, Ava?"

We'd covered so much ground, yet a giant boulder sat between us.

"I've gotten a lot from our sessions, and I've learned about myself."

"You're always welcome to discontinue our meetings, but in my professional opinion, we still have lots to work on."

"I know. It's just—"

"You can trust me."

It was now or never. "When Nick and I were married, we fell in love with the Southwest. We took a trip to Arizona and promised ourselves we'd move. It was the perfect dream until we came home and realized we'd take a financial hit on our condo. We decided to wait a year or two, but by that time Nick fell in love with someone else and destroyed our dream. So now, I'm living in a condo I can't afford, full of southwestern decor. Every time I come home, I'm reminded of what I've lost."

Dr. Brenner stared at me and said simply, "Why can't it be your dream?"

I stared at her in silence.

"Why do you need a man to fulfill your dream?"

I'd never imagined moving or doing anything so huge by myself. "But it would be like I was running away from New Jersey and my problems."

"Or you could be running toward Arizona and *your* dream."

My head exploded with possibilities.

eighty-two

Arizona Again

As the calendar turned to 1996, I called a realtor who warned me I'd take a loss on my condo. I knew if I didn't take a loss in real estate, I'd take a greater loss in life. I signed the listing agreement.

In June, I celebrated my ten-year anniversary of sobriety and mourned the one-year end of my marriage. But my realtor had lined up a buyer.

I had a vacation coming up in late July. I needed to see Arizona one more time to make sure my dream was still alive. I wanted Suzi to make the trip with me, but she was needed at the salon, so I decided to make the trip solo. I booked a flight to Phoenix and five nights at a small boutique hotel. The trip would put me in debt, but if I didn't go, I'd always regret it.

I deserve to live my dream. Those words kept me going until my plane landed. Once I left the airport in my rental car, I felt I was where I belonged.

Give it time. Don't just assume. Those words ran through my head on the way to Scottsdale. Once I parked the car and stood on the adobe porch of my hotel, I knew for certain I was home.

How would I coordinate the move? Details and obstacles assaulted me until I let it all go. I told myself at best, I'd find a job and a place to live. At worst, I'd fly back to Jersey, rent a small apartment, and keep my job at Blissful.

If it's meant to happen, everything will fall into place.

My hotel offered free copies of the *Arizona Republic*, the state's largest daily newspaper. I combed the classifieds for salon jobs and found several that looked promising. I bought a detailed map of Phoenix and Scottsdale and circled the locations. I knew I wanted to work and live in Scottsdale, but I needed guidance.

Guidance came in the form of an elderly couple who joined me on the porch. They were elegantly dressed, and the woman's nails were done to perfection.

"Your manicure is beautiful," I said.

"I found the best manicurist not far from here. I've got her card here somewhere." She rummaged through her handbag and handed me a business card.

"Thank you."

"Are you here on holiday?" she asked.

"I'm hoping to move here. I'm on a fact-finding mission."

She laughed. "My name is Charlotte. My husband is Harold."

"I'm Ava. Nice to meet you."

Harold nodded and picked up his newspaper.

"What kind of work are you looking for?"

"I'm a nail technician. I saw some ads in the paper, but I know nothing about which areas are good."

"Maybe I can help. We've wintered here for the past fifteen years. We're down from Canada for a wedding."

I handed Charlotte the map. She took a mechanical pencil and circled different areas. "Here and here are the best neighborhoods for shopping and business. Are you looking to buy or rent?"

"Rent, at least for now."

"And what about your husband and children?"

A cloud passed across my vision, but it soon passed. "I'm divorced. My children are grown."

"You may want to check out rentals over here." Charlotte drew another circle. "They built apartments and condominiums back in the '70s."

We chatted until she and Harold left for dinner. I thanked her and wondered if I'd just met another angel.

I ordered room service and spent the rest of my evening scanning the Yellow Pages and mapping out a route for the following day.

My first stop was Glamour Nails, the salon Charlotte recommended. They had no openings but took a copy of my resume and a letter of recommendation written by one of my favorite clients.

It's not meant to be.

I drove through the business district, stopping at every salon with no luck.

It's not meant to be. How many times would I repeat the phrase before giving up?

I checked my watch and saw it was after two o'clock. I needed a break and stopped at a café near the residential area Charlotte had pointed out. Even though the mercury was topping 110 degrees, I sat outside, greedy for every breath of dry heat.

My avocado salad was total perfection, not like the avocados back home that were hard one day and rotten the next. As I nibbled, I noticed Harmony Spa in an upscale strip mall across the street. I didn't remember seeing it in the Yellow Pages. I decided to check it out.

A smiling receptionist greeted me when I entered.

"I'm here about a job. I'm a nail tech," I said, trying to radiate confidence.

"Really? Let me get Rebecca, the owner."

I couldn't imagine why she acted so surprised and eager to find her boss.

As I waited, I checked out the business. Their overhead menu included hair, facials, waxing, and massage in addition to nails. Prices were in line with New Jersey prices, unlike the other salons I'd visited, whose prices were significantly lower.

Despite the pricing, the place hummed with activity. Soft background music blended with the southwestern decor. A light scent of lavender floated through the air.

"Hi, I'm Rebecca." A forty-something brunette held out her hand.

"I'm Ava Stanton." I loved saying my new name.

"How did you know we were hiring?" she asked.

They're hiring! "I took a chance and walked in. Here's my resume and a letter of recommendation."

"You're from New Jersey?"

"I'm moving to Scottsdale," I said. "I'm here for a few days looking for a job and a place to live."

"Well, Ava Stanton, you're in luck. Our lead manicurist gave notice today. When can you start?"

When can I start? I hadn't thought that far ahead.

"I need to go back to Jersey, give notice at my job, and arrange for a mover. Probably not for two weeks."

"Hmm, two weeks? Our manicurist will be leaving in ten days," Rebecca said.

Please, God, make it work.

"I'm a great believer in fate," Rebecca said after a moment. "It's summer, our slow season. We should be able to work things out. Okay, you're hired!"

If it's meant to happen, everything will fall into place.

"Thank you! Now all I need is a place to live."

"That shouldn't be hard," Rebecca said. "Come with me. We'll fill out some paperwork, and I'll give you leads on apartments."

July and August were prime months to find rentals, as most snowbirds had flown home for the summer. Landlords were eager to rent to a year-round tenant. The apartments were nice enough, but none felt right.

If it's meant to happen, everything will fall into place. I had two more days to find my ideal home.

The next morning, I stopped at a charming adobe community a few miles from Harmony Spa. The manager showed me two units overlooking garages and dumpsters—not my idea of a southwestern landscape.

"I got one more unit, but it's fifty bucks more a month," the manager said.

"Fifty bucks more than what?" I asked.

He quoted me the monthly rent. I knew salaries were lower in Arizona than New Jersey, but judging from what I'd seen at Harmony Spa, I was confident I could earn enough to swing it.

He took me to a one-bedroom apartment on the second floor. The living room and bedroom floors were done in deep-pile, beige carpeting, the bathroom and kitchen in beige tile. From a small balcony, I had a view of the community pool and distant mountains.

Without hesitation I said, "I'll take it!"

Back at my hotel, I sat on the porch and contemplated my good fortune. At age fifty-two, when most lives were winding down, mine was beginning to take shape. I spent my final day in Scottsdale enjoying the sights and sounds of the city.

eighty-three

Goodbye . . . Hello

The first thing I did when I returned to New Jersey was to transfer my professional license from New Jersey to Arizona. Next, I arranged for a mover and a company to ship my 1986 Pontiac Sunbird. I then stopped at Blissful to give my notice. Two weeks later, Suzi, Katie, and I said our private goodbyes, then joined the entire salon for my going-away party.

I was leaving behind my AA sponsor and those I had sponsored. I thought back on the woman I'd been when I attended my first meeting. That woman would never have had the courage to move across the country alone, confident her sobriety would travel with her.

I was proud of who I'd become, but that didn't mean I was leaving without remorse. The distance between my boys and me would be there no matter where I lived. I prayed that over time, we could heal our broken lives.

Saying goodbye to Warren was bittersweet. He'd been my lifesaver, my friend, the father I never had. He'd remarried and had his sister and family, so I knew he'd be taken care of.

"I wouldn't be here today if it wasn't for you, Warren," I confided at our last meeting.

"Sure ya would've. Ya didn't need me. All I did was be yer friend."

"I'll treasure your friendship forever," I said.

~~~

For five days I lived out of a suitcase and slept on an air mattress until my things arrived. I danced around the empty apartment singing, "It's all mine!" The dream belonged to me and no one else. I'd begun a new chapter with a clear and sober mind. Nobody could take that from me.

At Harmony Spa, Rebecca introduced me to the other employees and some regular clients. I agreed to do a few manis and pedis gratis. Soon, women were asking for me, tipping generously, and making regular appointments. Before long, I was earning enough to cover my living expenses and more.

Three days after my arrival, I plugged myself into local AA meetings, which was where I met Shelley, my Scottsdale sponsor. Back in New Jersey, I'd had a positive relationship with my sponsor, but it never grew beyond the parameters of addiction. Shelley was different. We clicked and became best friends.

By October, the one-hundred-degree days slid into the eighties, and the snowbirds arrived. My chair was booked every day, and I began paying off my debts. Business boomed through early spring, when our weather warmed, and the northerners returned home.

I began sponsoring other alcoholics, mostly younger women. I'd let them know I was a no-nonsense sponsor.

"If you're not serious about getting sober, don't even ask me to sponsor you," I'd say and wait for their response. Some brushed me off; others agreed and soon gave up. I saw myself in them and hoped eventually they'd find the serenity I'd known for many years.

After two years in Scottsdale, I began sponsoring a thirty-something woman who'd recently gotten her real estate license.

"You should really buy a place, Ava," she said.

"I lost so much on my Jersey condo. I don't think I could do it again."
~~~

She knew some of my story, including my disastrous third marriage. "Just 'cause you got burned once doesn't mean it'll happen again."

I still hesitated.

"Every month you pay rent is like throwing your money down the drain."

She had a point. "Okay, why not?"

Like most Scottsdale communities, Desert View featured adobe buildings landscaped with cactus and palms.

"They cater to seniors and snowbirds," my realtor said. "I know you're neither, but it'll be quiet, and you won't have to worry about a bunch of twenty-somethings moving in."

The second-floor condo was about the size of my apartment, which suited me perfectly. A small gym, pool, and clubhouse were included with my monthly fee.

"The original owner upgraded everything." She showed me an up-to-date kitchen and bath, hardwood floors, and gorgeous lighting.

"It's perfect," I said. "I'd like to bring a friend to see the place before I commit."

At age fifty-four, I'd finally learned to think before acting.

I brought Shelley to see the place.

"Ava, it's you," Shelley said.

"And it won't cost much more than my apartment."

"What about a down payment?" she asked.

"It's only $92,000. They're asking 10 percent down. I think I can swing it."

Shelley looked at me with concern. "You'll be back where you started when you moved here."

"Financially, yes, but look what I'm gaining."

"What about your debts?"

I still had credit card debt from my move and first few months in Scottsdale. "You're good at math, Shelley. Let's do the numbers."

We sat on a bench outside the condo. Shelley played with her calculator, then turned to me.

"If you don't mind carrying your current debt for a while longer, you can swing it."

The next day, I put in my offer. Three months later, I moved into my new home.

Before I unpacked a single box, I poured a glass of sparkling cider, stood on my balcony, and toasted. "To me!"

I thought back to the day nearly thirty-six years before when my mother threw me out of the house. I reflected on the loss of family, home, and security. I'd never been shown unconditional love, never had peace of mind, yet I'd survived.

Three failed marriages, a child whom I hadn't seen in thirteen years, another child who barely acknowledged me. Prison, addiction, and sorrow, yet I'd survived.

There must be a higher purpose. I promised myself I'd find that purpose.

eighty-four

Home

I settled into my new home and prepared for the onslaught of snowbirds. Once the 1998-1999 season wound down, I began to feel an emptiness. I had a career I loved, a roof over my head, and a network of friends. I'd come to realize money and things were no substitute for a sober life.

Still, something was missing. Had I become complacent now that I'd achieved my dream? Was I craving the excitement of my past life? Why couldn't I relax in my success?

I was coming up on thirteen years of sobriety and invited Shelley to celebrate my anniversary. We met at our favorite Mexican restaurant and ordered fish tacos. The aroma arrived seconds before our food. We couldn't resist a few bites before getting down to business.

"Don't get me wrong," I began. "I'm grateful for my life in Scottsdale. I never thought I'd live past forty, and here I am in paradise with my best friend."

"What's the problem?"

"Something's missing. There's a piece of my heart that hasn't healed. I've asked myself if I'm still searching for the man of my dreams, but I know that's not it."

"Guess you've come to the same place as me," Shelley said. "No man is going to make you happy. It's gotta come from within."

"Right," I agreed. "If a guy does come along, he'll be the catsup on the burger, not the burger."

She broke out in laughter. "You sure have a way of phrasing things!"

My mood lifted. We enjoyed our tacos. My questions could wait until after we indulged in dulce de leche, the house dessert specialty. Once we'd eaten our fill and sat with our coffee, Shelley brought our conversation back to me.

"I think I know what's bugging you," she said. "You're looking for more than AA."

I nodded. "I keep asking myself if I'll be going to meetings, repeating the same phrases over and over, till I die."

"I asked myself the same question after I celebrated ten years of sobriety."

"What'd you do?" I asked.

"I found Jesus."

I thought back to my time in prison, how I turned to my little blue Bible for peace, and how God's words soothed me. Perhaps Shelley was onto something.

"AA taught me that running on my own steam and doing things my way wasn't working," I said, "but they rarely mention Jesus."

"That's 'cause they're appealing to a cross section of the population," Shelley explained. "They want you to realize there's a power greater than yourself, but they leave it up to you to define that power."

"It's like they take spirituality only so far. It's all about the Twelve Steps, listening to war stories, repeating the serenity prayer. I need more."

"Now you're talking," Shelley said.

"It's almost like Jesus has been out there waiting for me. Boy, has he been waiting a long time."

Shelley smiled. "He's patient and never gives up."

"I was thinking about Kenya and how my Bible saved me. But it was all selfish prayers. 'Foxhole prayers,' I think they're called. 'Get me outta here,' I'd pray. And once I was out, I forgot about God."

"The road to hell is paved with good intentions." Shelley's cliché hit home. "Come to church with me this Sunday."

This wasn't the first time Shelley had mentioned her church. She'd hinted at me joining her, but I had more important things to do on a Sunday—like clean my condo, shop, or sleep in after a hectic week at the salon.

I hesitated. "Sunday's always been *my* day."

"It's my day, too, but now I share it with Jesus," Shelley said. "You've been working your tail off for months. You deserve to treat yourself to something special. I promise you won't be disappointed."

"Well, maybe just this once."

Shelley's smile was infectious. "My church is amazing. The congregation is kind and welcoming; the music will blow you away. Once won't be enough."

That Sunday I put on my best slacks and a silk blouse and met Shelley outside Praise Him Bible Church. The building was nothing like the Gothic-style churches of my youth. The church had taken over an abandoned strip mall and turned it into a house of worship. Hundreds of cars filled the parking lot. Parishioners, young and old, in jeans or Sunday best, filed into the entrance.

"I had no idea so many people worshiped on Sunday," I said.

Shelley laughed. "Follow me."

The anchor store had been turned into a sanctuary. Tiered seats rose on three sides. Seats on the ground level faced an enormous platform with a bandstand, pulpits, and risers for a choir. A massive TV screen played videos of prior services, baptisms, and more. Recorded praise music welcomed us to join the celebration.

"The energy is intense!"

"This is nothing. Wait'll the service starts." Shelley led me to second-tier seats.

"Can't we sit up front?"

"I think you'll be happier up here," she said. "You're close enough to see everything, and the perfect distance from the TV."

A band and choir appeared first. The crowd stood and joined in the singing. I swayed to the music and looked forward to the day I'd know the lyrics.

Once the service began, I was mesmerized.

"Once a person accepts Jesus into their heart, they become reborn," the pastor preached. "You, as a brand-new creation, become the living representation of Christ. Jesus died on the cross to save every one of us. By accepting and believing in Him, you will be empowered."

I could swear he looked directly at me. As we bowed our heads in prayer, the congregation stood, joined hands, and became a single, powerful embodiment of the Holy Spirit.

My only disappointment was how quickly the service ended.

"I could stay here all day," I said.

"I told you. This is the absolute best!"

"It's almost as though I had to go through my marriages, prison, dancing, drinking, and drugging to get to this place."

Shelley nodded. "Don't forget AA. It saved your life and brought you to me."

"It's all part of the journey. I wish I didn't have to wait till next Sunday to come back."

"You don't have to," Shelley said. "They have Bible study on Wednesday evenings. You'll get to meet more people and study the Word of God."

"Care to join me?" I asked.

"Absolutely! Now, my friend, how about lunch?"

I arrived at the Wednesday evening Bible study bathed in nervous excitement. A group of thirty men and women greeted me. My initial self-consciousness faded the moment the meeting began.

We opened with a prayer and discussion. Members shared their challenges and triumphs and how Jesus had spoken to them during the week.

John, the leader, turned to me. "Would you like to introduce yourself and tell us what brought you here?"

I stood proudly. "My name's Ava Stanton. I attended the Sunday service and knew I'd found my home. I want to learn everything I can, to know Jesus, and what His purpose is for me."

Everyone smiled and clapped. Murmurs of "Welcome" and "Praise Jesus" floated through the room.

"Thank you," John said. "Let's open our Bibles to Galatians 2:20. Ava, as our newest member, would you like to read the passage?"

I felt heat rise into my cheeks. Would I stumble on the words or give them meaning?

"'I have been crucified with Christ and I no longer live, but Christ lives in me. The life I now live in the body, I live by faith in the Son of God, who loved me and gave himself for me.'"

God's words spoke to me through that passage. I knew my knowledge of the Bible was limited, but not until that evening did I realize the depth of meaning in the scriptures and how much there was to learn.

John addressed the group. "What does tonight's passage say?"

A few members shared their interpretations. I'd brought a notebook and scribbled their responses.

John then asked, "Who would like to share how God's words spoke to you personally?"

John's goal was to help each of us build a bridge between observation and interpretation. He stressed the importance of reading the Bible daily.

"And if you're reading a difficult passage, relax." He looked directly at me. "I've been studying the Word of God for years and there's still much I don't understand. Bible study is a lifelong endeavor."

We discussed a few more passages from the New Testament before we broke for coffee and fellowship. The warmth emanating from the group was contagious.

"What did you think of tonight's study group?" John asked.

"I loved every minute," I said.

"I felt God's love radiate from you."

"I felt it, too," I agreed. "It's like I've come home."

"You have. Will we see you next Wednesday?"

"Absolutely. And you'll see me Sunday."

"Praise Jesus," John said.

I attended services on Sundays and Bible study on Wednesdays. I immersed myself in God's teachings and read His word daily. At a Bible study several months later, John approached me.

"Ava, have you been baptized?"

"I assume I was when I was a baby."

"That was for your parents, not you," John explained. "Baptizing you as a conscious adult means you are publicly declaring you belong to Christ."

"I'm ready."

On a Sunday a few weeks later, I was baptized along with several other adults. I'd watched baptisms and been instructed in what to expect, but I was still anxious and excited to experience the ritual for myself.

I wore shorts and a Praise Him T-shirt for the ceremony and brought a change of clothes for later. When it was my turn, the pastor recited a short prayer and asked if I'd accepted Christ as my savior. Once I agreed, I was led to a tank that had been wheeled into the sanctuary. John escorted me up a short ladder to enter the tank. Randy, an assistant pastor, assisted me down another ladder, where I joined him in the waist-high warm water. A volunteer stood nearby.

He gently placed one arm on my shoulder and gazed into my eyes. "It is our honor to baptize you today," he began. "I baptize you in the name of the Father, the Son, and the Holy Spirit. Amen."

Randy gave me a gentle nudge. I held my nose, leaned backward into the arms of the volunteer, and immersed myself in the water. I was only under water for a few seconds, but when I emerged, I felt reborn. The entire congregation applauded as I stood drenched and dripping.

After the ceremony I was led backstage to a room where I could change, dry my hair, and apply makeup. Friends and strangers congratulated me after the service. I don't think I ever felt as loved as I did that day.

I knew life would continue to present me with struggles, and I knew I still carried pain in my heart. But now I had Jesus walking beside me and bringing the right experiences and people into my life.

eighty-five

Moving On

Praise Him Bible Church had given me salvation. It was time to give back. I approached John a few months after my baptism. "The church has done so much for me—"

John didn't give me time to finish. "You're not the same person who walked in here last year."

"Thank you. But—"

He interrupted again. "You've flourished in God's love. And you'll continue to grow as you study the scriptures."

"I want to give back." I finally got my words out.

John's smile lit up his face. "Why didn't you say so?"

"I thought maybe I could do something to help other lost women. If I could work with them, it would make everything I went through worthwhile."

"Funny you should ask," John said. "The church has begun working with a women's shelter in Phoenix. We're hoping to coordinate with the counseling staff to bring the women into our fold."

"That's exactly what I've been looking for!"

A few days later, John and I met with the staff at the shelter. I had no degree or experience leading groups, but the church and the home were eager to form a liaison and saw me as the link between the two.

Most women had experienced the emotional and physical pain

of sexual abuse. I became the leader of a group that met weekly at my church. Using a format similar to AA, we supported one another. Had I not suffered abuse in my past, I wouldn't be the pillar these women needed in their lives.

Over the next two years, I shared in the joy of faith and renewal for many of my charges. I watched, helpless, as some women returned to their tormenters. I began each meeting by reading Proverbs 26:11: "As a dog that returns to his vomit, so is a fool that misbehaves in his folly."

Some got it, some didn't. I was grateful for my successes and turned my failures over to Jesus. But it wasn't always easy. The stress of the group often left me exhausted. I considered resigning but refused to admit defeat. I prayed for a solution to my dilemma.

In the meantime, a new man began attending Bible study. He approached me one evening during fellowship.

"I've seen you at Sunday services but never had the chance to introduce myself. My name's Dan."

"Ava. Nice to meet you."

He appeared to be about my age—nearly sixty—gray hair and mustache, average height, a muscular build, and a radiant smile. I hadn't thought about dating in years. Maybe Dan would change that.

Dan was separated from his wife and wanted to wait until his divorce was finalized before taking things to the next level. I respected his decision.

We met for lunch a few times, always keeping it short since I had to get back to the salon. One evening after Bible study, he asked if I'd like to join him for coffee. We met at a café not far from church. We sat opposite one another in a booth near the entrance and reviewed the evening's lesson while waiting to be served.

John and Randy, the assistant pastor, arrived shortly after we did. I waved them over to join us. John nodded, looked to Randy, who shook his head, and moved to a table in the main dining room.

~~~

Randy approached me at Sunday's fellowship gathering.

"We need to talk," he said in a strained whisper. He led me by my elbow to a back corner where John waited. Neither man looked happy.

"Ava, you have violated God's seventh commandment, 'Thou shalt not commit adultery,'" John said.

I looked at the men, stunned. "I have not!"

"We saw you with Dan, a married man," Randy said.

"He's separated, waiting for his divorce. We had coffee—"

"He's still married in the eyes of the church."

How dare these men judge me for something I hadn't done?

"You are immediately stripped of your leadership position with the women's group," the assistant pastor said. "We will pray for your forgiveness. We suggest you do the same."

"But—"

"That's all, Ava."

The men left me and approached Dan. I watched as they accused him, watched as he hung his head in shame. What punishment would they inflict on him?

Dan shuffled toward the exit. I followed him to the parking lot.

"Those men had no right to accuse us. We've done nothing wrong."

"Stay away from me, Ava." He hurried into his car.

I never went back to Praise Him Bible Church.

"You're not the only one they've done this to," Shelley said. "Seems like a lot of people are finding Praise Him too judgmental."

"I felt like they were imposing man-made rules on me," I said.

"You know the assistant worship leader, Patrick?"

"I haven't seen him for a while," I said.

"He had enough, too. He's at Grande View Bible Church. How about we check it out this Sunday?"
~~~

"Absolutely." My only concern was for the women in my sexual abuse group. What would the church tell them about me? I decided the best thing to do would be to write a letter to the women's shelter saying I needed to resign for personal reasons. I never received a response.

Grande View Bible Church became my home for the next several years. In addition to Sunday services, I enrolled in a program called "My Identity in Christ," which took my faith and understanding to a new level.

I'd been living with guilt and shame my entire adult life: guilt for my bad decisions, for my parenting skills, and for people I'd wronged, either intentionally or unintentionally. Though I'd been a Christian for years and outwardly accepted that my sins had been forgiven, I'd been unable to accept the totality of God's forgiveness in my heart.

"What are you getting out of your guilt?" Paul, the workshop leader, asked me.

"Nothing."

"You are getting something." Paul looked into my eyes. "You're getting something out of the bitterness you feel. Why can't you let it go?"

I wanted to scream, "I don't know!" but stayed silent, afraid of giving the wrong answer.

"It means you don't have to change," he said. "It's easier to live in misery than take a bold step into the unknown. Until you can forgive yourself, you can't receive God's forgiveness."

A light switch clicked on in my brain. I was awakened to the reality of what it meant to be a Christian and living life in Christ. Over time, I learned to exchange the cloak of guilt and shame for one of peace and joy.

"My Identity in Christ" taught me that doing good in the world is great but being the good in the world is greater. I learned that God is in me, for me, and with me every moment of every day.

After three years with the group, I emerged a new person. My demeanor changed, even my facial expression. I walked taller, prouder, more confident, knowing the Holy Spirit lived within me.

As I looked back, I realized God and Jesus had been with me since the beginning. An invisible thread—God's thread—carried me through the abuse, mistakes, and darkness. God's thread allowed me to survive the horrors of my life to bring me to a place of peace.

eighty-six

The Unexpected

At age sixty-one, life was good. While most people my age looked toward retirement, I looked toward a life of working, sharing, and giving. It all came crashing down one December morning in 2005.

I'd just returned from visiting my friend Suzi in New Jersey. By the time I'd unpacked and made a salad, I felt nauseous and exhausted. I threw out the salad and climbed into bed. Had I caught the flu on the flight home?

When I woke the next morning, I felt like vomiting. I tried getting out of bed, but my legs had turned to rubber bands and wouldn't support me.

I managed to crawl to the living room and dialed my friend Shelley.

"I'll be right over. Don't move," she said.

I couldn't move if I wanted to.

Shelley let herself in with a key I kept hidden outside. She took one look at me. "I think you've had a stroke."

She called 9-1-1.

"You're crazy," I mumbled.

She held a mirror in front of my face. My mouth drooped on the left side. I realized my left arm felt invisible. I knew these were signs of a stroke, but how could it have happened? I'd always tried to eat healthy food, exercise, and take vitamins even in the worse days of my addiction.

The EMTs arrived within minutes. As they loaded me onto a stretcher, I turned to Shelley. "Get my hairbrush and my makeup."

My words sounded unintelligible, even to me.

My memory blurs when I try to recall the early moments in the hospital. What I do remember is the neurologist explaining that my carotid artery on one side was 90 percent blocked. He recommended surgery to remove the blockage and prescribed a strong cholesterol medication to prevent a reoccurrence.

Shelley went back to my condo for a few things, including my little blue Bible. The cover was worn and the pages frayed, but the book had saved me in Kenya. I prayed it would save me again.

She sat at my bedside and read words of hope and healing. I received comfort from Jeremiah 17:14: "Heal me, O Lord, and I shall be healed; save me, and I shall be saved, for thou art my praise."

My voice slurred, so I prayed silently while Shelley prayed aloud. "Dear God, give Ava the strength to know in her heart that you are there for her every minute of every day. May the Holy Spirit live within her and guide her to full recovery. Amen."

I couldn't believe the outpouring of prayers and good wishes from my church and my friends. Phone calls occupied my morning, and visitors kept me busy from afternoon through early evening. In the moments I spent alone, I had time to reflect on how my life had morphed from an abused young woman and addict to a sober, independent mature woman: from a down-and-out dancer to a successful nail technician. I'd given my life over to Christ and in return, I was free from my past. I prayed God would see fit to give me a future.

I spent six days in the hospital before I was ready for surgery. Slowly, I regained control of my legs and left arm. Each day my mouth drooped less.

My surgery was successful. Rest and physical therapy restored all movement and brain function. Within a few weeks, I returned to work and to church.

I'd had several brushes with death over the years but none as profound as my stroke. When you're young, you feel invincible. When you're sixty-one, you realize death has its hand out waiting for you. Without my friends, the phenomenal hospital staff, prayers, and my faith in God, I wouldn't have survived. Time and life had become precious commodities.

eighty-seven

Reflections Church

Time, like God, works in mysterious ways. When you're young, a day lasts forever, and a year is an eternity. As you grow older, a year passes as quickly as a month once did.

Before I realized what had happened, ten years had flown by. I'd built up a successful clientele, Shelley and I continued to be best buddies, and I'd deepened my relationship with Jesus.

One of my newer clients, Vera, sat in my chair for a mani and pedi. "You're a Christian, aren't you, Ava?"

"Yes, how'd you know?"

"The cross around your neck, your manner, your speech. It's all there."

My hand went to the gold cross I wore day and night. "It's my life."

"Mine, too," Vera agreed. "Where do you worship?"

"Grande View. And you?"

"I was at Grande View for years," she said. "Then I felt like I was outgrowing the church."

I interrupted, something I rarely did. "I feel the same way. It's gotten stale."

"I started church shopping a while back. I finally settled on Reflections Church. The music will blow you away."

On my break, I did an Internet search for Reflections. I loved what I read: Reflections believed in diversity, authenticity, and celebrating Jesus. They spoke of the Trinity—God the Father, Jesus his son, and the Holy Spirit that lives in every Christian. Reflections was led by a team of men and women—young and old, white, black, and brown. Their photos on the website welcomed me.

I called Shelley. "Have you heard of Reflections Church?"

"Funny you should ask," she replied. "I just read some good stuff about the place. Why, do you want to go this Sunday?"

"Yes, ma'am!"

"Wow," I whispered to Shelley as we entered Reflections. "I wish we'd known about this place sooner. Think of all the Sundays we could've worshipped here."

Shelley nodded. "But we're here now."

The music, the energy, and the pastor's message were spot-on. The sanctuary was enormous and resonated with the Holy Spirit. Dress was casual, and the congregants enthusiastic and friendly. I never wanted to leave.

eighty-eight

Celebrate Recovery

Each Sunday I left Reflections filled with God's love. I joined Wednesday night Bible study, which deepened my faith and understanding of the Word. The community welcomed Shelley and me. Life was amazing.

I'd often reminisce about the work I'd done with abused women at Praise Him Bible Church. I enjoyed giving back, sharing my sobriety story and my love for Jesus. I longed for an opportunity to contribute to my new community.

That opportunity came in the form of Celebrate Recovery, a faith-based, twelve-step recovery program I'd learned about from a client a year after I joined Reflections. They encouraged me to read *The Purpose Driven Life* by Rick Warren, a forty-two-day study guide, which provided daily meditation and steps to help discover and live your life's purpose.

As I worked my way through each day, I thought about the self-help books I'd read during my addiction. I asked myself if my life would've been different if I'd discovered Rick Warren's book earlier. Once again, I came to the realization that I needed to go through the pain, suffering, and confusion to get to where I was at that moment. I no longer carried regrets about my past, only joy in my present and the will to create a better future for myself and those I might help.

Celebrate Recovery began in 1991 at Saddleback Church in Lake Forest, California, with support and study groups for codependency and chemical dependency. The difference between Alcoholics Anonymous and Celebrate Recovery was Celebrate's focus on Christianity. In the years since its inception, the organization had become worldwide, bringing the healing power of Christ to those in need. By the time I'd found the organization, it had spread beyond churches to recovery houses, rescue missions, prisons, and universities.

What I loved about Celebrate Recovery was its emphasis on recovery, not only for substances but for pain and addiction of any kind. I summoned up the courage to speak to Assistant Pastor Robert at Bible study.

"Have you heard about Celebrate Recovery?" I asked.

"There are several groups here in the Phoenix area," Robert said. "I could recommend a group if you're interested."

"Actually, I thought we could start a group here at Reflections."

His eyes lit up. "Let me talk it over with the other pastors. I'll get back to you."

"Thanks, Robert."

"No, thank you, Ava."

I loved Reflection's willingness to explore new ideas. Within a month, we had a team of four, including me, that formed our own Celebrate Recovery group. We began with a Saturday evening meeting in which members were invited to share their story or, in Celebrate Recovery's words, give their testimony. From there, we formed a study group on Tuesday evenings in which we discussed their twelve steps and eight principles, all faith-based.

Members arrived with issues of anger, resentment, codependency, addiction, and more. Through studying, journaling, and sharing, we worked through our hurts, habits, and hang-ups. We became aware of the difference between making amends to those we've hurt versus lip service. We learned to avoid worry by staying present in the moment.

The greatest lesson for me was to stop searching for approval and to stop feeling unworthy of love. I came to trust in God's love for me, flawed and imperfect as I am. I continue to pray one day my children will find it in their hearts to forgive me and truly know the depth of my love for them.

At times, I wished I'd gotten sober through Celebrate Recovery rather than Alcoholics Anonymous, but then I'd remind myself that AA had worked for me for thirteen years. Instead, I chose to celebrate my journey and express gratitude for who I had been and who I am at this moment.

As I did in AA, I began sponsoring other women.

My first question to a new member is always, "What are you getting out of your addiction, your thought process, or your codependency?"

Invariably, they'd reply, "Nothing."

"That's not true," I'd say. "You have to be getting something or you'd get out."

Some women would become defensive, others angry or confused.

"Change is scary. By staying in your addiction, you don't have to change. Your misery becomes your safety net. It's always easier to stay where you are. Chase sobriety as hard as you chased your drug. Don't think of your life as over; think of your new life in Christ."

I'd watch their expressions and body language. Some women broke down; some got it, and others didn't. I'd celebrate those who tore down the curtain of denial and pray for those who weren't ready.

I give my testimony at Celebrate Recovery twice a year. I continue to work on myself, and as Celebrate Recovery says, I turned my mess into a message.

~~~
~~~

I've found my calling—to help free abused, broken-hearted women from their prison. My greatest joy in life is watching their growth and transformation, knowing God is working through me every minute of every day.

acknowledgments

I'd like to thank all those who inspired me and offered their ideas and suggestions. I would especially like to thank the Watchung Writers, fearlessly led by Pat Rydberg. Thank you all for your patience, insight, and friendship. You are my inspiration and motivation.Thank you to everyone at She Writes Press—especially Brooke Warner; Addison Gallegos, my project manager; Lorraine White and Melinda Andrews, my editors; my book designers Rebecca Lown and Stacey Aaronson; and my fellow authors. I am proud and honored to be a She Writes Press Author.

To my husband, Bob, thank you for giving me the space to write, and for the hours you spent reading draft after draft. I love you today and always.

And finally, to Ava. Thank you . . . for everything.

about the author

Photo credit: Bob Edwards

Susen Edwards is the founder and former director of Somerset School of Massage Therapy, New Jersey's first state-approved and nationally accredited postsecondary school for massage therapy. During her tenure she was nominated by Merrill Lynch for *Inc. Magazine*'s Entrepreneur of the Year Award. After the successful sale of the business, she became an administrator at her local community college. Susen is currently secretary for the board of trustees for her town library and a full-time writer. She is the author of *Doctor Whisper and Nurse Willow*, a children's fantasy, and *What a Trip*, an adult novel. Her articles have appeared on Residence11.com, BooksBy-Women.org, and DIYMFA.com. Susen lives in Middlesex, New Jersey, with her husband, Bob, and her two fuzzy feline babies, Harold and Maude.

Learn more about Susen:

http://www.SusenEdwardsAuthor.com
https://www.facebook.com/SusenEdwardsAuthor
https://www.instagram.com/susenedwards/
https://www.linkedin.com/in/susenedwards/

Looking for your next great read?

We can help!

Visit www.shewritespress.com/next-read
or scan the QR code below for a list
of our recommended titles.

She Writes Press is an award-winning
independent publishing company founded to
serve women writers everywhere.